GIANT DAYS

VOLUME THREE

BOOM! BOX

Ross Richie CEO & FOUNDER
Matt Gagnon EDITOR-IN-CHIEF
Filip Sablik PRESIDENT OF PUBLISHING & MARKETING
Stephen Christy PRESIDENT OF DEVELOPMENT
Lance Kreiter VP OF LICENSING & MERCHANDISING
Phil Barbaro VP OF FINANCE
Arune Singh VP OF MARKETING
Bryce Carlson MANAGING EDITOR
Mel Caylo MARKETING MANAGER
Scott Newman PRODUCTION DESIGN MANAGER
Kate Henning OPERATIONS MANAGER
Sierra Hahn SENIOR EDITOR
Dafna Pleban EDITOR, TALENT DEVELOPMENT
Shannon Watters EDITOR
Eric Harburn EDITOR
Whitney Leopard EDITOR

Jasmine Amiri EDITOR
Chris Rosa ASSOCIATE EDITOR
Alex Galer ASSOCIATE EDITOR
Cameron Chittock ASSOCIATE EDITOR
Matthew Levine ASSISTANT EDITOR
Sophie Philips-Roberts ASSISTANT EDITOR
Kelsey Dieterich DESIGNER
Jillian Crab PRODUCTION DESIGNER
Michelle Ankley PRODUCTION DESIGNER
Grace Park PRODUCTION DESIGN ASSISTANT
Elizabeth Loughridge ACCOUNTING COORDINATOR
Stephanie Hocutt SOCIAL MEDIA COORDINATOR
José Meza EVENT COORDINATOR
James Arriola MAILROOM ASSISTANT
Holly Aitchison OPERATIONS ASSISTANT
Amber Parker ADMINISTRATIVE ASSISTANT

BOOM! BOX

GIANT DAYS Volume Three, February 2017. Published by BOOM! Box, a division of Boom Entertainment, Inc. Giant Days is ™ & © 2017 John Allison. Originally published in single magazine form as GIANT DAYS No. 9-12. ™ & © 2015, 2016 John Allison. All rights reserved. BOOM! Box™ and the BOOM! Box logo are trademarks of Boom Entertainment, Inc., registered in various countries and categories. All characters, events, and institutions depicted herein are fictional. Any similarity between any of the names, characters, persons, events, and/or institutions in this publication to actual names, characters, and persons, whether living or dead, events, and/or institutions is unintended and purely coincidental. BOOM! Box does not read or accept unsolicited submissions of ideas, stories, or artwork.

For information regarding the CPSIA on this printed material, call: (203) 595-3636 and provide reference #RICH – 724678.

BOOM! Studios, 5670 Wilshire Boulevard, Suite 450, Los Angeles, CA 90036-5679. Printed in USA. Second Printing.

ISBN: 978-1-60886-851-3, eISBN: 978-1-61398-522-9

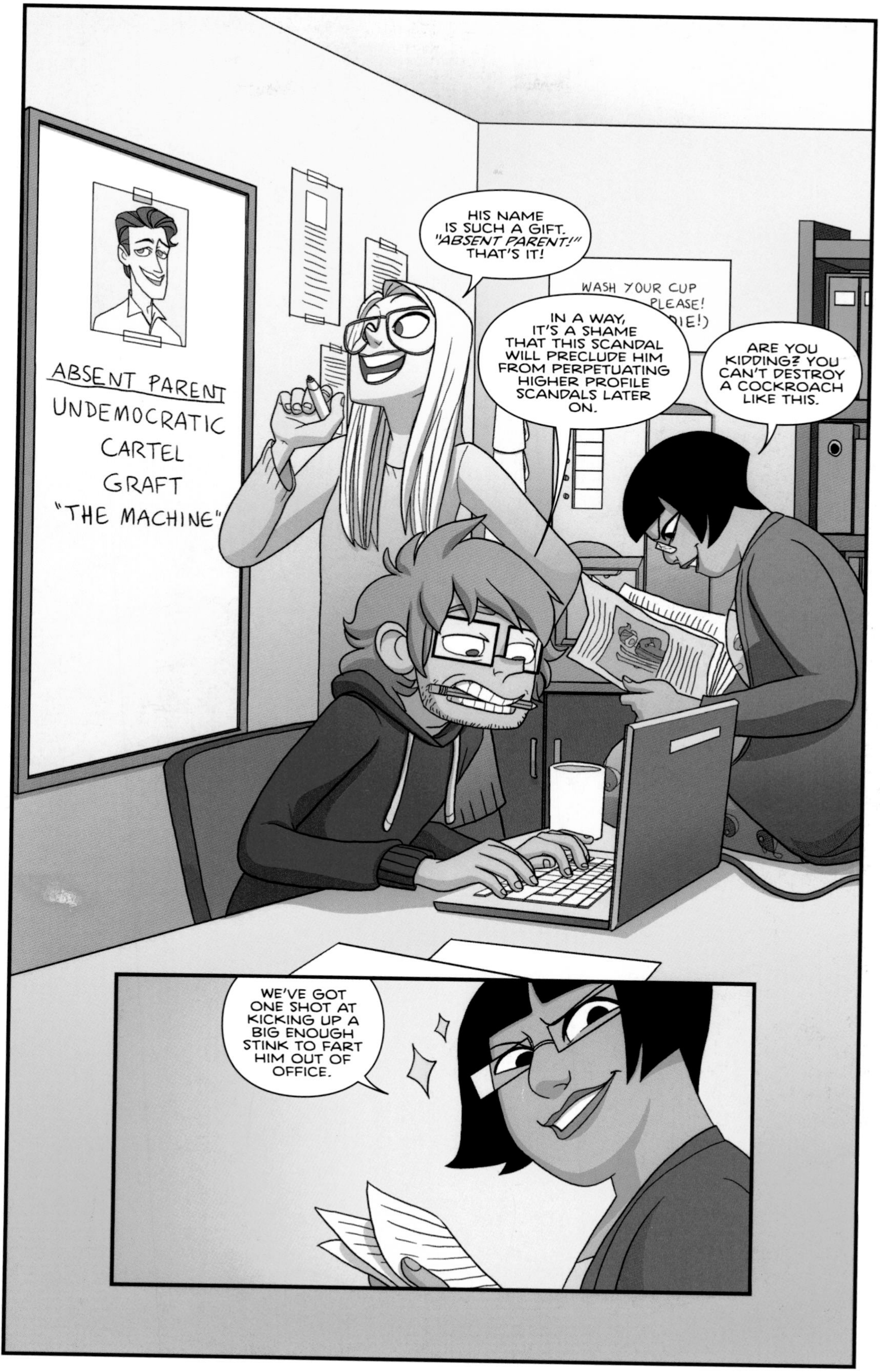
ABSENT PARENT
UNDEMOCRATIC
CARTEL
GRAFT
"THE MACHINE"
HIS NAME IS SUCH A GIFT. *"ABSENT PARENT!"* THAT'S IT!
WASH YOUR CUP
PLEASE!
IN A WAY, IT'S A SHAME THAT THIS SCANDAL WILL PRECLUDE HIM FROM PERPETUATING HIGHER PROFILE SCANDALS LATER ON.
ARE YOU KIDDING? YOU CAN'T DESTROY A COCKROACH LIKE THIS.
WE'VE GOT ONE SHOT AT KICKING UP A BIG ENOUGH STINK TO FART HIM OUT OF OFFICE.

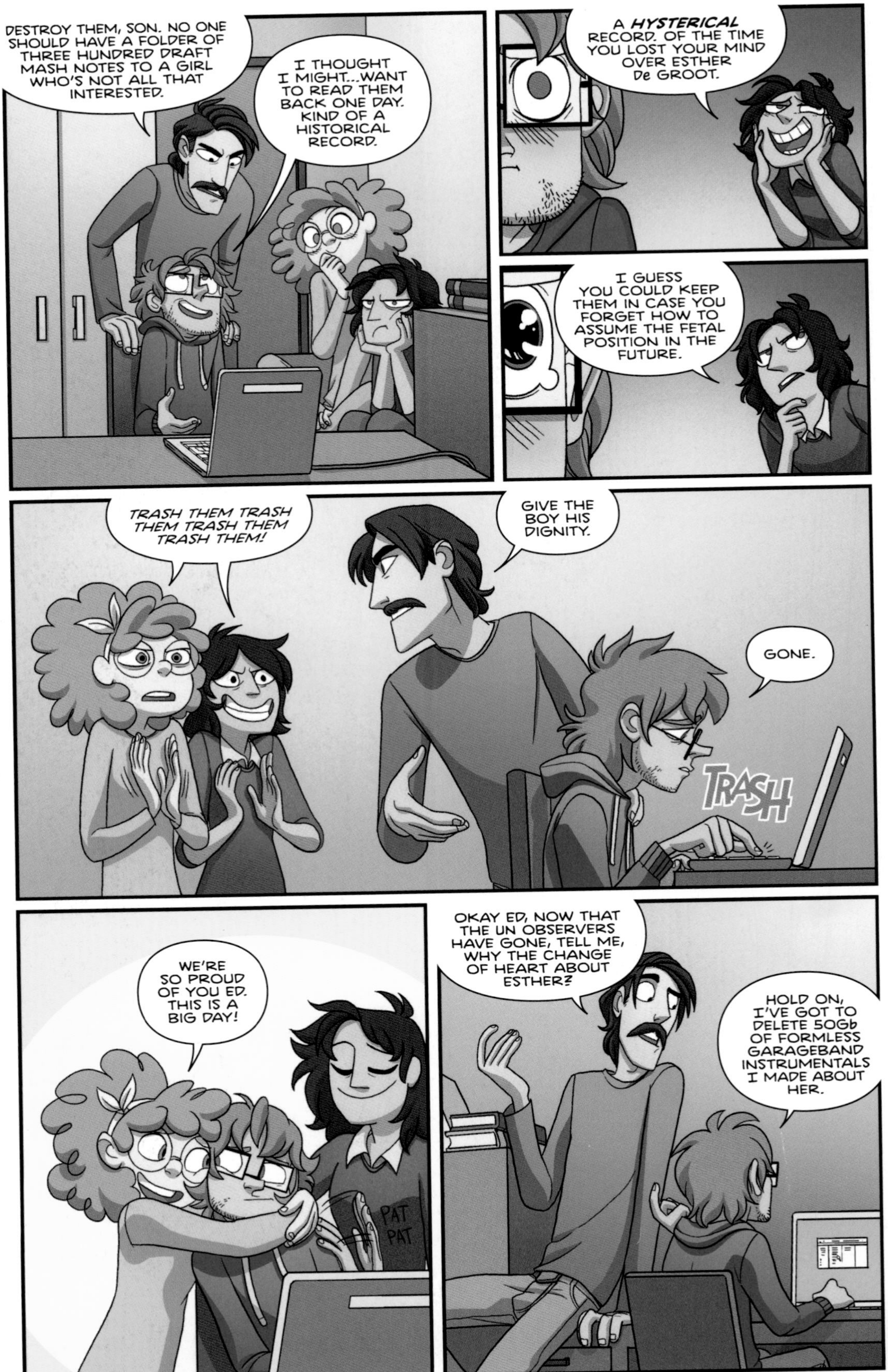
DESTROY THEM, SON. NO ONE SHOULD HAVE A FOLDER OF THREE HUNDRED DRAFT MASH NOTES TO A GIRL WHO'S NOT ALL THAT INTERESTED.
I THOUGHT I MIGHT...WANT TO READ THEM BACK ONE DAY. KIND OF A HISTORICAL RECORD.
A *HYSTERICAL* RECORD. OF THE TIME YOU LOST YOUR MIND OVER ESTHER De GROOT.
I GUESS YOU COULD KEEP THEM IN CASE YOU FORGET HOW TO ASSUME THE FETAL POSITION IN THE FUTURE.
TRASH THEM TRASH THEM TRASH THEM TRASH THEM!
GIVE THE BOY HIS DIGNITY.
GONE.
TRASH
WE'RE SO PROUD OF YOU ED. THIS IS A BIG DAY!
PAT PAT
OKAY ED, NOW THAT THE UN OBSERVERS HAVE GONE, TELL ME, WHY THE CHANGE OF HEART ABOUT ESTHER?
HOLD ON, I'VE GOT TO DELETE 50Gb OF FORMLESS GARAGEBAND INSTRUMENTALS I MADE ABOUT HER.

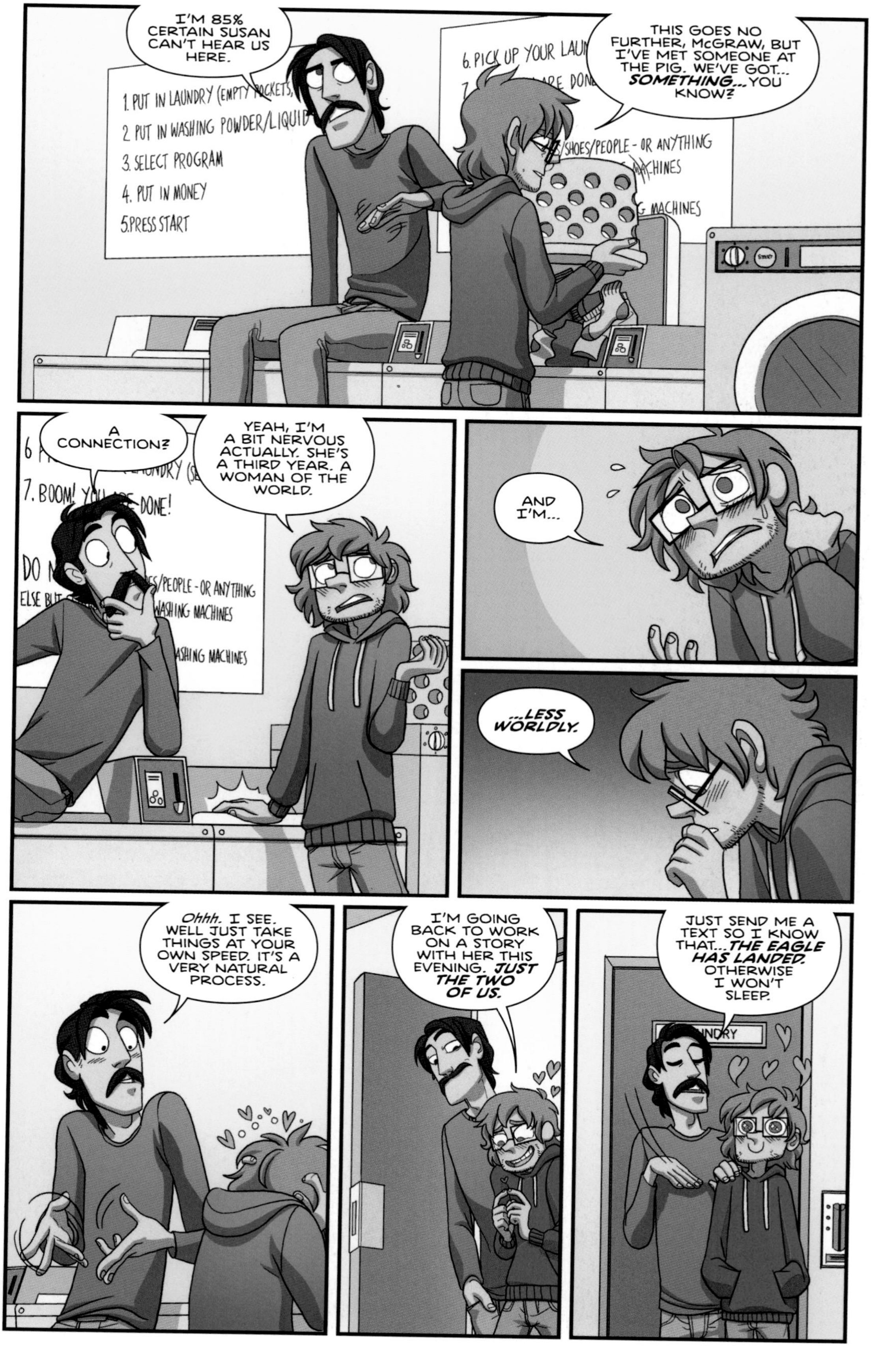

I'M 85% CERTAIN SUSAN CAN'T HEAR US HERE.
1. PUT IN LAUNDRY (EMPTY POCKETS,
2. PUT IN WASHING POWDER/LIQUID
3. SELECT PROGRAM
4. PUT IN MONEY
5.PRESS START
6. PICK UP YOUR LAUN
THIS GOES NO FURTHER, McGRAW, BUT I'VE MET SOMEONE AT THE PIG. WE'VE GOT... *SOMETHING...* YOU KNOW?
A CONNECTION?
YEAH, I'M A BIT NERVOUS ACTUALLY. SHE'S A THIRD YEAR. A WOMAN OF THE WORLD.
AND I'M...
...LESS WORLDLY.
Ohhh. I SEE. WELL JUST TAKE THINGS AT YOUR OWN SPEED. IT'S A VERY NATURAL PROCESS.
I'M GOING BACK TO WORK ON A STORY WITH HER THIS EVENING. *JUST THE TWO OF US.*
JUST SEND ME A TEXT SO I KNOW THAT... *THE EAGLE HAS LANDED.* OTHERWISE I WON'T SLEEP.

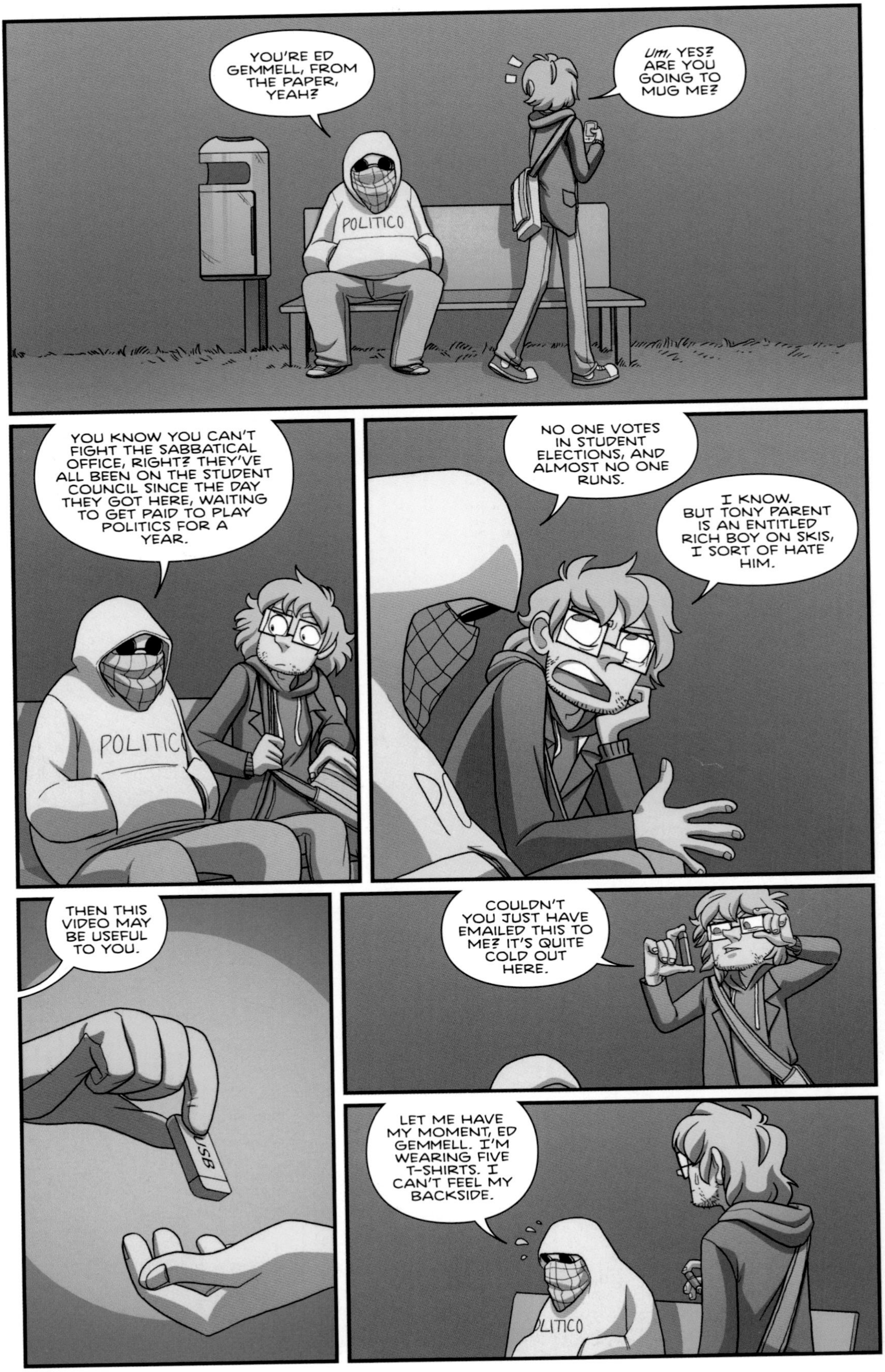
YOU'RE ED GEMMELL, FROM THE PAPER, YEAH?
UM, YES? ARE YOU GOING TO MUG ME?
POLITICO
YOU KNOW YOU CAN'T FIGHT THE SABBATICAL OFFICE, RIGHT? THEY'VE ALL BEEN ON THE STUDENT COUNCIL SINCE THE DAY THEY GOT HERE, WAITING TO GET PAID TO PLAY POLITICS FOR A YEAR.
POLITICO
NO ONE VOTES IN STUDENT ELECTIONS, AND ALMOST NO ONE RUNS.
I KNOW. BUT TONY PARENT IS AN ENTITLED RICH BOY ON SKIS, I SORT OF HATE HIM.
THEN THIS VIDEO MAY BE USEFUL TO YOU.
USB
COULDN'T YOU JUST HAVE EMAILED THIS TO ME? IT'S QUITE COLD OUT HERE.
LET ME HAVE MY MOMENT, ED GEMMELL. I'M WEARING FIVE T-SHIRTS. I CAN'T FEEL MY BACKSIDE.
OLITICO

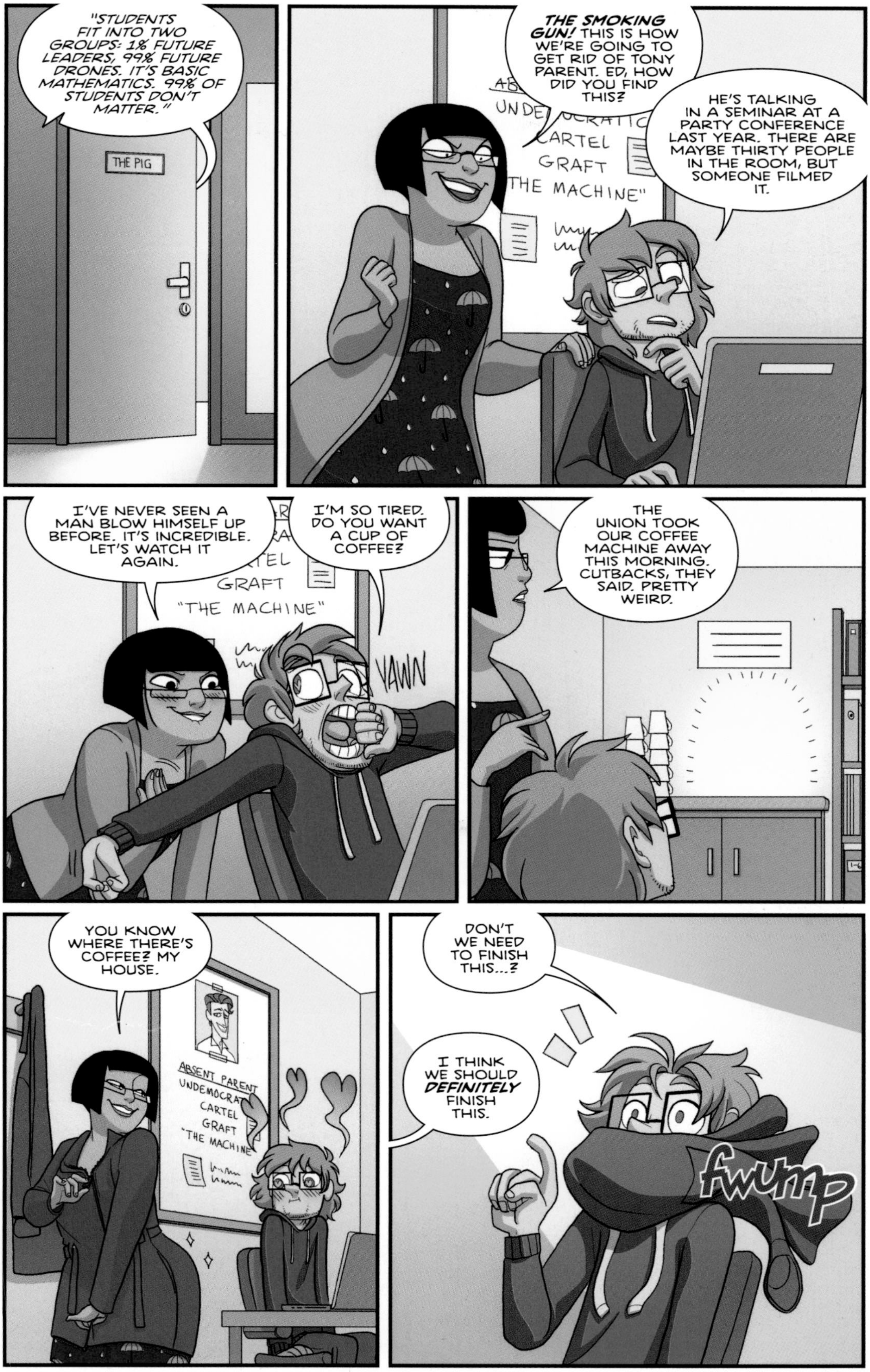
"STUDENTS FIT INTO TWO GROUPS: 1% FUTURE LEADERS, 99% FUTURE DRONES. IT'S BASIC MATHEMATICS. 99% OF STUDENTS DON'T MATTER."
THE PIG
THE SMOKING GUN! THIS IS HOW WE'RE GOING TO GET RID OF TONY PARENT. ED, HOW DID YOU FIND THIS?
HE'S TALKING IN A SEMINAR AT A PARTY CONFERENCE LAST YEAR. THERE ARE MAYBE THIRTY PEOPLE IN THE ROOM, BUT SOMEONE FILMED IT.
CARTEL
GRAFT
"THE MACHINE"
I'VE NEVER SEEN A MAN BLOW HIMSELF UP BEFORE. IT'S INCREDIBLE. LET'S WATCH IT AGAIN.
I'M SO TIRED. DO YOU WANT A CUP OF COFFEE?
YAWN
THE UNION TOOK OUR COFFEE MACHINE AWAY THIS MORNING. CUTBACKS, THEY SAID. PRETTY WEIRD.
YOU KNOW WHERE THERE'S COFFEE? MY HOUSE.
ABSENT PARENT
UNDEMOCRATIC
CARTEL
GRAFT
"THE MACHINE"
DON'T WE NEED TO FINISH THIS...?
I THINK WE SHOULD DEFINITELY FINISH THIS.
fwump

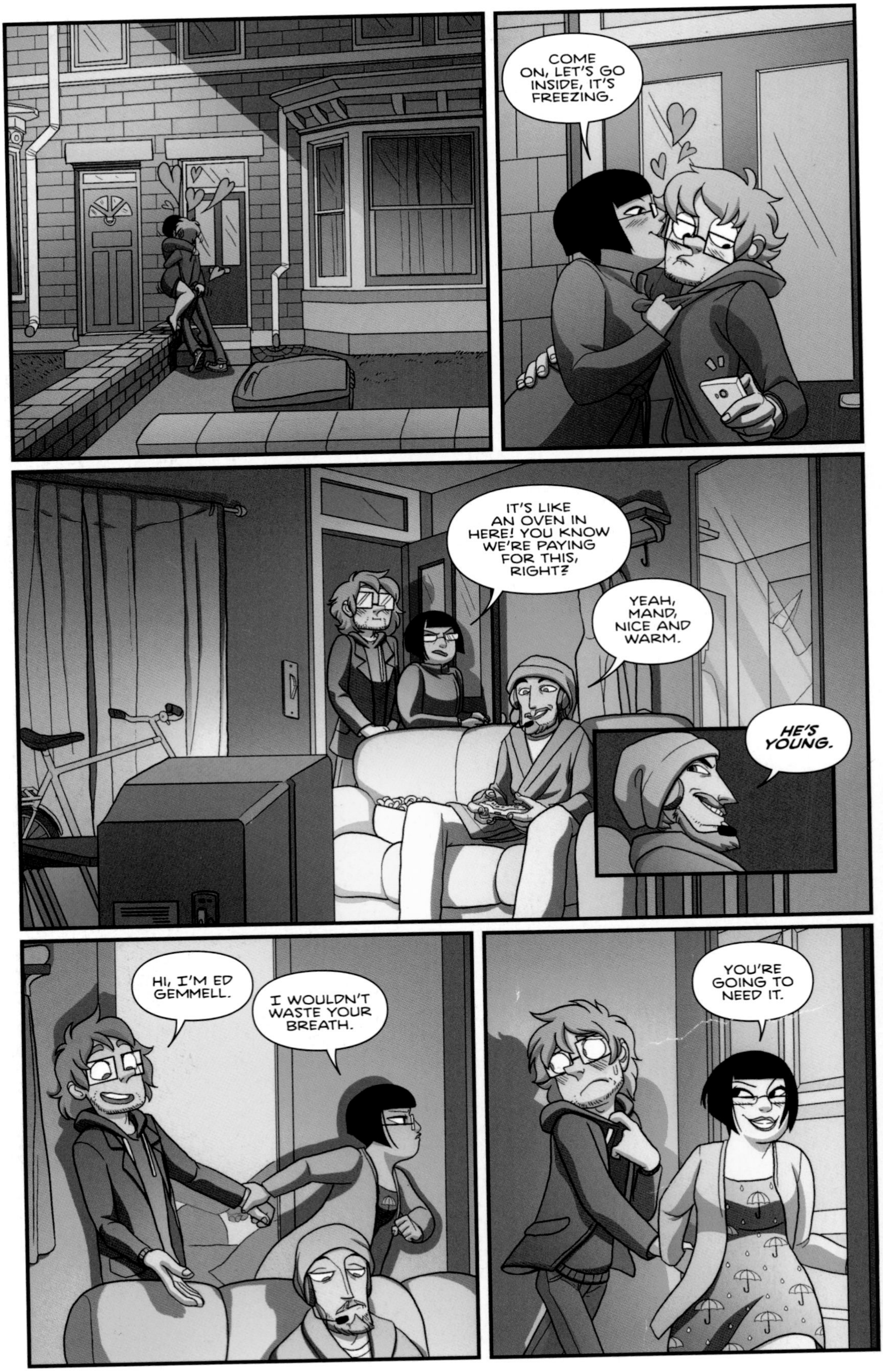
COME ON, LET'S GO INSIDE, IT'S FREEZING.
IT'S LIKE AN OVEN IN HERE! YOU KNOW WE'RE PAYING FOR THIS, RIGHT?
YEAH, MAND, NICE AND WARM.
HE'S YOUNG.
HI, I'M ED GEMMELL.
I WOULDN'T WASTE YOUR BREATH.
YOU'RE GOING TO NEED IT.

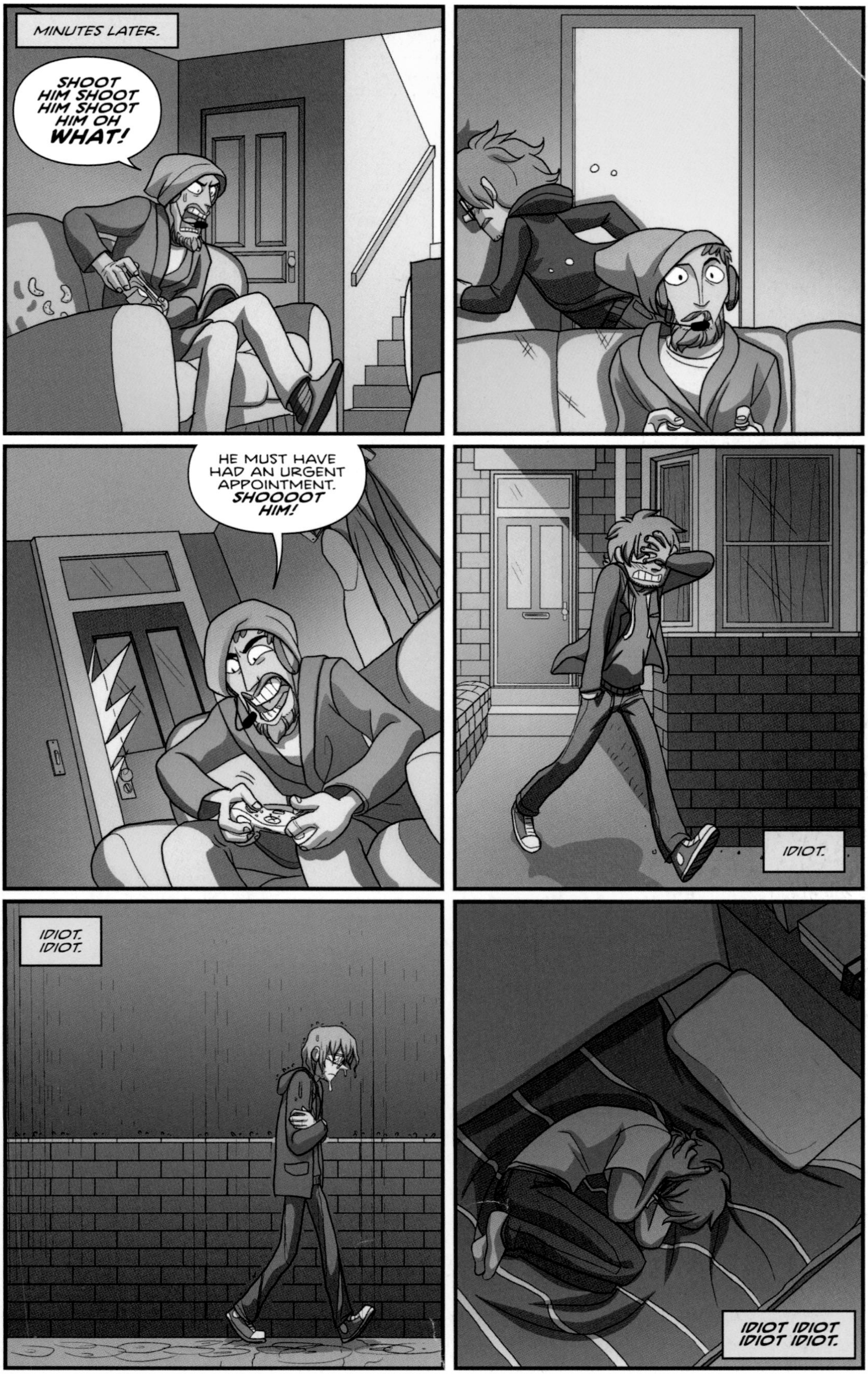
MINUTES LATER.
SHOOT HIM SHOOT HIM SHOOT HIM OH WHAT!
HE MUST HAVE HAD AN URGENT APPOINTMENT. SHOOOOT HIM!
IDIOT.
IDIOT. IDIOT.
IDIOT IDIOT IDIOT IDIOT.

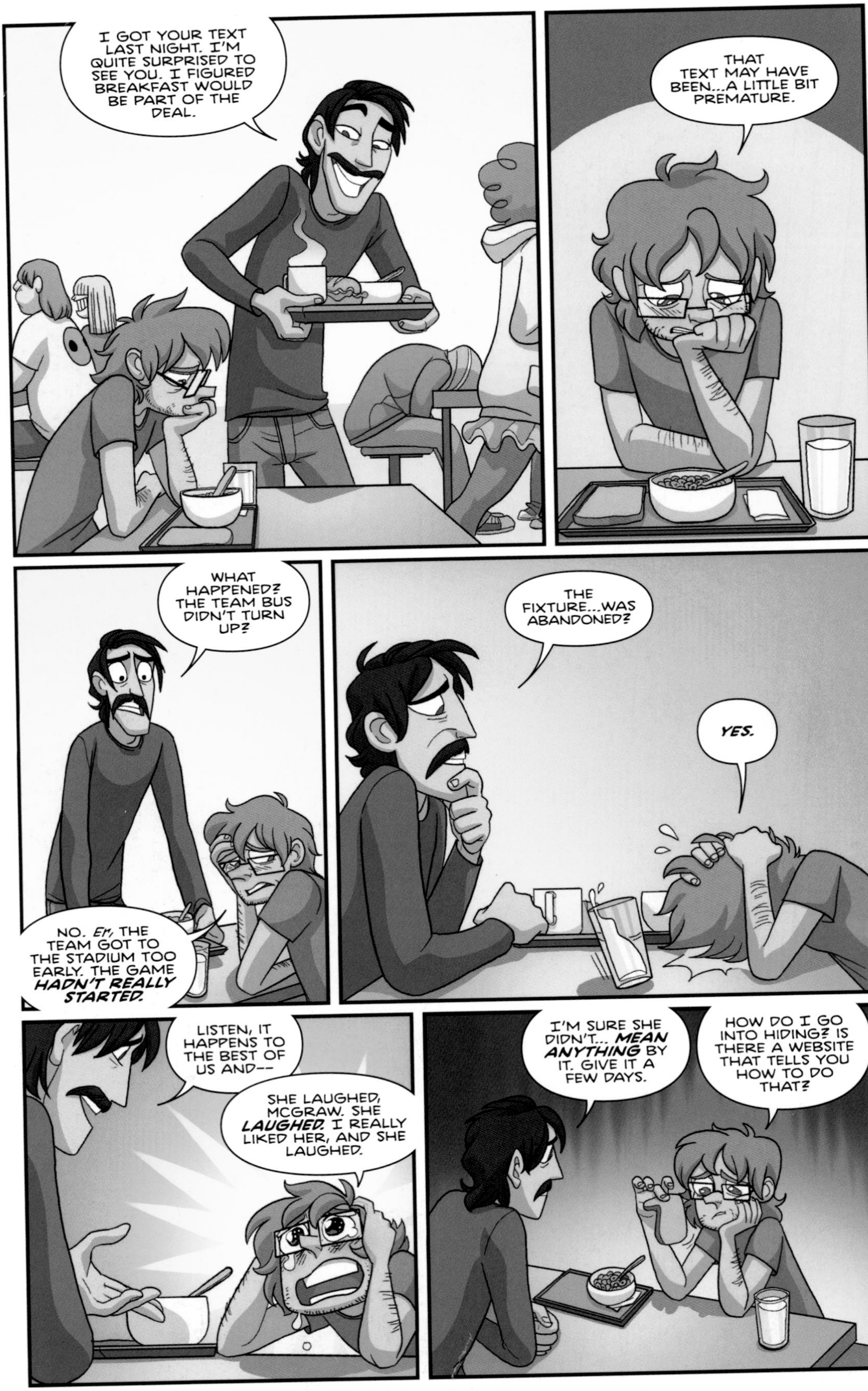
I GOT YOUR TEXT LAST NIGHT. I'M QUITE SURPRISED TO SEE YOU. I FIGURED BREAKFAST WOULD BE PART OF THE DEAL.
THAT TEXT MAY HAVE BEEN...A LITTLE BIT PREMATURE.
WHAT HAPPENED? THE TEAM BUS DIDN'T TURN UP?
NO. *Er*, THE TEAM GOT TO THE STADIUM TOO EARLY. THE GAME ***HADN'T REALLY STARTED.***
THE FIXTURE...WAS ABANDONED?
YES.
LISTEN, IT HAPPENS TO THE BEST OF US AND--
SHE LAUGHED, MCGRAW. SHE ***LAUGHED.*** I REALLY LIKED HER, AND SHE LAUGHED.
I'M SURE SHE DIDN'T... ***MEAN ANYTHING*** BY IT. GIVE IT A FEW DAYS.
HOW DO I GO INTO HIDING? IS THERE A WEBSITE THAT TELLS YOU HOW TO DO THAT?

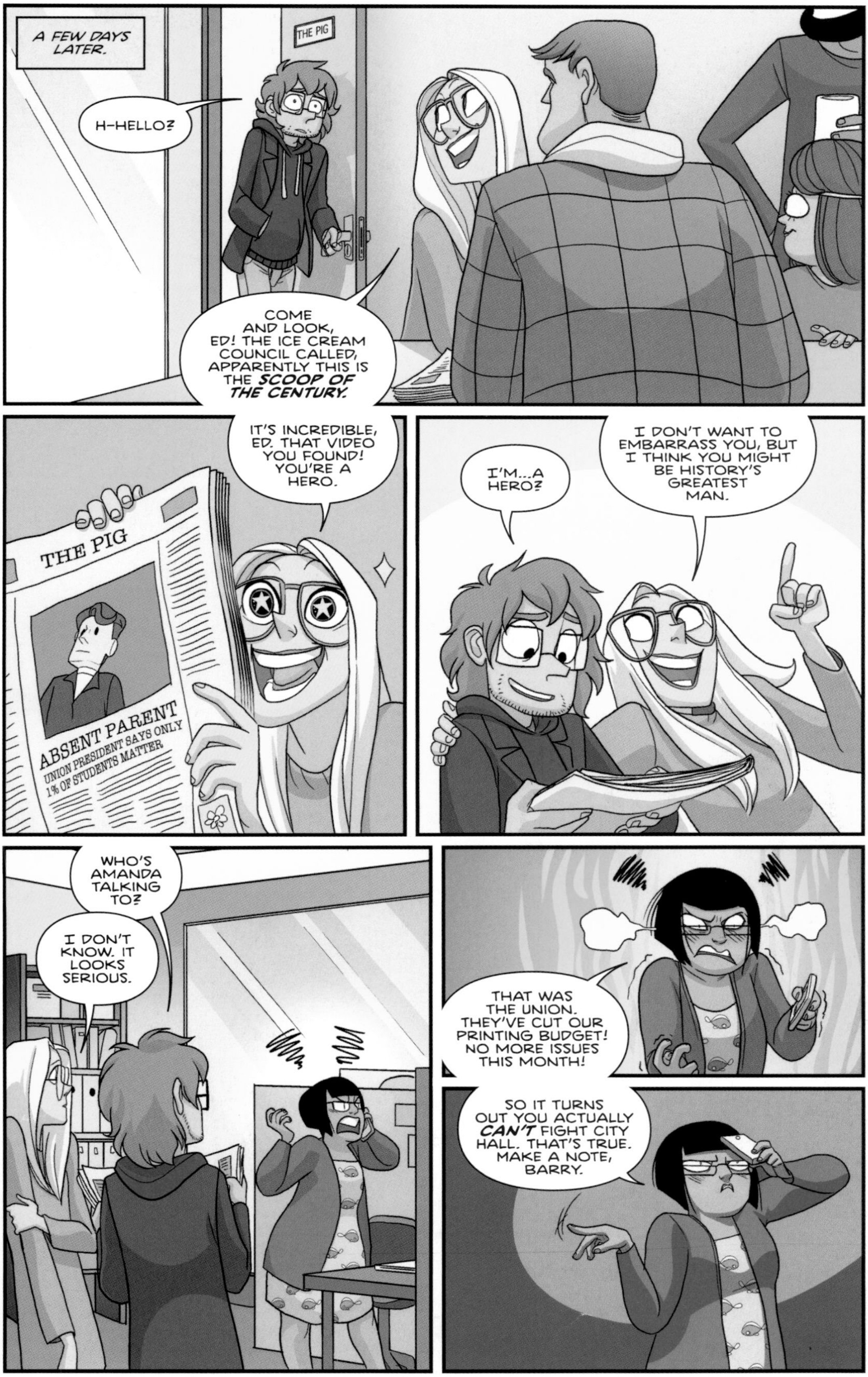
A FEW DAYS LATER.
THE PIG
H-HELLO?
COME AND LOOK, ED! THE ICE CREAM COUNCIL CALLED, APPARENTLY THIS IS THE ***SCOOP OF THE CENTURY.***
IT'S INCREDIBLE, ED. THAT VIDEO YOU FOUND! YOU'RE A HERO.
THE PIG
ABSENT PARENT
UNION PRESIDENT SAYS ONLY 1% OF STUDENTS MATTER
I'M...A HERO?
I DON'T WANT TO EMBARRASS YOU, BUT I THINK YOU MIGHT BE HISTORY'S GREATEST MAN.
WHO'S AMANDA TALKING TO?
I DON'T KNOW. IT LOOKS SERIOUS.
THAT WAS THE UNION. THEY'VE CUT OUR PRINTING BUDGET! NO MORE ISSUES THIS MONTH!
SO IT TURNS OUT YOU ACTUALLY ***CAN'T*** FIGHT CITY HALL. THAT'S TRUE. MAKE A NOTE, BARRY.

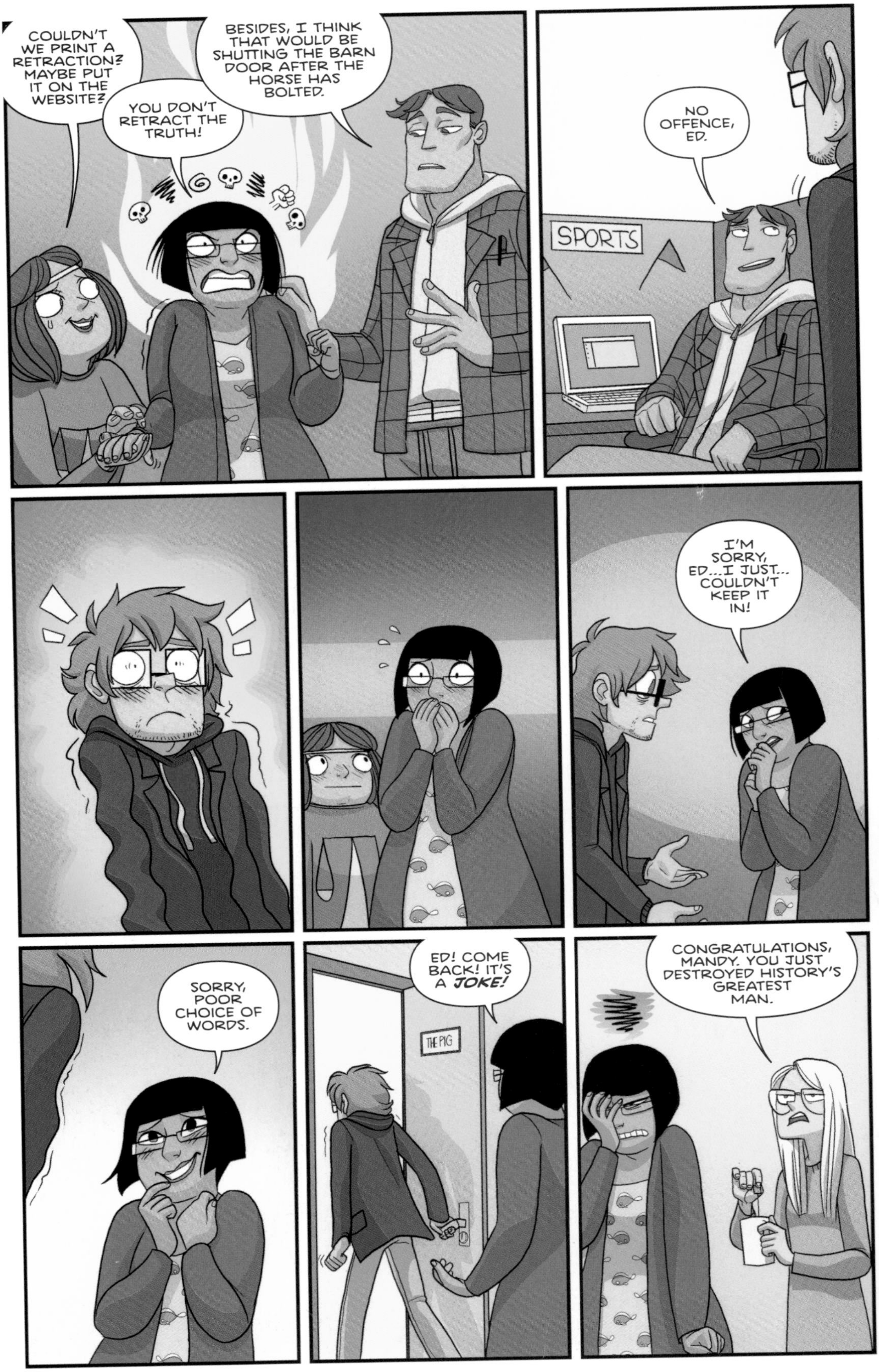
COULDN'T WE PRINT A RETRACTION? MAYBE PUT IT ON THE WEBSITE?
YOU DON'T RETRACT THE TRUTH!
BESIDES, I THINK THAT WOULD BE SHUTTING THE BARN DOOR AFTER THE HORSE HAS BOLTED.
NO OFFENCE, ED.
SPORTS
I'M SORRY, ED... I JUST... COULDN'T KEEP IT IN!
SORRY, POOR CHOICE OF WORDS.
ED! COME BACK! IT'S A ***JOKE!***
THE PIG
CONGRATULATIONS, MANDY. YOU JUST DESTROYED HISTORY'S GREATEST MAN.

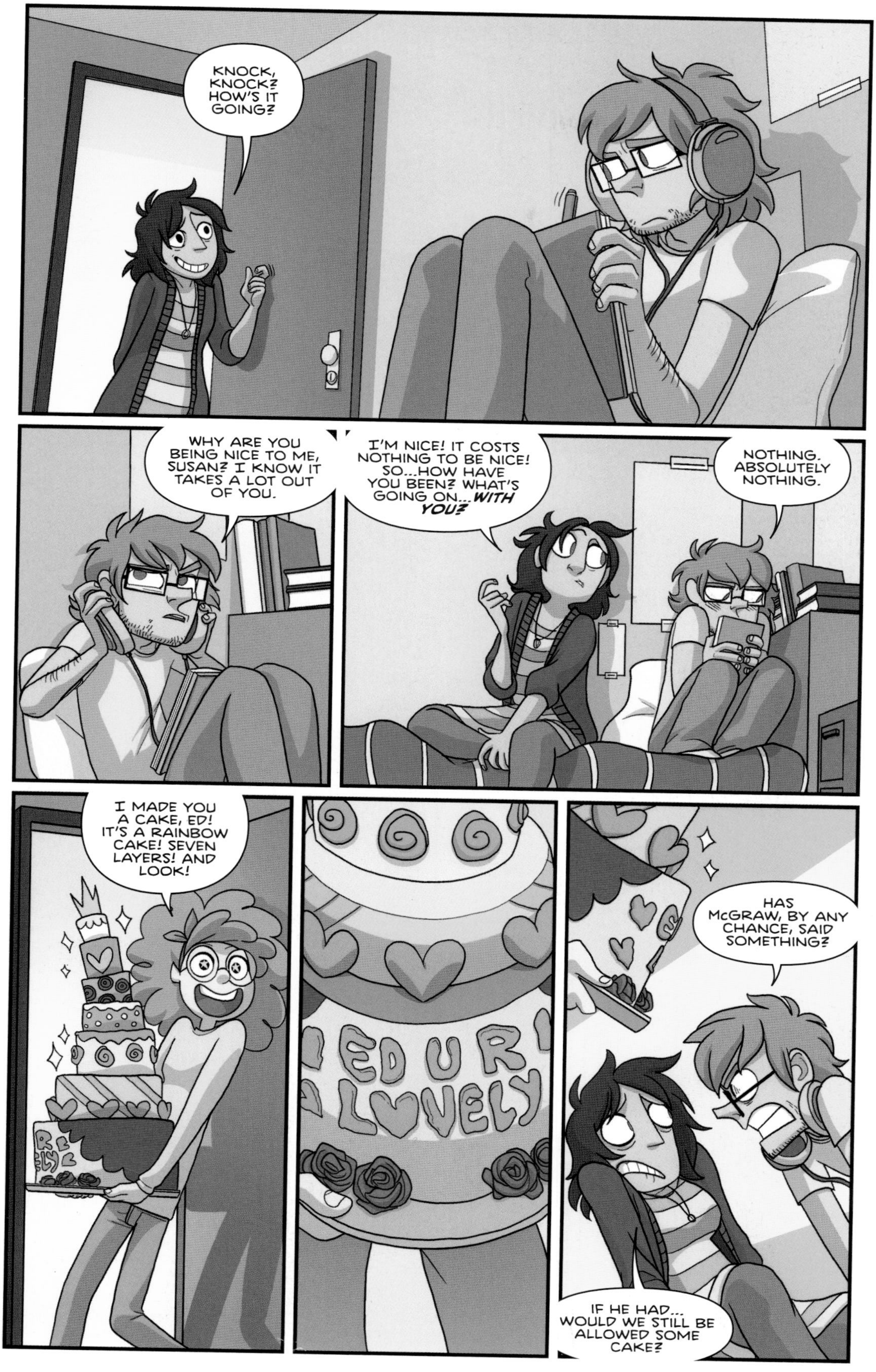
KNOCK, KNOCK? HOW'S IT GOING?
WHY ARE YOU BEING NICE TO ME, SUSAN? I KNOW IT TAKES A LOT OUT OF YOU.
I'M NICE! IT COSTS NOTHING TO BE NICE! SO...HOW HAVE YOU BEEN? WHAT'S GOING ON...WITH YOU?
NOTHING. ABSOLUTELY NOTHING.
I MADE YOU A CAKE, ED! IT'S A RAINBOW CAKE! SEVEN LAYERS! AND LOOK!
ED U R LOVELY
HAS McGRAW, BY ANY CHANCE, SAID SOMETHING?
IF HE HAD... WOULD WE STILL BE ALLOWED SOME CAKE?

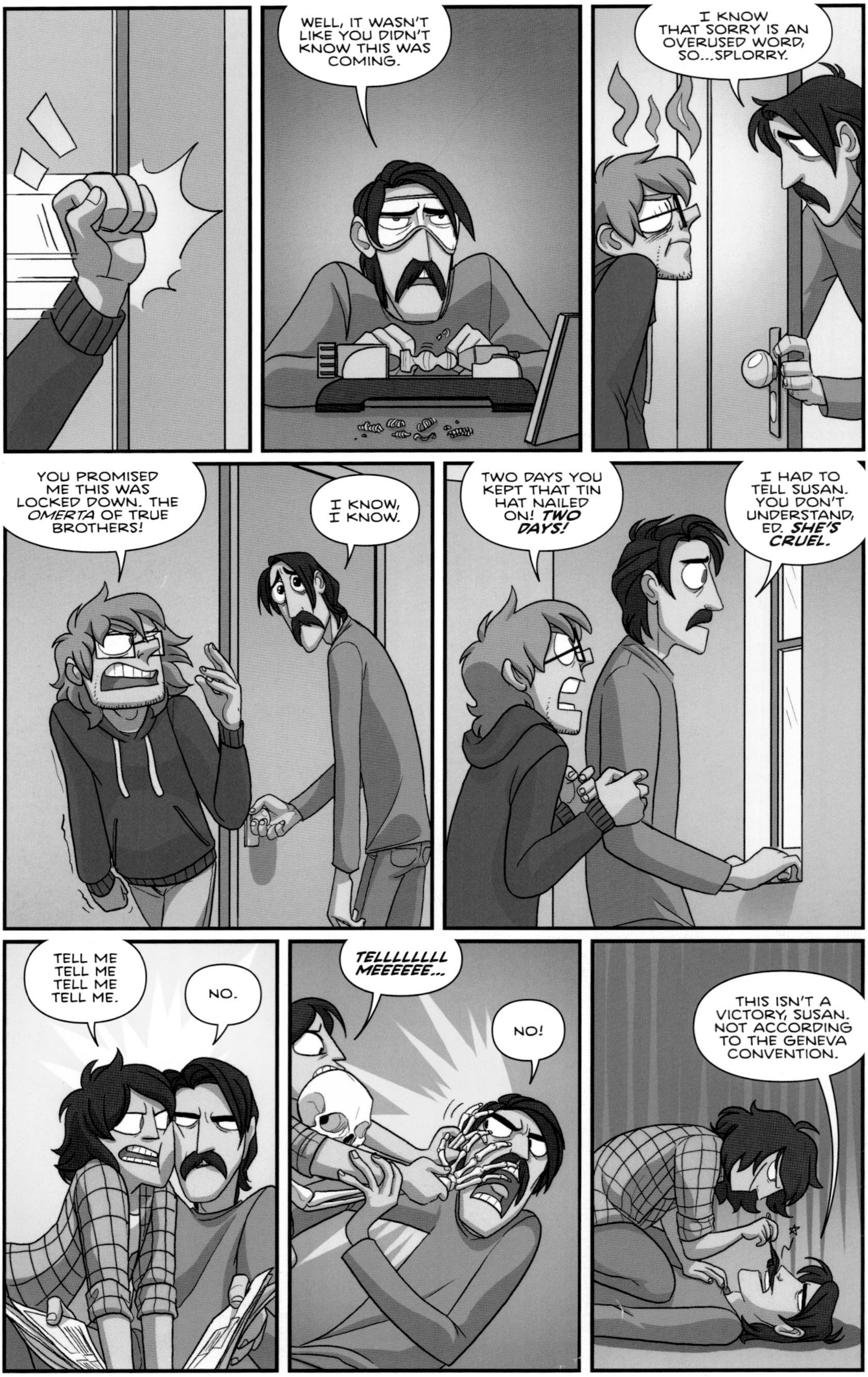
WELL, IT WASN'T LIKE YOU DIDN'T KNOW THIS WAS COMING.
I KNOW THAT SORRY IS AN OVERUSED WORD, SO...SPLORRY.
YOU PROMISED ME THIS WAS LOCKED DOWN. THE *OMERTA* OF TRUE BROTHERS!
I KNOW, I KNOW.
TWO DAYS YOU KEPT THAT TIN HAT NAILED ON! ***TWO DAYS!***
I HAD TO TELL SUSAN. YOU DON'T UNDERSTAND, ED. ***SHE'S CRUEL.***
TELL ME TELL ME TELL ME TELL ME.
NO.
TELLLLLLLLL MEEEEEE...
NO!
THIS ISN'T A VICTORY, SUSAN. NOT ACCORDING TO THE GENEVA CONVENTION.

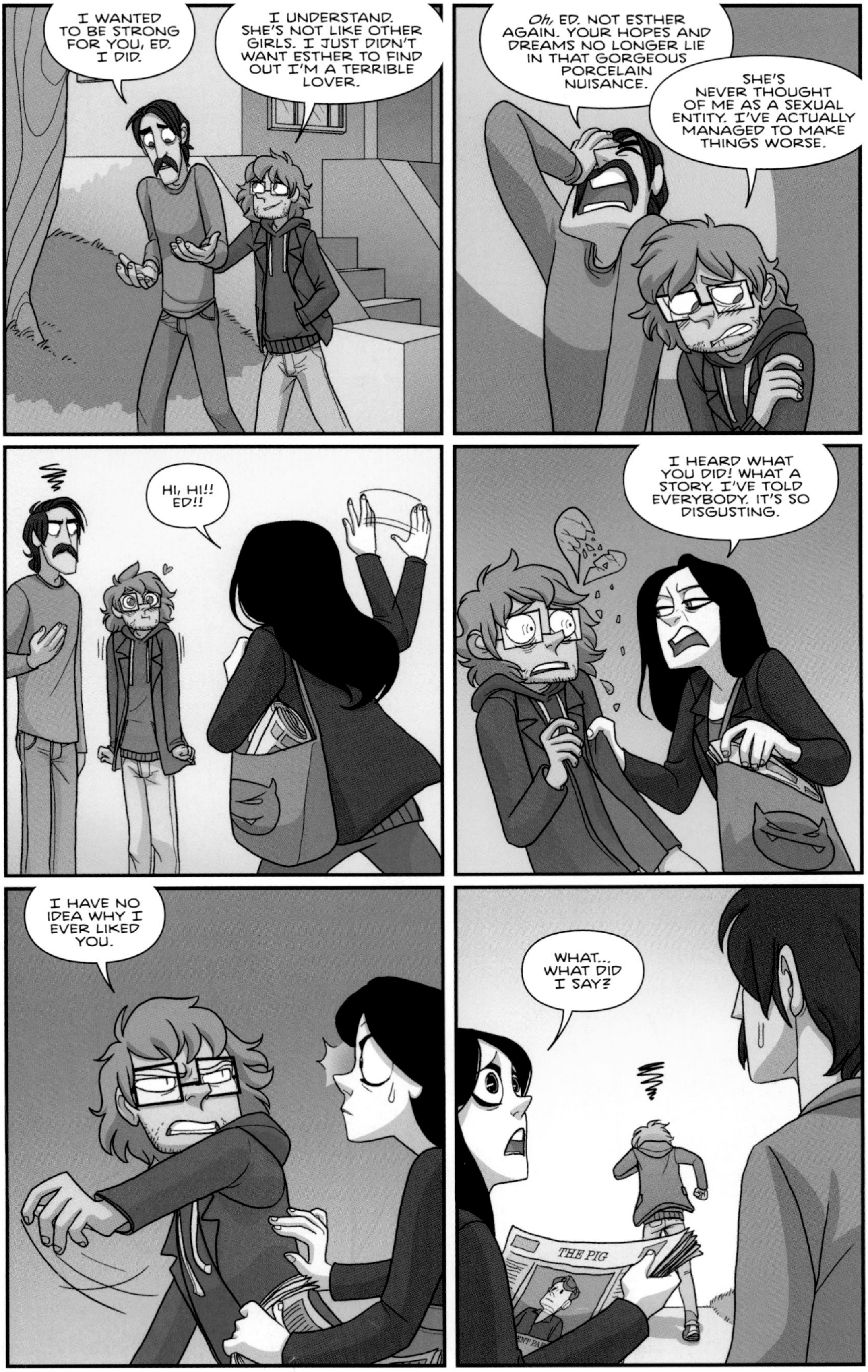
I WANTED TO BE STRONG FOR YOU, ED. I DID.
I UNDERSTAND. SHE'S NOT LIKE OTHER GIRLS. I JUST DIDN'T WANT ESTHER TO FIND OUT I'M A TERRIBLE LOVER.
Oh, ED. NOT ESTHER AGAIN. YOUR HOPES AND DREAMS NO LONGER LIE IN THAT GORGEOUS PORCELAIN NUISANCE.
SHE'S NEVER THOUGHT OF ME AS A SEXUAL ENTITY. I'VE ACTUALLY MANAGED TO MAKE THINGS WORSE.
HI, HI!! ED!!
I HEARD WHAT YOU DID! WHAT A STORY. I'VE TOLD EVERYBODY. IT'S SO DISGUSTING.
I HAVE NO IDEA WHY I EVER LIKED YOU.
WHAT... WHAT DID I SAY?
THE PIG

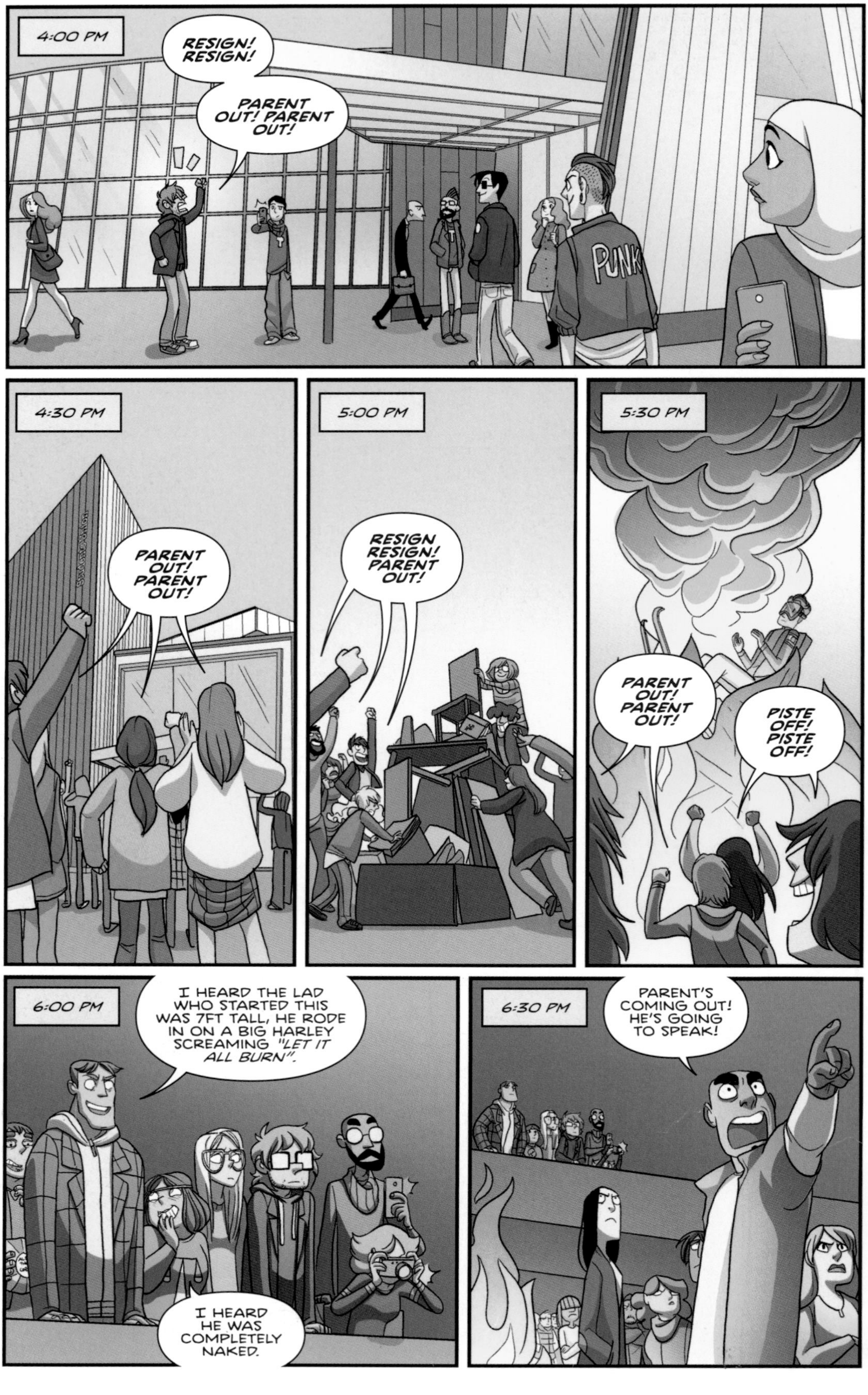
4:00 PM
RESIGN! RESIGN!
PARENT OUT! PARENT OUT!
PUNK
4:30 PM
PARENT OUT! PARENT OUT!
5:00 PM
RESIGN RESIGN! PARENT OUT!
5:30 PM
PARENT OUT! PARENT OUT!
PISTE OFF! PISTE OFF!
6:00 PM
I HEARD THE LAD WHO STARTED THIS WAS 7FT TALL, HE RODE IN ON A BIG HARLEY SCREAMING "LET IT ALL BURN".
I HEARD HE WAS COMPLETELY NAKED.
6:30 PM
PARENT'S COMING OUT! HE'S GOING TO SPEAK!

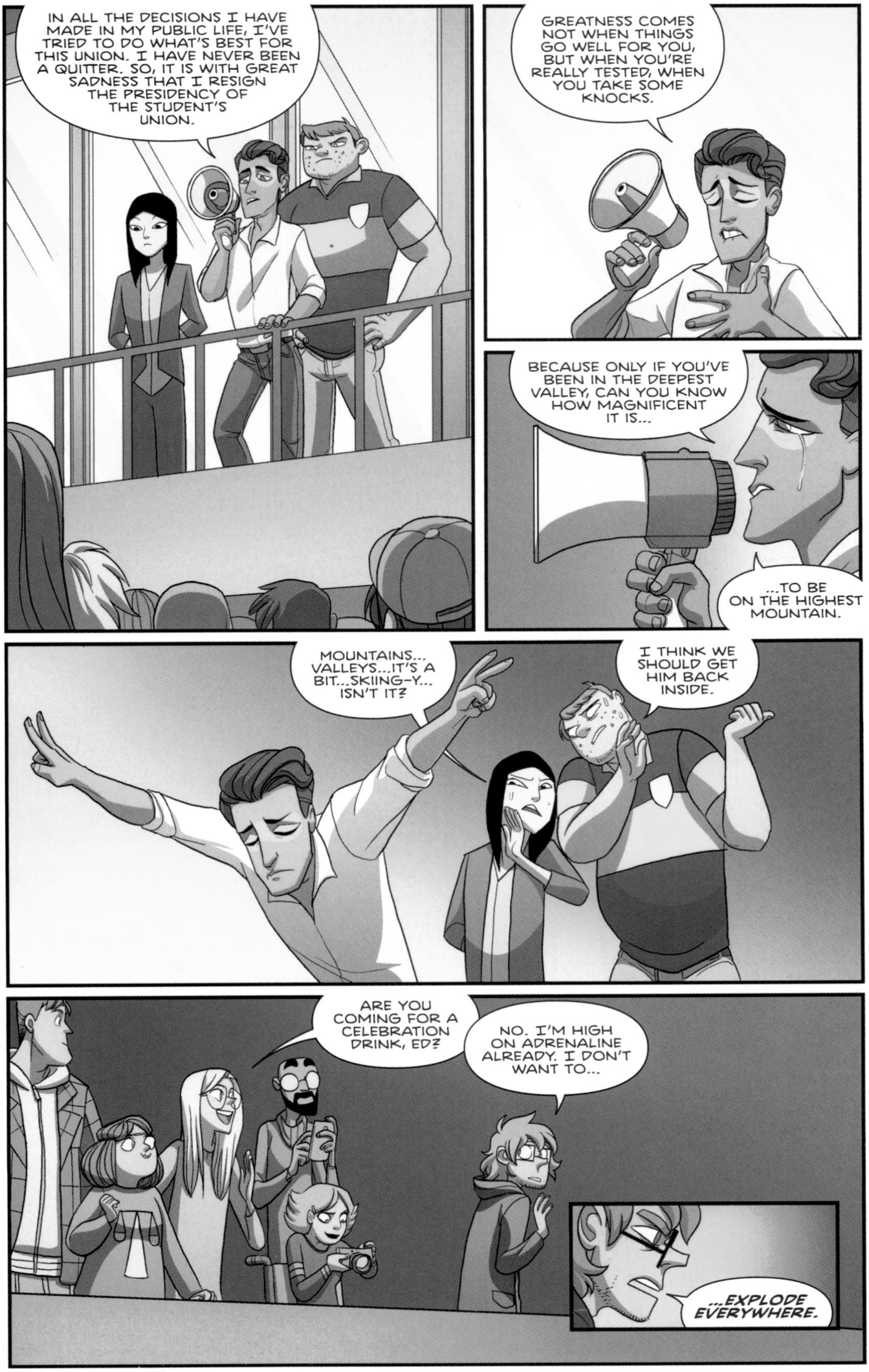
IN ALL THE DECISIONS I HAVE MADE IN MY PUBLIC LIFE, I'VE TRIED TO DO WHAT'S BEST FOR THIS UNION. I HAVE NEVER BEEN A QUITTER. SO, IT IS WITH GREAT SADNESS THAT I RESIGN THE PRESIDENCY OF THE STUDENT'S UNION.
GREATNESS COMES NOT WHEN THINGS GO WELL FOR YOU, BUT WHEN YOU'RE REALLY TESTED, WHEN YOU TAKE SOME KNOCKS.
BECAUSE ONLY IF YOU'VE BEEN IN THE DEEPEST VALLEY, CAN YOU KNOW HOW MAGNIFICENT IT IS...
...TO BE ON THE HIGHEST MOUNTAIN.
MOUNTAINS... VALLEYS...IT'S A BIT...SKIING-Y... ISN'T IT?
I THINK WE SHOULD GET HIM BACK INSIDE.
ARE YOU COMING FOR A CELEBRATION DRINK, ED?
NO. I'M HIGH ON ADRENALINE ALREADY. I DON'T WANT TO...
...EXPLODE EVERYWHERE.

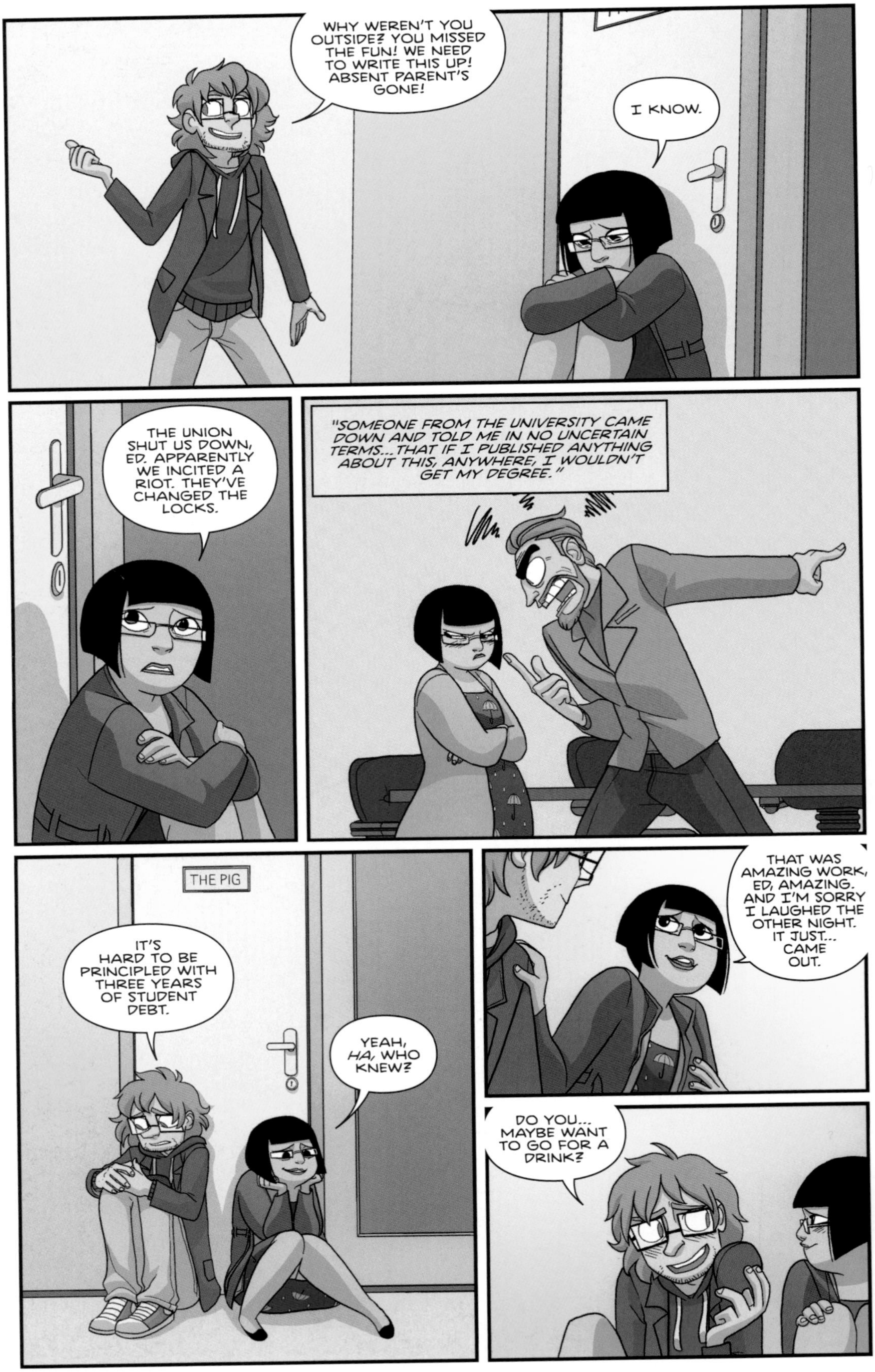
WHY WEREN'T YOU OUTSIDE? YOU MISSED THE FUN! WE NEED TO WRITE THIS UP! ABSENT PARENT'S GONE!
I KNOW.
THE UNION SHUT US DOWN, ED. APPARENTLY WE INCITED A RIOT. THEY'VE CHANGED THE LOCKS.
"SOMEONE FROM THE UNIVERSITY CAME DOWN AND TOLD ME IN NO UNCERTAIN TERMS... THAT IF I PUBLISHED ANYTHING ABOUT THIS, ANYWHERE, I WOULDN'T GET MY DEGREE."
THE PIG
IT'S HARD TO BE PRINCIPLED WITH THREE YEARS OF STUDENT DEBT.
YEAH, *HA*, WHO KNEW?
THAT WAS AMAZING WORK, ED, AMAZING. AND I'M SORRY I LAUGHED THE OTHER NIGHT. IT JUST... CAME OUT.
DO YOU... MAYBE WANT TO GO FOR A DRINK?

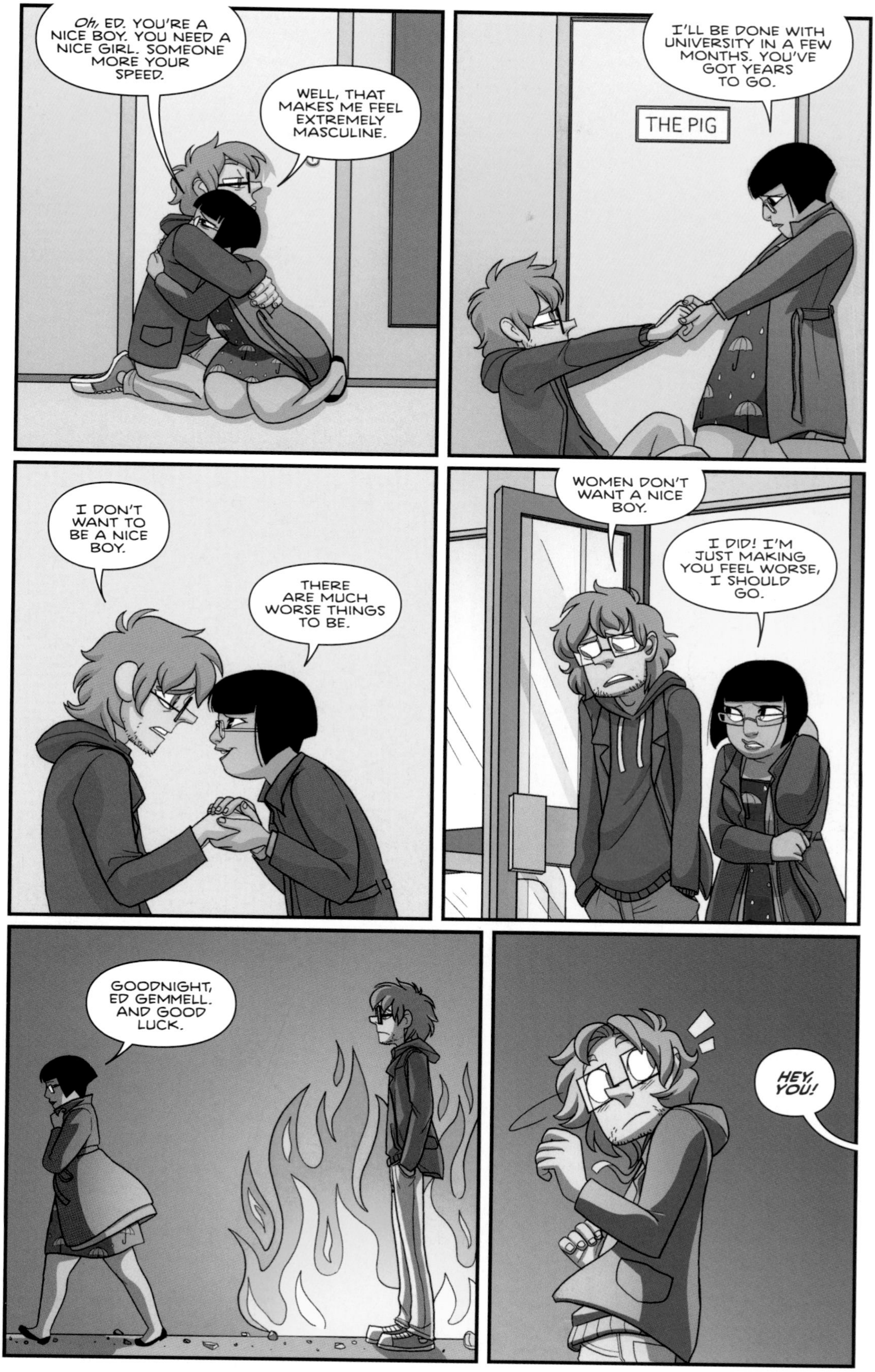
Oh, ED. YOU'RE A NICE BOY. YOU NEED A NICE GIRL. SOMEONE MORE YOUR SPEED.
WELL, THAT MAKES ME FEEL EXTREMELY MASCULINE.
I'LL BE DONE WITH UNIVERSITY IN A FEW MONTHS. YOU'VE GOT YEARS TO GO.
THE PIG
I DON'T WANT TO BE A NICE BOY.
THERE ARE MUCH WORSE THINGS TO BE.
WOMEN DON'T WANT A NICE BOY.
I DID! I'M JUST MAKING YOU FEEL WORSE, I SHOULD GO.
GOODNIGHT, ED GEMMELL. AND GOOD LUCK.
HEY, YOU!

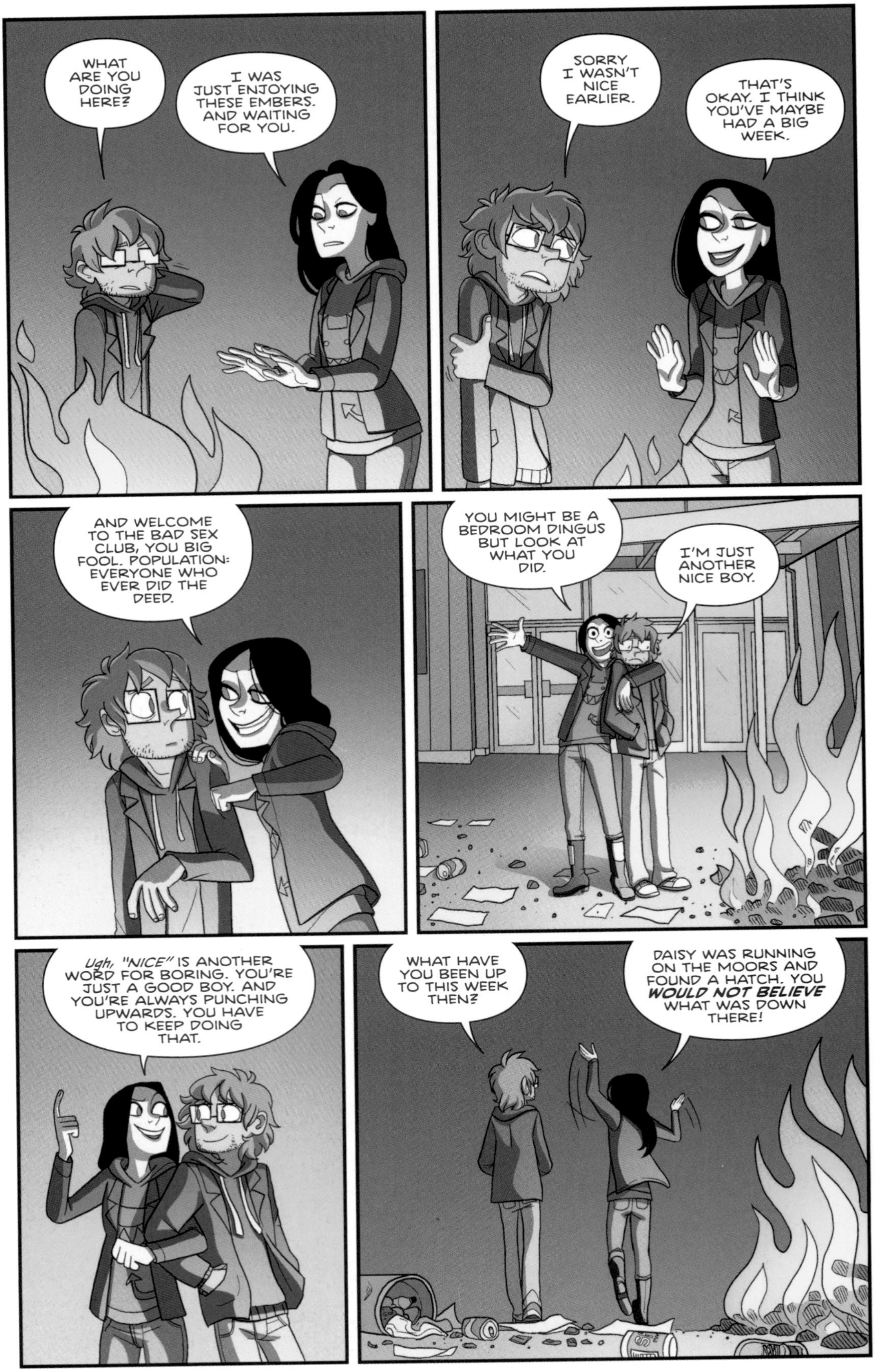
WHAT ARE YOU DOING HERE?
I WAS JUST ENJOYING THESE EMBERS. AND WAITING FOR YOU.
SORRY I WASN'T NICE EARLIER.
THAT'S OKAY. I THINK YOU'VE MAYBE HAD A BIG WEEK.
AND WELCOME TO THE BAD SEX CLUB, YOU BIG FOOL. POPULATION: EVERYONE WHO EVER DID THE DEED.
YOU MIGHT BE A BEDROOM DINGUS BUT LOOK AT WHAT YOU DID.
I'M JUST ANOTHER NICE BOY.
Ugh, "NICE" IS ANOTHER WORD FOR BORING. YOU'RE JUST A GOOD BOY. AND YOU'RE ALWAYS PUNCHING UPWARDS. YOU HAVE TO KEEP DOING THAT.
WHAT HAVE YOU BEEN UP TO THIS WEEK THEN?
DAISY WAS RUNNING ON THE MOORS AND FOUND A HATCH. YOU ***WOULD NOT BELIEVE*** WHAT WAS DOWN THERE!

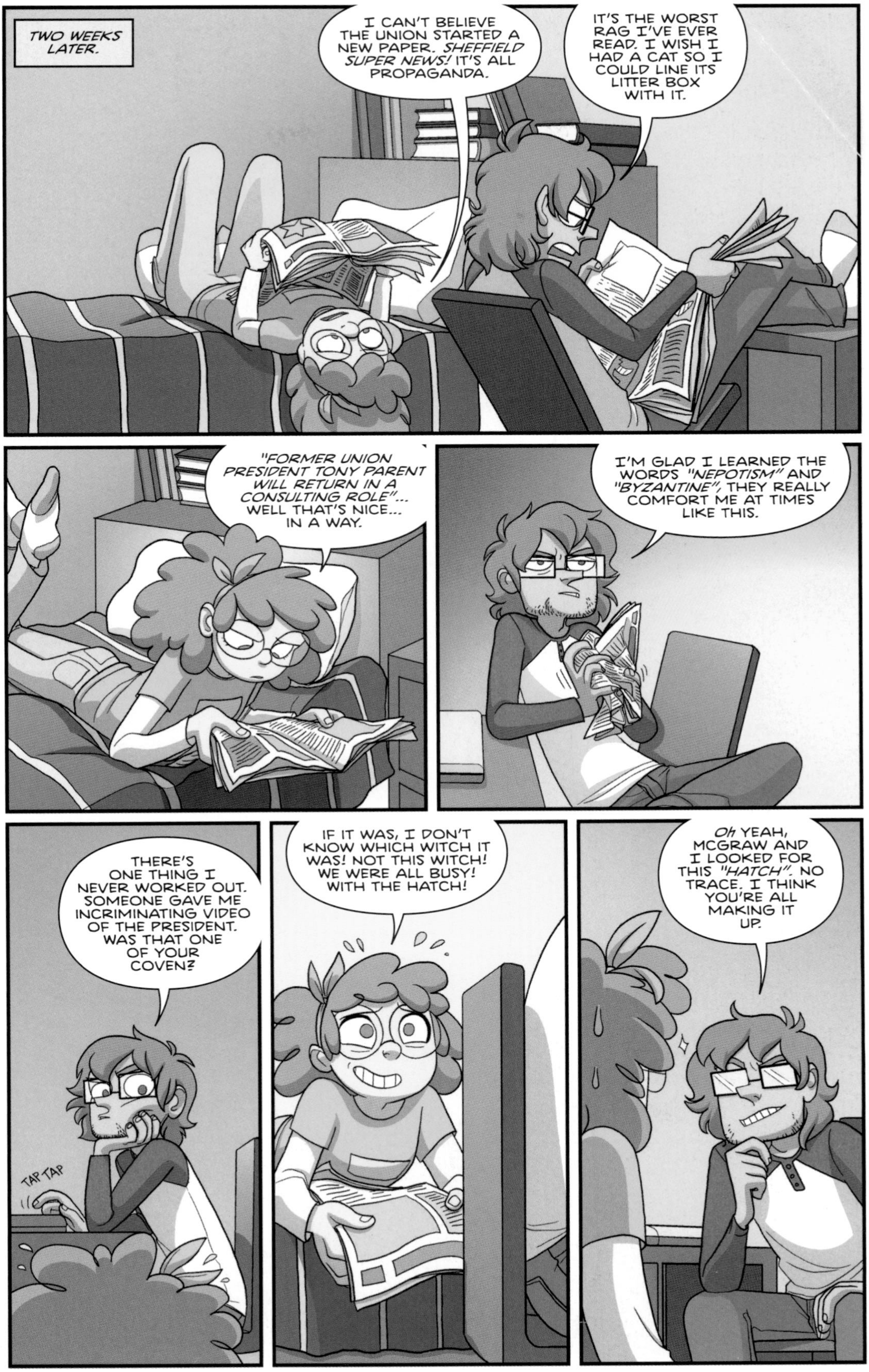
TWO WEEKS LATER.
I CAN'T BELIEVE THE UNION STARTED A NEW PAPER. SHEFFIELD SUPER NEWS! IT'S ALL PROPAGANDA.
IT'S THE WORST RAG I'VE EVER READ. I WISH I HAD A CAT SO I COULD LINE ITS LITTER BOX WITH IT.
"FORMER UNION PRESIDENT TONY PARENT WILL RETURN IN A CONSULTING ROLE"... WELL THAT'S NICE... IN A WAY.
I'M GLAD I LEARNED THE WORDS "NEPOTISM" AND "BYZANTINE", THEY REALLY COMFORT ME AT TIMES LIKE THIS.
THERE'S ONE THING I NEVER WORKED OUT. SOMEONE GAVE ME INCRIMINATING VIDEO OF THE PRESIDENT. WAS THAT ONE OF YOUR COVEN?
TAP TAP
IF IT WAS, I DON'T KNOW WHICH WITCH IT WAS! NOT THIS WITCH! WE WERE ALL BUSY! WITH THE HATCH!
Oh YEAH, MCGRAW AND I LOOKED FOR THIS "HATCH". NO TRACE. I THINK YOU'RE ALL MAKING IT UP.

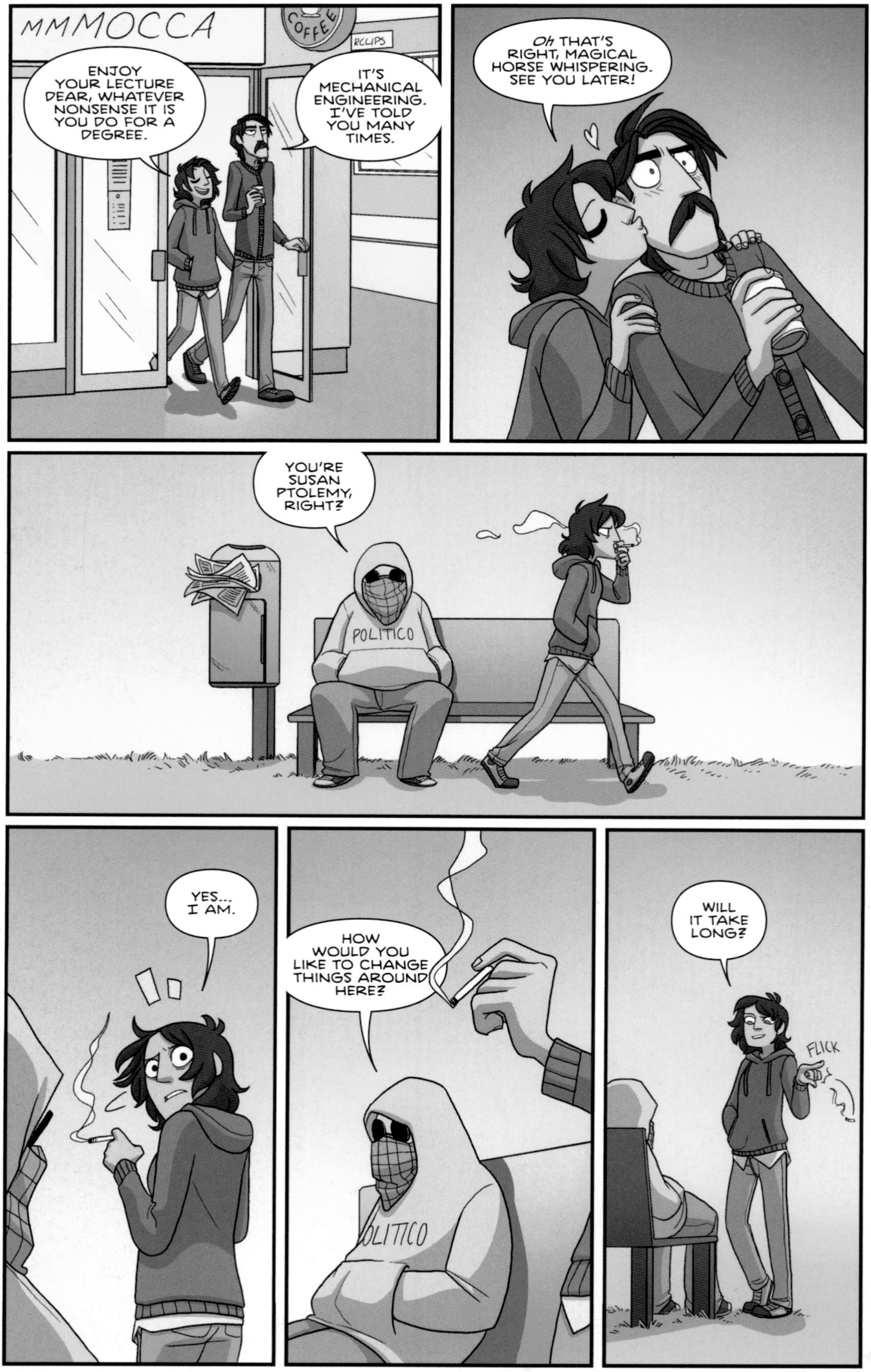
MMMOCCA
COFFEE
RCLIPS
ENJOY YOUR LECTURE DEAR, WHATEVER NONSENSE IT IS YOU DO FOR A DEGREE.
IT'S MECHANICAL ENGINEERING. I'VE TOLD YOU MANY TIMES.
Oh THAT'S RIGHT, MAGICAL HORSE WHISPERING. SEE YOU LATER!
YOU'RE SUSAN PTOLEMY, RIGHT?
POLITICO
YES... I AM.
HOW WOULD YOU LIKE TO CHANGE THINGS AROUND HERE?
OLITICO
WILL IT TAKE LONG?
FLICK

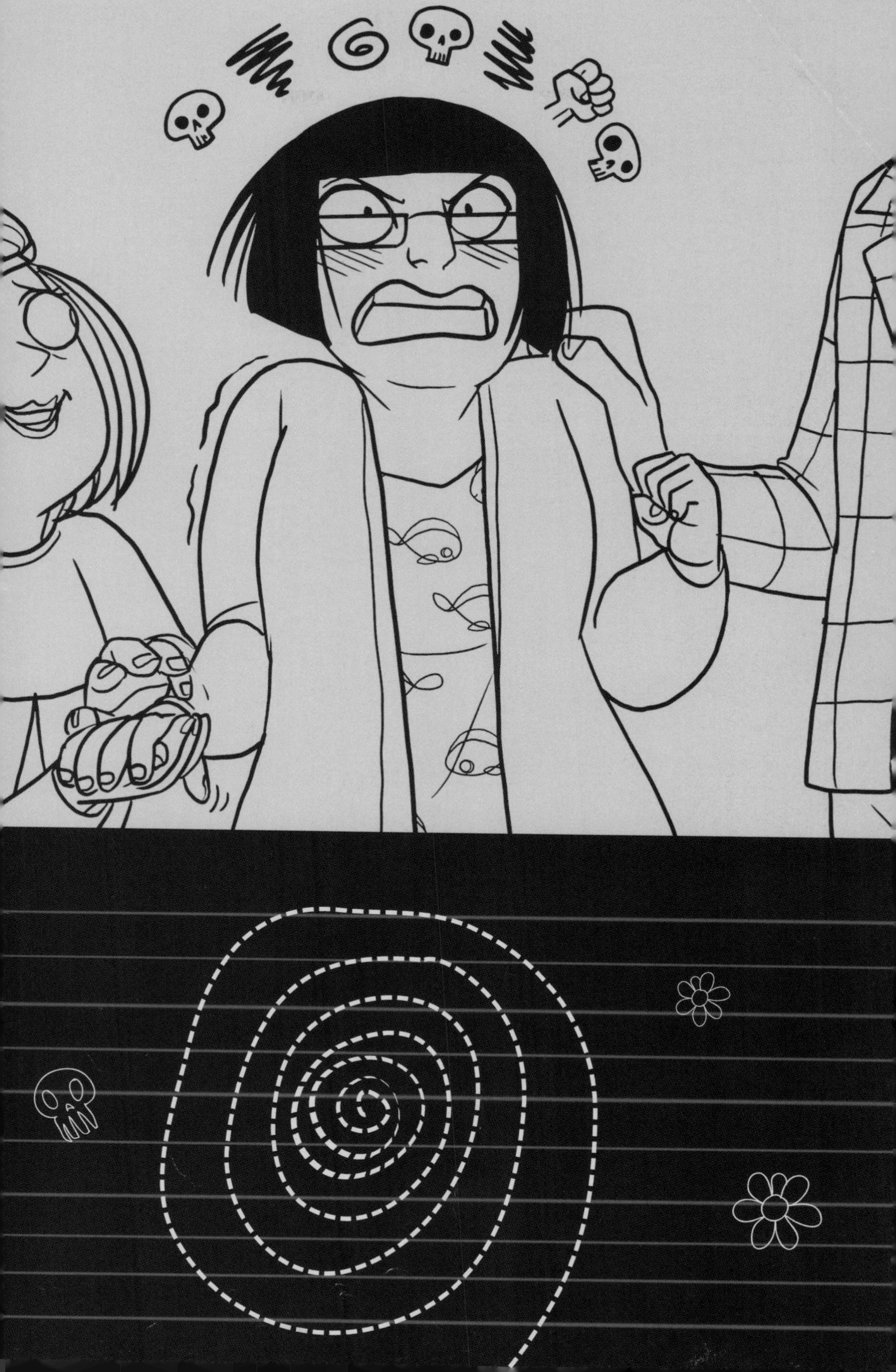

CHAPTER TEN

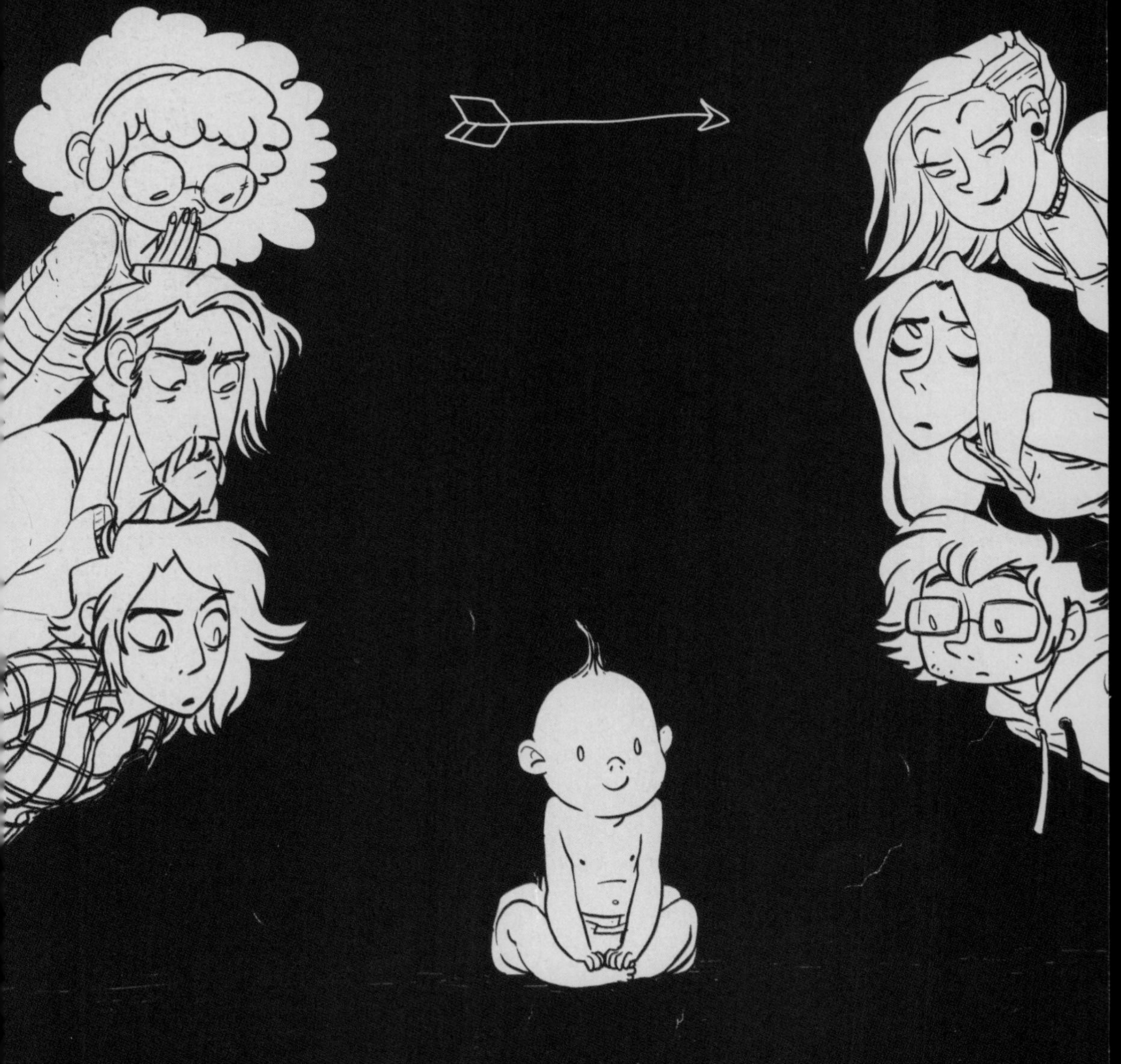

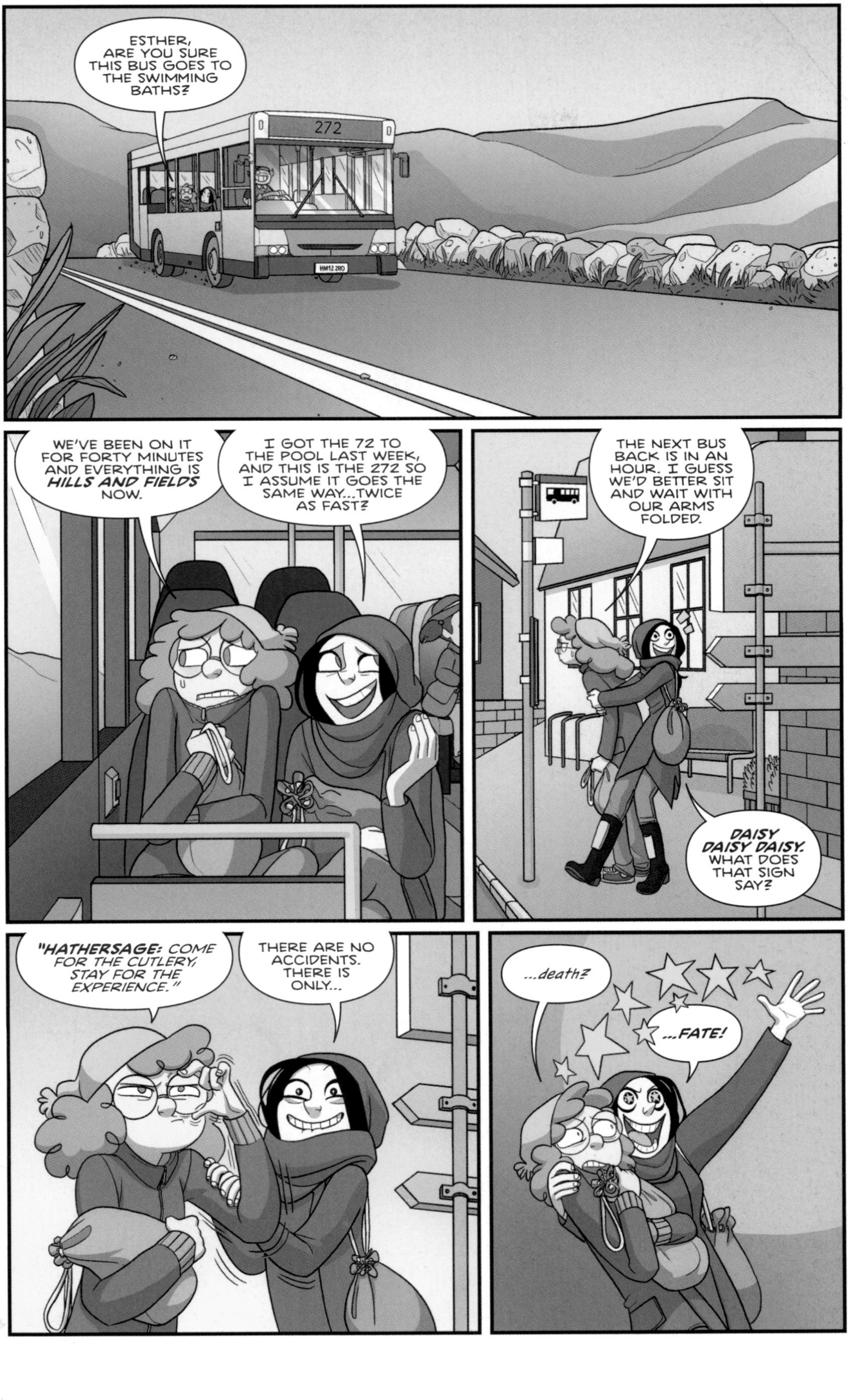
ESTHER, ARE YOU SURE THIS BUS GOES TO THE SWIMMING BATHS?
272
WE'VE BEEN ON IT FOR FORTY MINUTES AND EVERYTHING IS **HILLS AND FIELDS** NOW.
I GOT THE 72 TO THE POOL LAST WEEK, AND THIS IS THE 272 SO I ASSUME IT GOES THE SAME WAY... TWICE AS FAST?
THE NEXT BUS BACK IS IN AN HOUR. I GUESS WE'D BETTER SIT AND WAIT WITH OUR ARMS FOLDED.
DAISY DAISY DAISY. WHAT DOES THAT SIGN SAY?
"**HATHERSAGE:** COME FOR THE CUTLERY, STAY FOR THE EXPERIENCE."
THERE ARE NO ACCIDENTS. THERE IS ONLY...
...death?
...FATE!

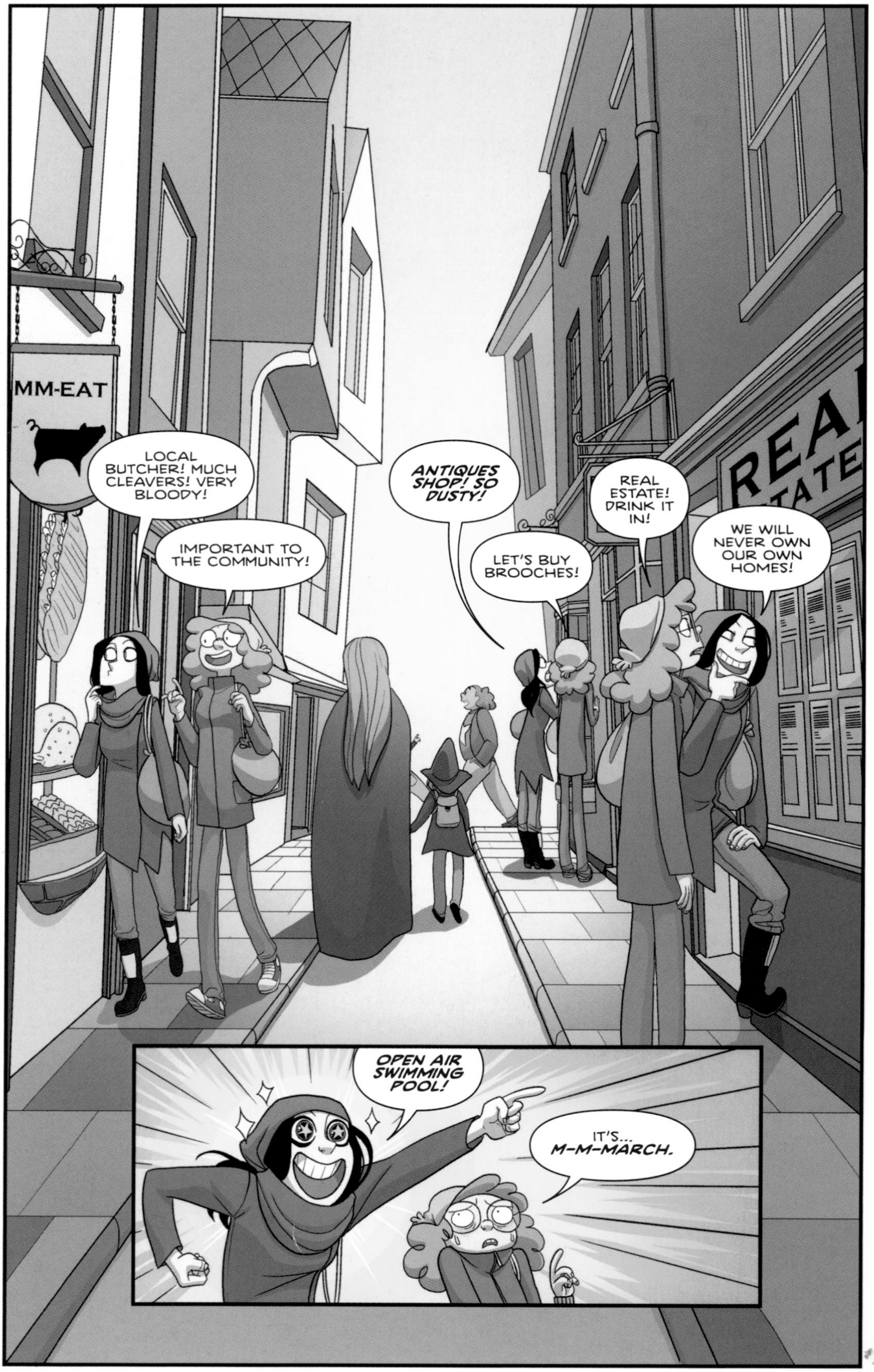
MM-EAT
LOCAL BUTCHER! MUCH CLEAVERS! VERY BLOODY!
IMPORTANT TO THE COMMUNITY!
ANTIQUES SHOP! SO DUSTY!
LET'S BUY BROOCHES!
REAL ESTATE! DRINK IT IN!
REAL ESTATE
WE WILL NEVER OWN OUR OWN HOMES!
OPEN AIR SWIMMING POOL!
IT'S... M-M-MARCH.

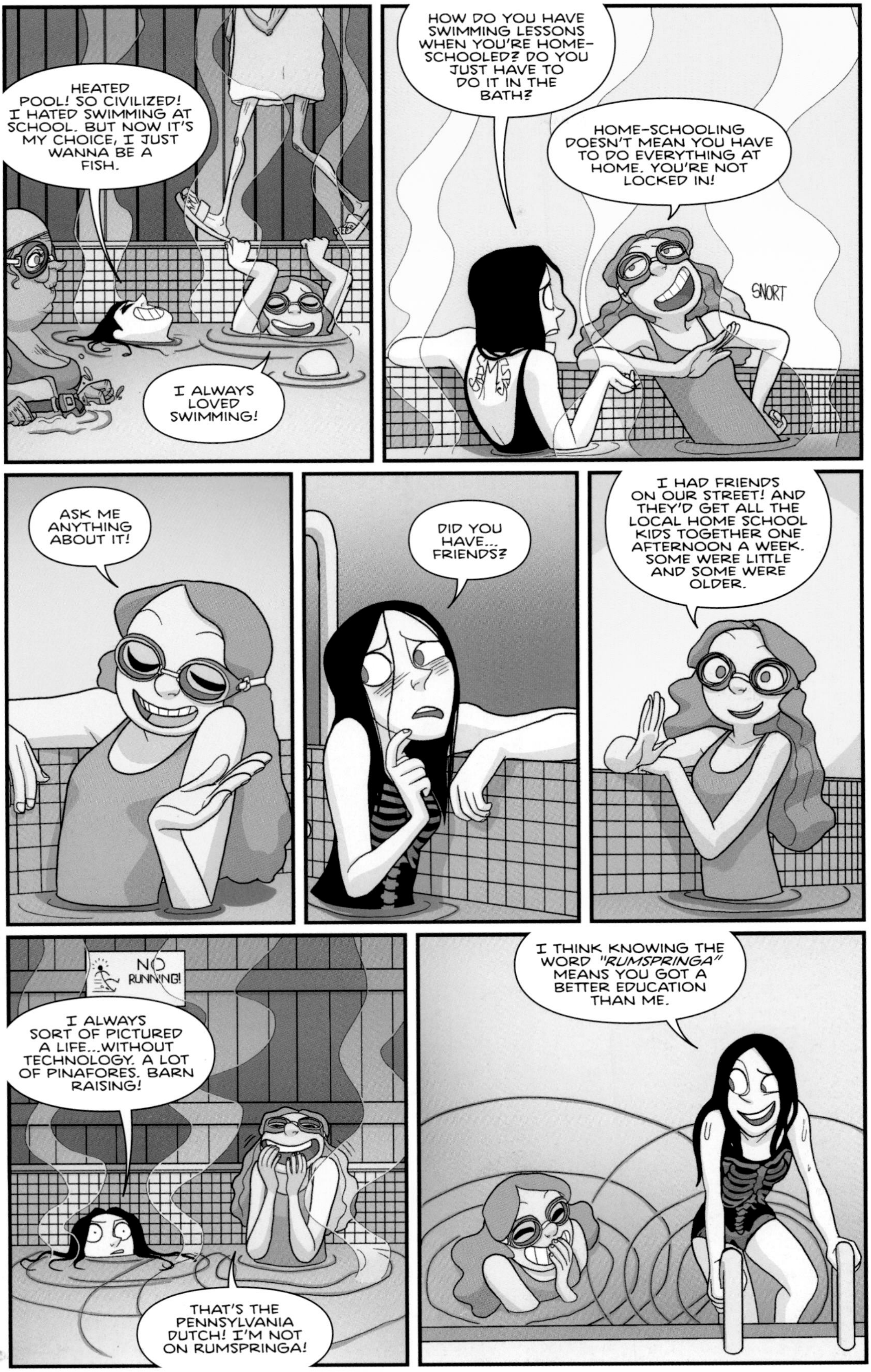
HEATED POOL! SO CIVILIZED! I HATED SWIMMING AT SCHOOL. BUT NOW IT'S MY CHOICE, I JUST WANNA BE A FISH.
I ALWAYS LOVED SWIMMING!
HOW DO YOU HAVE SWIMMING LESSONS WHEN YOU'RE HOME-SCHOOLED? DO YOU JUST HAVE TO DO IT IN THE BATH?
HOME-SCHOOLING DOESN'T MEAN YOU HAVE TO DO EVERYTHING AT HOME. YOU'RE NOT LOCKED IN!
SNORT
ASK ME ANYTHING ABOUT IT!
DID YOU HAVE... FRIENDS?
I HAD FRIENDS ON OUR STREET! AND THEY'D GET ALL THE LOCAL HOME SCHOOL KIDS TOGETHER ONE AFTERNOON A WEEK. SOME WERE LITTLE AND SOME WERE OLDER.
NO RUNNING!
I ALWAYS SORT OF PICTURED A LIFE...WITHOUT TECHNOLOGY. A LOT OF PINAFORES. BARN RAISING!
THAT'S THE PENNSYLVANIA DUTCH! I'M NOT ON RUMSPRINGA!
I THINK KNOWING THE WORD "RUMSPRINGA" MEANS YOU GOT A BETTER EDUCATION THAN ME.

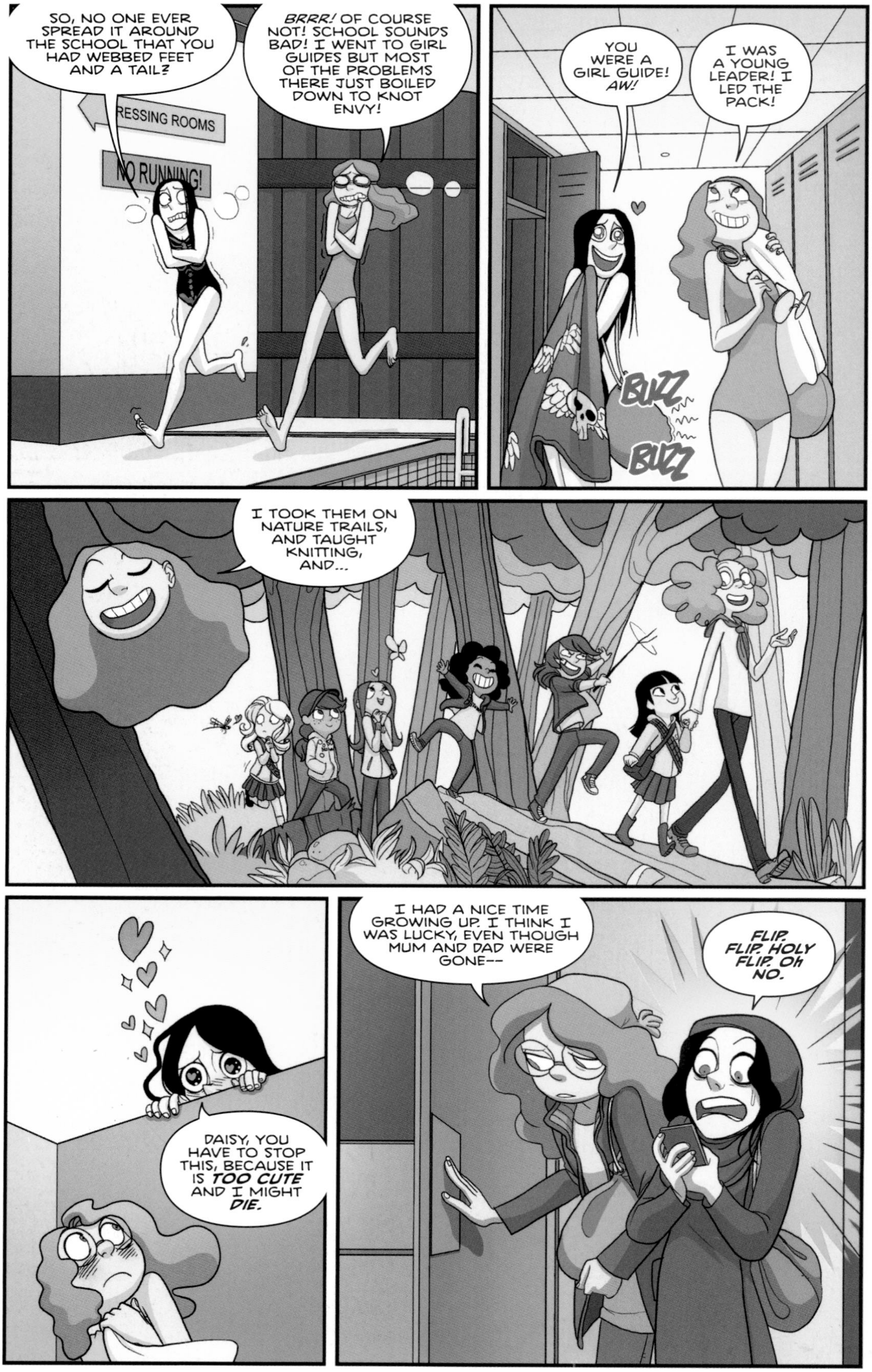
SO, NO ONE EVER SPREAD IT AROUND THE SCHOOL THAT YOU HAD WEBBED FEET AND A TAIL?
BRRR! OF COURSE NOT! SCHOOL SOUNDS BAD! I WENT TO GIRL GUIDES BUT MOST OF THE PROBLEMS THERE JUST BOILED DOWN TO KNOT ENVY!
RESSING ROOMS
NO RUNNING!
YOU WERE A GIRL GUIDE! AW!
I WAS A YOUNG LEADER! I LED THE PACK!
BUZZ
BUZZ
I TOOK THEM ON NATURE TRAILS, AND TAUGHT KNITTING, AND...
DAISY, YOU HAVE TO STOP THIS, BECAUSE IT IS TOO CUTE AND I MIGHT DIE.
I HAD A NICE TIME GROWING UP. I THINK I WAS LUCKY, EVEN THOUGH MUM AND DAD WERE GONE--
FLIP. FLIP. HOLY FLIP. Oh NO.

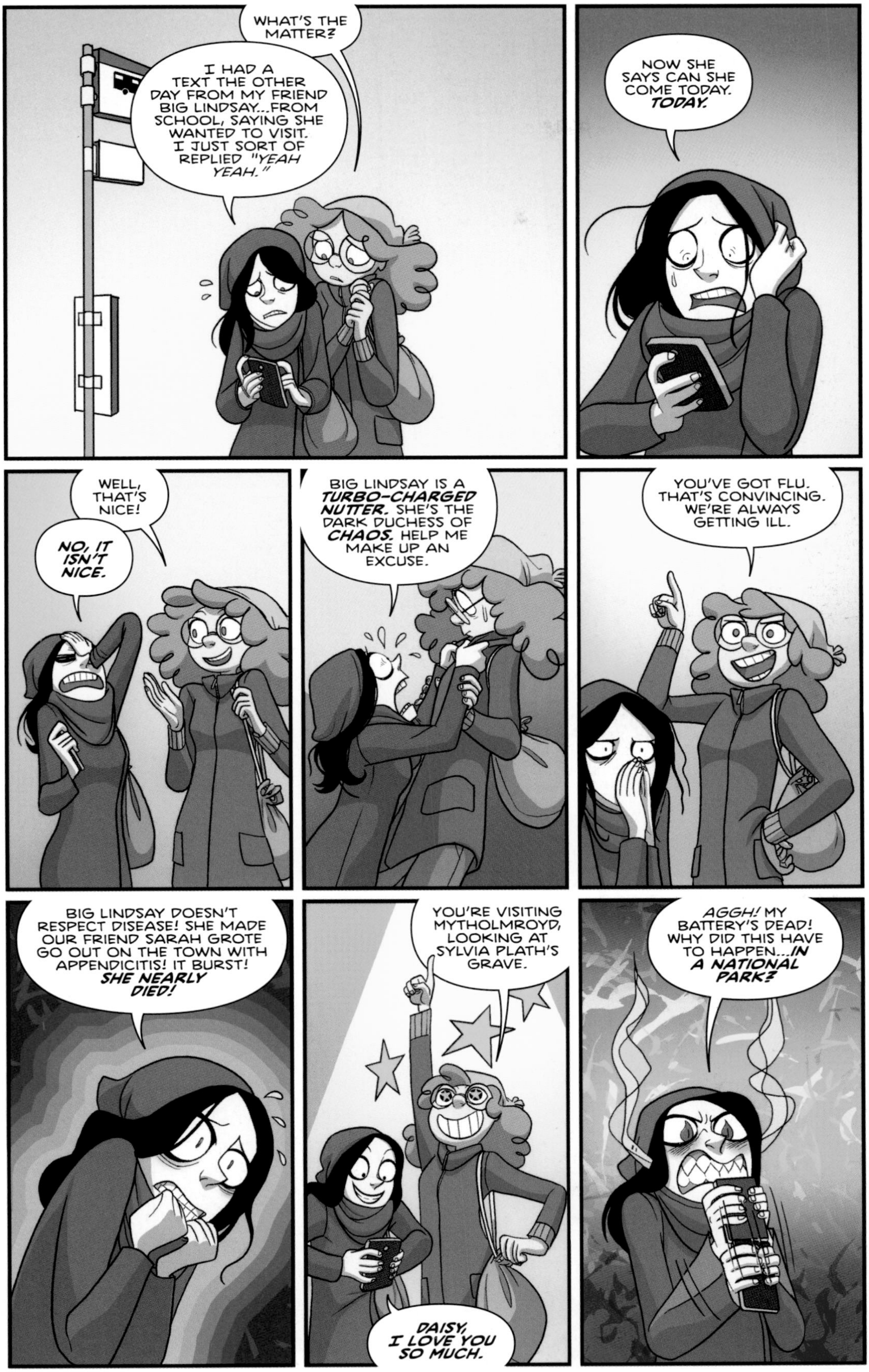
WHAT'S THE MATTER?
I HAD A TEXT THE OTHER DAY FROM MY FRIEND BIG LINDSAY...FROM SCHOOL, SAYING SHE WANTED TO VISIT. I JUST SORT OF REPLIED "YEAH YEAH."
NOW SHE SAYS CAN SHE COME TODAY. TODAY.
WELL, THAT'S NICE!
NO, IT ISN'T NICE.
BIG LINDSAY IS A TURBO-CHARGED NUTTER. SHE'S THE DARK DUCHESS OF CHAOS. HELP ME MAKE UP AN EXCUSE.
YOU'VE GOT FLU. THAT'S CONVINCING. WE'RE ALWAYS GETTING ILL.
BIG LINDSAY DOESN'T RESPECT DISEASE! SHE MADE OUR FRIEND SARAH GROTE GO OUT ON THE TOWN WITH APPENDICITIS! IT BURST! SHE NEARLY DIED!
YOU'RE VISITING MYTHOLMROYD, LOOKING AT SYLVIA PLATH'S GRAVE.
DAISY, I LOVE YOU SO MUCH.
AGGH! MY BATTERY'S DEAD! WHY DID THIS HAVE TO HAPPEN...IN A NATIONAL PARK?

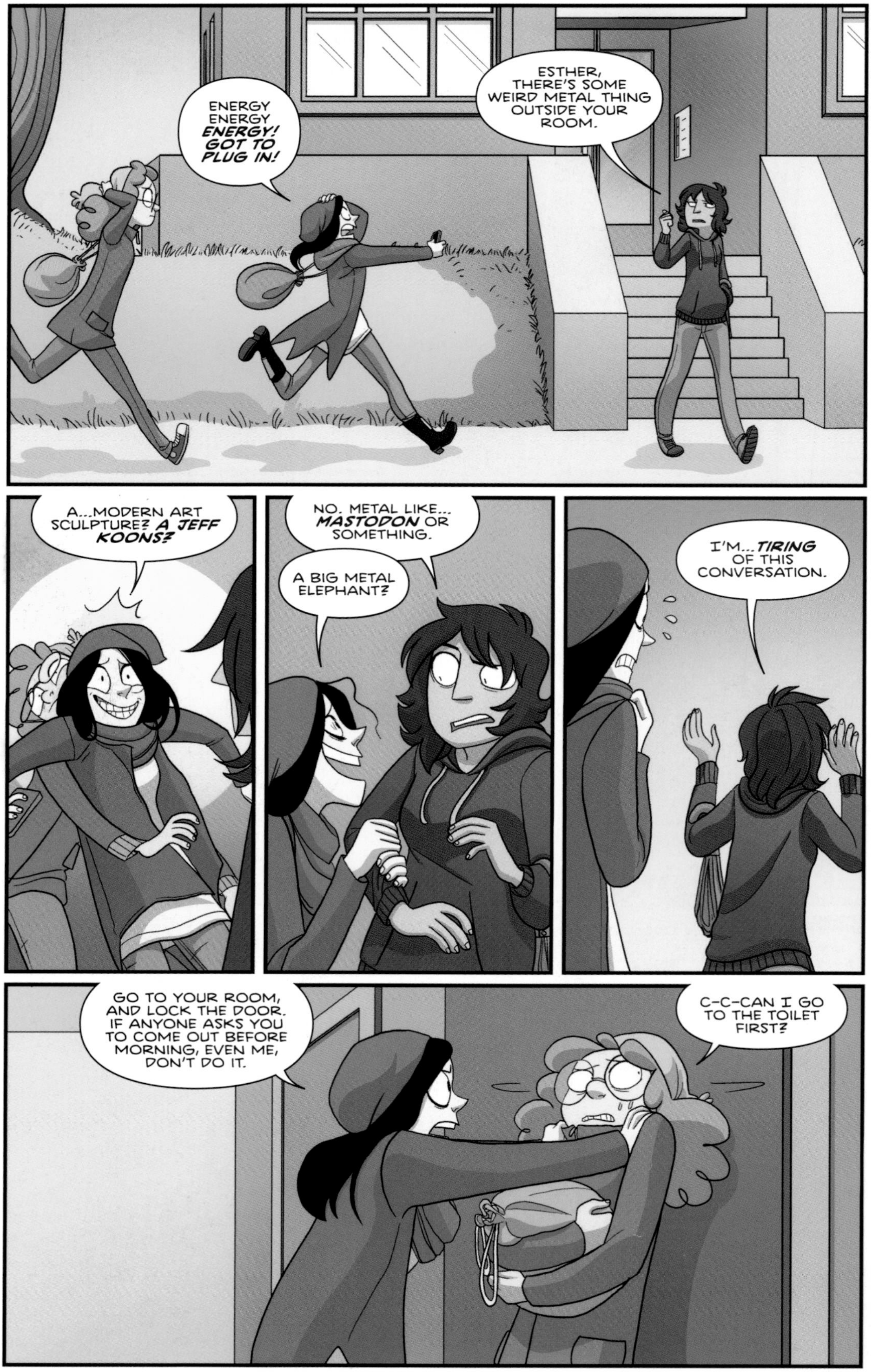
ENERGY ENERGY *ENERGY! GOT TO PLUG IN!*
ESTHER, THERE'S SOME WEIRD METAL THING OUTSIDE YOUR ROOM.
A...MODERN ART SCULPTURE? *A JEFF KOONS?*
NO. METAL LIKE... *MASTODON* OR SOMETHING.
A BIG METAL ELEPHANT?
I'M...*TIRING* OF THIS CONVERSATION.
GO TO YOUR ROOM, AND LOCK THE DOOR. IF ANYONE ASKS YOU TO COME OUT BEFORE MORNING, EVEN ME, DON'T DO IT.
C-C-CAN I GO TO THE TOILET FIRST?

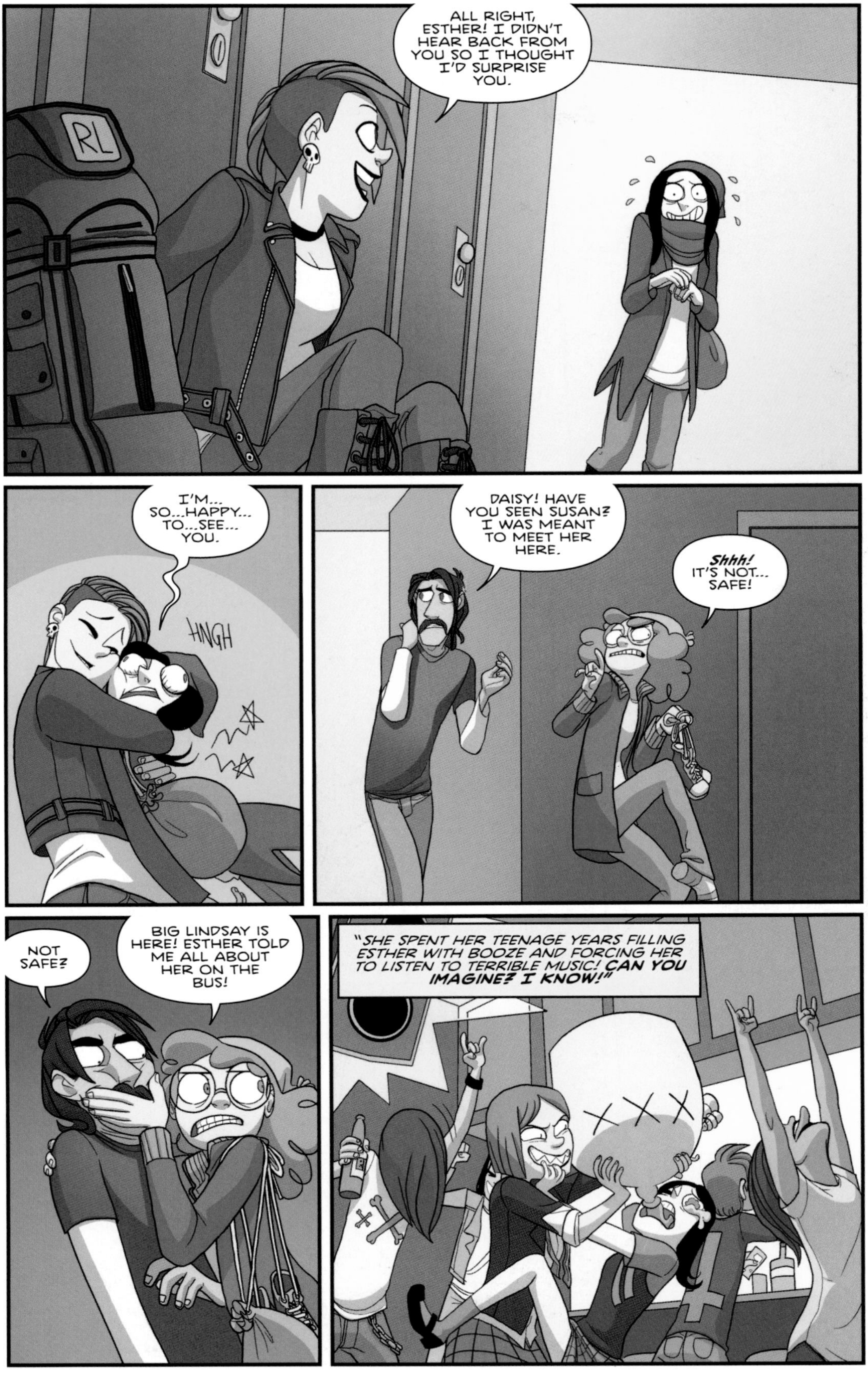
ALL RIGHT, ESTHER! I DIDN'T HEAR BACK FROM YOU SO I THOUGHT I'D SURPRISE YOU.
RL
I'M... SO...HAPPY... TO...SEE... YOU.
HNGH
DAISY! HAVE YOU SEEN SUSAN? I WAS MEANT TO MEET HER HERE.
Shhh! IT'S NOT... SAFE!
NOT SAFE?
BIG LINDSAY IS HERE! ESTHER TOLD ME ALL ABOUT HER ON THE BUS!
"SHE SPENT HER TEENAGE YEARS FILLING ESTHER WITH BOOZE AND FORCING HER TO LISTEN TO TERRIBLE MUSIC! **CAN YOU IMAGINE? I KNOW!**"

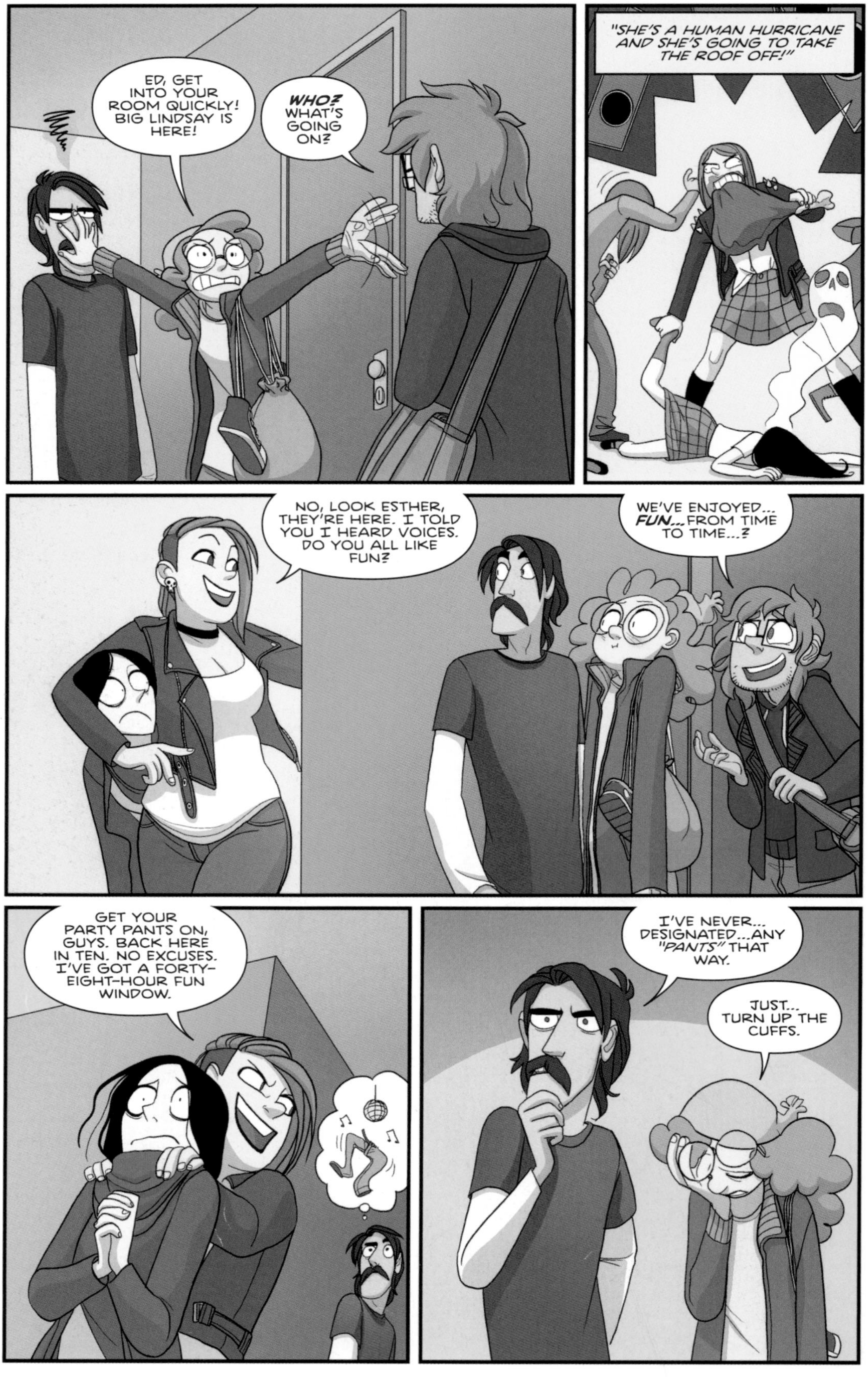
ED, GET INTO YOUR ROOM QUICKLY! BIG LINDSAY IS HERE!
WHO? WHAT'S GOING ON?
"SHE'S A HUMAN HURRICANE AND SHE'S GOING TO TAKE THE ROOF OFF!"
NO, LOOK ESTHER, THEY'RE HERE. I TOLD YOU I HEARD VOICES. DO YOU ALL LIKE FUN?
WE'VE ENJOYED... FUN... FROM TIME TO TIME...?
GET YOUR PARTY PANTS ON, GUYS. BACK HERE IN TEN. NO EXCUSES. I'VE GOT A FORTY-EIGHT-HOUR FUN WINDOW.
I'VE NEVER... DESIGNATED...ANY "PANTS" THAT WAY.
JUST... TURN UP THE CUFFS.

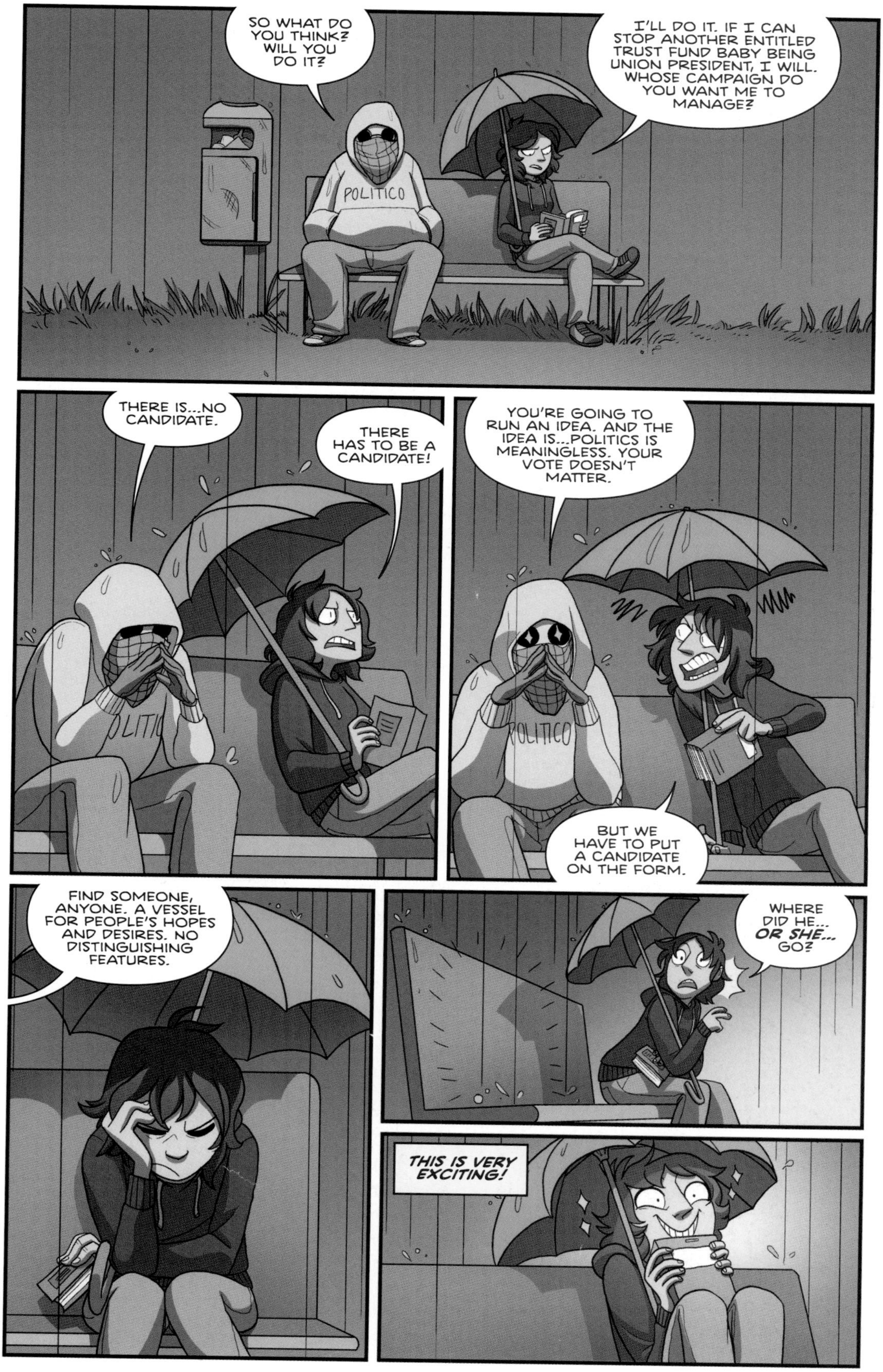
SO WHAT DO YOU THINK? WILL YOU DO IT?
I'LL DO IT. IF I CAN STOP ANOTHER ENTITLED TRUST FUND BABY BEING UNION PRESIDENT, I WILL. WHOSE CAMPAIGN DO YOU WANT ME TO MANAGE?
POLITICO
THERE IS...NO CANDIDATE.
THERE HAS TO BE A CANDIDATE!
YOU'RE GOING TO RUN AN IDEA. AND THE IDEA IS...POLITICS IS MEANINGLESS. YOUR VOTE DOESN'T MATTER.
BUT WE HAVE TO PUT A CANDIDATE ON THE FORM.
FIND SOMEONE, ANYONE. A VESSEL FOR PEOPLE'S HOPES AND DESIRES. NO DISTINGUISHING FEATURES.
WHERE DID HE... OR SHE... GO?
THIS IS VERY EXCITING!

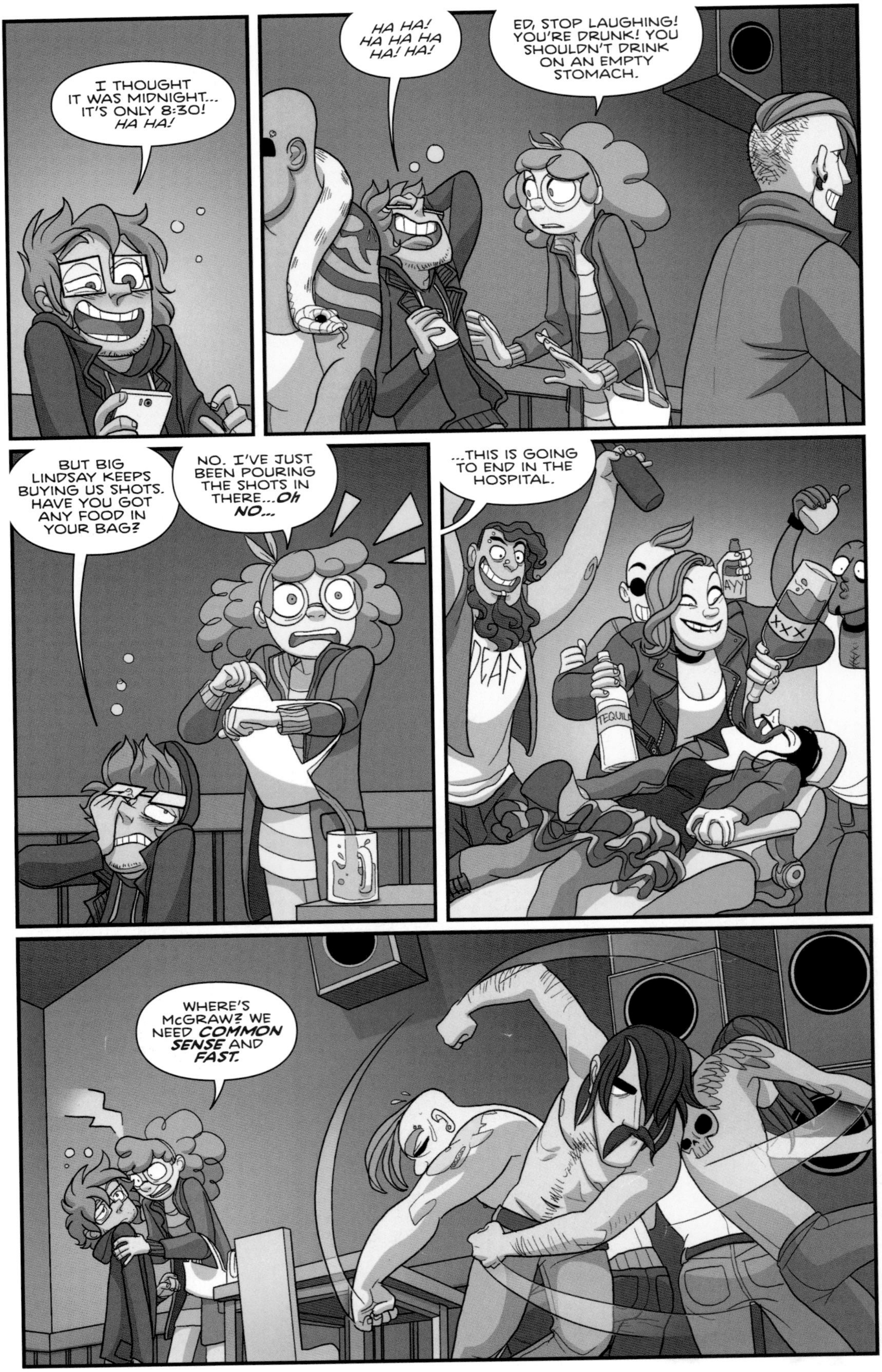
I THOUGHT IT WAS MIDNIGHT... IT'S ONLY 8:30! *HA HA!*
HA HA! HA HA HA HA! HA!
ED, STOP LAUGHING! YOU'RE DRUNK! YOU SHOULDN'T DRINK ON AN EMPTY STOMACH.
BUT BIG LINDSAY KEEPS BUYING US SHOTS. HAVE YOU GOT ANY FOOD IN YOUR BAG?
NO. I'VE JUST BEEN POURING THE SHOTS IN THERE...*Oh NO...*
...THIS IS GOING TO END IN THE HOSPITAL.
DEAF
TEQUILA
AYY
XXX
WHERE'S McGRAW? WE NEED *COMMON SENSE* AND *FAST.*

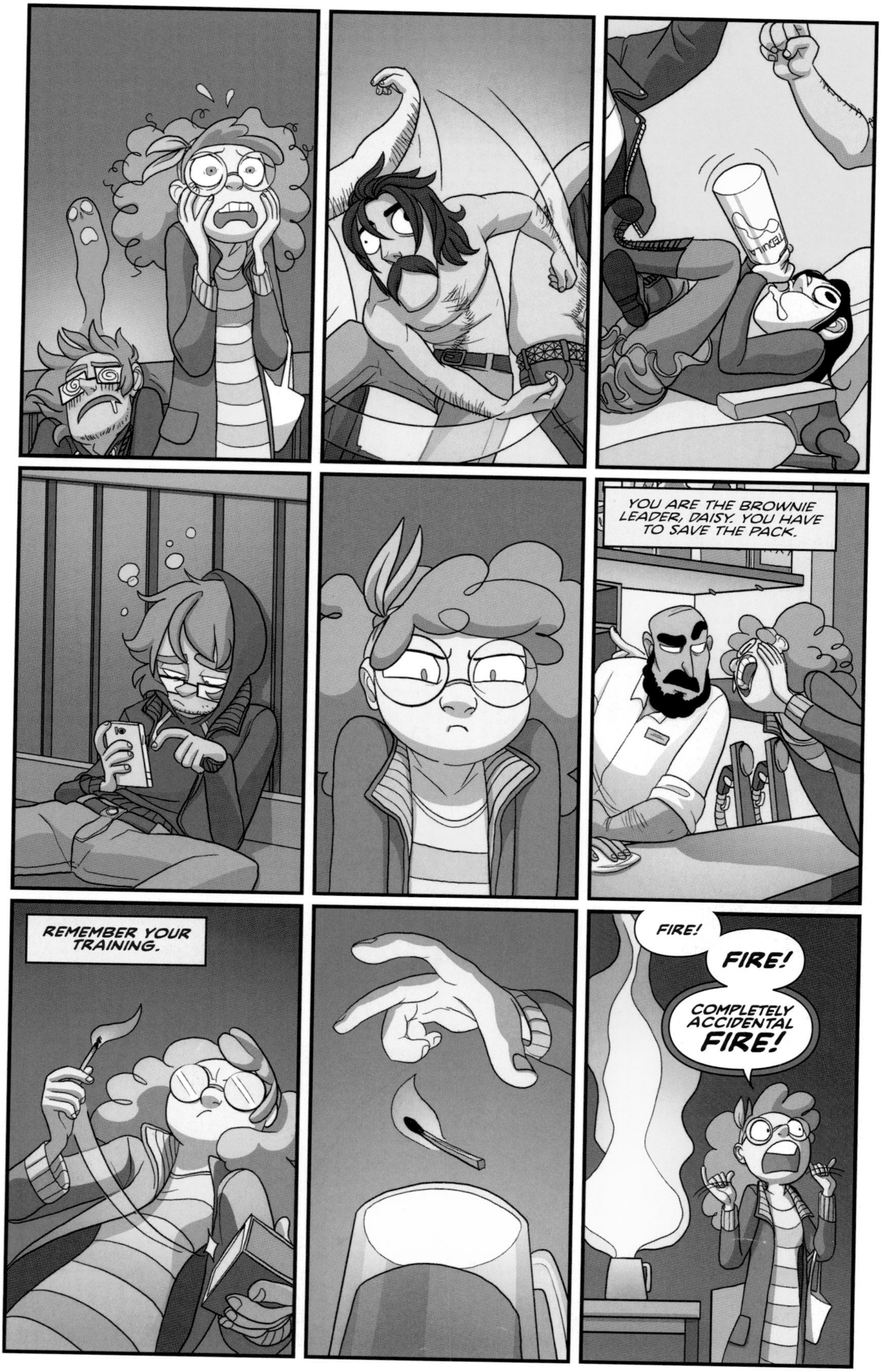
TEQUILA
YOU ARE THE BROWNIE LEADER, DAISY. YOU HAVE TO SAVE THE PACK.
REMEMBER YOUR TRAINING.
FIRE!
FIRE!
COMPLETELY ACCIDENTAL FIRE!

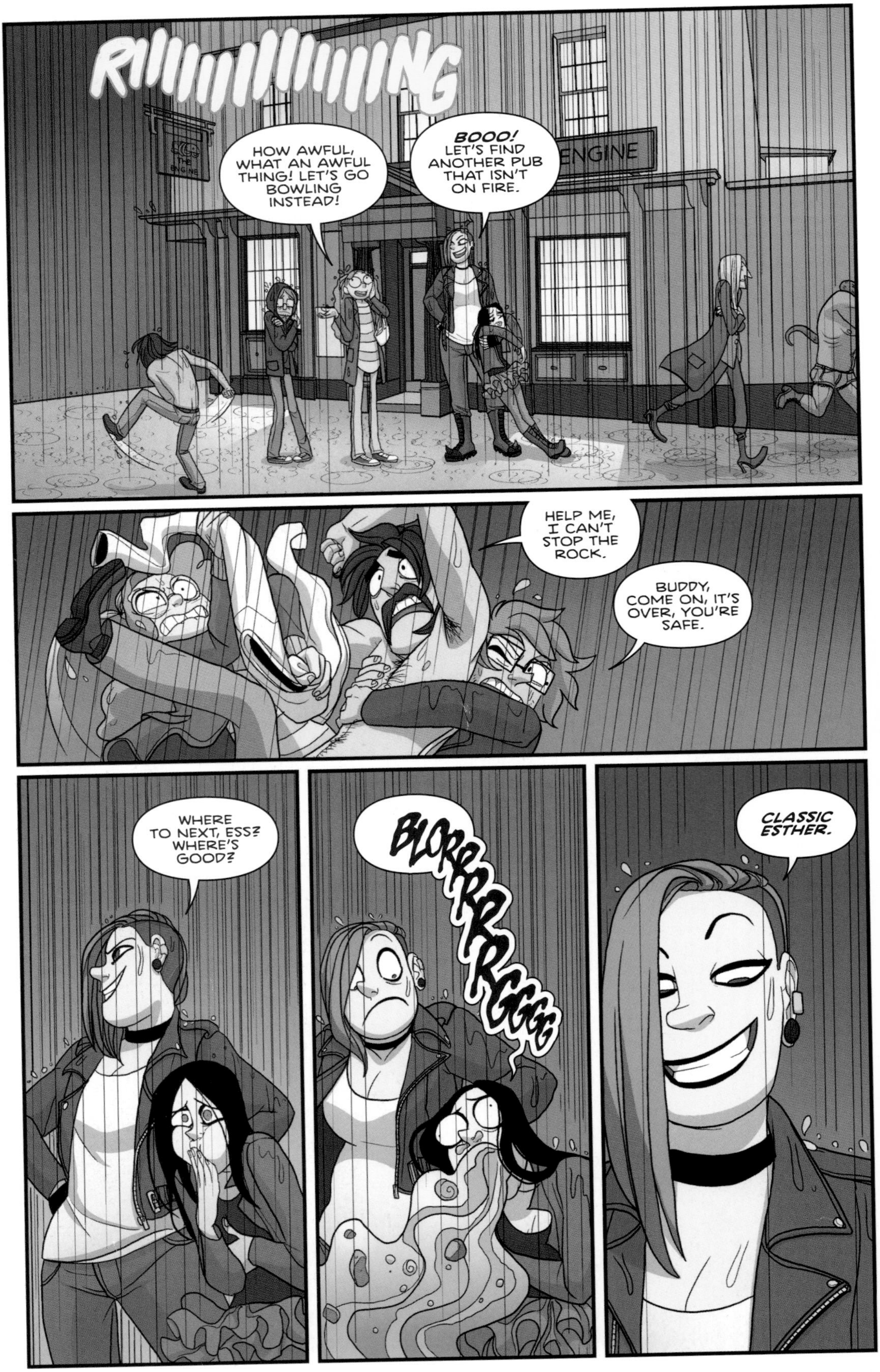
RIIIIIIIIIIIIIIING
THE ENGINE
HOW AWFUL, WHAT AN AWFUL THING! LET'S GO BOWLING INSTEAD!
BOOO! LET'S FIND ANOTHER PUB THAT ISN'T ON FIRE.
ENGINE
HELP ME, I CAN'T STOP THE ROCK.
BUDDY, COME ON, IT'S OVER, YOU'RE SAFE.
WHERE TO NEXT, ESS? WHERE'S GOOD?
BLORRRRRRGGGG
CLASSIC ESTHER.

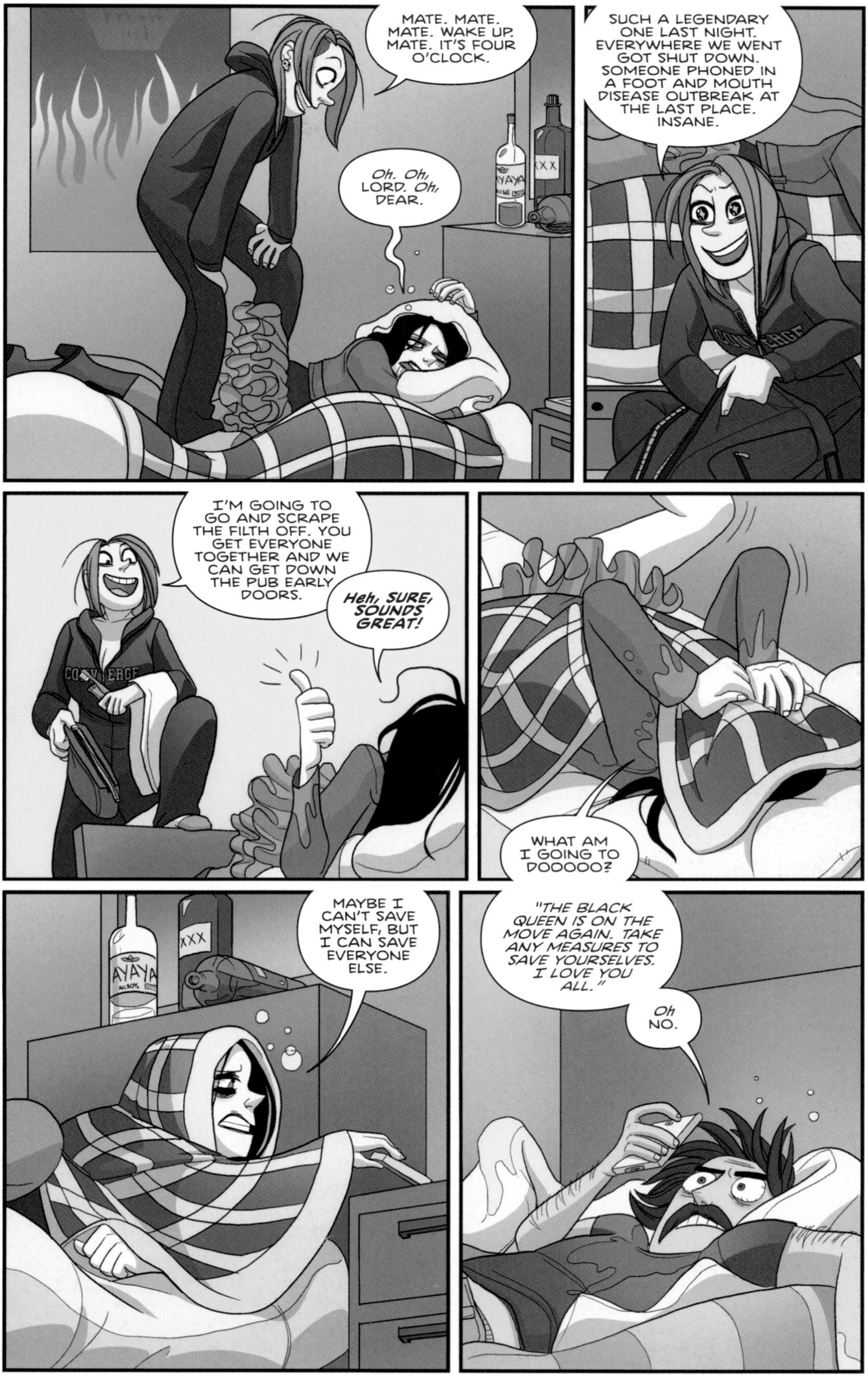
MATE. MATE. MATE. WAKE UP. MATE. IT'S FOUR O'CLOCK.
Oh. Oh, LORD. Oh, DEAR.
SUCH A LEGENDARY ONE LAST NIGHT. EVERYWHERE WE WENT GOT SHUT DOWN. SOMEONE PHONED IN A FOOT AND MOUTH DISEASE OUTBREAK AT THE LAST PLACE. INSANE.
I'M GOING TO GO AND SCRAPE THE FILTH OFF. YOU GET EVERYONE TOGETHER AND WE CAN GET DOWN THE PUB EARLY DOORS.
Heh, SURE, SOUNDS GREAT!
WHAT AM I GOING TO DOOOOO?
MAYBE I CAN'T SAVE MYSELF, BUT I CAN SAVE EVERYONE ELSE.
"THE BLACK QUEEN IS ON THE MOVE AGAIN. TAKE ANY MEASURES TO SAVE YOURSELVES. I LOVE YOU ALL."
Oh NO.

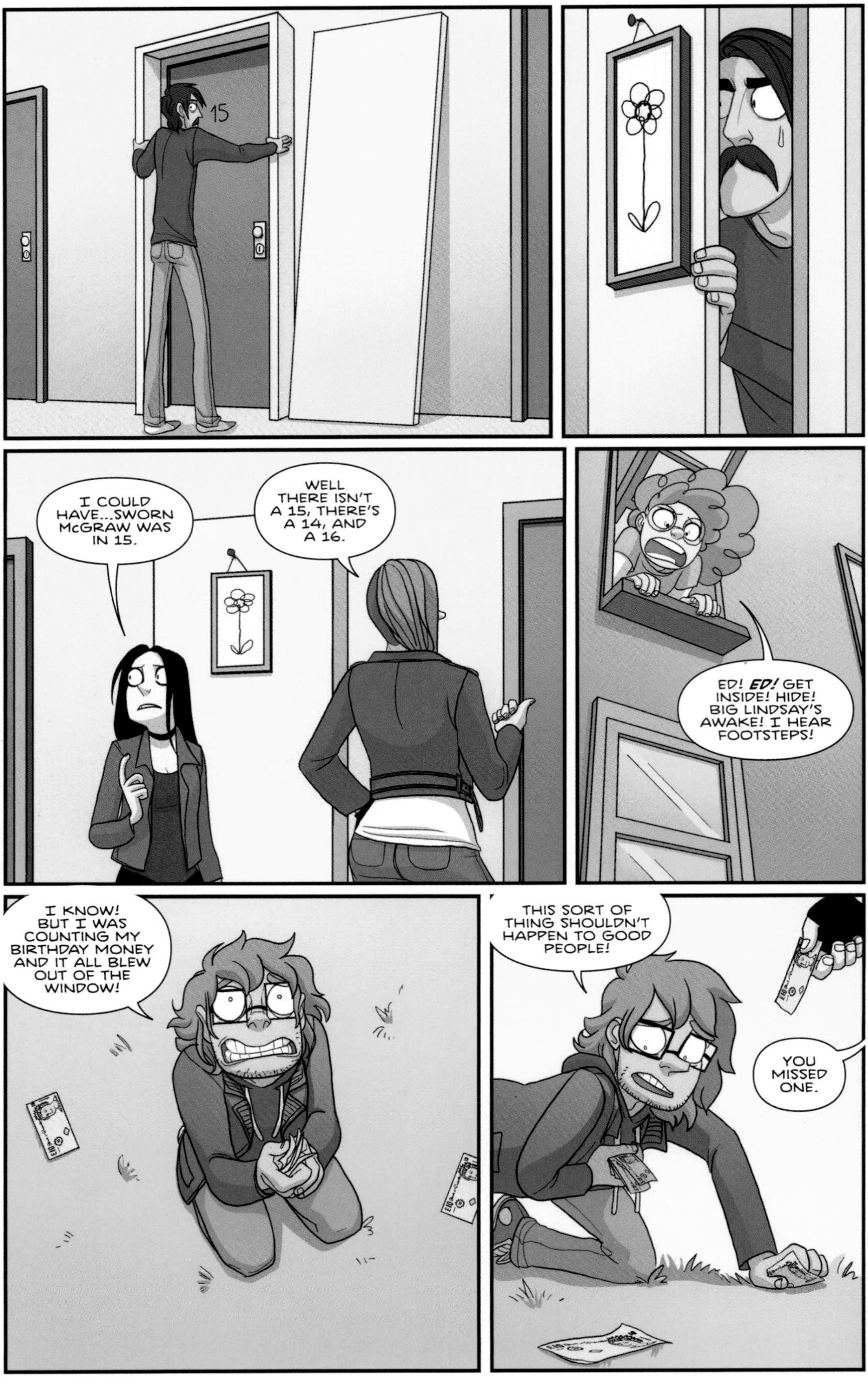
I COULD HAVE...SWORN McGRAW WAS IN 15.
WELL THERE ISN'T A 15, THERE'S A 14, AND A 16.
ED! ED! GET INSIDE! HIDE! BIG LINDSAY'S AWAKE! I HEAR FOOTSTEPS!
I KNOW! BUT I WAS COUNTING MY BIRTHDAY MONEY AND IT ALL BLEW OUT OF THE WINDOW!
THIS SORT OF THING SHOULDN'T HAPPEN TO GOOD PEOPLE!
YOU MISSED ONE.

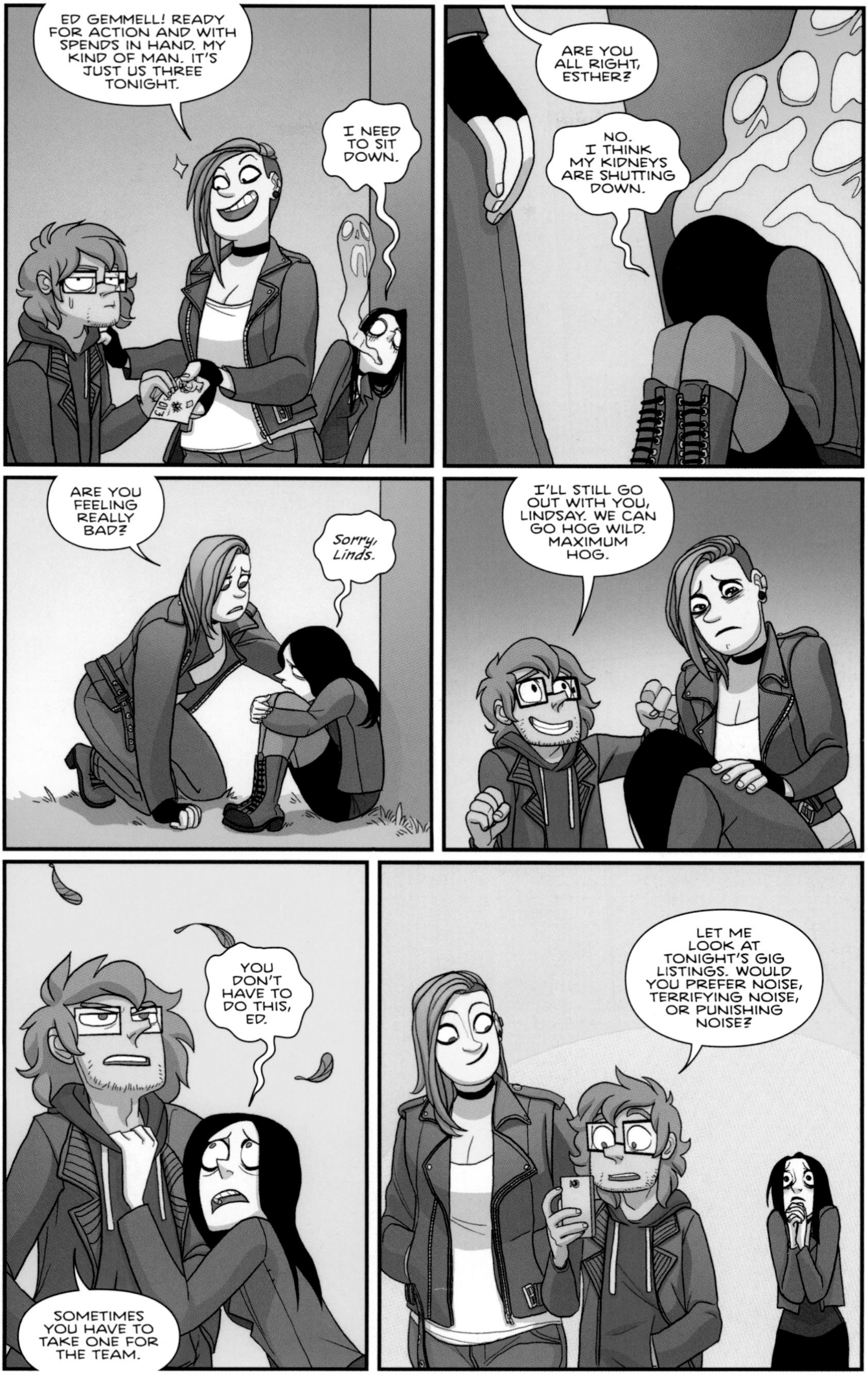
ED GEMMELL! READY FOR ACTION AND WITH SPENDS IN HAND. MY KIND OF MAN. IT'S JUST US THREE TONIGHT.
I NEED TO SIT DOWN.
ARE YOU ALL RIGHT, ESTHER?
NO. I THINK MY KIDNEYS ARE SHUTTING DOWN.
ARE YOU FEELING REALLY BAD?
Sorry, Linds.
I'LL STILL GO OUT WITH YOU, LINDSAY. WE CAN GO HOG WILD. MAXIMUM HOG.
YOU DON'T HAVE TO DO THIS, ED.
SOMETIMES YOU HAVE TO TAKE ONE FOR THE TEAM.
LET ME LOOK AT TONIGHT'S GIG LISTINGS. WOULD YOU PREFER NOISE, TERRIFYING NOISE, OR PUNISHING NOISE?

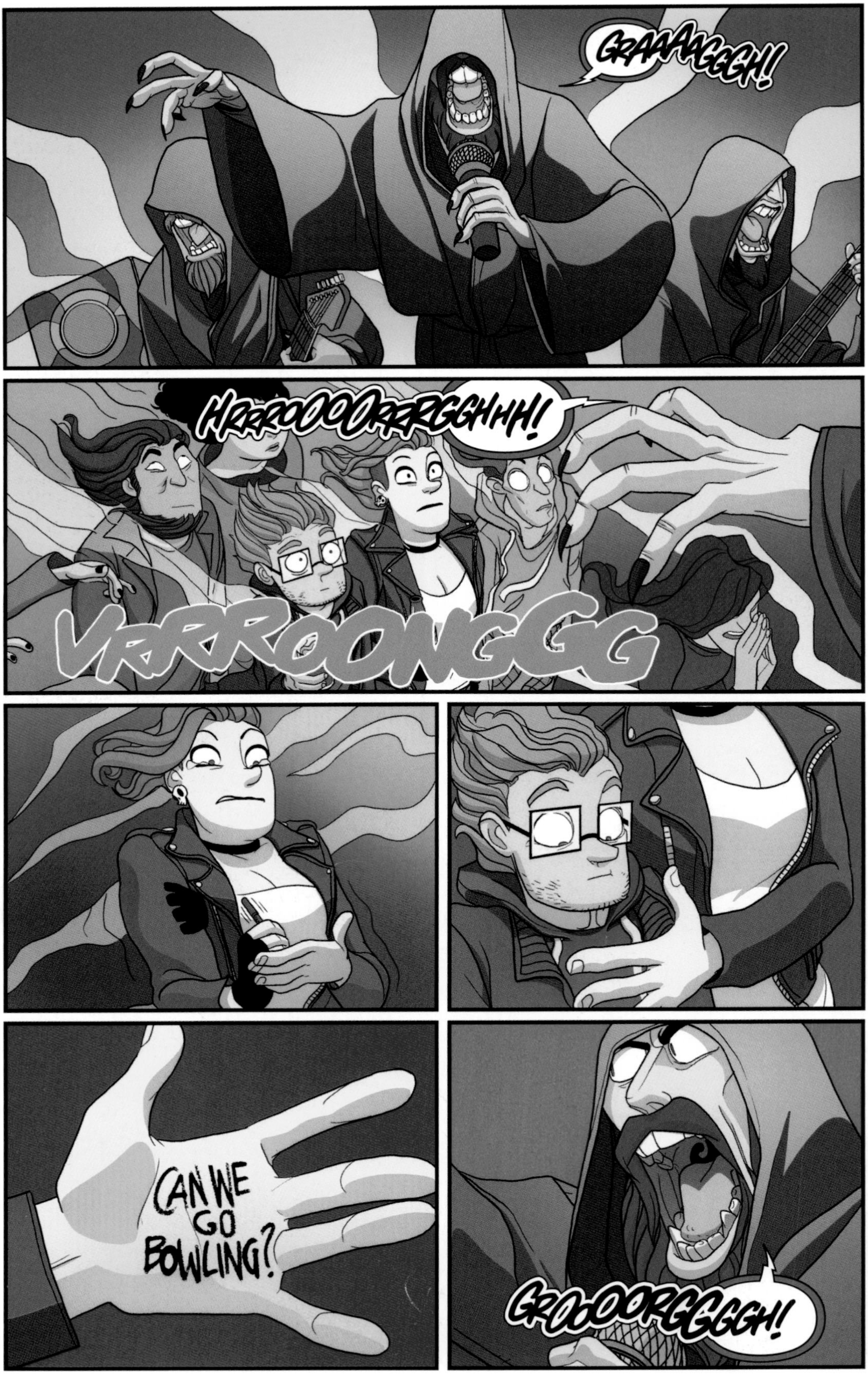
GRAAAAGGGH!
HRRROOOORRRGGHHH!
VRRROONGGG
CAN WE GO BOWLING?
GROOOORGGGGH!

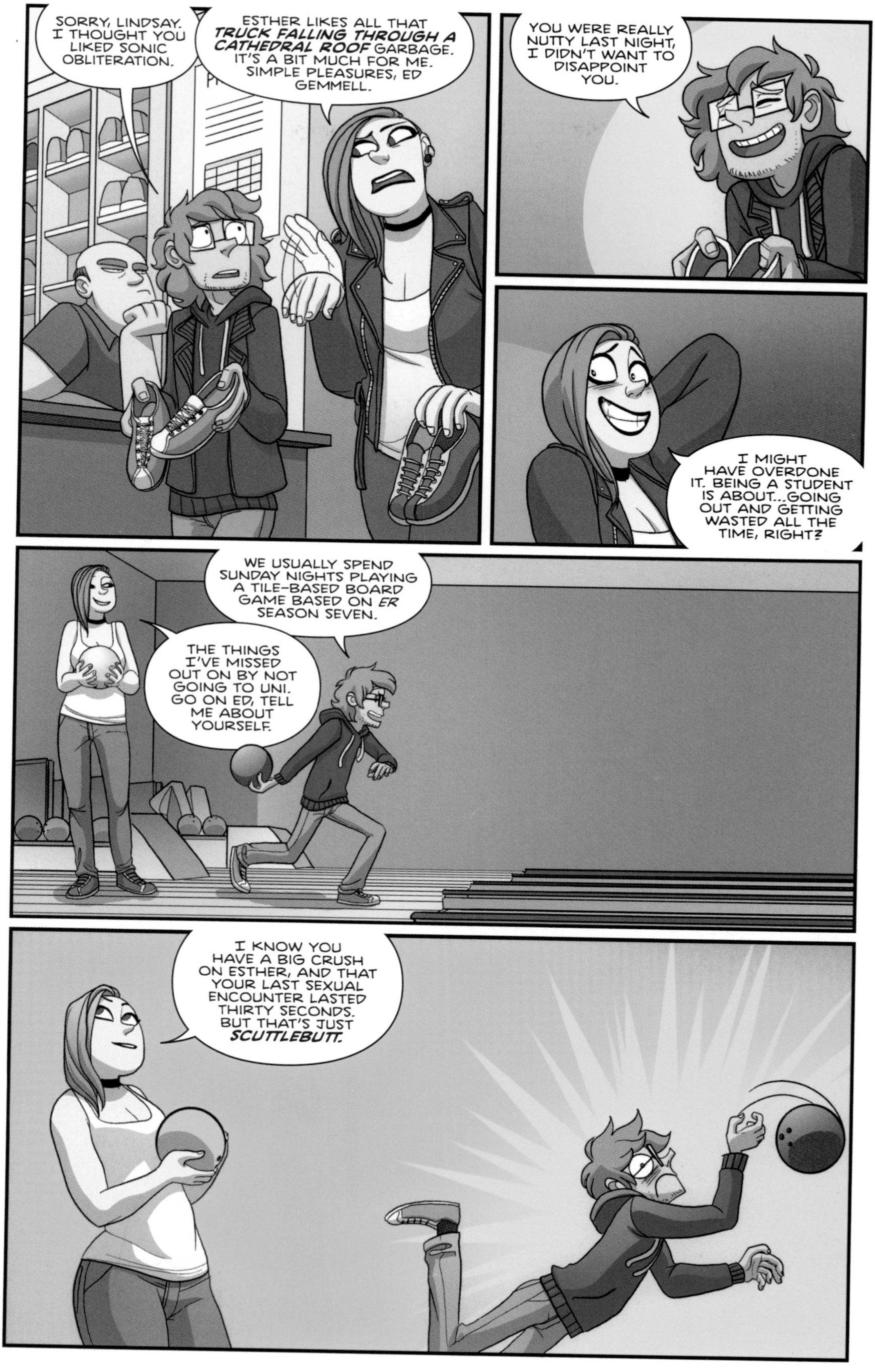
SORRY, LINDSAY. I THOUGHT YOU LIKED SONIC OBLITERATION.
ESTHER LIKES ALL THAT TRUCK FALLING THROUGH A CATHEDRAL ROOF GARBAGE. IT'S A BIT MUCH FOR ME. SIMPLE PLEASURES, ED GEMMELL.
YOU WERE REALLY NUTTY LAST NIGHT, I DIDN'T WANT TO DISAPPOINT YOU.
I MIGHT HAVE OVERDONE IT. BEING A STUDENT IS ABOUT...GOING OUT AND GETTING WASTED ALL THE TIME, RIGHT?
WE USUALLY SPEND SUNDAY NIGHTS PLAYING A TILE-BASED BOARD GAME BASED ON ER SEASON SEVEN.
THE THINGS I'VE MISSED OUT ON BY NOT GOING TO UNI. GO ON ED, TELL ME ABOUT YOURSELF.
I KNOW YOU HAVE A BIG CRUSH ON ESTHER, AND THAT YOUR LAST SEXUAL ENCOUNTER LASTED THIRTY SECONDS. BUT THAT'S JUST SCUTTLEBUTT.

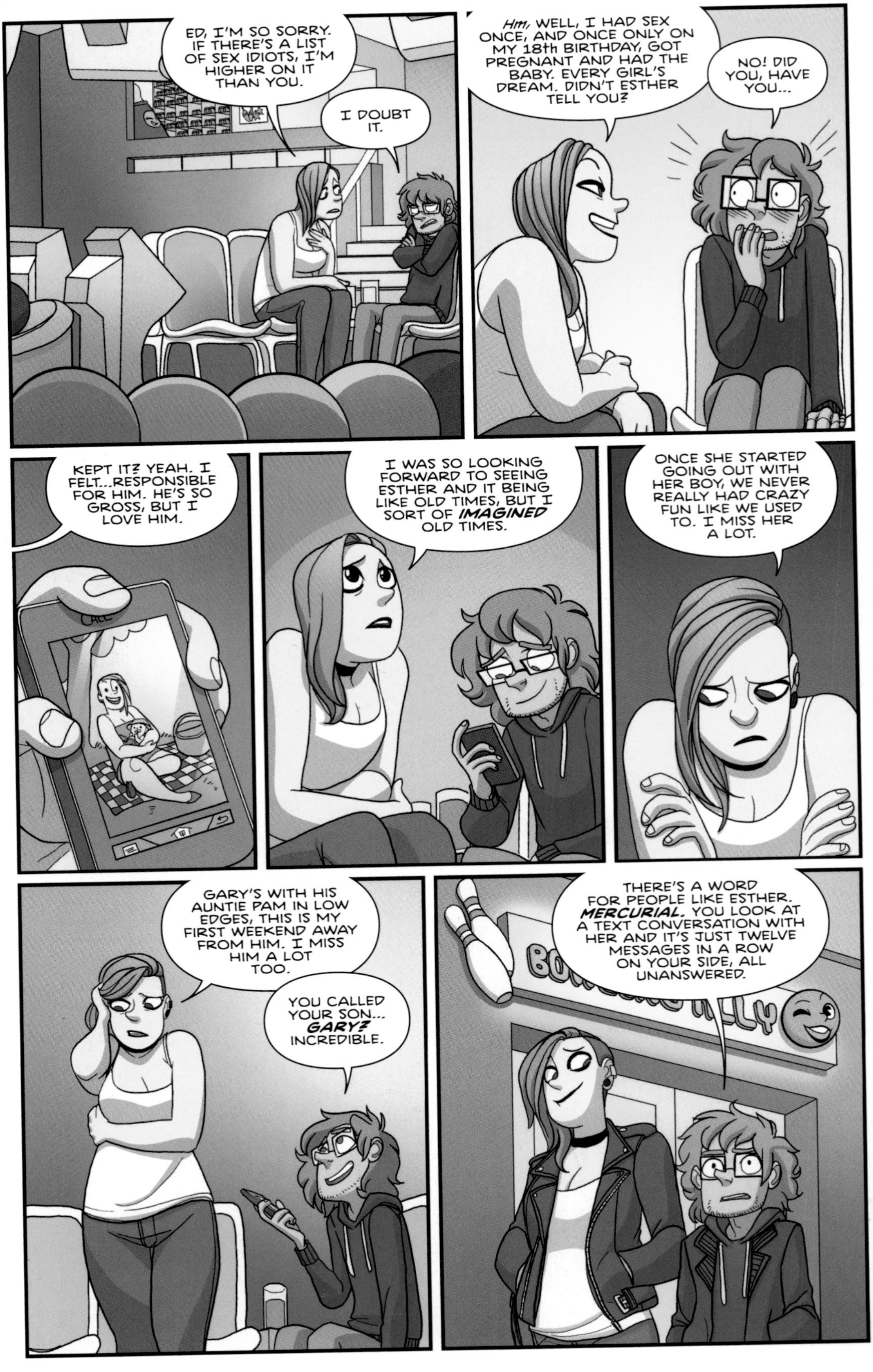
ED, I'M SO SORRY. IF THERE'S A LIST OF SEX IDIOTS, I'M HIGHER ON IT THAN YOU.
I DOUBT IT.
HM, WELL, I HAD SEX ONCE, AND ONCE ONLY ON MY 18th BIRTHDAY, GOT PREGNANT AND HAD THE BABY. EVERY GIRL'S DREAM. DIDN'T ESTHER TELL YOU?
NO! DID YOU, HAVE YOU...
KEPT IT? YEAH. I FELT...RESPONSIBLE FOR HIM. HE'S SO GROSS, BUT I LOVE HIM.
I WAS SO LOOKING FORWARD TO SEEING ESTHER AND IT BEING LIKE OLD TIMES, BUT I SORT OF IMAGINED OLD TIMES.
ONCE SHE STARTED GOING OUT WITH HER BOY, WE NEVER REALLY HAD CRAZY FUN LIKE WE USED TO. I MISS HER A LOT.
GARY'S WITH HIS AUNTIE PAM IN LOW EDGES, THIS IS MY FIRST WEEKEND AWAY FROM HIM. I MISS HIM A LOT TOO.
YOU CALLED YOUR SON... GARY? INCREDIBLE.
THERE'S A WORD FOR PEOPLE LIKE ESTHER. MERCURIAL. YOU LOOK AT A TEXT CONVERSATION WITH HER AND IT'S JUST TWELVE MESSAGES IN A ROW ON YOUR SIDE, ALL UNANSWERED.

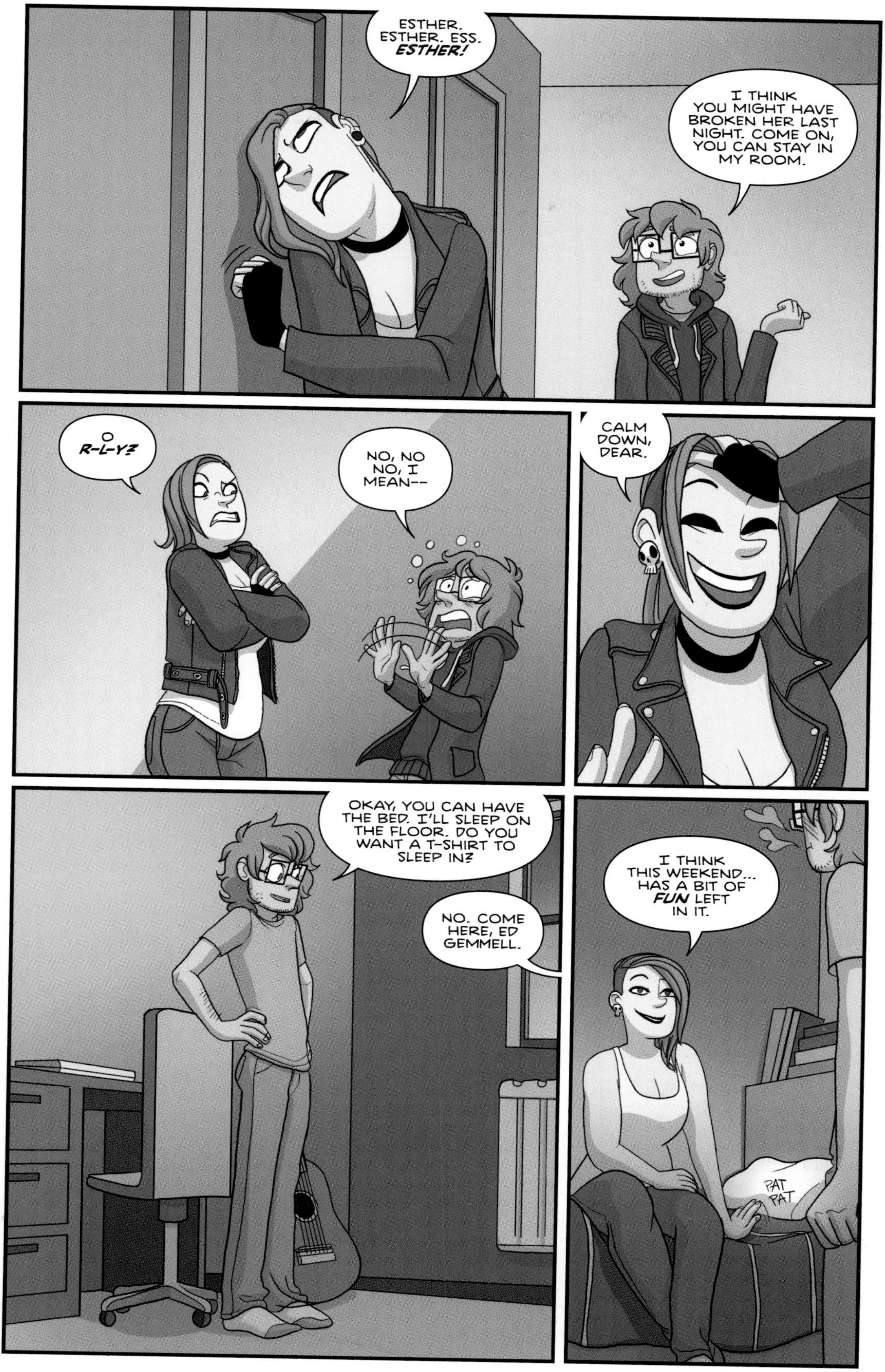
ESTHER. ESTHER. ESS. ESTHER!
I THINK YOU MIGHT HAVE BROKEN HER LAST NIGHT. COME ON, YOU CAN STAY IN MY ROOM.
O R-L-Y?
NO, NO NO, I MEAN--
CALM DOWN, DEAR.
OKAY, YOU CAN HAVE THE BED. I'LL SLEEP ON THE FLOOR. DO YOU WANT A T-SHIRT TO SLEEP IN?
NO. COME HERE, ED GEMMELL.
I THINK THIS WEEKEND... HAS A BIT OF FUN LEFT IN IT.
PAT PAT

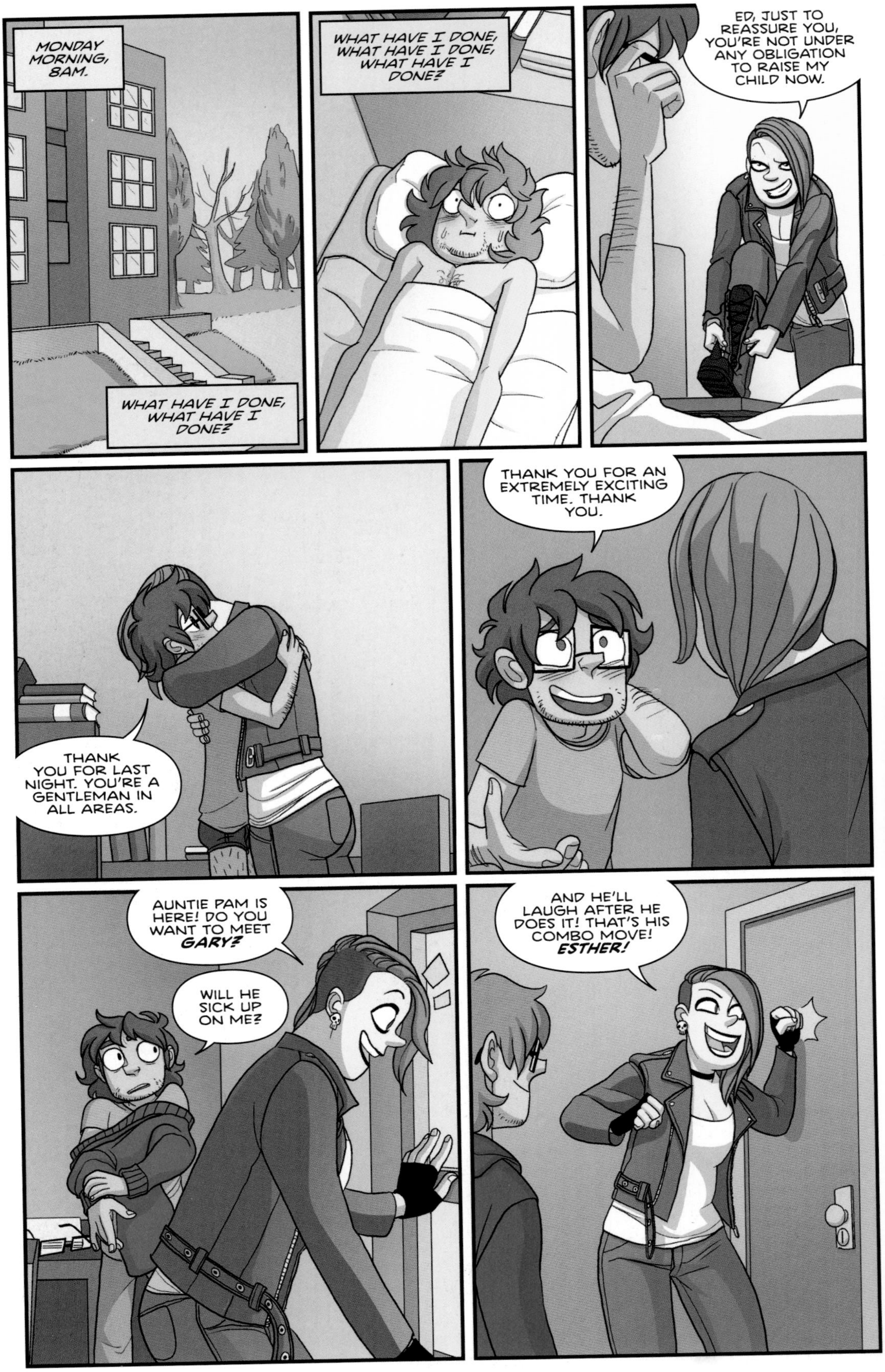
MONDAY MORNING, 8AM.
WHAT HAVE I DONE, WHAT HAVE I DONE?
WHAT HAVE I DONE, WHAT HAVE I DONE, WHAT HAVE I DONE?
ED, JUST TO REASSURE YOU, YOU'RE NOT UNDER ANY OBLIGATION TO RAISE MY CHILD NOW.
THANK YOU FOR LAST NIGHT. YOU'RE A GENTLEMAN IN ALL AREAS.
THANK YOU FOR AN EXTREMELY EXCITING TIME. THANK YOU.
AUNTIE PAM IS HERE! DO YOU WANT TO MEET *GARY?*
WILL HE SICK UP ON ME?
AND HE'LL LAUGH AFTER HE DOES IT! THAT'S HIS COMBO MOVE! ***ESTHER!***

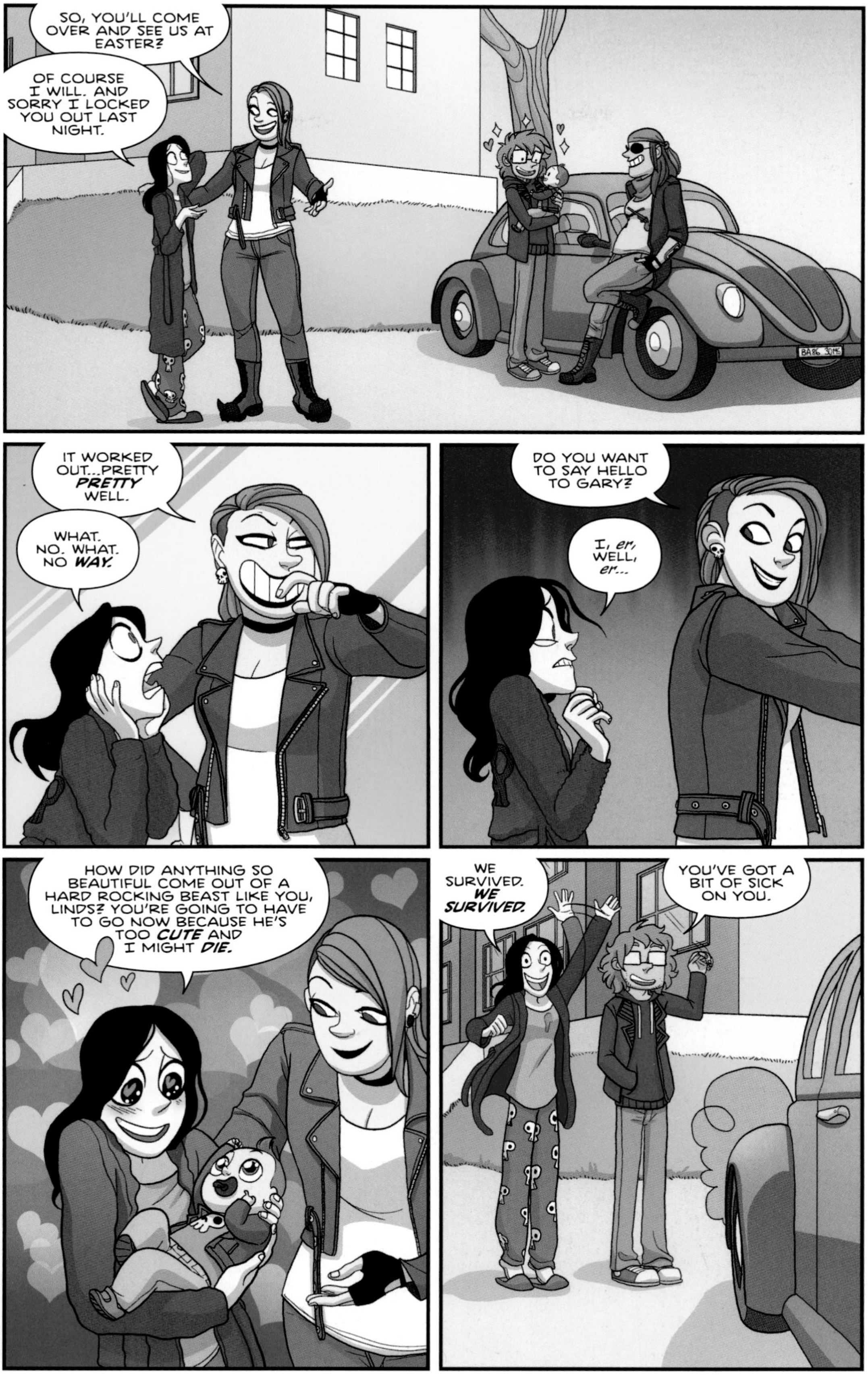
SO, YOU'LL COME OVER AND SEE US AT EASTER?
OF COURSE I WILL. AND SORRY I LOCKED YOU OUT LAST NIGHT.
BA86 30MS
IT WORKED OUT...PRETTY *PRETTY* WELL.
WHAT. NO. WHAT. NO *WAY.*
DO YOU WANT TO SAY HELLO TO GARY?
I, *er,* WELL, *er...*
HOW DID ANYTHING SO BEAUTIFUL COME OUT OF A HARD ROCKING BEAST LIKE YOU, LINDS? YOU'RE GOING TO HAVE TO GO NOW BECAUSE HE'S TOO *CUTE* AND I MIGHT *DIE.*
WE SURVIVED. *WE SURVIVED.*
YOU'VE GOT A BIT OF SICK ON YOU.

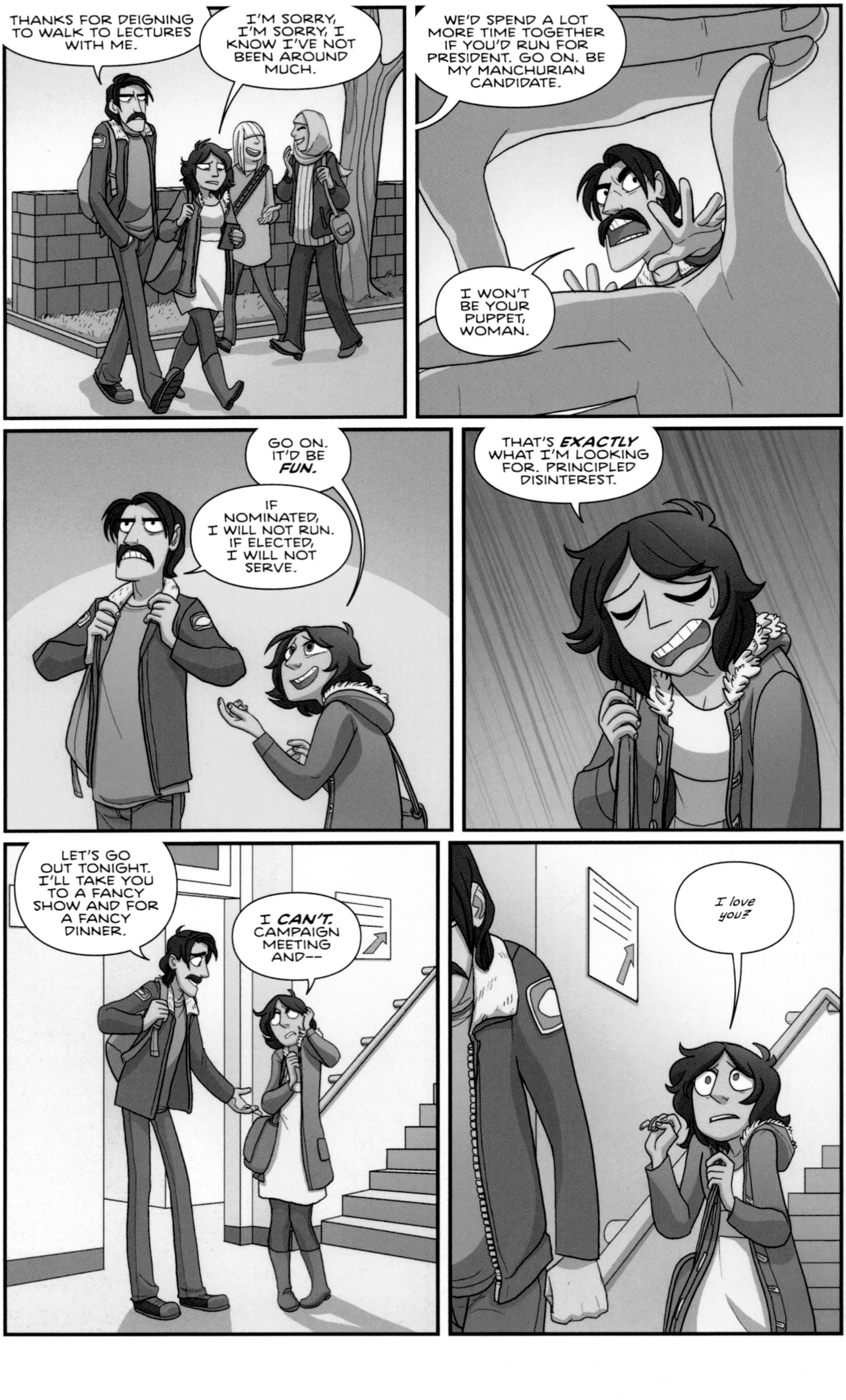
THANKS FOR DEIGNING TO WALK TO LECTURES WITH ME.
I'M SORRY, I'M SORRY, I KNOW I'VE NOT BEEN AROUND MUCH.
WE'D SPEND A LOT MORE TIME TOGETHER IF YOU'D RUN FOR PRESIDENT. GO ON. BE MY MANCHURIAN CANDIDATE.
I WON'T BE YOUR PUPPET, WOMAN.
GO ON. IT'D BE ***FUN.***
IF NOMINATED, I WILL NOT RUN. IF ELECTED, I WILL NOT SERVE.
THAT'S ***EXACTLY*** WHAT I'M LOOKING FOR. PRINCIPLED DISINTEREST.
LET'S GO OUT TONIGHT. I'LL TAKE YOU TO A FANCY SHOW AND FOR A FANCY DINNER.
I ***CAN'T.*** CAMPAIGN MEETING AND--
I love you?

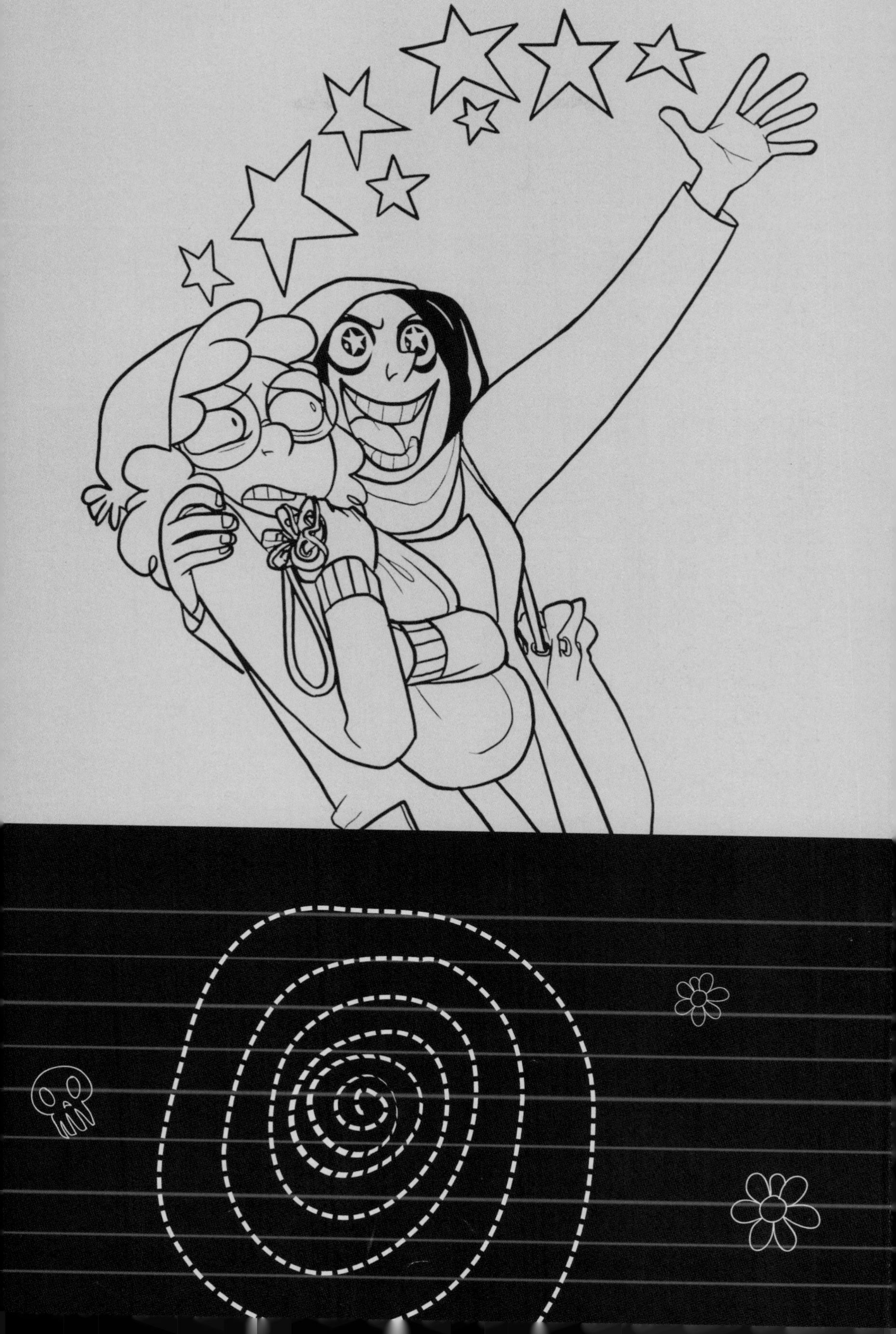

CHAPTER
ELEVEN

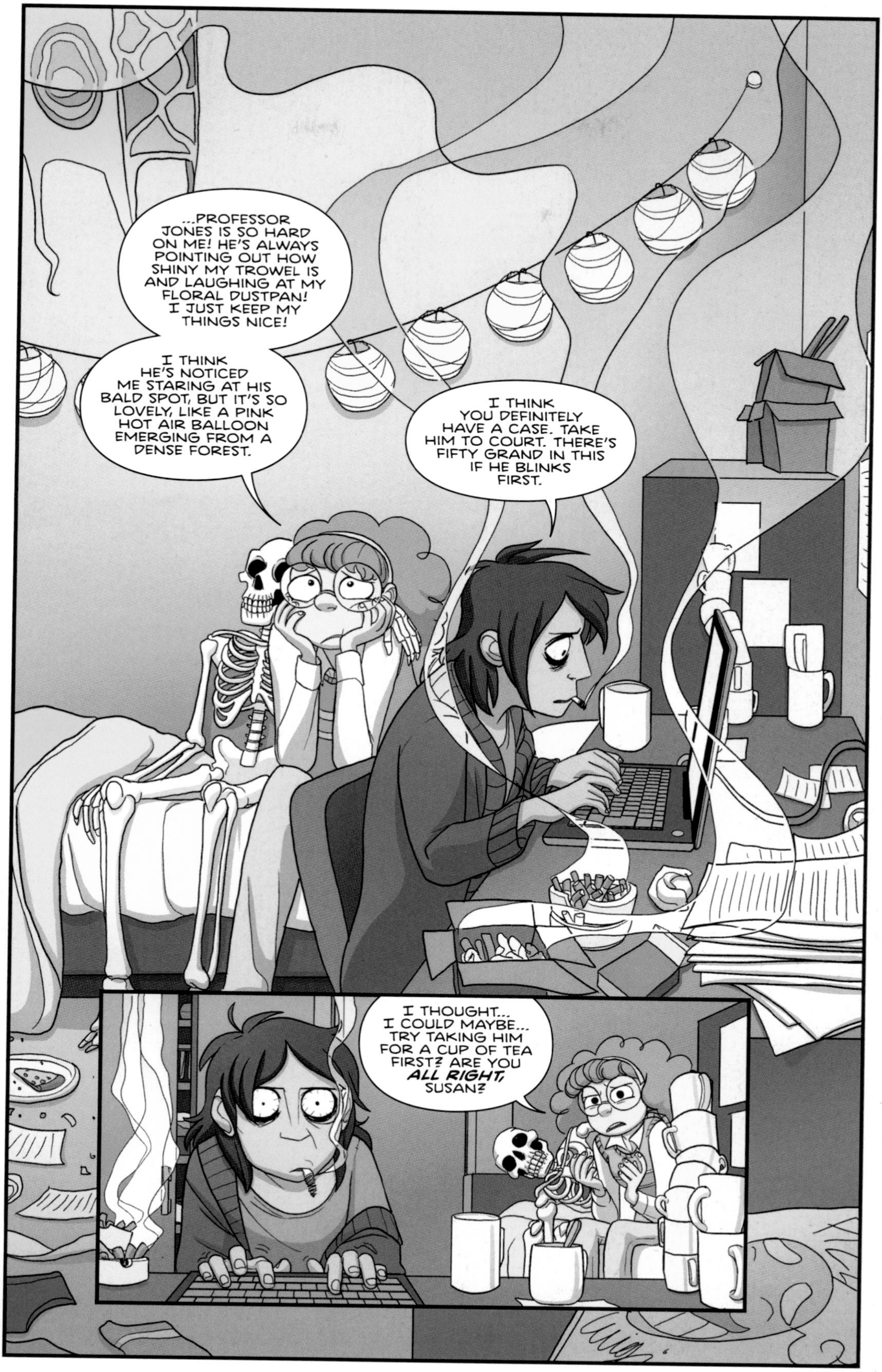
...PROFESSOR JONES IS SO HARD ON ME! HE'S ALWAYS POINTING OUT HOW SHINY MY TROWEL IS AND LAUGHING AT MY FLORAL DUSTPAN! I JUST KEEP MY THINGS NICE!
I THINK HE'S NOTICED ME STARING AT HIS BALD SPOT, BUT IT'S SO LOVELY, LIKE A PINK HOT AIR BALLOON EMERGING FROM A DENSE FOREST.
I THINK YOU DEFINITELY HAVE A CASE. TAKE HIM TO COURT. THERE'S FIFTY GRAND IN THIS IF HE BLINKS FIRST.
I THOUGHT... I COULD MAYBE... TRY TAKING HIM FOR A CUP OF TEA FIRST? ARE YOU ***ALL RIGHT,*** SUSAN?

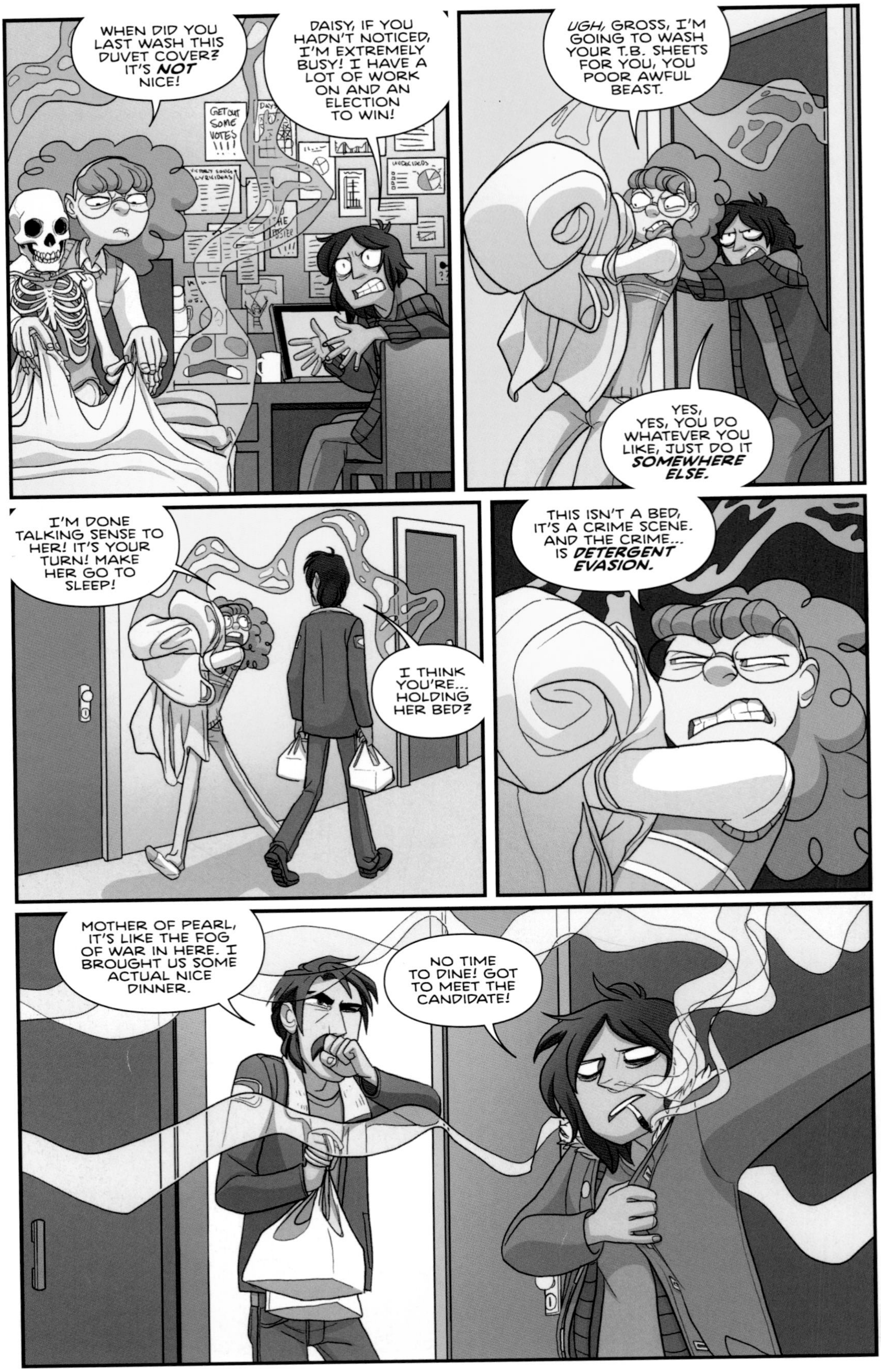
WHEN DID YOU LAST WASH THIS DUVET COVER? IT'S **NOT** NICE!
DAISY, IF YOU HADN'T NOTICED, I'M EXTREMELY BUSY! I HAVE A LOT OF WORK ON AND AN ELECTION TO WIN!
UGH, GROSS, I'M GOING TO WASH YOUR T.B. SHEETS FOR YOU, YOU POOR AWFUL BEAST.
YES, YES, YOU DO WHATEVER YOU LIKE, JUST DO IT ***SOMEWHERE ELSE.***
I'M DONE TALKING SENSE TO HER! IT'S YOUR TURN! MAKE HER GO TO SLEEP!
I THINK YOU'RE... HOLDING HER BED?
THIS ISN'T A BED, IT'S A CRIME SCENE. AND THE CRIME... IS ***DETERGENT EVASION.***
MOTHER OF PEARL, IT'S LIKE THE FOG OF WAR IN HERE. I BROUGHT US SOME ACTUAL NICE DINNER.
NO TIME TO DINE! GOT TO MEET THE CANDIDATE!

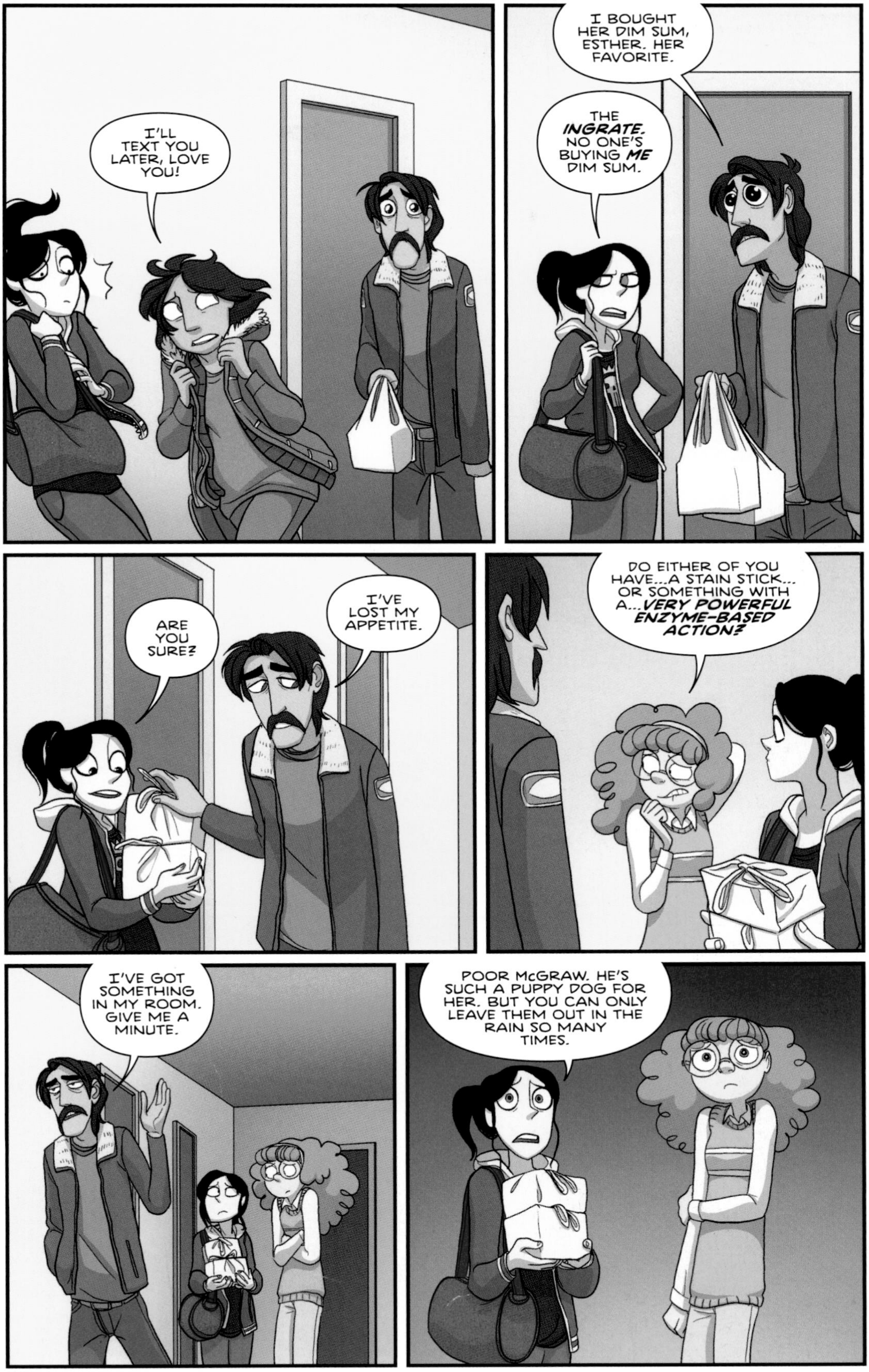
I'LL TEXT YOU LATER, LOVE YOU!
I BOUGHT HER DIM SUM, ESTHER. HER FAVORITE.
THE *INGRATE.* NO ONE'S BUYING *ME* DIM SUM.
ARE YOU SURE?
I'VE LOST MY APPETITE.
DO EITHER OF YOU HAVE...A STAIN STICK... OR SOMETHING WITH A...*VERY POWERFUL ENZYME-BASED ACTION?*
I'VE GOT SOMETHING IN MY ROOM. GIVE ME A MINUTE.
POOR McGRAW. HE'S SUCH A PUPPY DOG FOR HER. BUT YOU CAN ONLY LEAVE THEM OUT IN THE RAIN SO MANY TIMES.

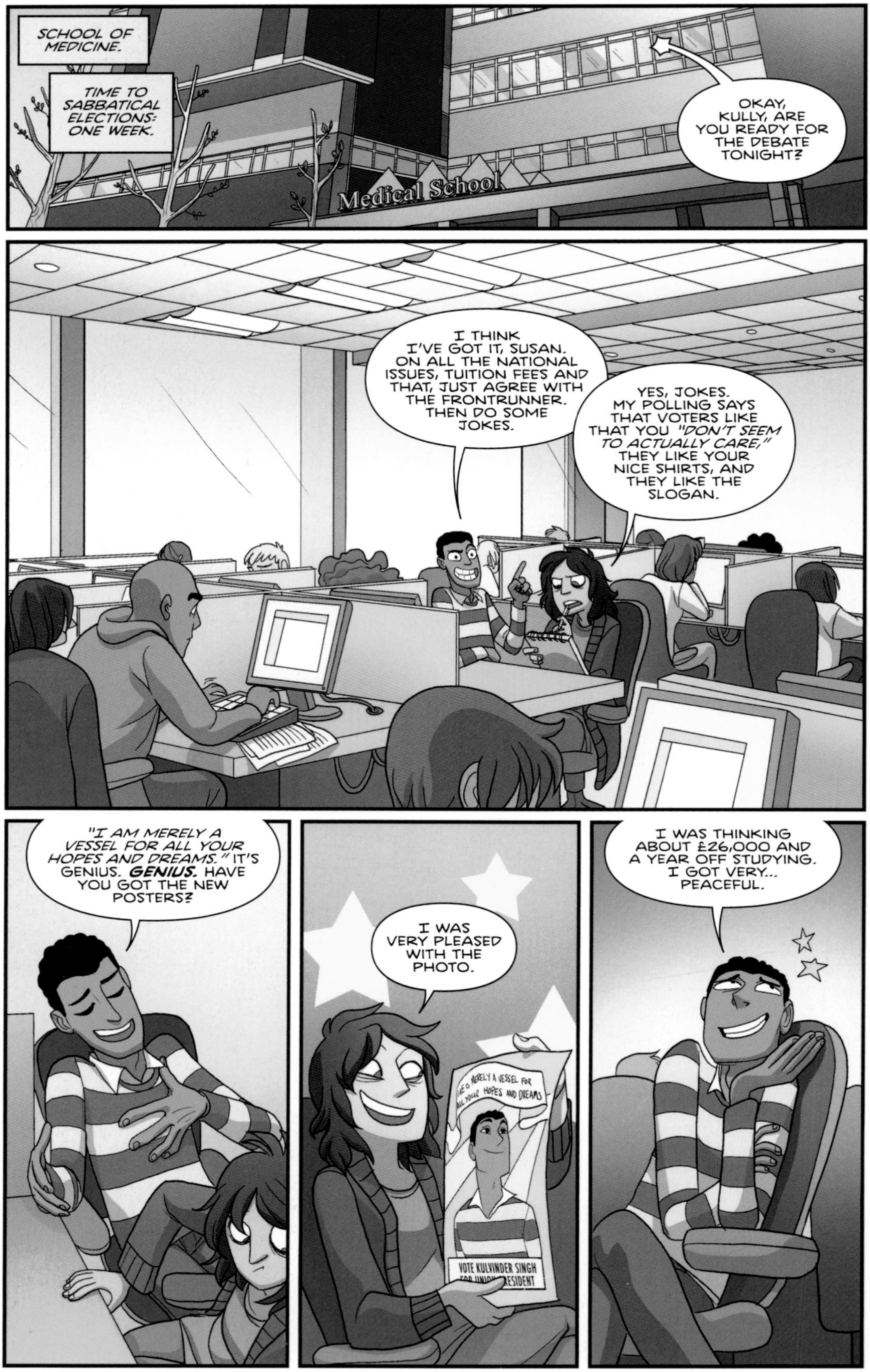
SCHOOL OF MEDICINE.
TIME TO SABBATICAL ELECTIONS: ONE WEEK.
Medical School
OKAY, KULLY, ARE YOU READY FOR THE DEBATE TONIGHT?
I THINK I'VE GOT IT, SUSAN. ON ALL THE NATIONAL ISSUES, TUITION FEES AND THAT, JUST AGREE WITH THE FRONTRUNNER. THEN DO SOME JOKES.
YES, JOKES. MY POLLING SAYS THAT VOTERS LIKE THAT YOU *"DON'T SEEM TO ACTUALLY CARE,"* THEY LIKE YOUR NICE SHIRTS, AND THEY LIKE THE SLOGAN.
"I AM MERELY A VESSEL FOR ALL YOUR HOPES AND DREAMS." IT'S GENIUS. ***GENIUS.*** HAVE YOU GOT THE NEW POSTERS?
I WAS VERY PLEASED WITH THE PHOTO.
VOTE KULVINDER SINGH
I WAS THINKING ABOUT £26,000 AND A YEAR OFF STUDYING. I GOT VERY... PEACEFUL.

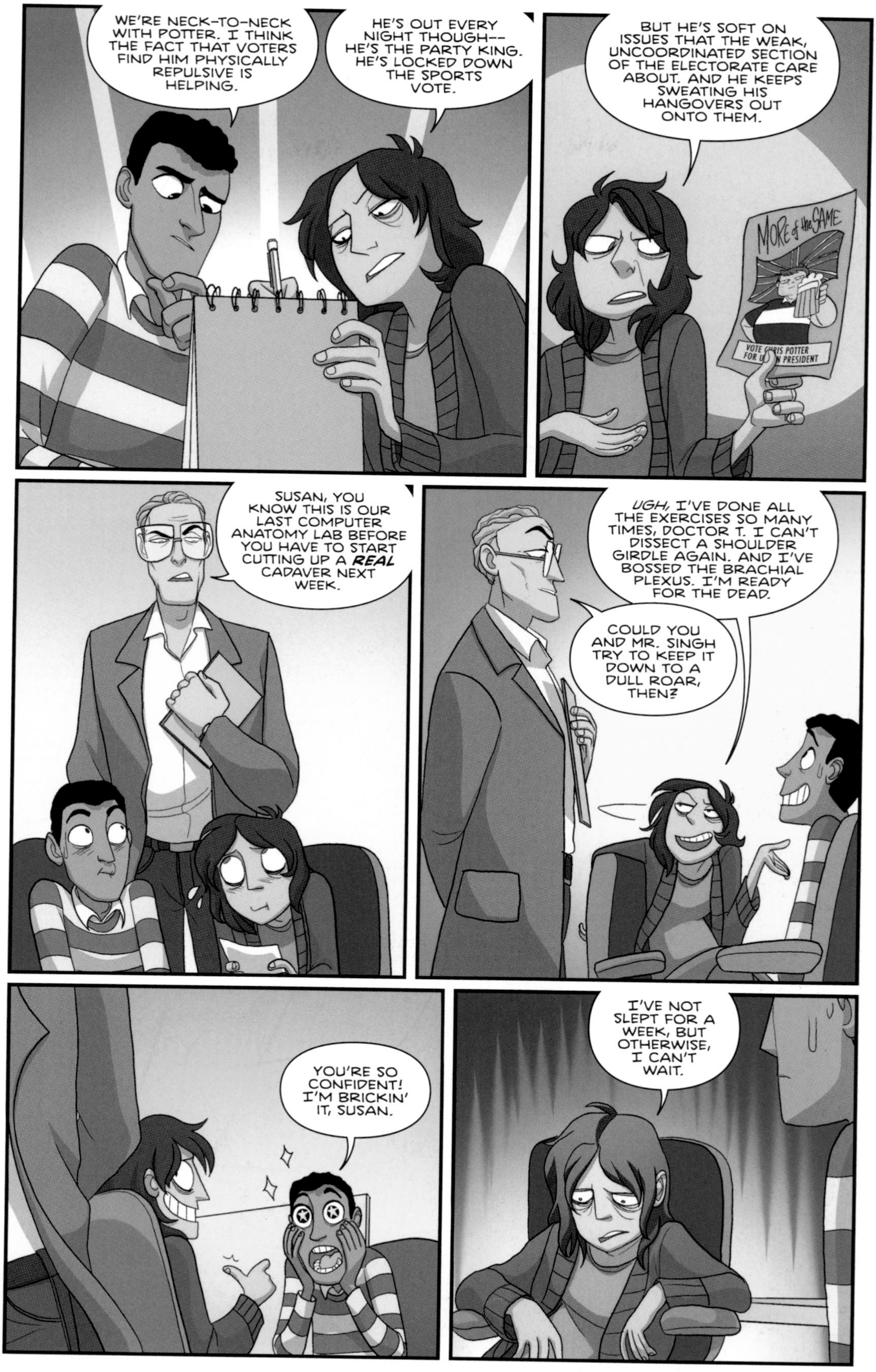
WE'RE NECK-TO-NECK WITH POTTER. I THINK THE FACT THAT VOTERS FIND HIM PHYSICALLY REPULSIVE IS HELPING.
HE'S OUT EVERY NIGHT THOUGH-- HE'S THE PARTY KING. HE'S LOCKED DOWN THE SPORTS VOTE.
BUT HE'S SOFT ON ISSUES THAT THE WEAK, UNCOORDINATED SECTION OF THE ELECTORATE CARE ABOUT. AND HE KEEPS SWEATING HIS HANGOVERS OUT ONTO THEM.
MORE of the SAME
FOR U N PRESIDENT
SUSAN, YOU KNOW THIS IS OUR LAST COMPUTER ANATOMY LAB BEFORE YOU HAVE TO START CUTTING UP A *REAL* CADAVER NEXT WEEK.
UGH, I'VE DONE ALL THE EXERCISES SO MANY TIMES, DOCTOR T. I CAN'T DISSECT A SHOULDER GIRDLE AGAIN. AND I'VE BOSSED THE BRACHIAL PLEXUS. I'M READY FOR THE DEAD.
COULD YOU AND MR. SINGH TRY TO KEEP IT DOWN TO A DULL ROAR, THEN?
YOU'RE SO CONFIDENT! I'M BRICKIN' IT, SUSAN.
I'VE NOT SLEPT FOR A WEEK, BUT OTHERWISE, I CAN'T WAIT.

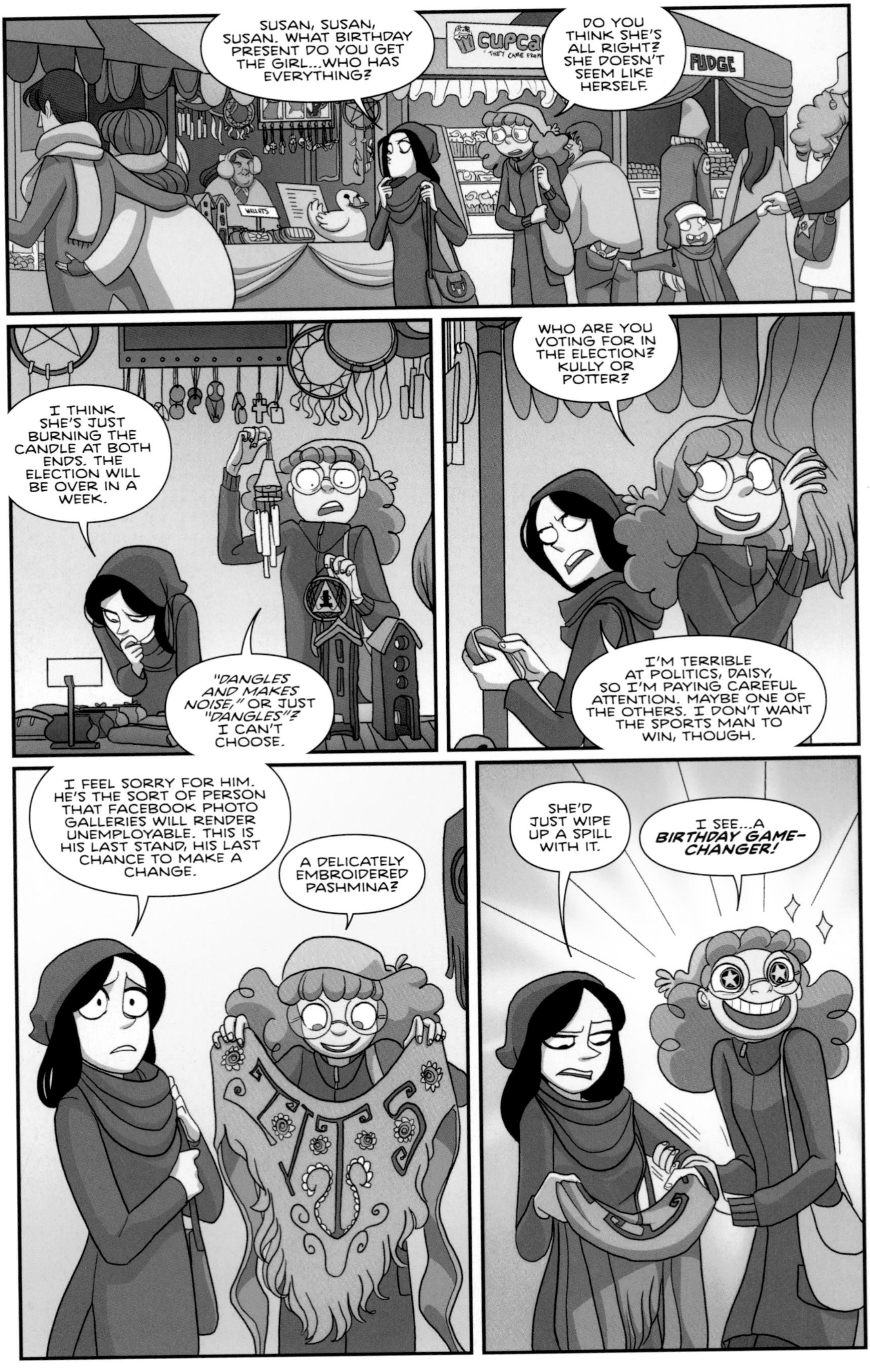
SUSAN, SUSAN, SUSAN. WHAT BIRTHDAY PRESENT DO YOU GET THE GIRL...WHO HAS EVERYTHING?
DO YOU THINK SHE'S ALL RIGHT? SHE DOESN'T SEEM LIKE HERSELF.
FUDGE
WALLETS
I THINK SHE'S JUST BURNING THE CANDLE AT BOTH ENDS. THE ELECTION WILL BE OVER IN A WEEK.
"DANGLES AND MAKES NOISE," OR JUST "DANGLES"? I CAN'T CHOOSE.
WHO ARE YOU VOTING FOR IN THE ELECTION? KULLY OR POTTER?
I'M TERRIBLE AT POLITICS, DAISY, SO I'M PAYING CAREFUL ATTENTION. MAYBE ONE OF THE OTHERS. I DON'T WANT THE SPORTS MAN TO WIN, THOUGH.
I FEEL SORRY FOR HIM. HE'S THE SORT OF PERSON THAT FACEBOOK PHOTO GALLERIES WILL RENDER UNEMPLOYABLE. THIS IS HIS LAST STAND, HIS LAST CHANCE TO MAKE A CHANGE.
A DELICATELY EMBROIDERED PASHMINA?
SHE'D JUST WIPE UP A SPILL WITH IT.
I SEE...A BIRTHDAY GAME-CHANGER!

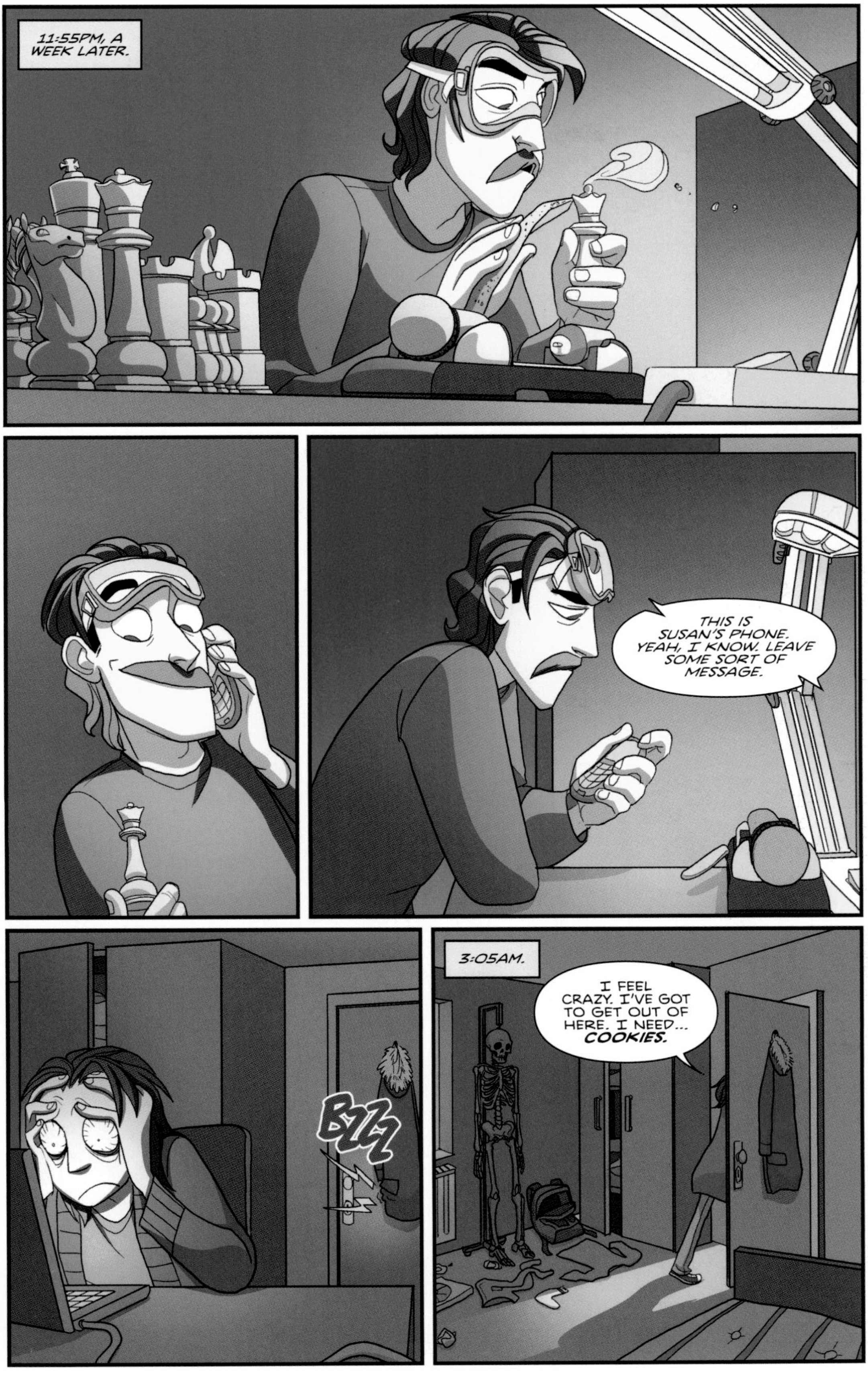
11:55PM, A WEEK LATER.
THIS IS SUSAN'S PHONE. YEAH, I KNOW. LEAVE SOME SORT OF MESSAGE.
BZZZ
3:05AM.
I FEEL CRAZY. I'VE GOT TO GET OUT OF HERE. I NEED... COOKIES.

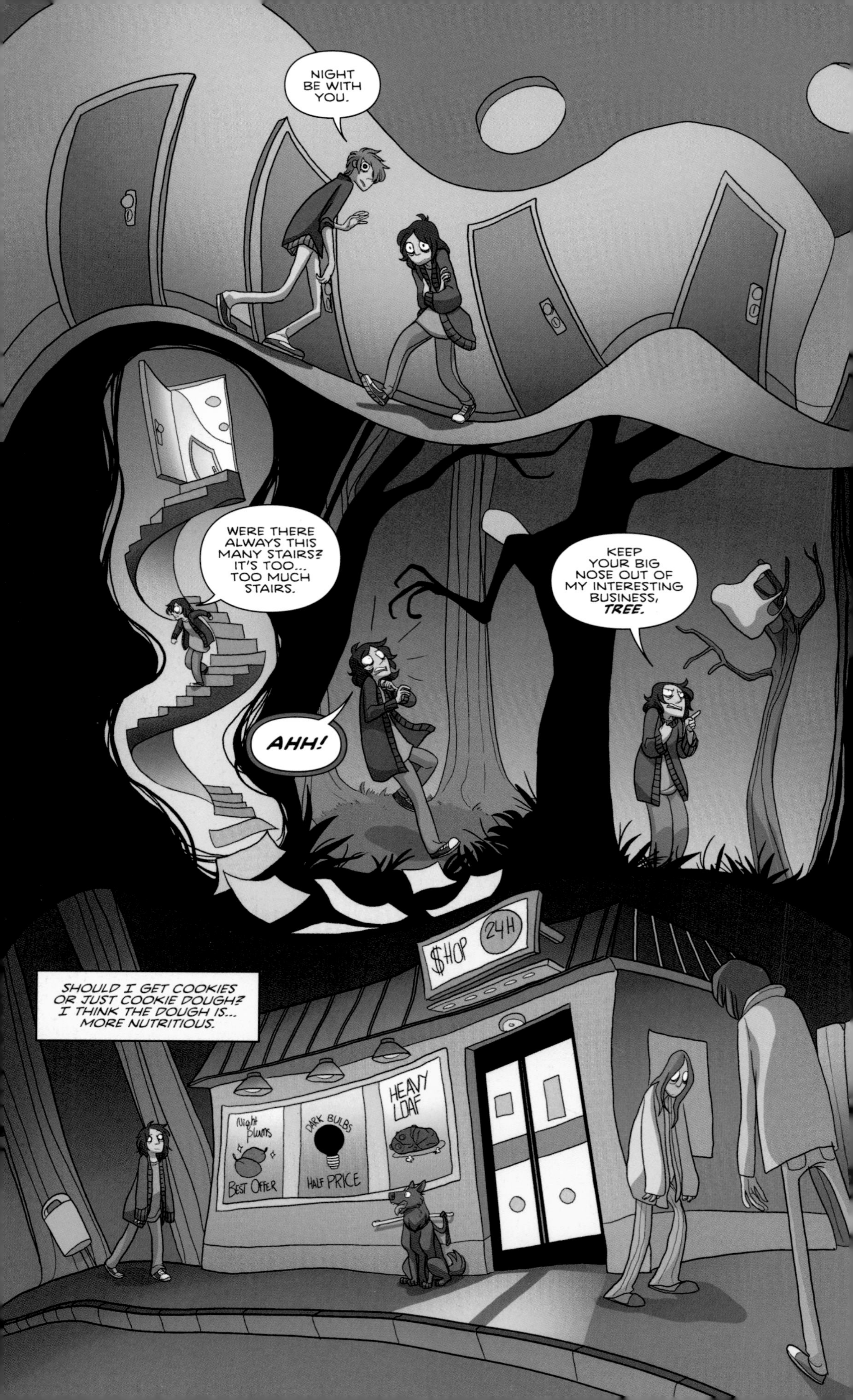
NIGHT BE WITH YOU.
WERE THERE ALWAYS THIS MANY STAIRS? IT'S TOO... TOO MUCH STAIRS.
AHH!
KEEP YOUR BIG NOSE OUT OF MY INTERESTING BUSINESS, TREE.
$HOP
24H
SHOULD I GET COOKIES OR JUST COOKIE DOUGH? I THINK THE DOUGH IS... MORE NUTRITIOUS.
HEAVY LOAF
Night Plums
BEST OFFER
DARK BULBS
HALF PRICE

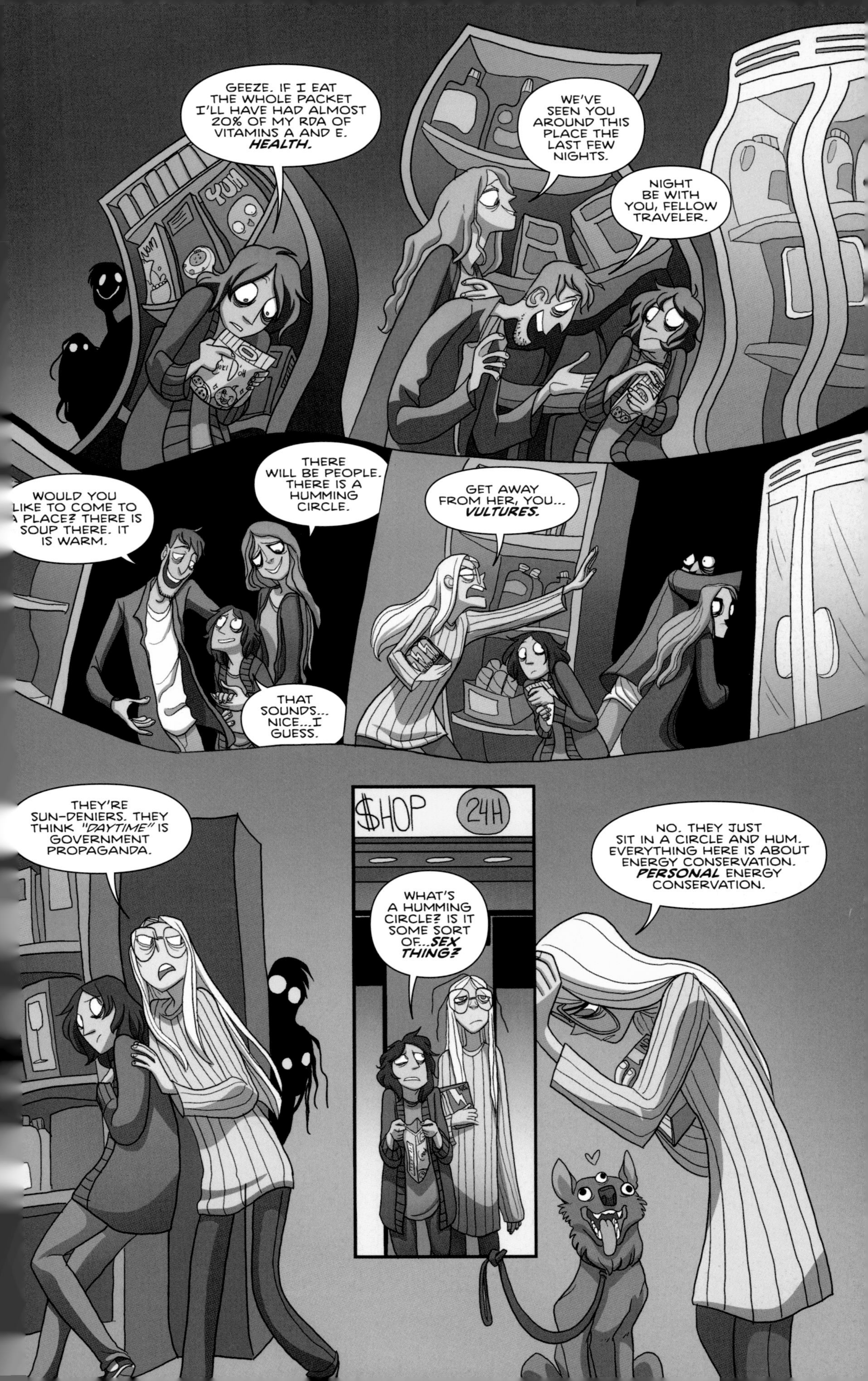
GEEZE. IF I EAT THE WHOLE PACKET I'LL HAVE HAD ALMOST 20% OF MY RDA OF VITAMINS A AND E. ***HEALTH.***
YUM
WE'VE SEEN YOU AROUND THIS PLACE THE LAST FEW NIGHTS.
NIGHT BE WITH YOU, FELLOW TRAVELER.
WOULD YOU LIKE TO COME TO A PLACE? THERE IS SOUP THERE. IT IS WARM.
THERE WILL BE PEOPLE. THERE IS A HUMMING CIRCLE.
THAT SOUNDS... NICE... I GUESS.
GET AWAY FROM HER, YOU... ***VULTURES.***
THEY'RE SUN-DENIERS. THEY THINK *"DAYTIME"* IS GOVERNMENT PROPAGANDA.
$HOP
24H
WHAT'S A HUMMING CIRCLE? IS IT SOME SORT OF... ***SEX THING?***
NO. THEY JUST SIT IN A CIRCLE AND HUM. EVERYTHING HERE IS ABOUT ENERGY CONSERVATION. ***PERSONAL*** ENERGY CONSERVATION.

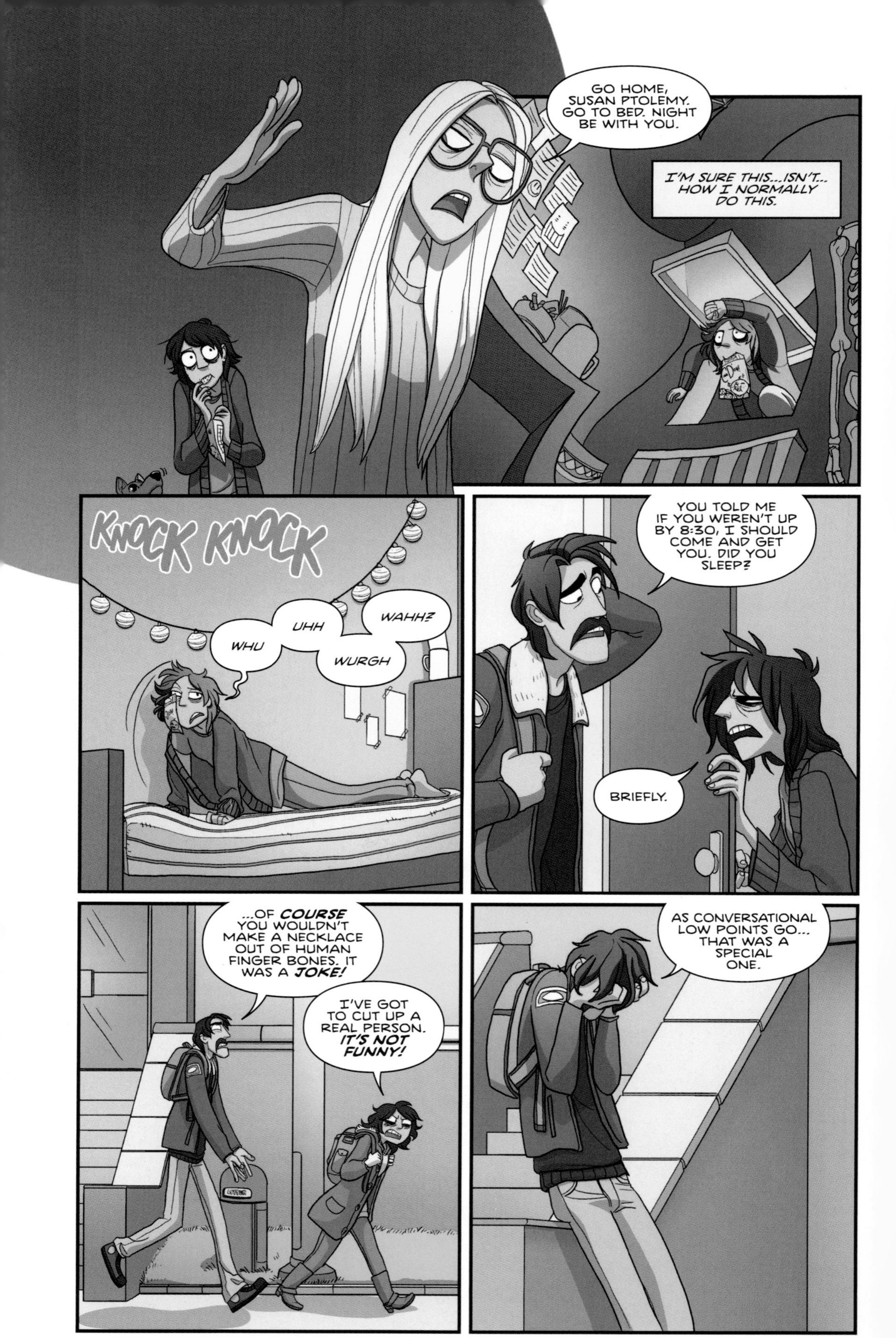
GO HOME, SUSAN PTOLEMY. GO TO BED. NIGHT BE WITH YOU.
I'M SURE THIS...ISN'T... HOW I NORMALLY DO THIS.
KNOCK KNOCK
WHU
UHH
WAHH?
WURGH
YOU TOLD ME IF YOU WEREN'T UP BY 8:30, I SHOULD COME AND GET YOU. DID YOU SLEEP?
BRIEFLY.
...OF COURSE YOU WOULDN'T MAKE A NECKLACE OUT OF HUMAN FINGER BONES. IT WAS A JOKE!
I'VE GOT TO CUT UP A REAL PERSON. IT'S NOT FUNNY!
AS CONVERSATIONAL LOW POINTS GO... THAT WAS A SPECIAL ONE.

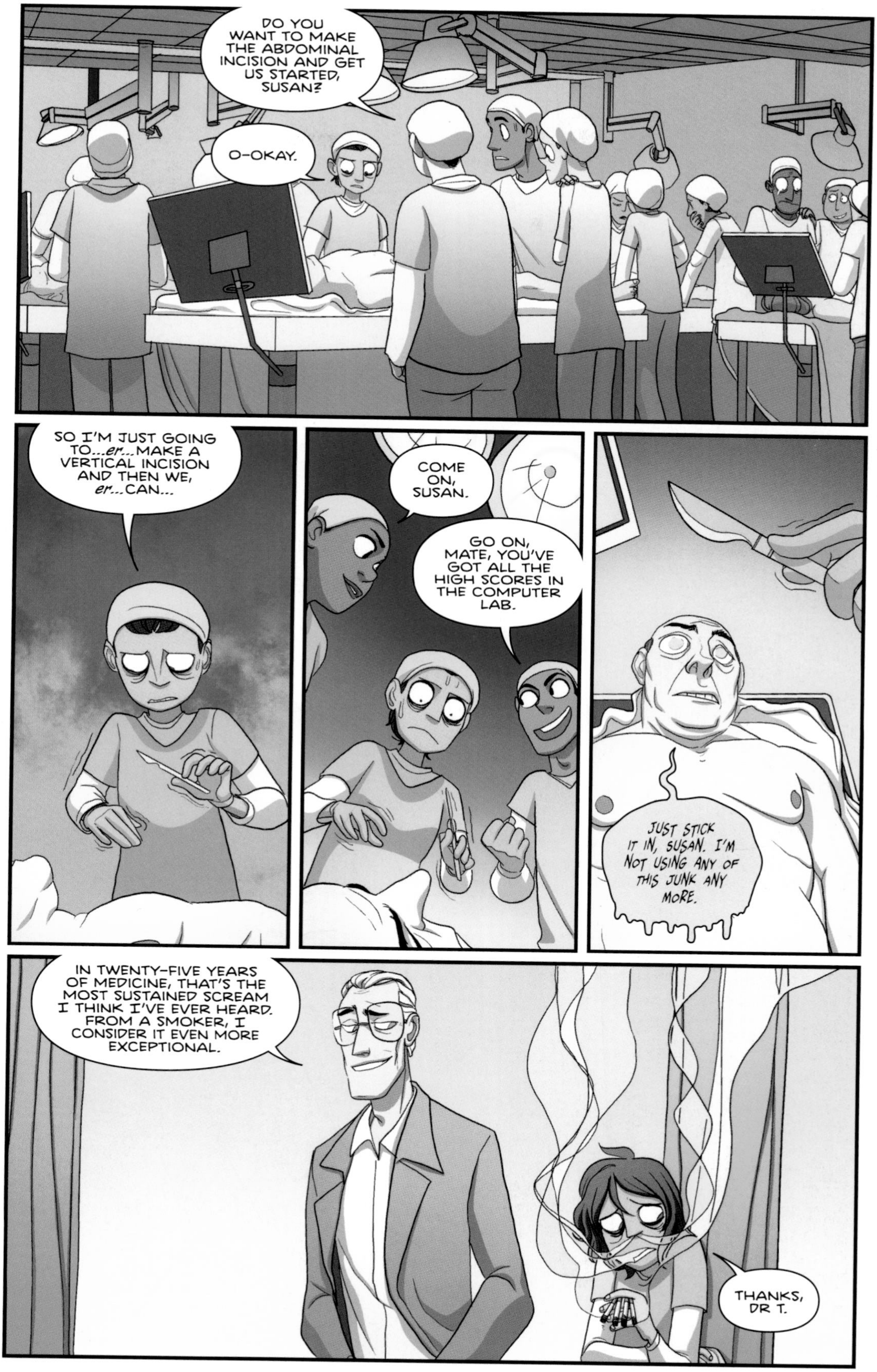
DO YOU WANT TO MAKE THE ABDOMINAL INCISION AND GET US STARTED, SUSAN?
O-OKAY.
SO I'M JUST GOING TO...er...MAKE A VERTICAL INCISION AND THEN WE, er...CAN...
COME ON, SUSAN.
GO ON, MATE, YOU'VE GOT ALL THE HIGH SCORES IN THE COMPUTER LAB.
JUST STICK IT IN, SUSAN. I'M NOT USING ANY OF THIS JUNK ANY MORE.
IN TWENTY-FIVE YEARS OF MEDICINE, THAT'S THE MOST SUSTAINED SCREAM I THINK I'VE EVER HEARD. FROM A SMOKER, I CONSIDER IT EVEN MORE EXCEPTIONAL.
THANKS, DR T.

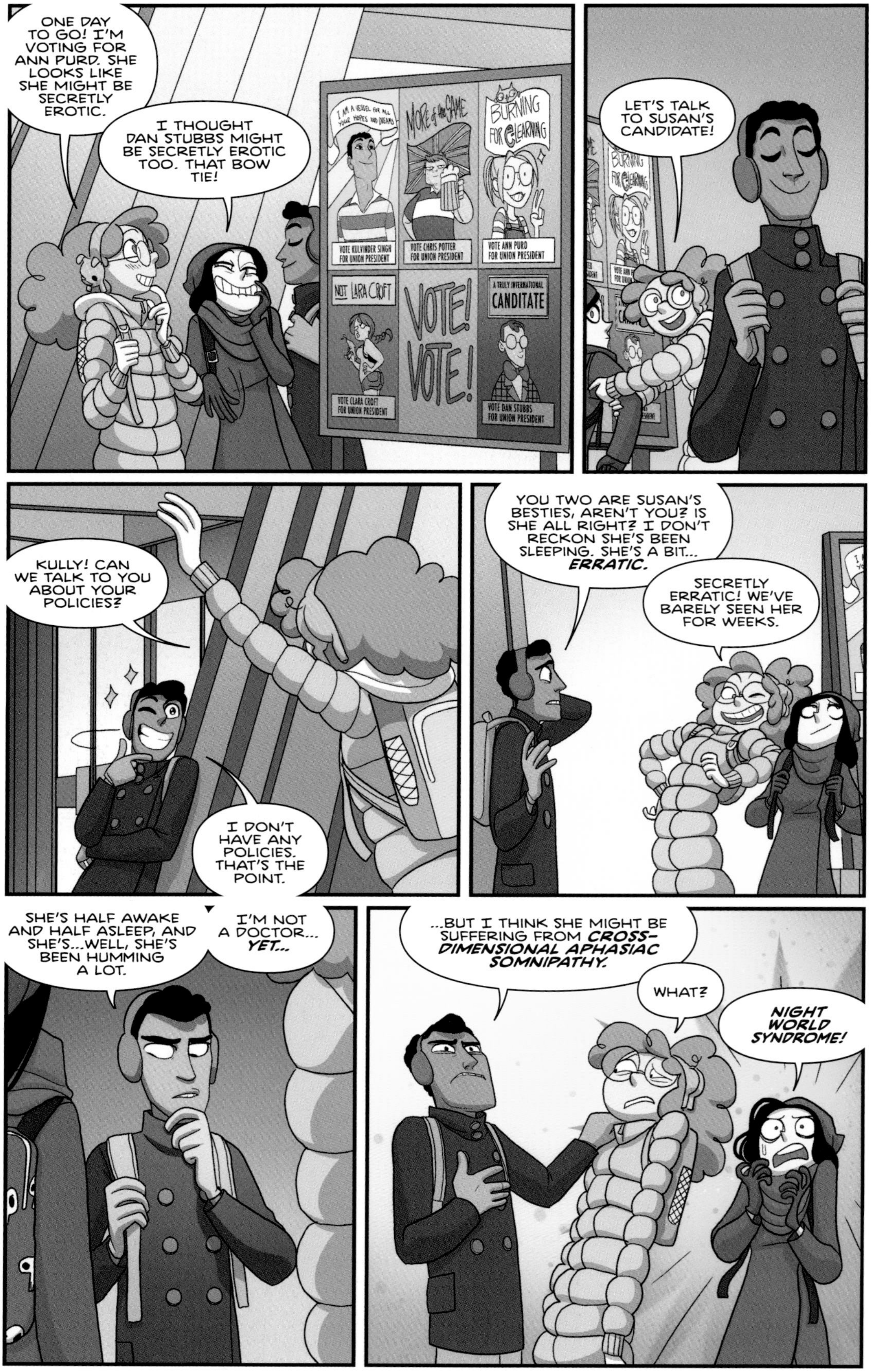
ONE DAY TO GO! I'M VOTING FOR ANN PURD. SHE LOOKS LIKE SHE MIGHT BE SECRETLY EROTIC.
I THOUGHT DAN STUBBS MIGHT BE SECRETLY EROTIC TOO. THAT BOW TIE!
I AM A VESSEL FOR ALL YOUR HOPES AND DREAMS
VOTE KULVINDER SINGH FOR UNION PRESIDENT
MORE of the SAME
VOTE CHRIS POTTER FOR UNION PRESIDENT
BURNING FOR LEARNING
VOTE ANN PURD FOR UNION PRESIDENT
NOT LARA CROFT
VOTE CLARA CROFT FOR UNION PRESIDENT
VOTE! VOTE!
A TRULY INTERNATIONAL CANDITATE
VOTE DAN STUBBS FOR UNION PRESIDENT
LET'S TALK TO SUSAN'S CANDIDATE!
KULLY! CAN WE TALK TO YOU ABOUT YOUR POLICIES?
I DON'T HAVE ANY POLICIES. THAT'S THE POINT.
YOU TWO ARE SUSAN'S BESTIES, AREN'T YOU? IS SHE ALL RIGHT? I DON'T RECKON SHE'S BEEN SLEEPING. SHE'S A BIT... ***ERRATIC.***
SECRETLY ERRATIC! WE'VE BARELY SEEN HER FOR WEEKS.
SHE'S HALF AWAKE AND HALF ASLEEP, AND SHE'S...WELL, SHE'S BEEN HUMMING A LOT.
I'M NOT A DOCTOR... ***YET...***
...BUT I THINK SHE MIGHT BE SUFFERING FROM ***CROSS-DIMENSIONAL APHASIAC SOMNIPATHY.***
WHAT?
NIGHT WORLD SYNDROME!

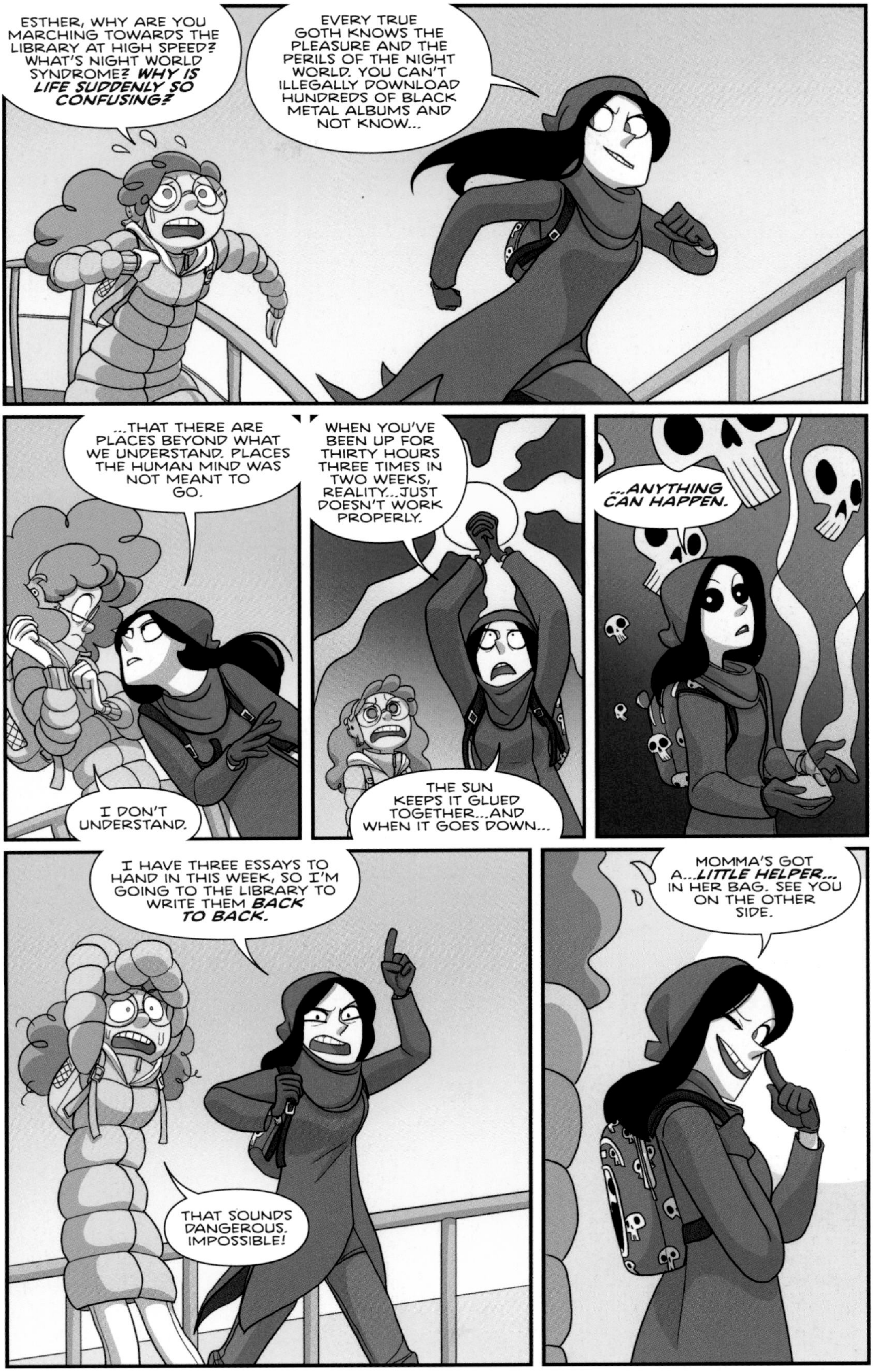
ESTHER, WHY ARE YOU MARCHING TOWARDS THE LIBRARY AT HIGH SPEED? WHAT'S NIGHT WORLD SYNDROME? ***WHY IS LIFE SUDDENLY SO CONFUSING?***
EVERY TRUE GOTH KNOWS THE PLEASURE AND THE PERILS OF THE NIGHT WORLD. YOU CAN'T ILLEGALLY DOWNLOAD HUNDREDS OF BLACK METAL ALBUMS AND NOT KNOW...
...THAT THERE ARE PLACES BEYOND WHAT WE UNDERSTAND. PLACES THE HUMAN MIND WAS NOT MEANT TO GO.
I DON'T UNDERSTAND.
WHEN YOU'VE BEEN UP FOR THIRTY HOURS THREE TIMES IN TWO WEEKS, REALITY...JUST DOESN'T WORK PROPERLY.
THE SUN KEEPS IT GLUED TOGETHER...AND WHEN IT GOES DOWN...
...ANYTHING CAN HAPPEN.
I HAVE THREE ESSAYS TO HAND IN THIS WEEK, SO I'M GOING TO THE LIBRARY TO WRITE THEM ***BACK TO BACK.***
THAT SOUNDS DANGEROUS. IMPOSSIBLE!
MOMMA'S GOT A...***LITTLE HELPER...*** IN HER BAG. SEE YOU ON THE OTHER SIDE.

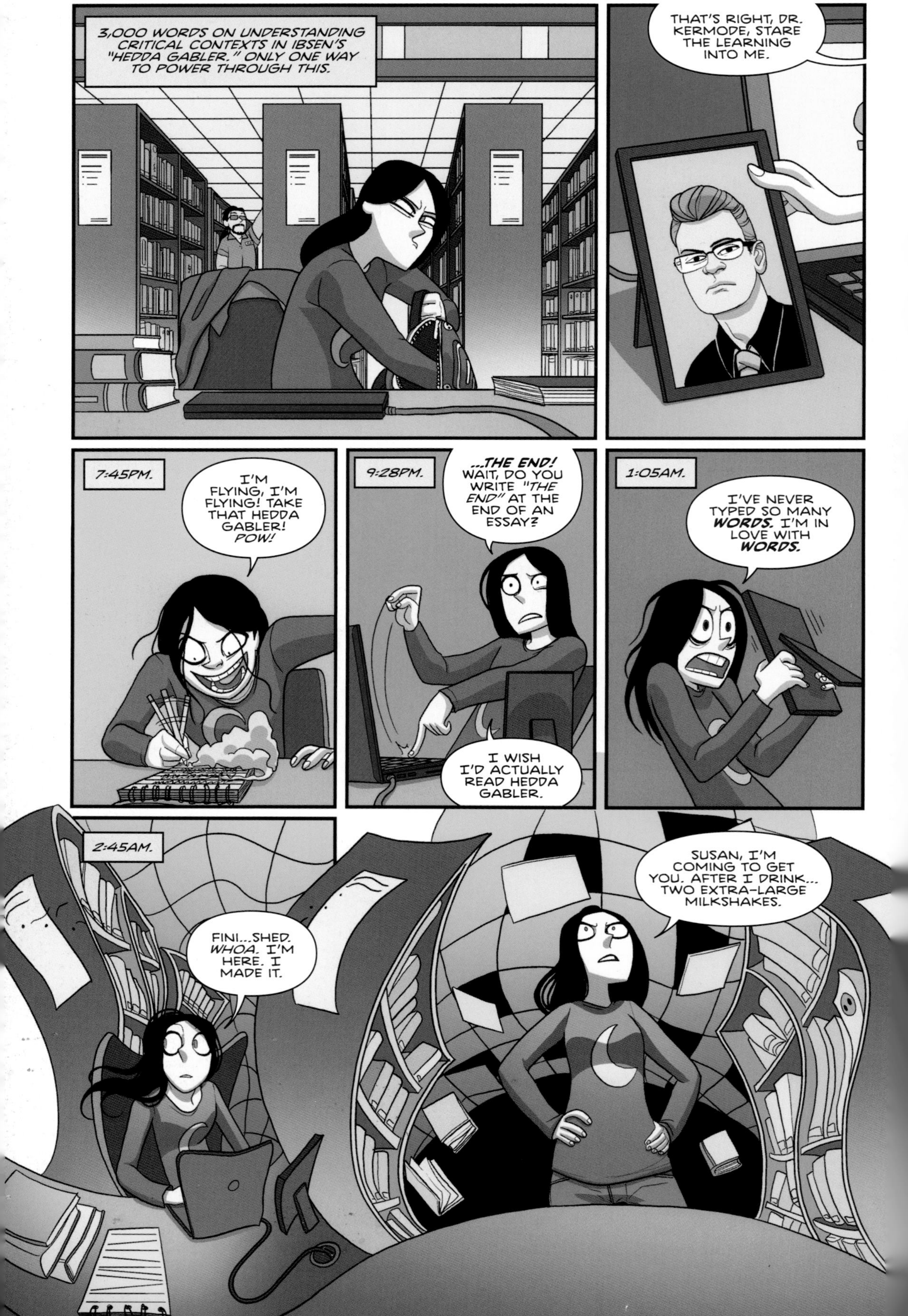
3,000 WORDS ON UNDERSTANDING CRITICAL CONTEXTS IN IBSEN'S "HEDDA GABLER." ONLY ONE WAY TO POWER THROUGH THIS.
THAT'S RIGHT, DR. KERMODE, STARE THE LEARNING INTO ME.
7:45PM.
I'M FLYING, I'M FLYING! TAKE THAT HEDDA GABLER! POW!
9:28PM.
...THE END! WAIT, DO YOU WRITE "THE END" AT THE END OF AN ESSAY?
I WISH I'D ACTUALLY READ HEDDA GABLER.
1:05AM.
I'VE NEVER TYPED SO MANY WORDS. I'M IN LOVE WITH WORDS.
2:45AM.
FINI...SHED. WHOA. I'M HERE. I MADE IT.
SUSAN, I'M COMING TO GET YOU. AFTER I DRINK... TWO EXTRA-LARGE MILKSHAKES.

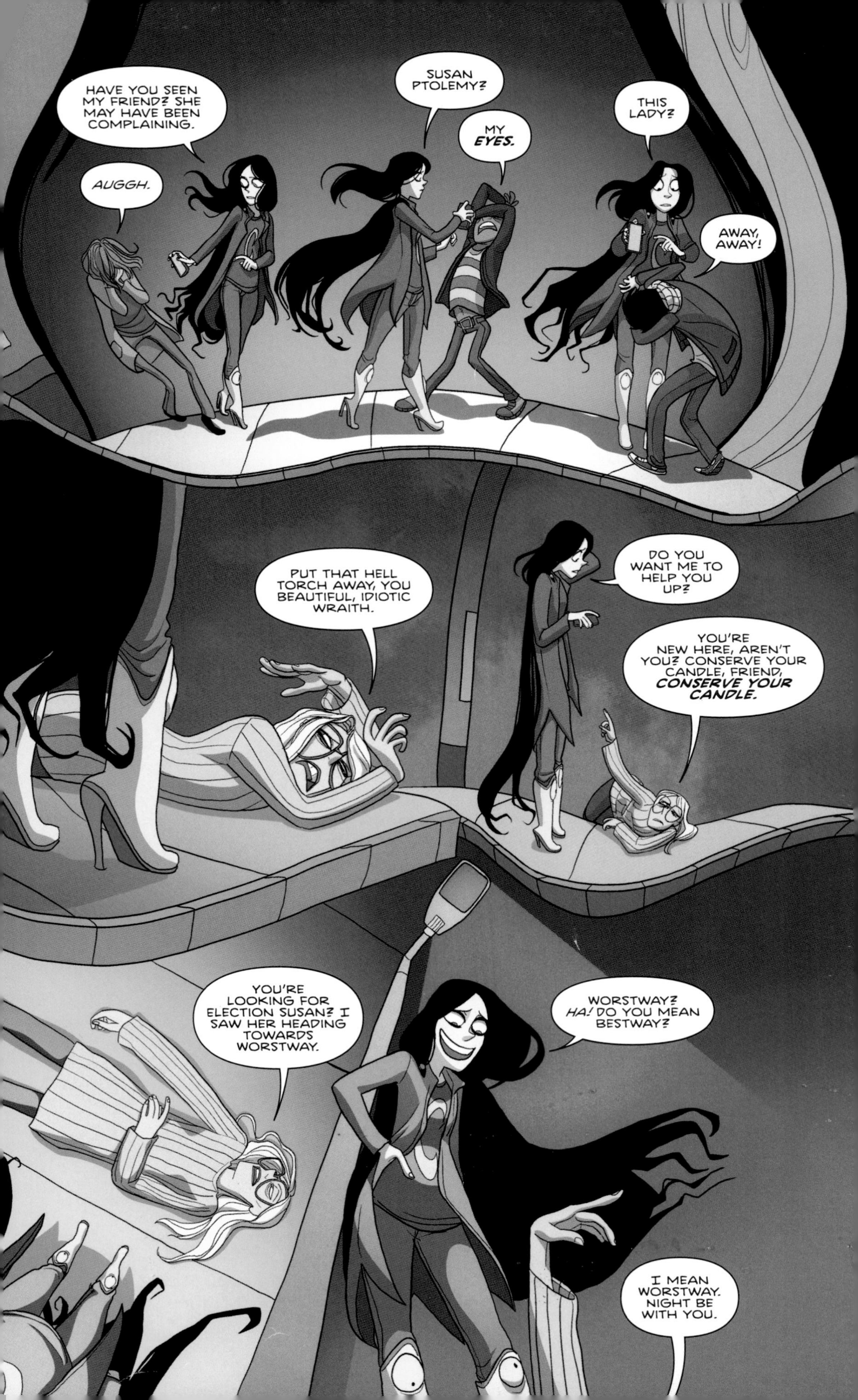
HAVE YOU SEEN MY FRIEND? SHE MAY HAVE BEEN COMPLAINING.
AUGGH.
SUSAN PTOLEMY?
MY *EYES.*
THIS LADY?
AWAY, AWAY!
PUT THAT HELL TORCH AWAY, YOU BEAUTIFUL, IDIOTIC WRAITH.
DO YOU WANT ME TO HELP YOU UP?
YOU'RE NEW HERE, AREN'T YOU? CONSERVE YOUR CANDLE, FRIEND, *CONSERVE YOUR CANDLE.*
YOU'RE LOOKING FOR ELECTION SUSAN? I SAW HER HEADING TOWARDS WORSTWAY.
WORSTWAY? *HA!* DO YOU MEAN BESTWAY?
I MEAN WORSTWAY. NIGHT BE WITH YOU.

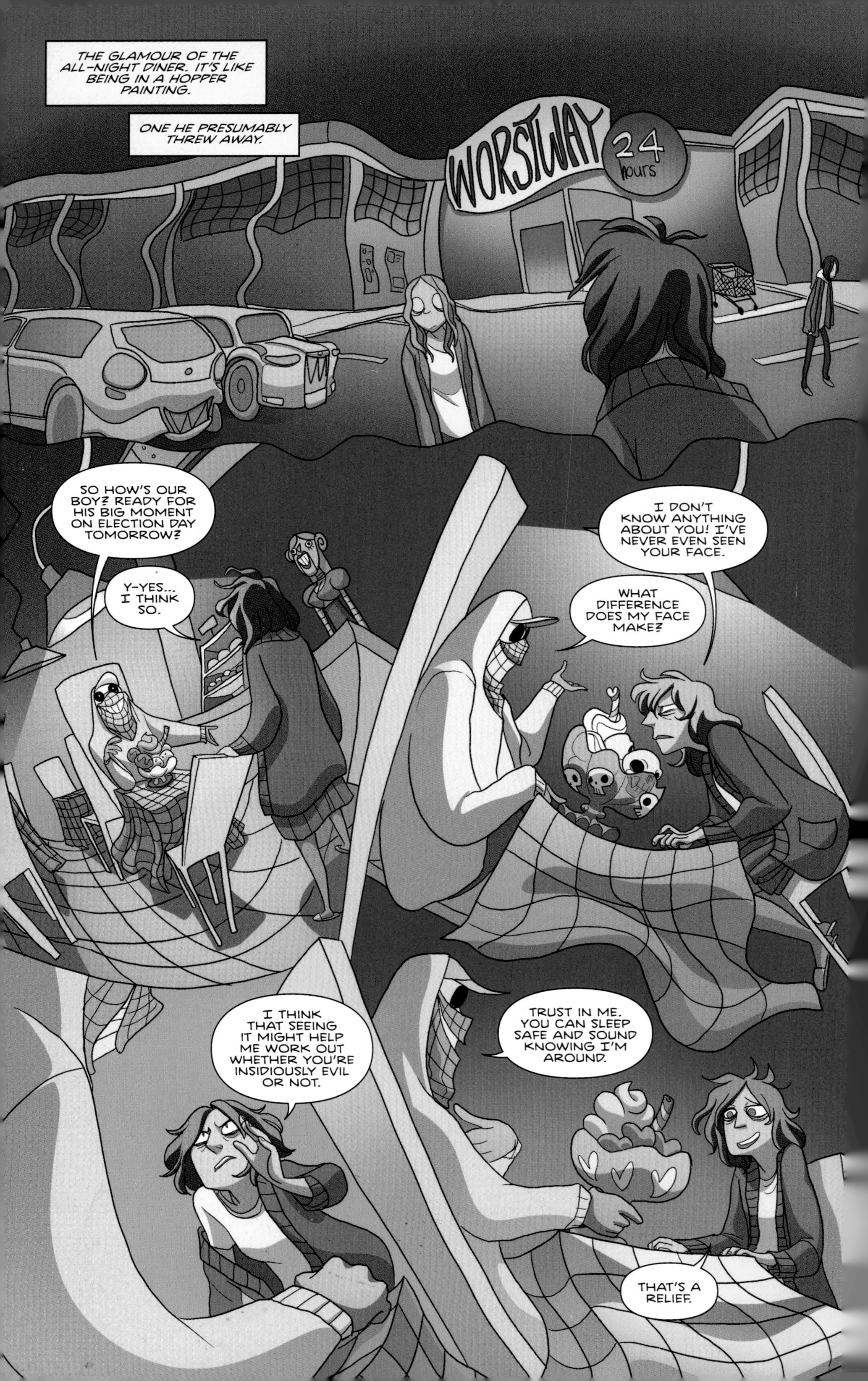
THE GLAMOUR OF THE ALL-NIGHT DINER. IT'S LIKE BEING IN A HOPPER PAINTING.
ONE HE PRESUMABLY THREW AWAY.
WORSTWAY
24 hours
SO HOW'S OUR BOY? READY FOR HIS BIG MOMENT ON ELECTION DAY TOMORROW?
Y-YES... I THINK SO.
I DON'T KNOW ANYTHING ABOUT YOU! I'VE NEVER EVEN SEEN YOUR FACE.
WHAT DIFFERENCE DOES MY FACE MAKE?
I THINK THAT SEEING IT MIGHT HELP ME WORK OUT WHETHER YOU'RE INSIDIOUSLY EVIL OR NOT.
TRUST IN ME. YOU CAN SLEEP SAFE AND SOUND KNOWING I'M AROUND.
THAT'S A RELIEF.

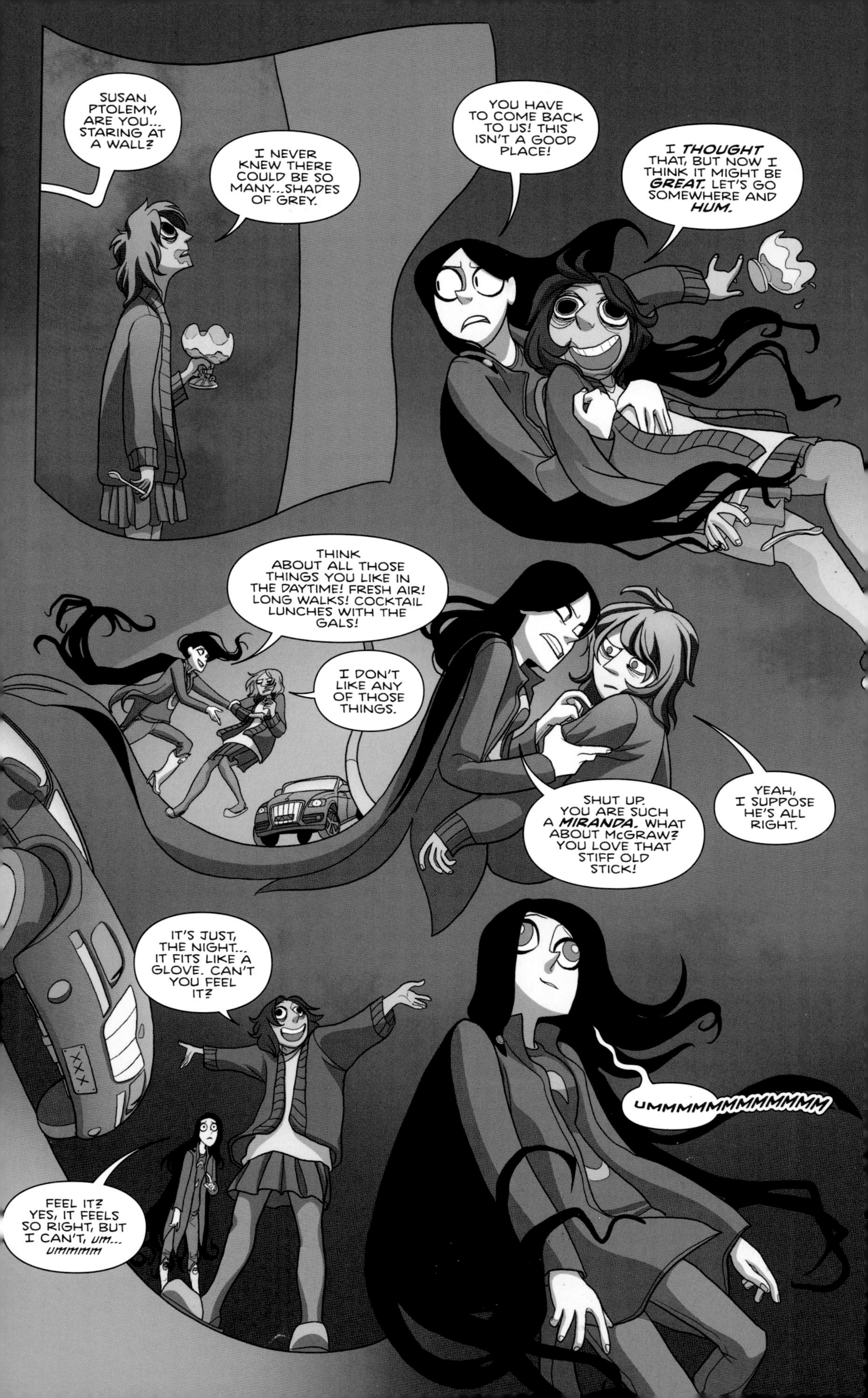
SUSAN PTOLEMY, ARE YOU... STARING AT A WALL?
I NEVER KNEW THERE COULD BE SO MANY...SHADES OF GREY.
YOU HAVE TO COME BACK TO US! THIS ISN'T A GOOD PLACE!
I THOUGHT THAT, BUT NOW I THINK IT MIGHT BE GREAT. LET'S GO SOMEWHERE AND HUM.
THINK ABOUT ALL THOSE THINGS YOU LIKE IN THE DAYTIME! FRESH AIR! LONG WALKS! COCKTAIL LUNCHES WITH THE GALS!
I DON'T LIKE ANY OF THOSE THINGS.
SHUT UP. YOU ARE SUCH A MIRANDA. WHAT ABOUT McGRAW? YOU LOVE THAT STIFF OLD STICK!
YEAH, I SUPPOSE HE'S ALL RIGHT.
IT'S JUST, THE NIGHT... IT FITS LIKE A GLOVE. CAN'T YOU FEEL IT?
FEEL IT? YES, IT FEELS SO RIGHT, BUT I CAN'T, UM... UMMMMM
UMMMMMMMMMMMM

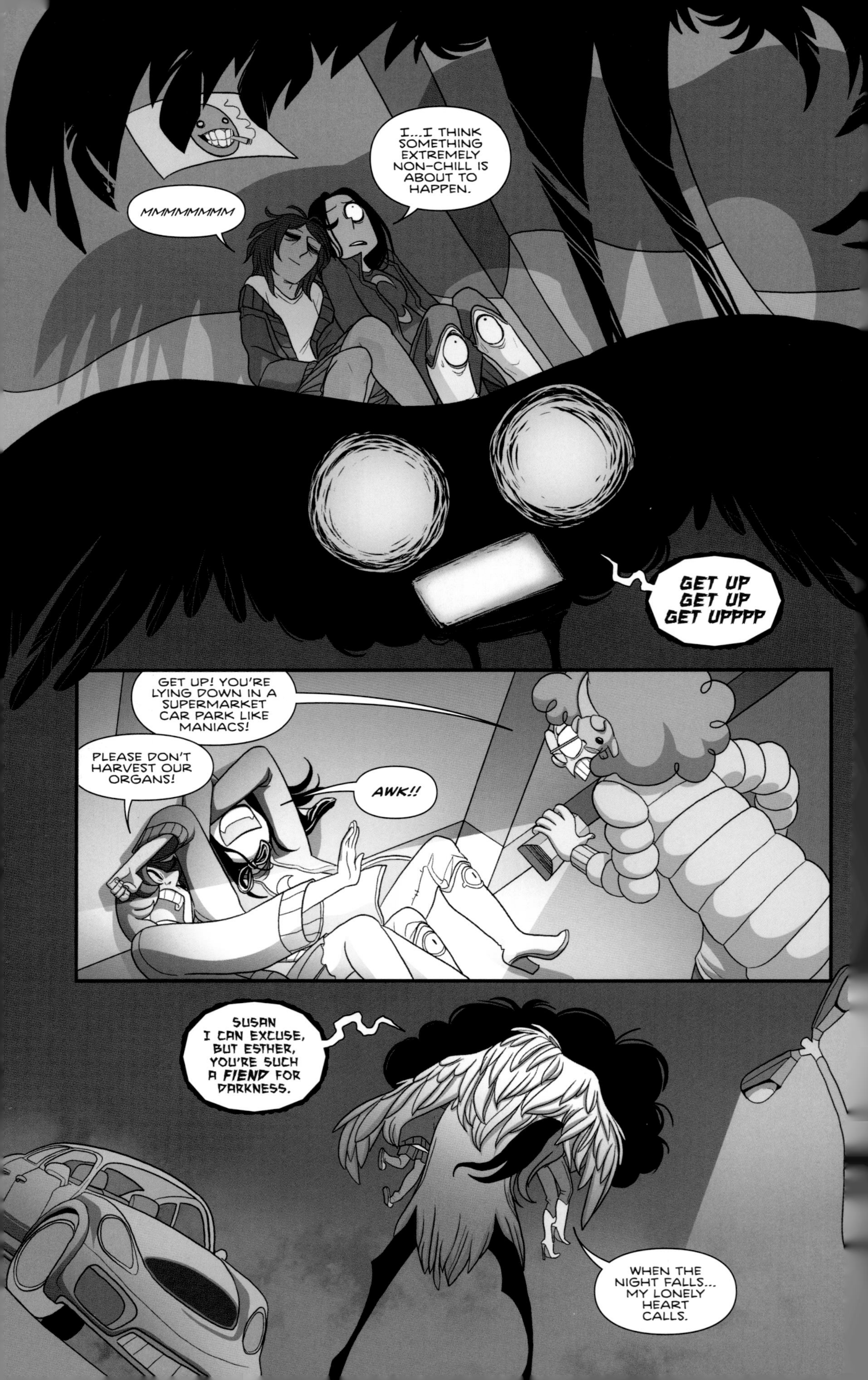

I...I THINK SOMETHING EXTREMELY NON-CHILL IS ABOUT TO HAPPEN.
MMMMMMMM
GET UP GET UP GET UPPPP
GET UP! YOU'RE LYING DOWN IN A SUPERMARKET CAR PARK LIKE MANIACS!
PLEASE DON'T HARVEST OUR ORGANS!
AWK!!
SUSAN I CAN EXCUSE, BUT ESTHER, YOU'RE SUCH A FIEND FOR DARKNESS.
WHEN THE NIGHT FALLS... MY LONELY HEART CALLS.

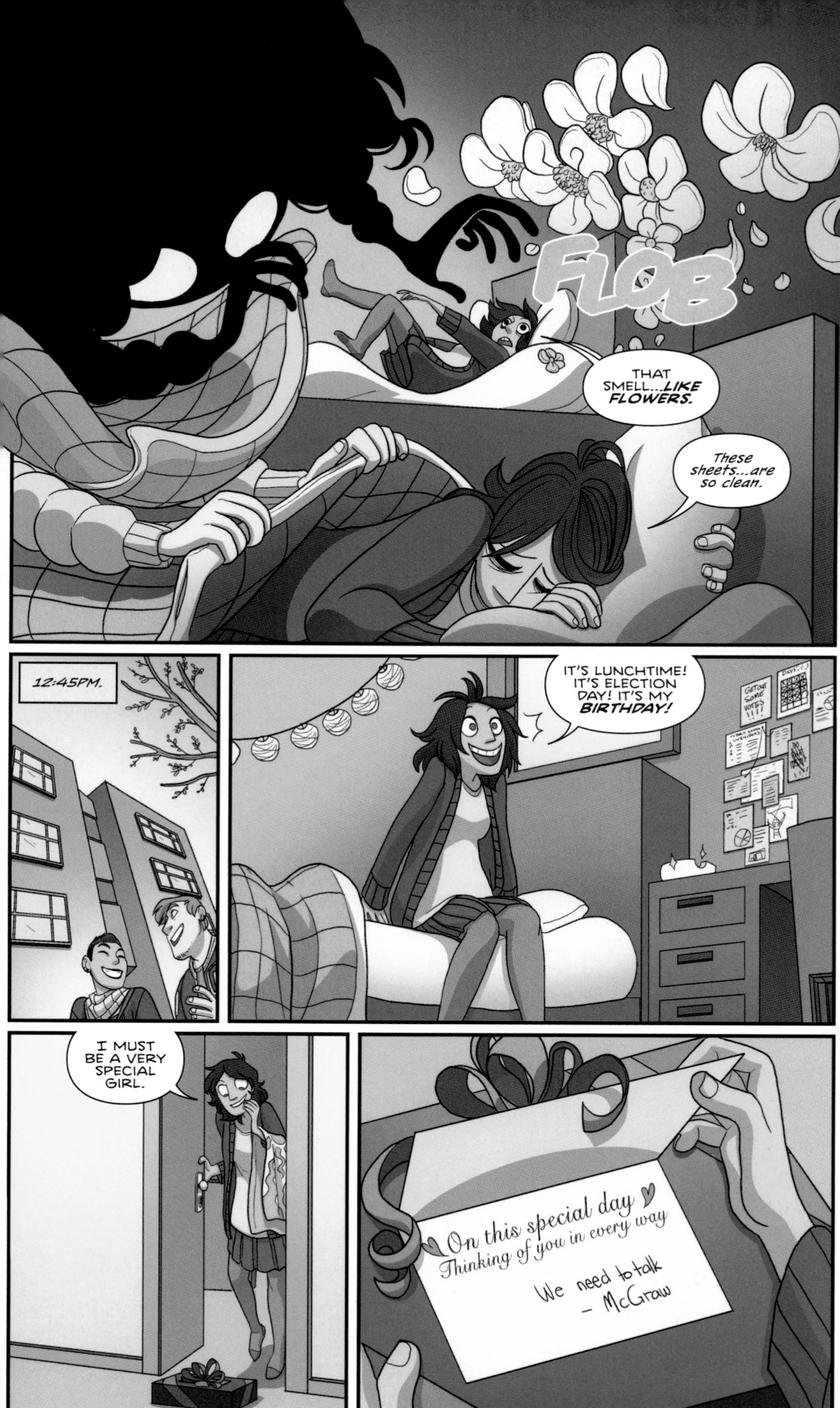
FLOB
THAT SMELL...LIKE FLOWERS.
These sheets...are so clean.
12:45PM.
IT'S LUNCHTIME! IT'S ELECTION DAY! IT'S MY BIRTHDAY!
GET OUT SOME VOTES!!!
I MUST BE A VERY SPECIAL GIRL.
On this special day
Thinking of you in every way
We need to talk
- McGraw

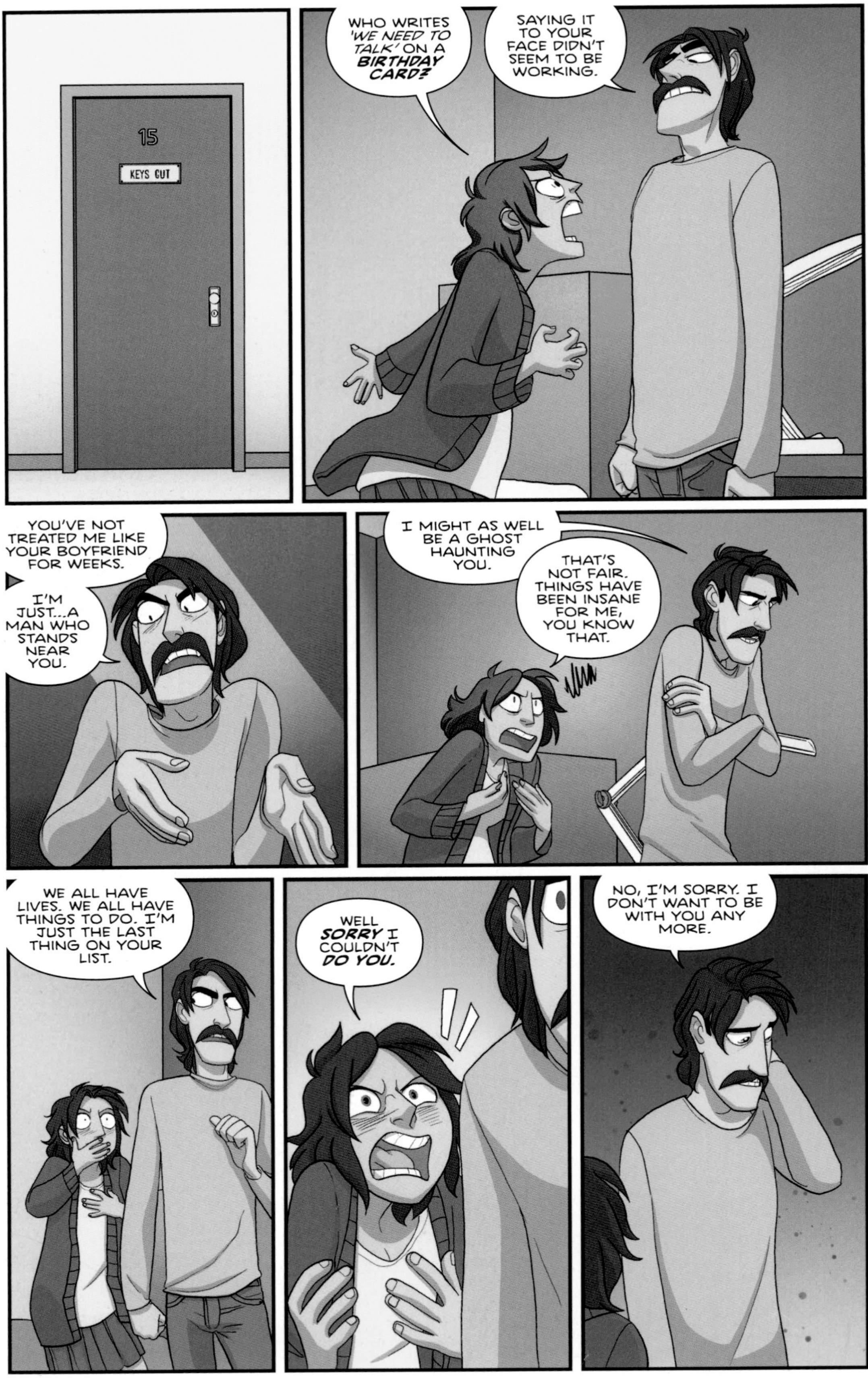
KEYS CUT
15
WHO WRITES 'WE NEED TO TALK' ON A BIRTHDAY CARD?
SAYING IT TO YOUR FACE DIDN'T SEEM TO BE WORKING.
YOU'VE NOT TREATED ME LIKE YOUR BOYFRIEND FOR WEEKS.
I'M JUST...A MAN WHO STANDS NEAR YOU.
I MIGHT AS WELL BE A GHOST HAUNTING YOU.
THAT'S NOT FAIR. THINGS HAVE BEEN INSANE FOR ME, YOU KNOW THAT.
WE ALL HAVE LIVES. WE ALL HAVE THINGS TO DO. I'M JUST THE LAST THING ON YOUR LIST.
WELL SORRY I COULDN'T DO YOU.
NO, I'M SORRY. I DON'T WANT TO BE WITH YOU ANY MORE.

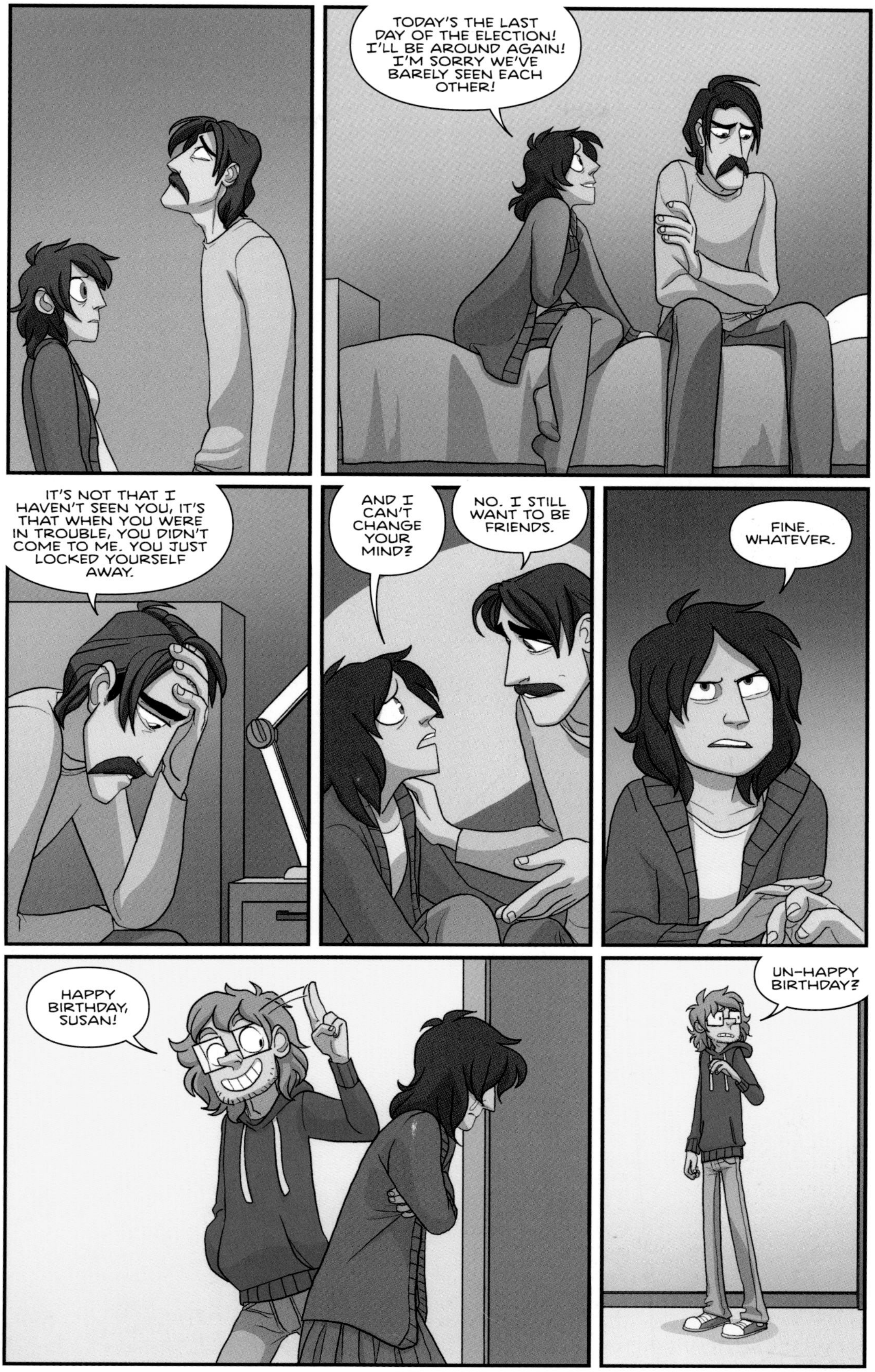
TODAY'S THE LAST DAY OF THE ELECTION! I'LL BE AROUND AGAIN! I'M SORRY WE'VE BARELY SEEN EACH OTHER!
IT'S NOT THAT I HAVEN'T SEEN YOU, IT'S THAT WHEN YOU WERE IN TROUBLE, YOU DIDN'T COME TO ME. YOU JUST LOCKED YOURSELF AWAY.
AND I CAN'T CHANGE YOUR MIND?
NO. I STILL WANT TO BE FRIENDS.
FINE. WHATEVER.
HAPPY BIRTHDAY, SUSAN!
UN-HAPPY BIRTHDAY?

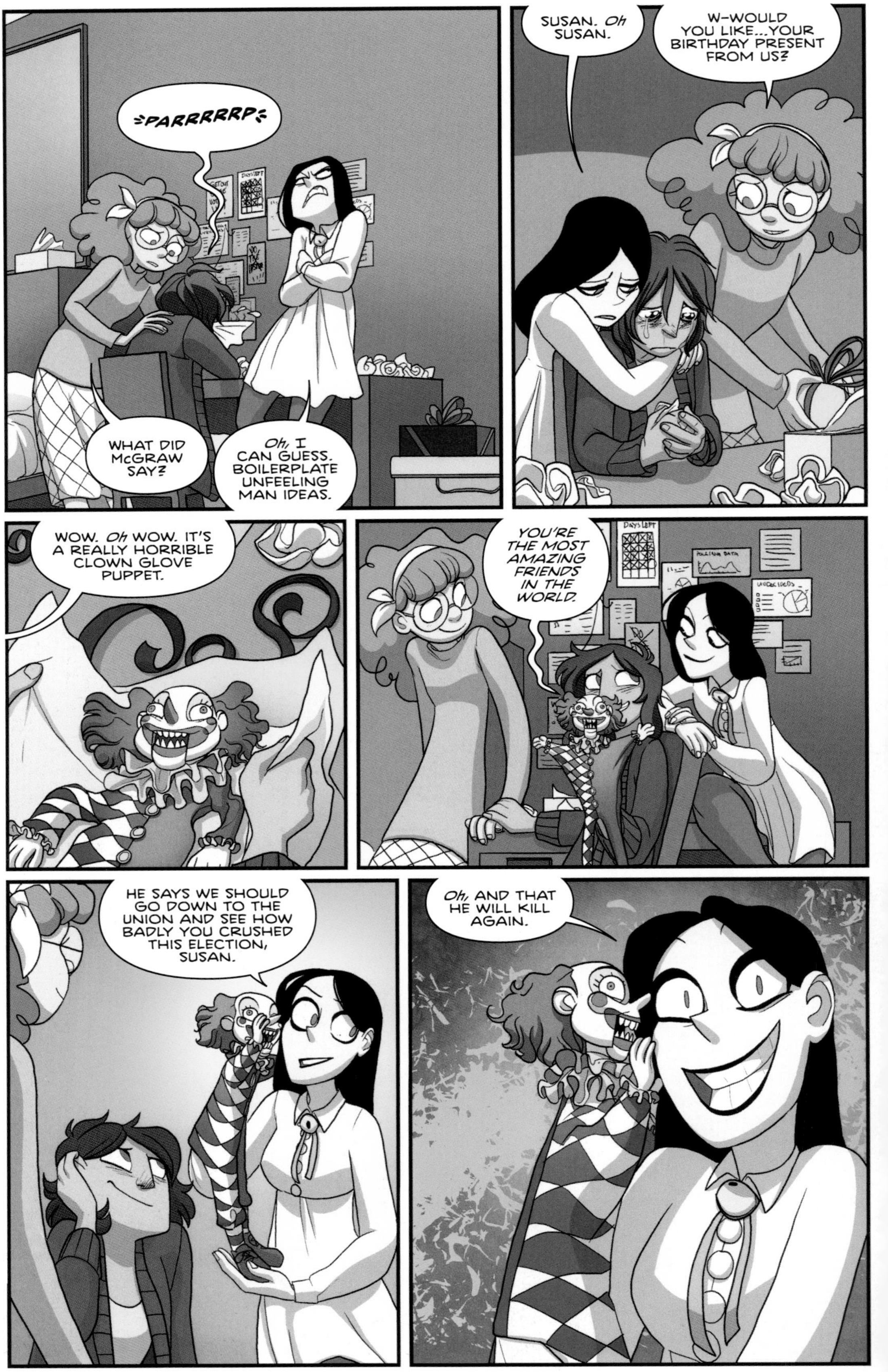
PARRRRRP
WHAT DID McGRAW SAY?
Oh, I CAN GUESS. BOILERPLATE UNFEELING MAN IDEAS.
SUSAN. Oh SUSAN.
W-WOULD YOU LIKE...YOUR BIRTHDAY PRESENT FROM US?
WOW. Oh WOW. IT'S A REALLY HORRIBLE CLOWN GLOVE PUPPET.
YOU'RE THE MOST AMAZING FRIENDS IN THE WORLD.
HE SAYS WE SHOULD GO DOWN TO THE UNION AND SEE HOW BADLY YOU CRUSHED THIS ELECTION, SUSAN.
Oh, AND THAT HE WILL KILL AGAIN.

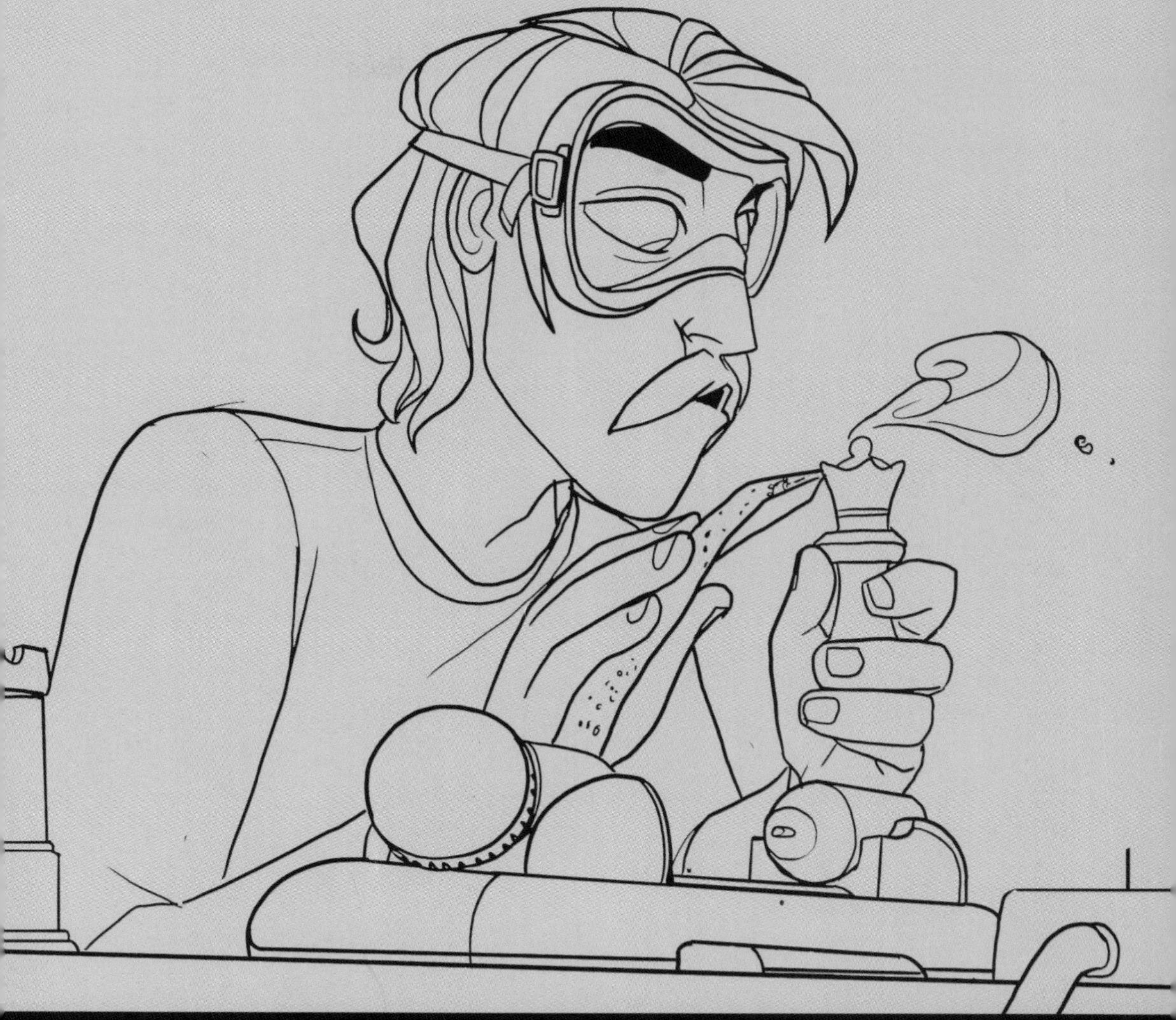

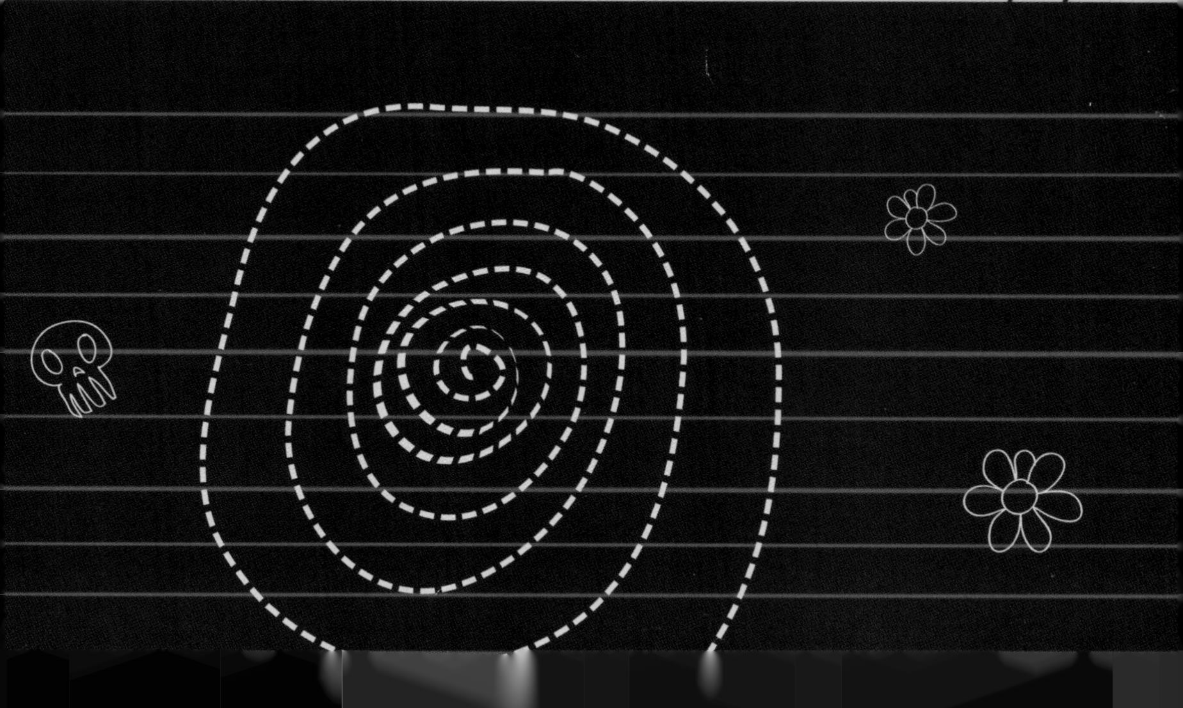

CHAPTER TWELEVE

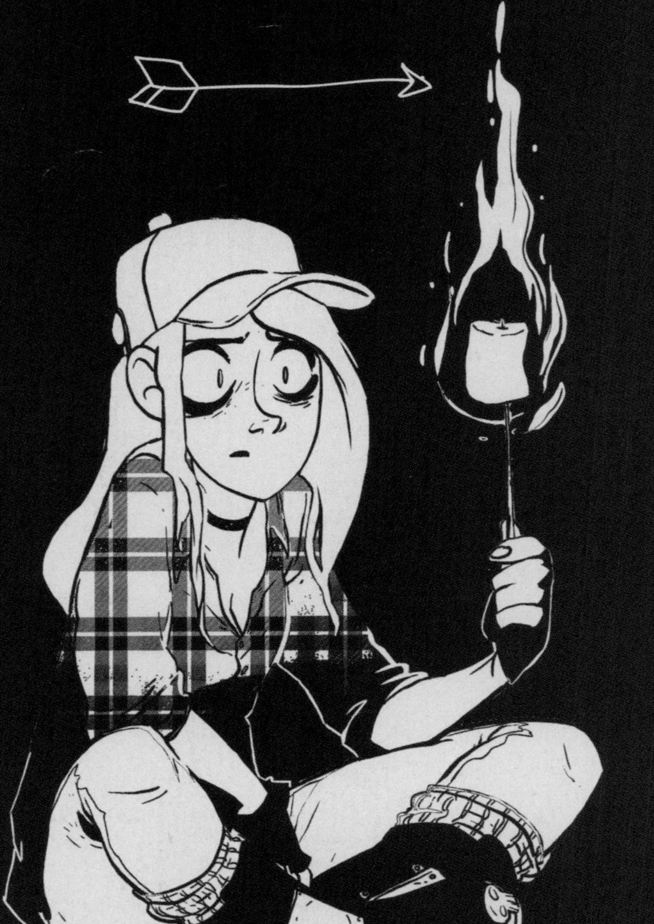

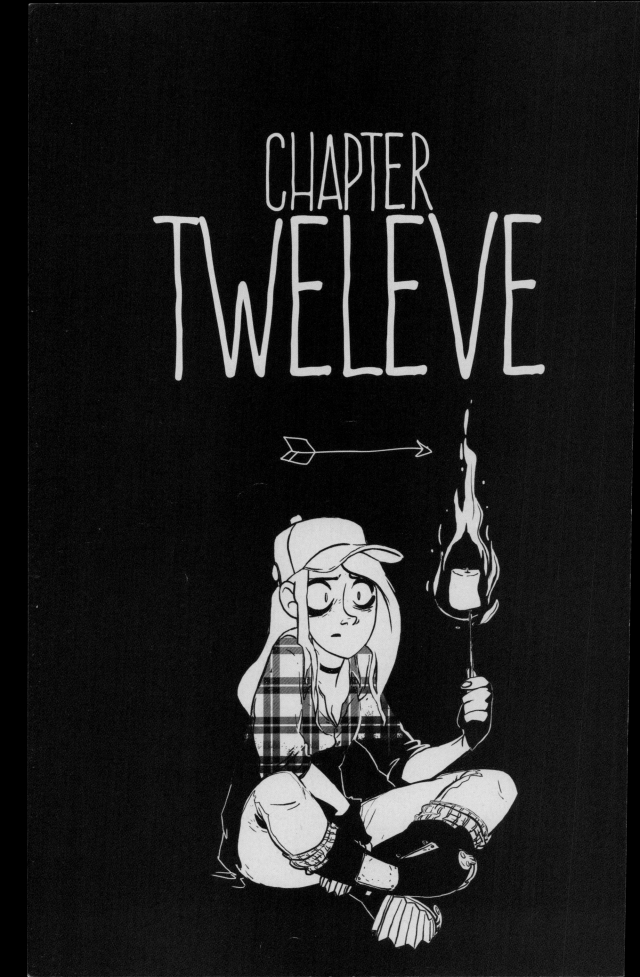

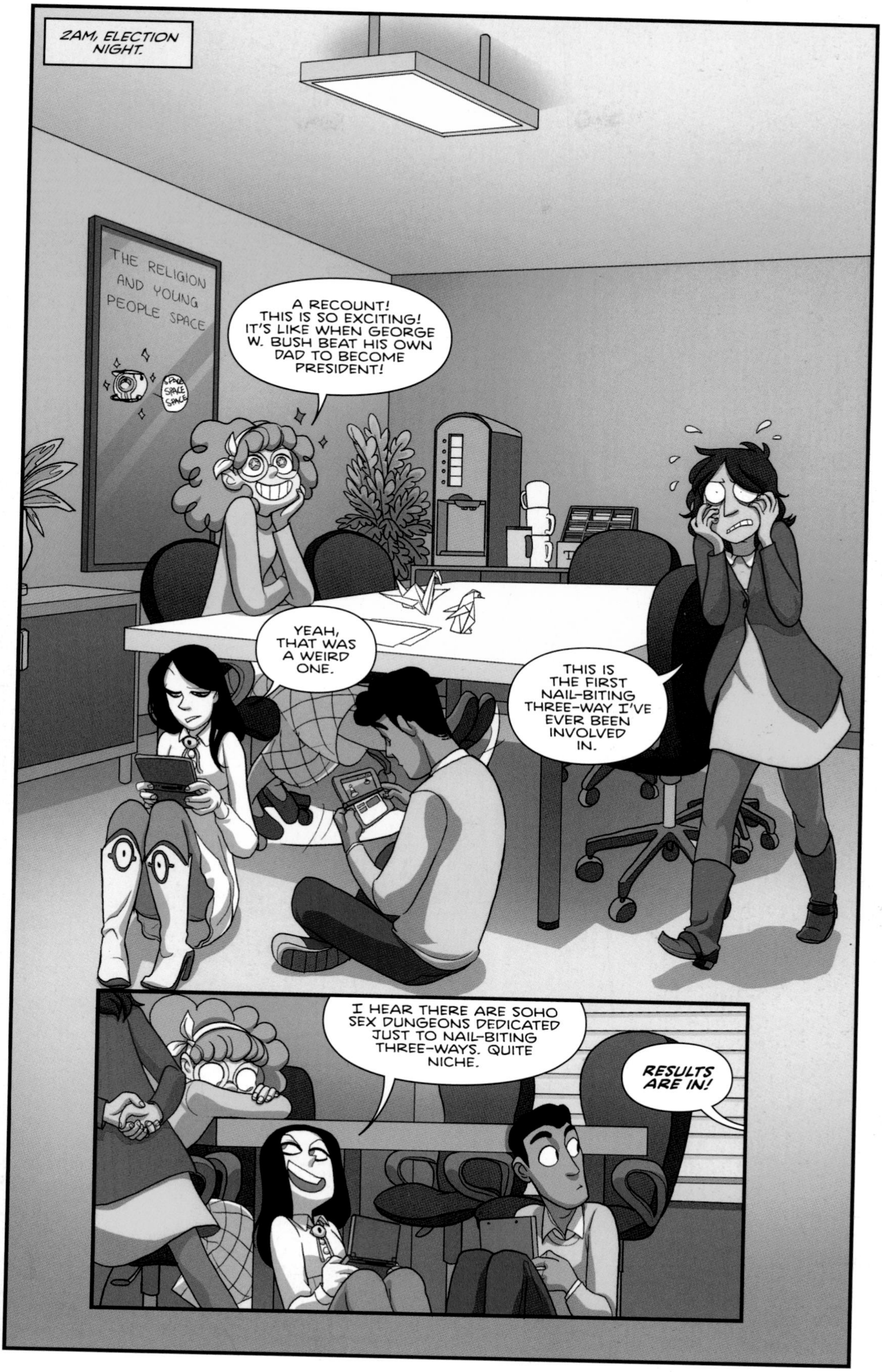
2AM, ELECTION NIGHT.
THE RELIGION AND YOUNG PEOPLE SPACE
SPACE SPACE SPACE
A RECOUNT! THIS IS SO EXCITING! IT'S LIKE WHEN GEORGE W. BUSH BEAT HIS OWN DAD TO BECOME PRESIDENT!
YEAH, THAT WAS A WEIRD ONE.
THIS IS THE FIRST NAIL-BITING THREE-WAY I'VE EVER BEEN INVOLVED IN.
I HEAR THERE ARE SOHO SEX DUNGEONS DEDICATED JUST TO NAIL-BITING THREE-WAYS. QUITE NICHE.
RESULTS ARE IN!

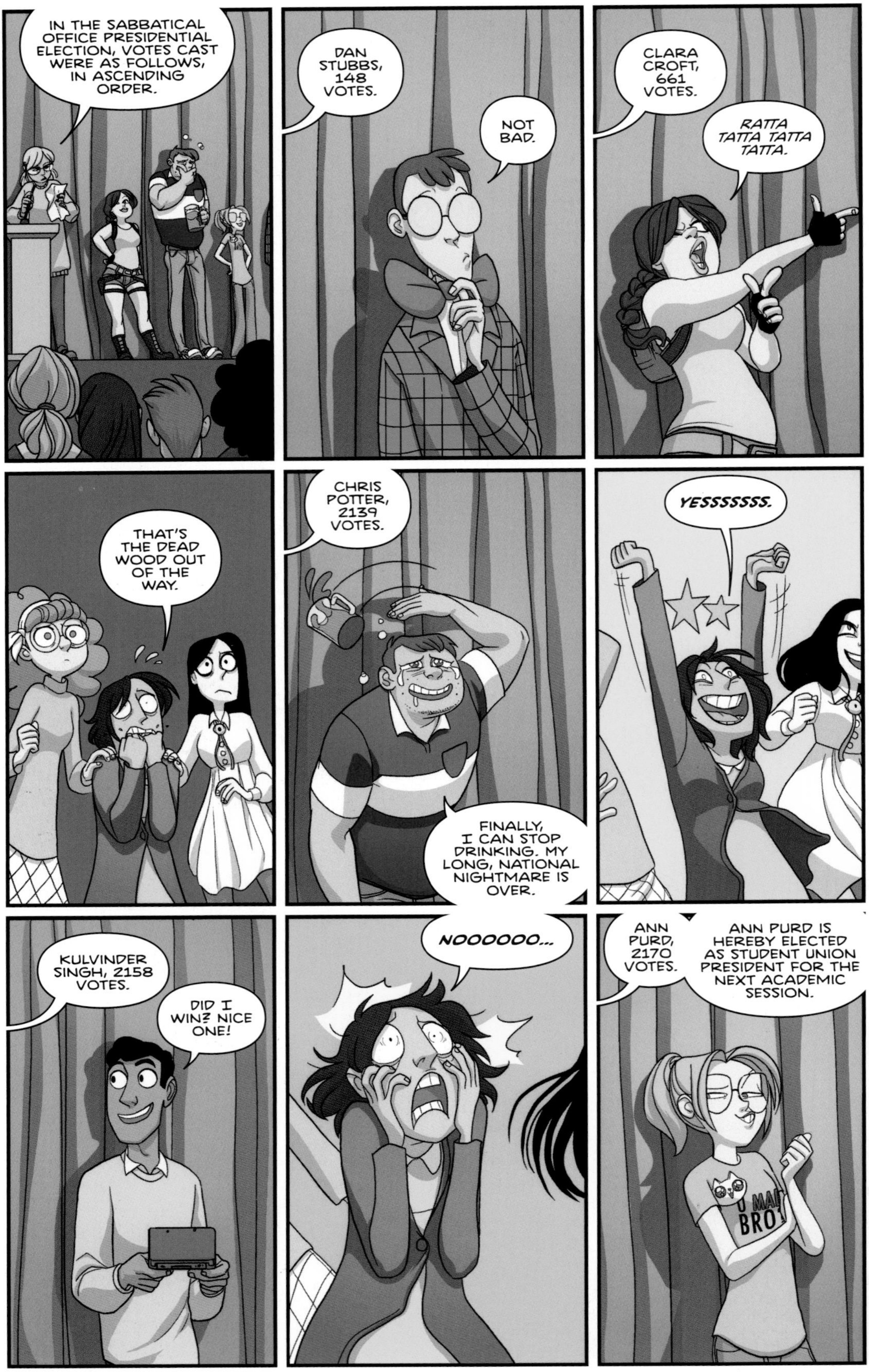
IN THE SABBATICAL OFFICE PRESIDENTIAL ELECTION, VOTES CAST WERE AS FOLLOWS, IN ASCENDING ORDER.
DAN STUBBS, 148 VOTES.
NOT BAD.
CLARA CROFT, 661 VOTES.
RATTA TATTA TATTA TATTA.
THAT'S THE DEAD WOOD OUT OF THE WAY.
CHRIS POTTER, 2139 VOTES.
FINALLY, I CAN STOP DRINKING. MY LONG, NATIONAL NIGHTMARE IS OVER.
YESSSSSSS.
KULVINDER SINGH, 2158 VOTES.
DID I WIN? NICE ONE!
NOOOOOO...
ANN PURD, 2170 VOTES.
ANN PURD IS HEREBY ELECTED AS STUDENT UNION PRESIDENT FOR THE NEXT ACADEMIC SESSION.

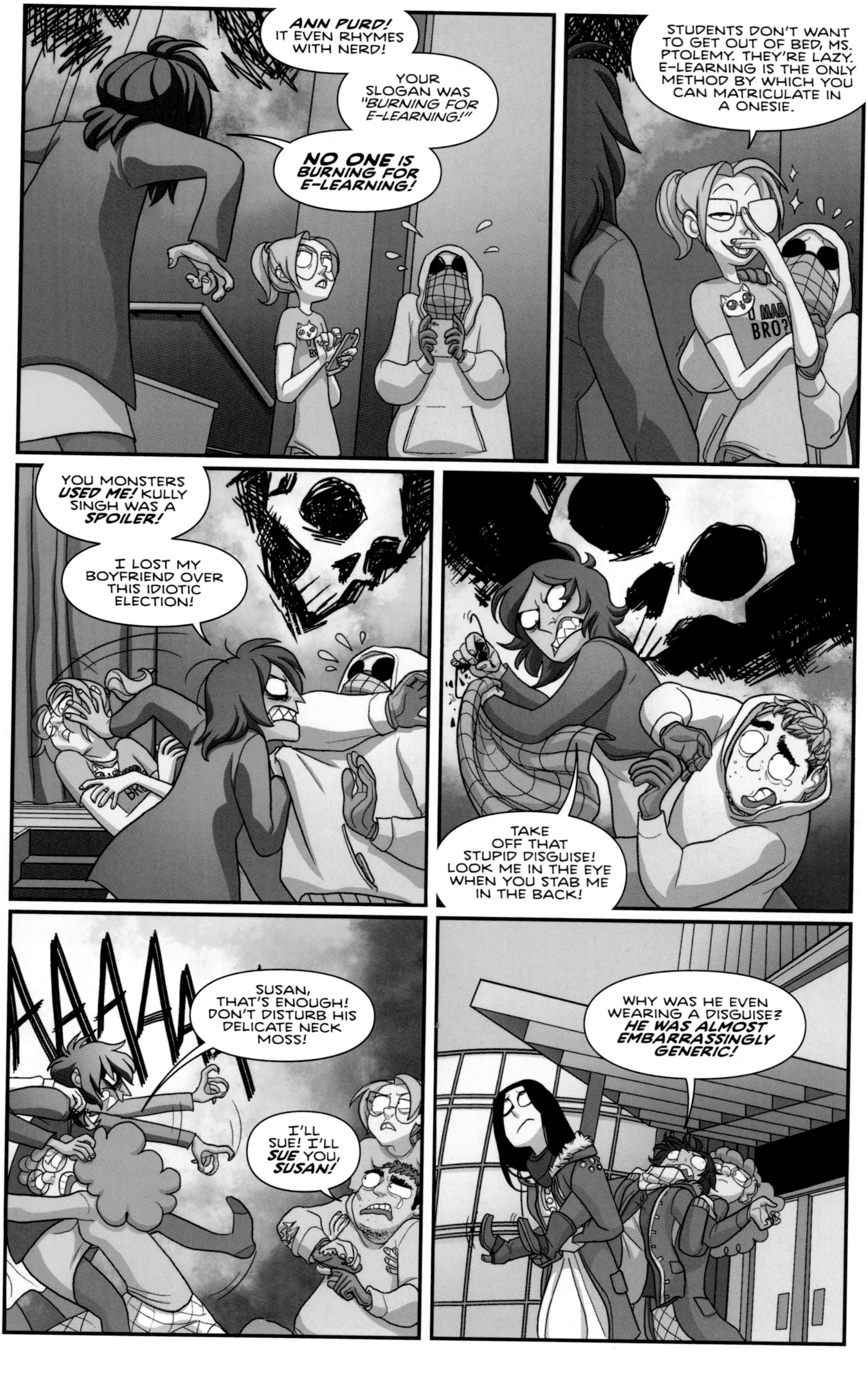
ANN PURD! IT EVEN RHYMES WITH NERD!
YOUR SLOGAN WAS "BURNING FOR E-LEARNING!"
NO ONE IS BURNING FOR E-LEARNING!
STUDENTS DON'T WANT TO GET OUT OF BED, MS. PTOLEMY. THEY'RE LAZY. E-LEARNING IS THE ONLY METHOD BY WHICH YOU CAN MATRICULATE IN A ONESIE.
U MAD BRO?
YOU MONSTERS USED ME! KULLY SINGH WAS A SPOILER!
I LOST MY BOYFRIEND OVER THIS IDIOTIC ELECTION!
TAKE OFF THAT STUPID DISGUISE! LOOK ME IN THE EYE WHEN YOU STAB ME IN THE BACK!
AAAAA
SUSAN, THAT'S ENOUGH! DON'T DISTURB HIS DELICATE NECK MOSS!
I'LL SUE! I'LL SUE YOU, SUSAN!
WHY WAS HE EVEN WEARING A DISGUISE? HE WAS ALMOST EMBARRASSINGLY GENERIC!

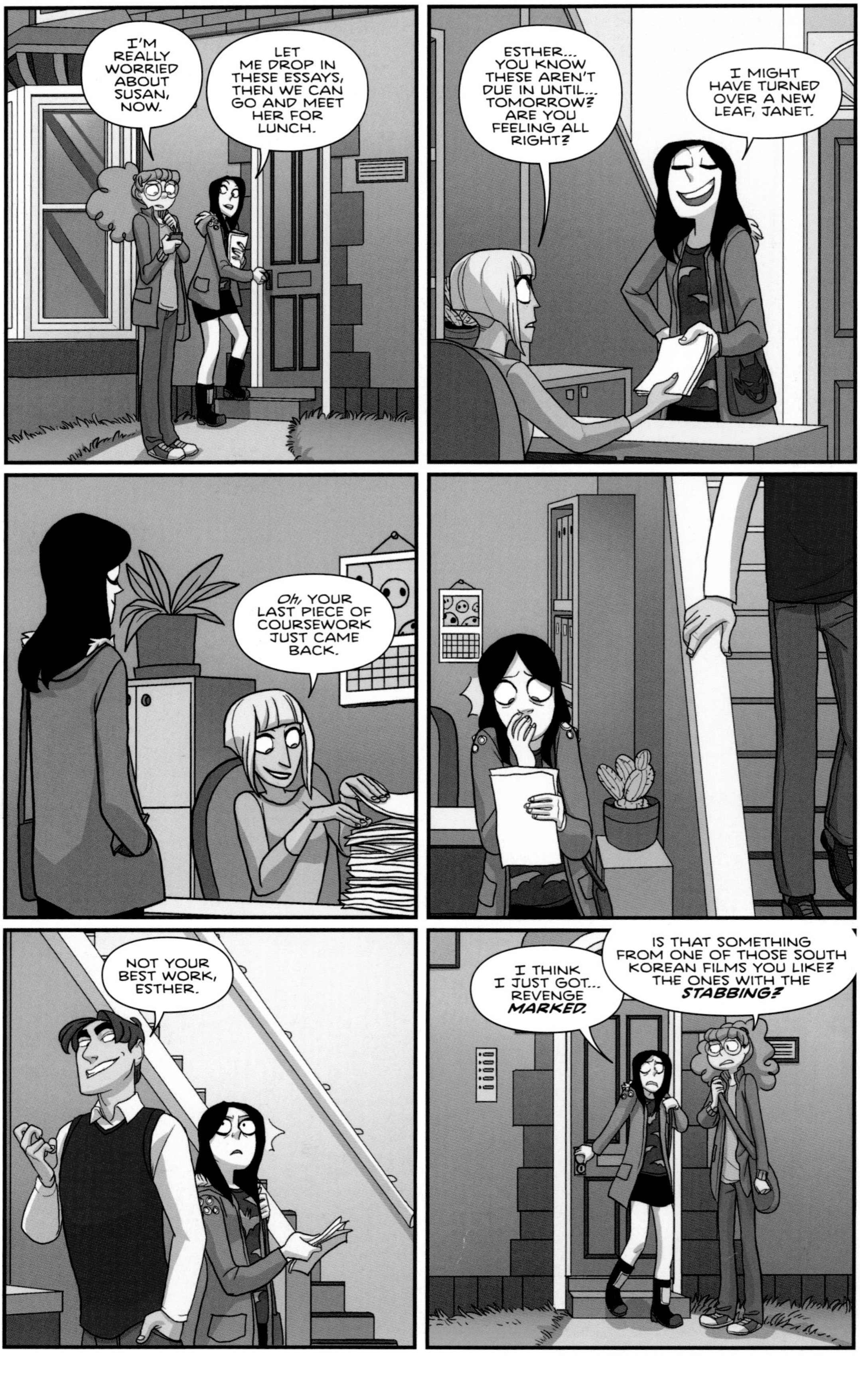
I'M REALLY WORRIED ABOUT SUSAN, NOW.
LET ME DROP IN THESE ESSAYS, THEN WE CAN GO AND MEET HER FOR LUNCH.
ESTHER... YOU KNOW THESE AREN'T DUE IN UNTIL... TOMORROW? ARE YOU FEELING ALL RIGHT?
I MIGHT HAVE TURNED OVER A NEW LEAF, JANET.
Oh, YOUR LAST PIECE OF COURSEWORK JUST CAME BACK.
NOT YOUR BEST WORK, ESTHER.
I THINK I JUST GOT... REVENGE MARKED.
IS THAT SOMETHING FROM ONE OF THOSE SOUTH KOREAN FILMS YOU LIKE? THE ONES WITH THE STABBING?

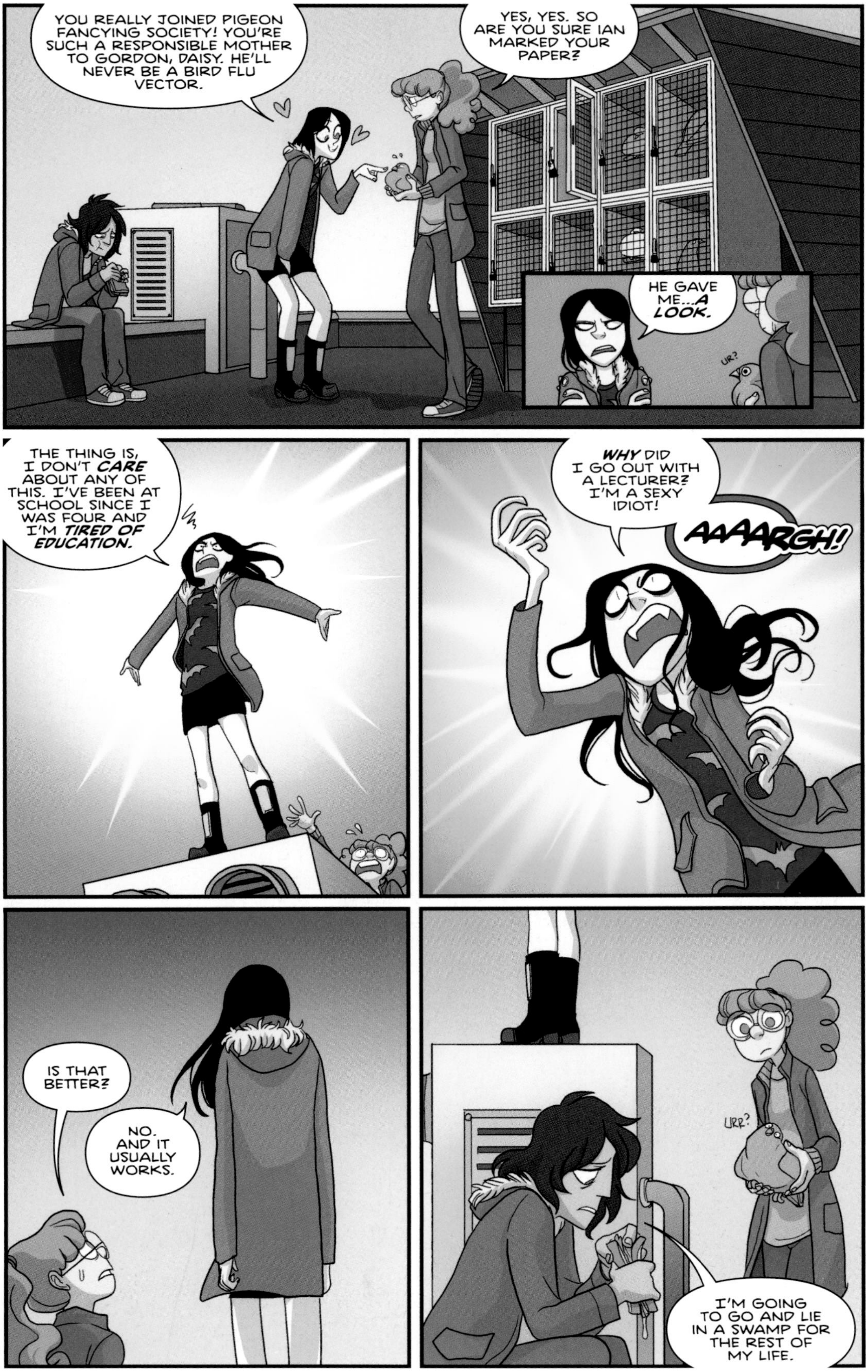
YOU REALLY JOINED PIGEON FANCYING SOCIETY! YOU'RE SUCH A RESPONSIBLE MOTHER TO GORDON, DAISY. HE'LL NEVER BE A BIRD FLU VECTOR.
YES, YES. SO ARE YOU SURE IAN MARKED YOUR PAPER?
HE GAVE ME... A LOOK.
UR?
THE THING IS, I DON'T CARE ABOUT ANY OF THIS. I'VE BEEN AT SCHOOL SINCE I WAS FOUR AND I'M TIRED OF EDUCATION.
WHY DID I GO OUT WITH A LECTURER? I'M A SEXY IDIOT!
AAAARGH!
IS THAT BETTER?
NO. AND IT USUALLY WORKS.
URR?
I'M GOING TO GO AND LIE IN A SWAMP FOR THE REST OF MY LIFE.

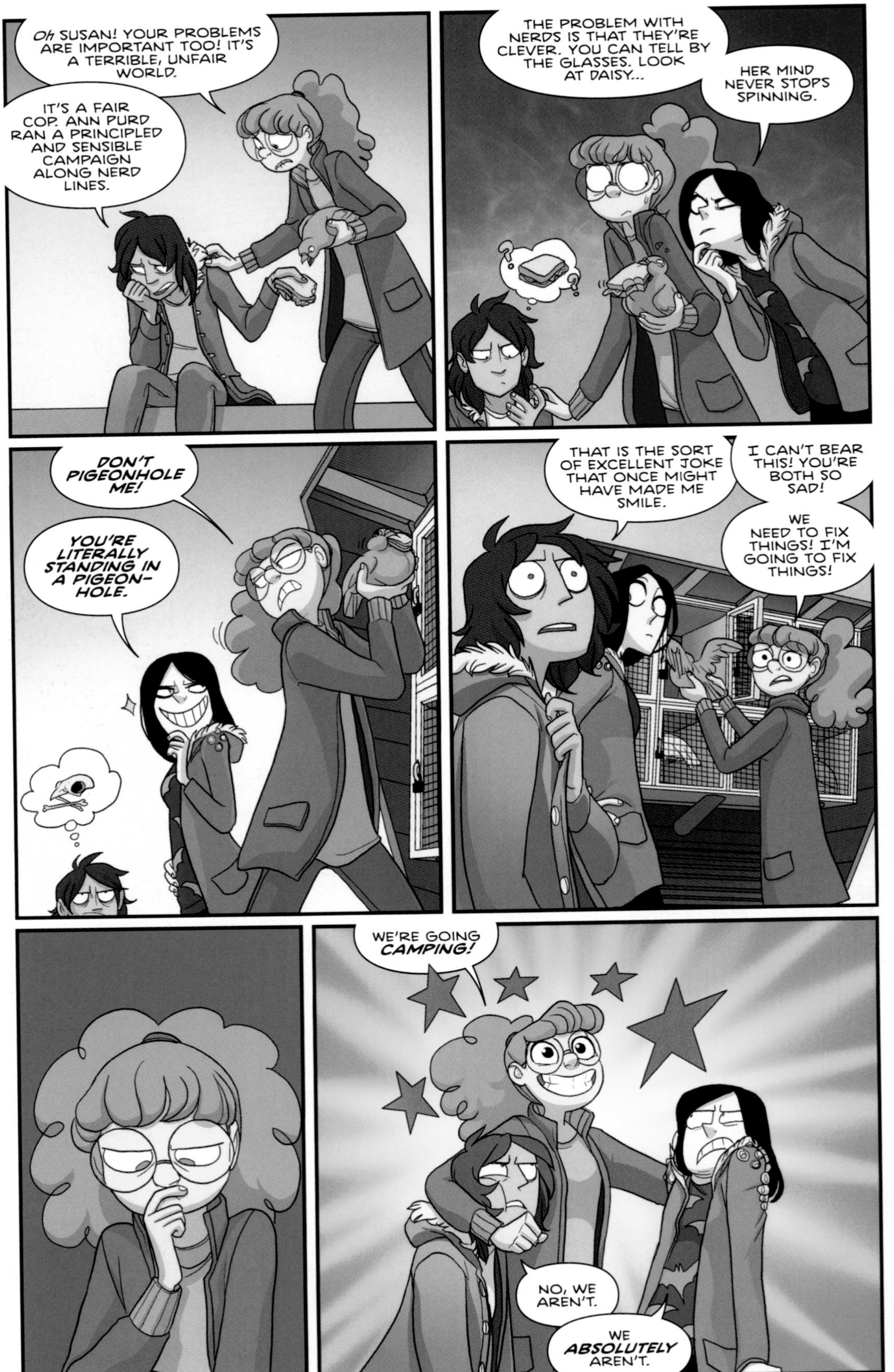
Oh SUSAN! YOUR PROBLEMS ARE IMPORTANT TOO! IT'S A TERRIBLE, UNFAIR WORLD.
IT'S A FAIR COP. ANN PURD RAN A PRINCIPLED AND SENSIBLE CAMPAIGN ALONG NERD LINES.
THE PROBLEM WITH NERDS IS THAT THEY'RE CLEVER. YOU CAN TELL BY THE GLASSES. LOOK AT DAISY...
HER MIND NEVER STOPS SPINNING.
DON'T PIGEONHOLE ME!
YOU'RE LITERALLY STANDING IN A PIGEON-HOLE.
THAT IS THE SORT OF EXCELLENT JOKE THAT ONCE MIGHT HAVE MADE ME SMILE.
I CAN'T BEAR THIS! YOU'RE BOTH SO SAD!
WE NEED TO FIX THINGS! I'M GOING TO FIX THINGS!
WE'RE GOING CAMPING!
NO, WE AREN'T.
WE ABSOLUTELY AREN'T.

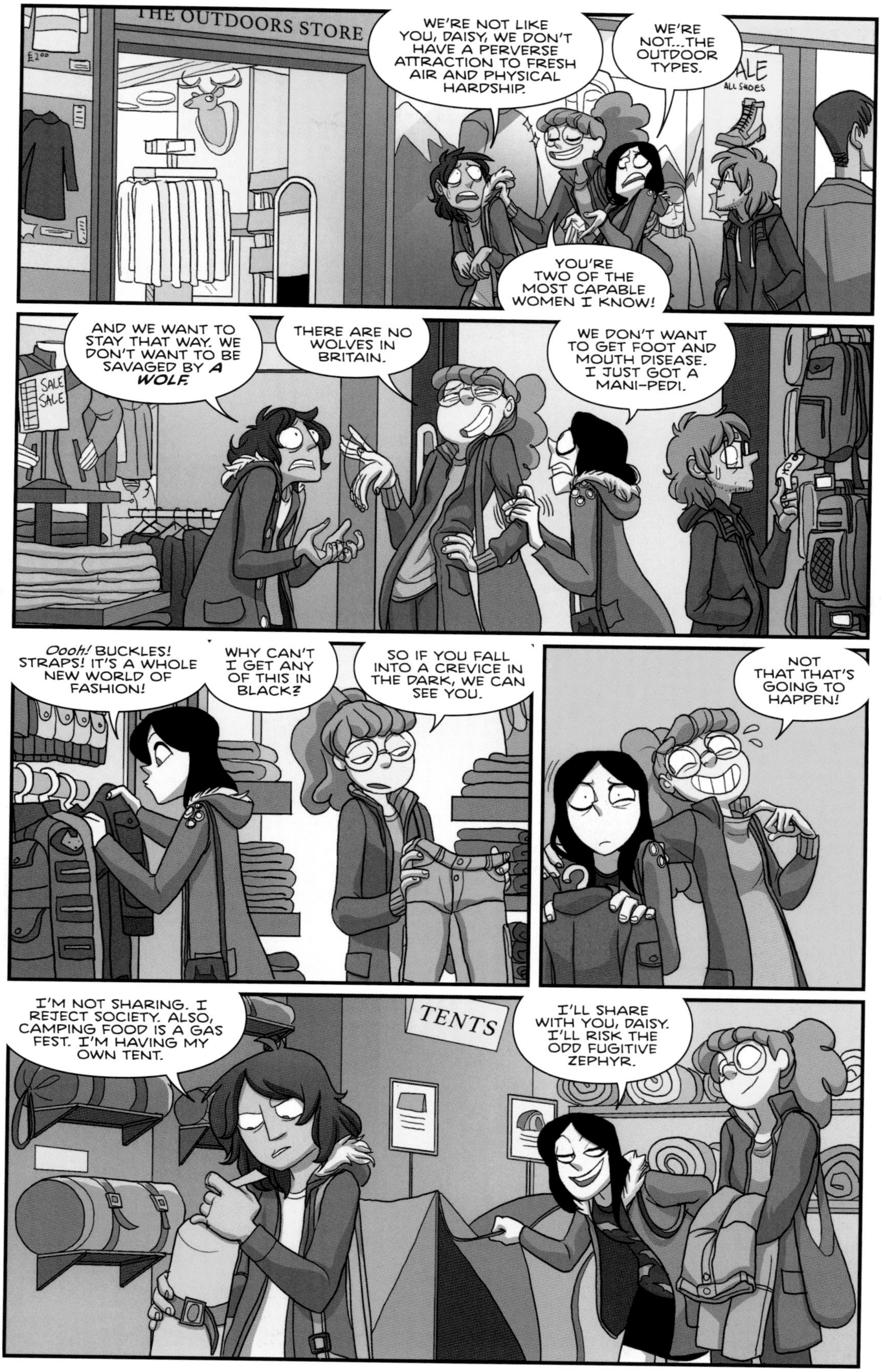
THE OUTDOORS STORE
WE'RE NOT LIKE YOU, DAISY, WE DON'T HAVE A PERVERSE ATTRACTION TO FRESH AIR AND PHYSICAL HARDSHIP.
WE'RE NOT...THE OUTDOOR TYPES.
YOU'RE TWO OF THE MOST CAPABLE WOMEN I KNOW!
AND WE WANT TO STAY THAT WAY. WE DON'T WANT TO BE SAVAGED BY *A WOLF.*
THERE ARE NO WOLVES IN BRITAIN.
WE DON'T WANT TO GET FOOT AND MOUTH DISEASE. I JUST GOT A MANI-PEDI.
Oooh! BUCKLES! STRAPS! IT'S A WHOLE NEW WORLD OF FASHION!
WHY CAN'T I GET ANY OF THIS IN BLACK?
SO IF YOU FALL INTO A CREVICE IN THE DARK, WE CAN SEE YOU.
NOT THAT THAT'S GOING TO HAPPEN!
I'M NOT SHARING. I REJECT SOCIETY. ALSO, CAMPING FOOD IS A GAS FEST. I'M HAVING MY OWN TENT.
TENTS
I'LL SHARE WITH YOU, DAISY. I'LL RISK THE ODD FUGITIVE ZEPHYR.

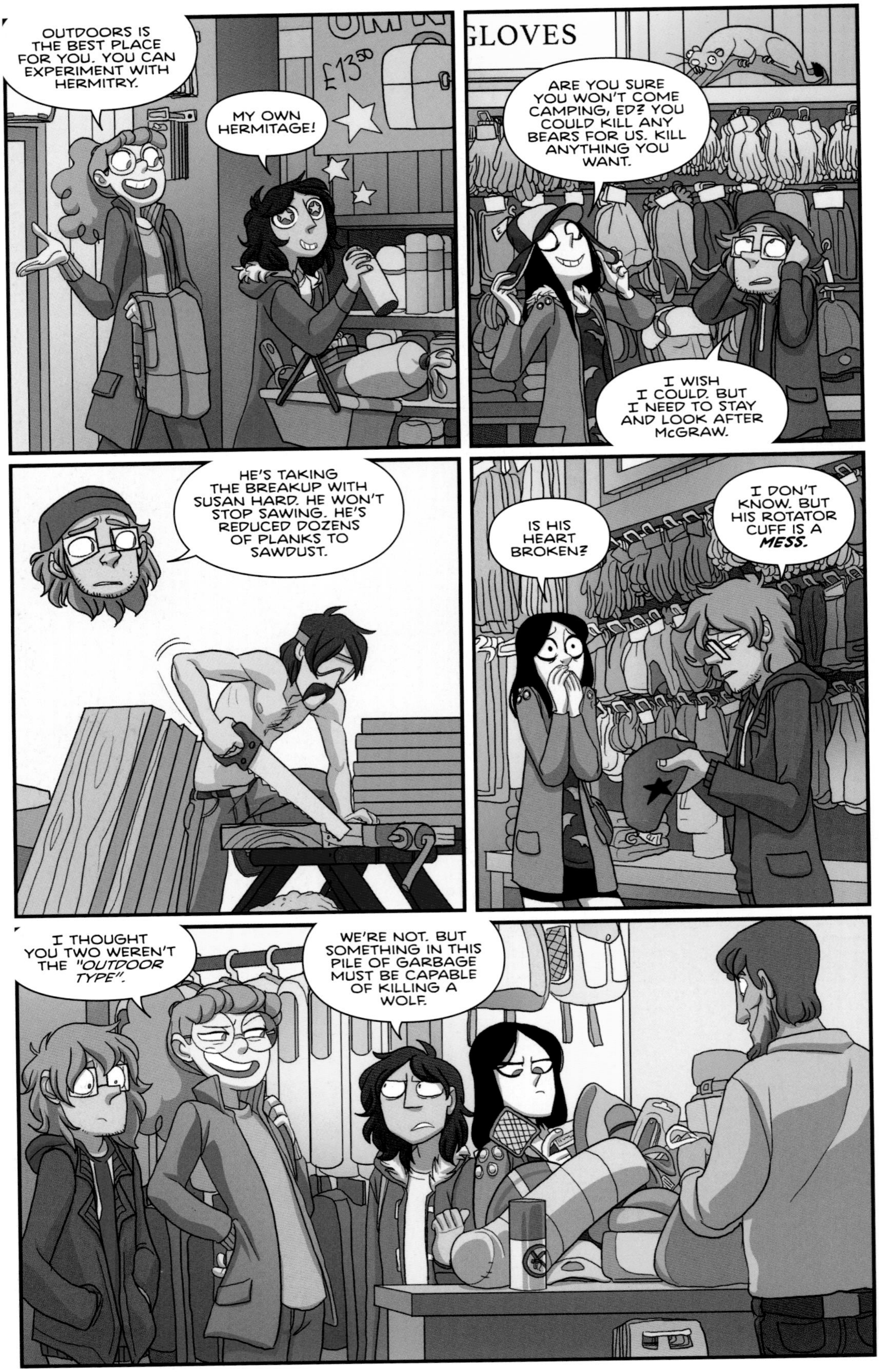

OUTDOORS IS THE BEST PLACE FOR YOU. YOU CAN EXPERIMENT WITH HERMITRY.
MY OWN HERMITAGE!
£13.50
GLOVES
ARE YOU SURE YOU WON'T COME CAMPING, ED? YOU COULD KILL ANY BEARS FOR US. KILL ANYTHING YOU WANT.
I WISH I COULD. BUT I NEED TO STAY AND LOOK AFTER McGRAW.
HE'S TAKING THE BREAKUP WITH SUSAN HARD. HE WON'T STOP SAWING. HE'S REDUCED DOZENS OF PLANKS TO SAWDUST.
IS HIS HEART BROKEN?
I DON'T KNOW. BUT HIS ROTATOR CUFF IS A *MESS.*
I THOUGHT YOU TWO WEREN'T THE *"OUTDOOR TYPE"*.
WE'RE NOT. BUT SOMETHING IN THIS PILE OF GARBAGE MUST BE CAPABLE OF KILLING A WOLF.

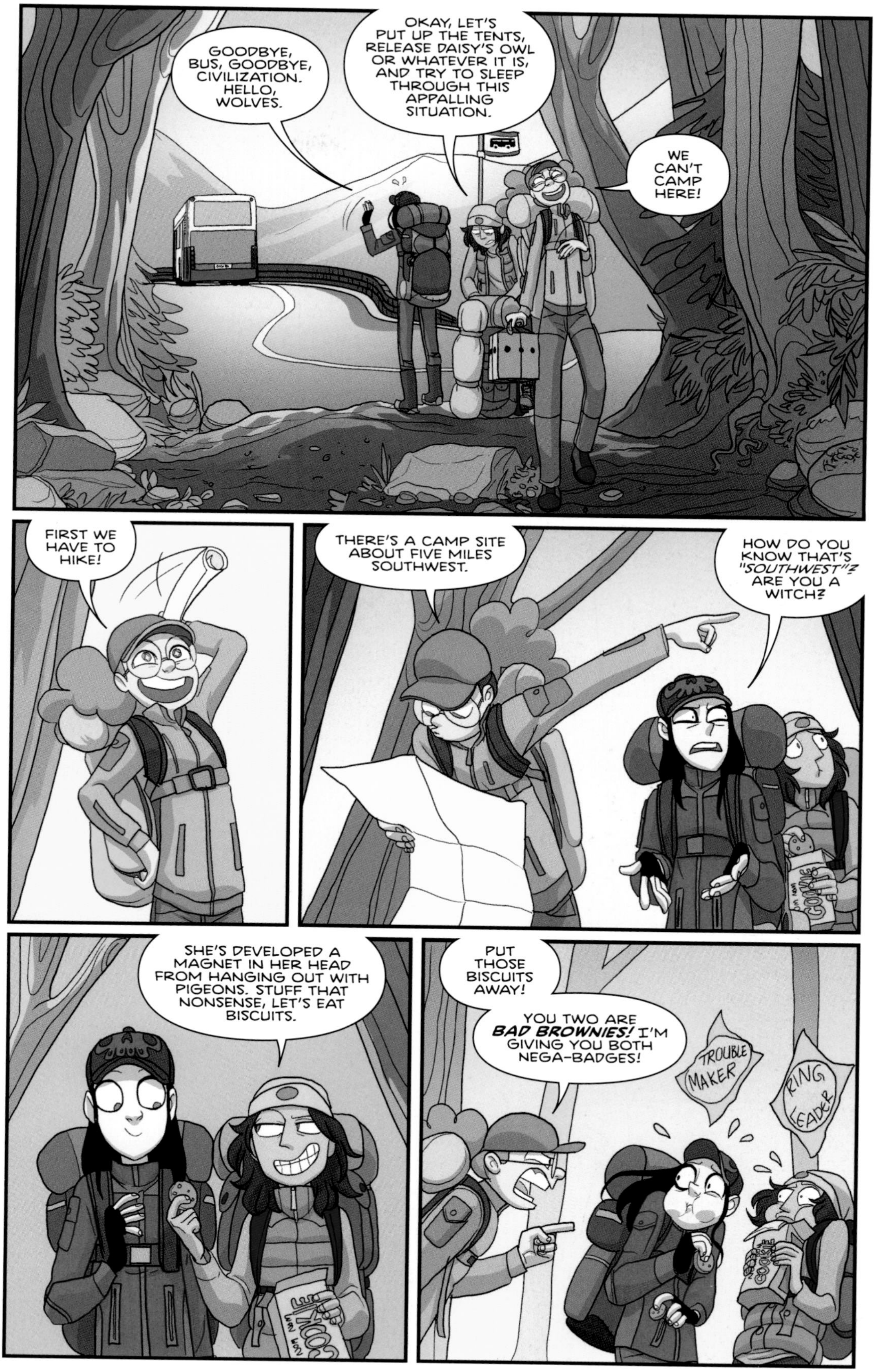
GOODBYE, BUS, GOODBYE, CIVILIZATION. HELLO, WOLVES.
OKAY, LET'S PUT UP THE TENTS, RELEASE DAISY'S OWL OR WHATEVER IT IS, AND TRY TO SLEEP THROUGH THIS APPALLING SITUATION.
WE CAN'T CAMP HERE!
FIRST WE HAVE TO HIKE!
THERE'S A CAMP SITE ABOUT FIVE MILES SOUTHWEST.
HOW DO YOU KNOW THAT'S "SOUTHWEST"? ARE YOU A WITCH?
SHE'S DEVELOPED A MAGNET IN HER HEAD FROM HANGING OUT WITH PIGEONS. STUFF THAT NONSENSE, LET'S EAT BISCUITS.
PUT THOSE BISCUITS AWAY!
YOU TWO ARE ***BAD BROWNIES!*** I'M GIVING YOU BOTH NEGA-BADGES!
TROUBLE MAKER
RING LEADER

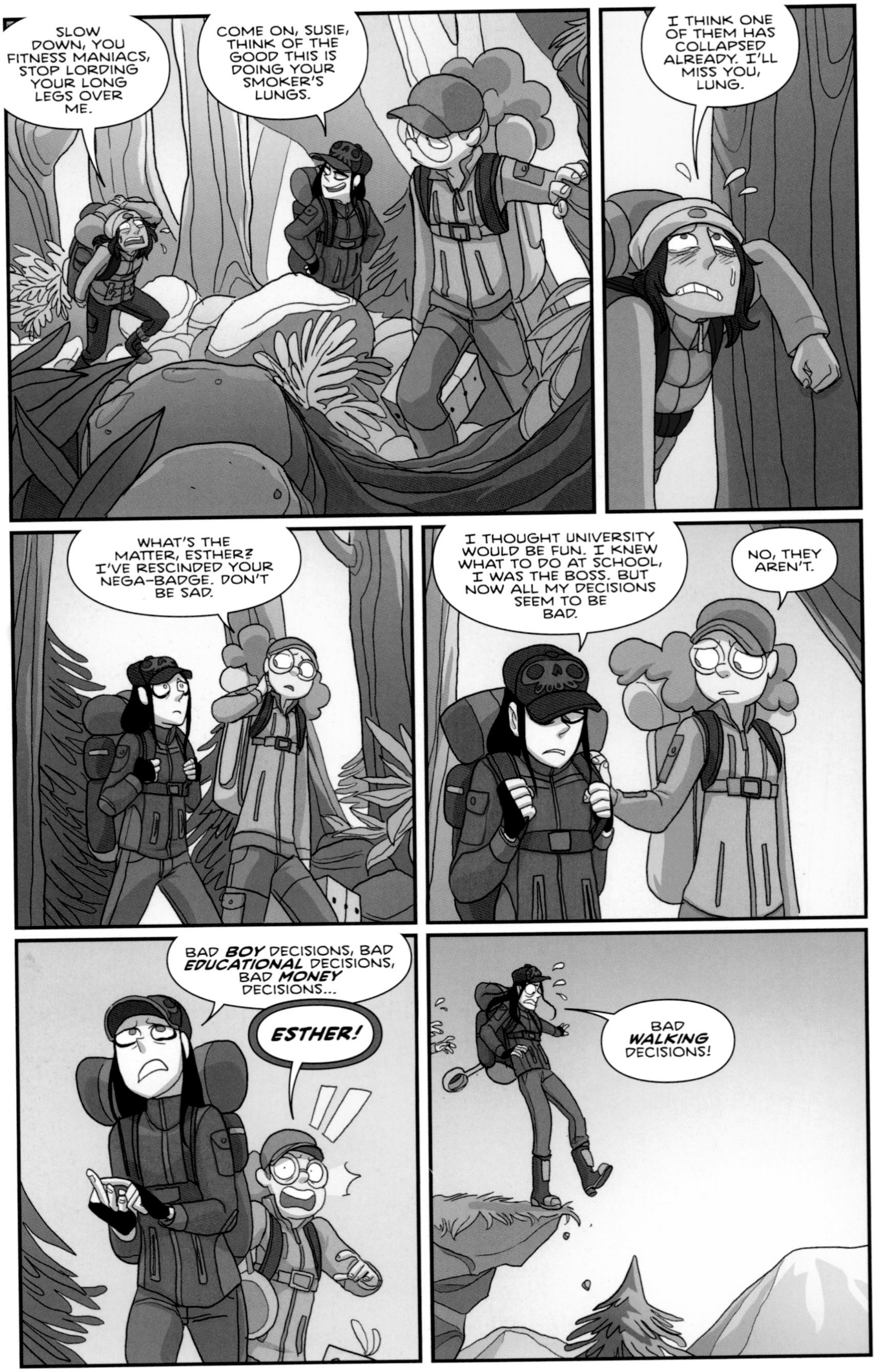
SLOW DOWN, YOU FITNESS MANIACS, STOP LORDING YOUR LONG LEGS OVER ME.
COME ON, SUSIE, THINK OF THE GOOD THIS IS DOING YOUR SMOKER'S LUNGS.
I THINK ONE OF THEM HAS COLLAPSED ALREADY. I'LL MISS YOU, LUNG.
WHAT'S THE MATTER, ESTHER? I'VE RESCINDED YOUR NEGA-BADGE. DON'T BE SAD.
I THOUGHT UNIVERSITY WOULD BE FUN. I KNEW WHAT TO DO AT SCHOOL, I WAS THE BOSS. BUT NOW ALL MY DECISIONS SEEM TO BE BAD.
NO, THEY AREN'T.
BAD **BOY** DECISIONS, BAD **EDUCATIONAL** DECISIONS, BAD **MONEY** DECISIONS...
ESTHER!
BAD **WALKING** DECISIONS!

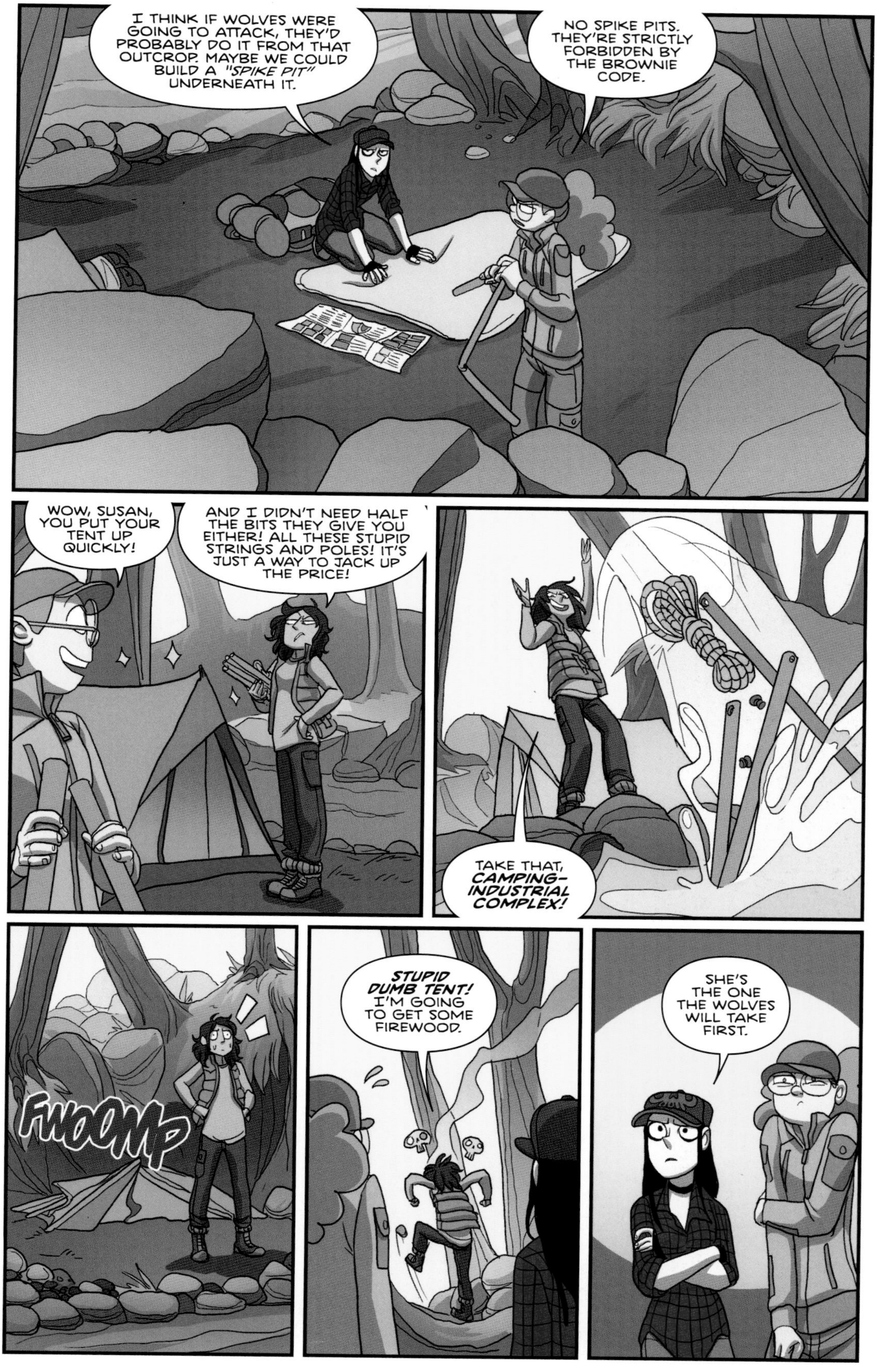
I THINK IF WOLVES WERE GOING TO ATTACK, THEY'D PROBABLY DO IT FROM THAT OUTCROP. MAYBE WE COULD BUILD A "SPIKE PIT" UNDERNEATH IT.
NO SPIKE PITS. THEY'RE STRICTLY FORBIDDEN BY THE BROWNIE CODE.
WOW, SUSAN, YOU PUT YOUR TENT UP QUICKLY!
AND I DIDN'T NEED HALF THE BITS THEY GIVE YOU EITHER! ALL THESE STUPID STRINGS AND POLES! IT'S JUST A WAY TO JACK UP THE PRICE!
TAKE THAT, CAMPING-INDUSTRIAL COMPLEX!
FWOOMP
STUPID DUMB TENT! I'M GOING TO GET SOME FIREWOOD.
SHE'S THE ONE THE WOLVES WILL TAKE FIRST.

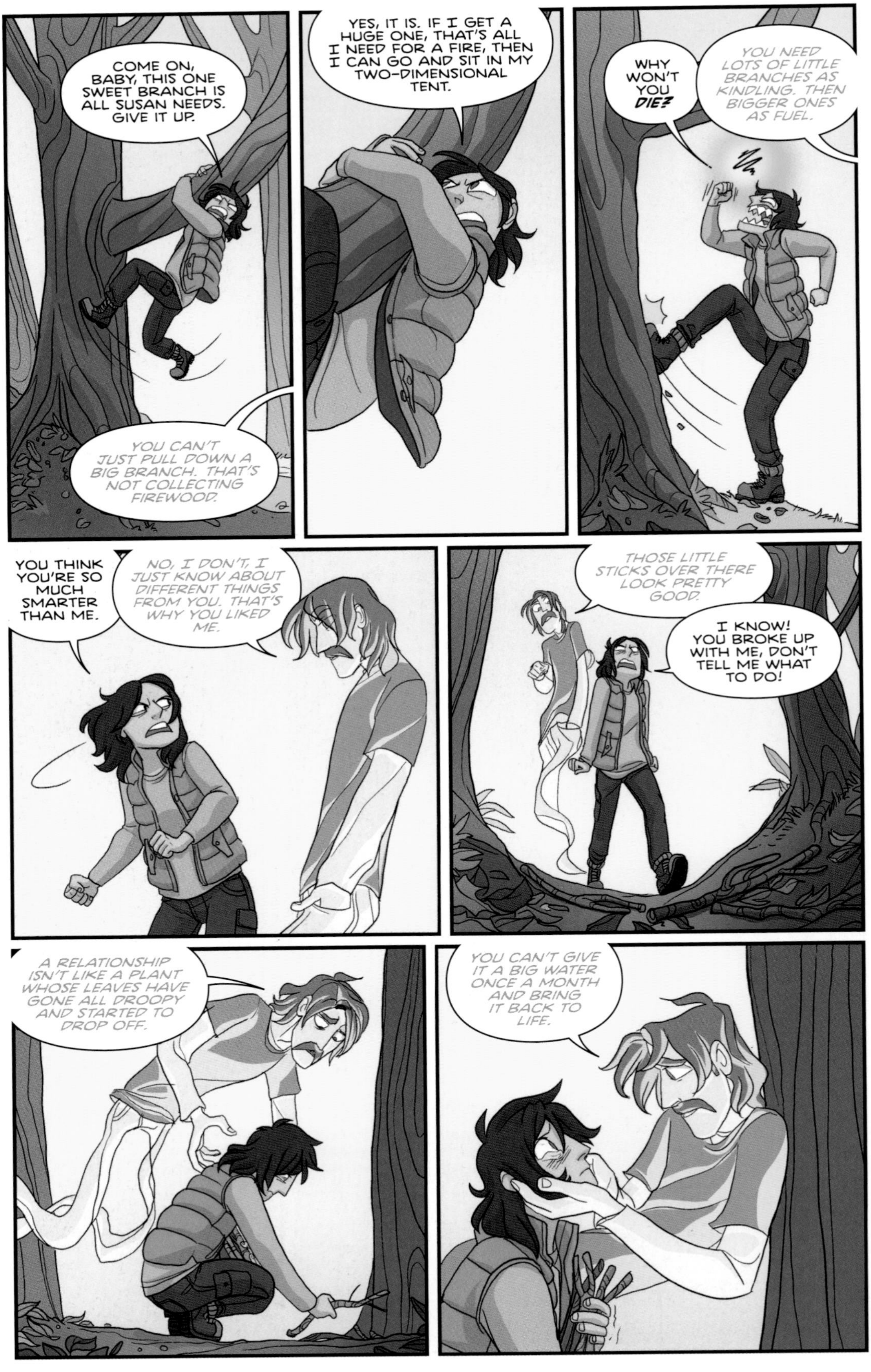
COME ON, BABY, THIS ONE SWEET BRANCH IS ALL SUSAN NEEDS. GIVE IT UP.
YOU CAN'T JUST PULL DOWN A BIG BRANCH. THAT'S NOT COLLECTING FIREWOOD.
YES, IT IS. IF I GET A HUGE ONE, THAT'S ALL I NEED FOR A FIRE, THEN I CAN GO AND SIT IN MY TWO-DIMENSIONAL TENT.
WHY WON'T YOU *DIE?*
YOU NEED LOTS OF LITTLE BRANCHES AS KINDLING. THEN BIGGER ONES AS FUEL.
YOU THINK YOU'RE SO MUCH SMARTER THAN ME.
NO, I DON'T, I JUST KNOW ABOUT DIFFERENT THINGS FROM YOU. THAT'S WHY YOU LIKED ME.
THOSE LITTLE STICKS OVER THERE LOOK PRETTY GOOD.
I KNOW! YOU BROKE UP WITH ME, DON'T TELL ME WHAT TO DO!
A RELATIONSHIP ISN'T LIKE A PLANT WHOSE LEAVES HAVE GONE ALL DROOPY AND STARTED TO DROP OFF.
YOU CAN'T GIVE IT A BIG WATER ONCE A MONTH AND BRING IT BACK TO LIFE.

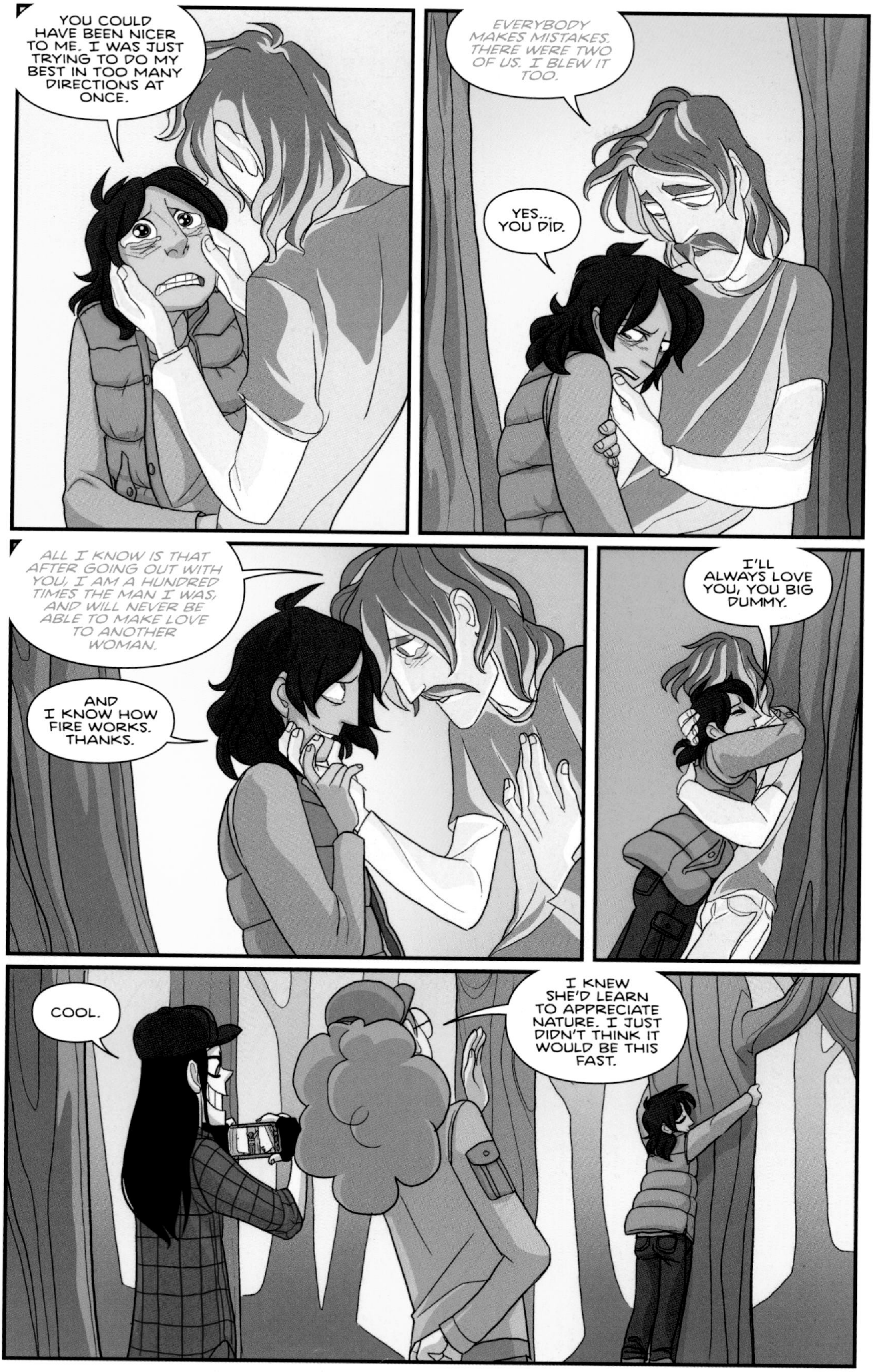
YOU COULD HAVE BEEN NICER TO ME. I WAS JUST TRYING TO DO MY BEST IN TOO MANY DIRECTIONS AT ONCE.
EVERYBODY MAKES MISTAKES. THERE WERE TWO OF US. I BLEW IT TOO.
YES... YOU DID.
ALL I KNOW IS THAT AFTER GOING OUT WITH YOU, I AM A HUNDRED TIMES THE MAN I WAS, AND WILL NEVER BE ABLE TO MAKE LOVE TO ANOTHER WOMAN.
AND I KNOW HOW FIRE WORKS. THANKS.
I'LL ALWAYS LOVE YOU, YOU BIG DUMMY.
COOL.
I KNEW SHE'D LEARN TO APPRECIATE NATURE. I JUST DIDN'T THINK IT WOULD BE THIS FAST.

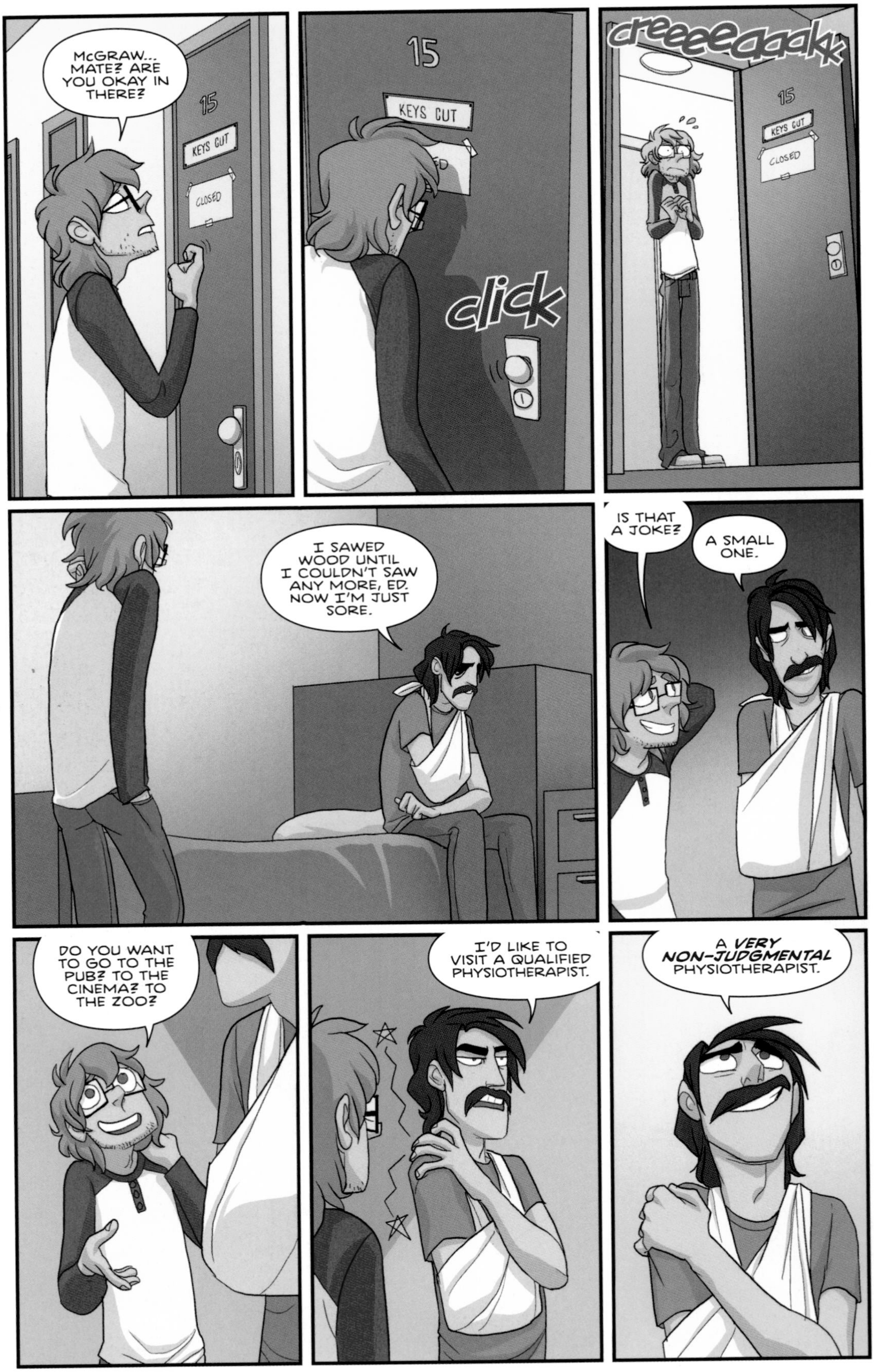
McGRAW... MATE? ARE YOU OKAY IN THERE?
15
KEYS CUT
CLOSED
click
creeeeaaakk
I SAWED WOOD UNTIL I COULDN'T SAW ANY MORE, ED. NOW I'M JUST SORE.
IS THAT A JOKE?
A SMALL ONE.
DO YOU WANT TO GO TO THE PUB? TO THE CINEMA? TO THE ZOO?
I'D LIKE TO VISIT A QUALIFIED PHYSIOTHERAPIST.
A VERY NON-JUDGMENTAL PHYSIOTHERAPIST.

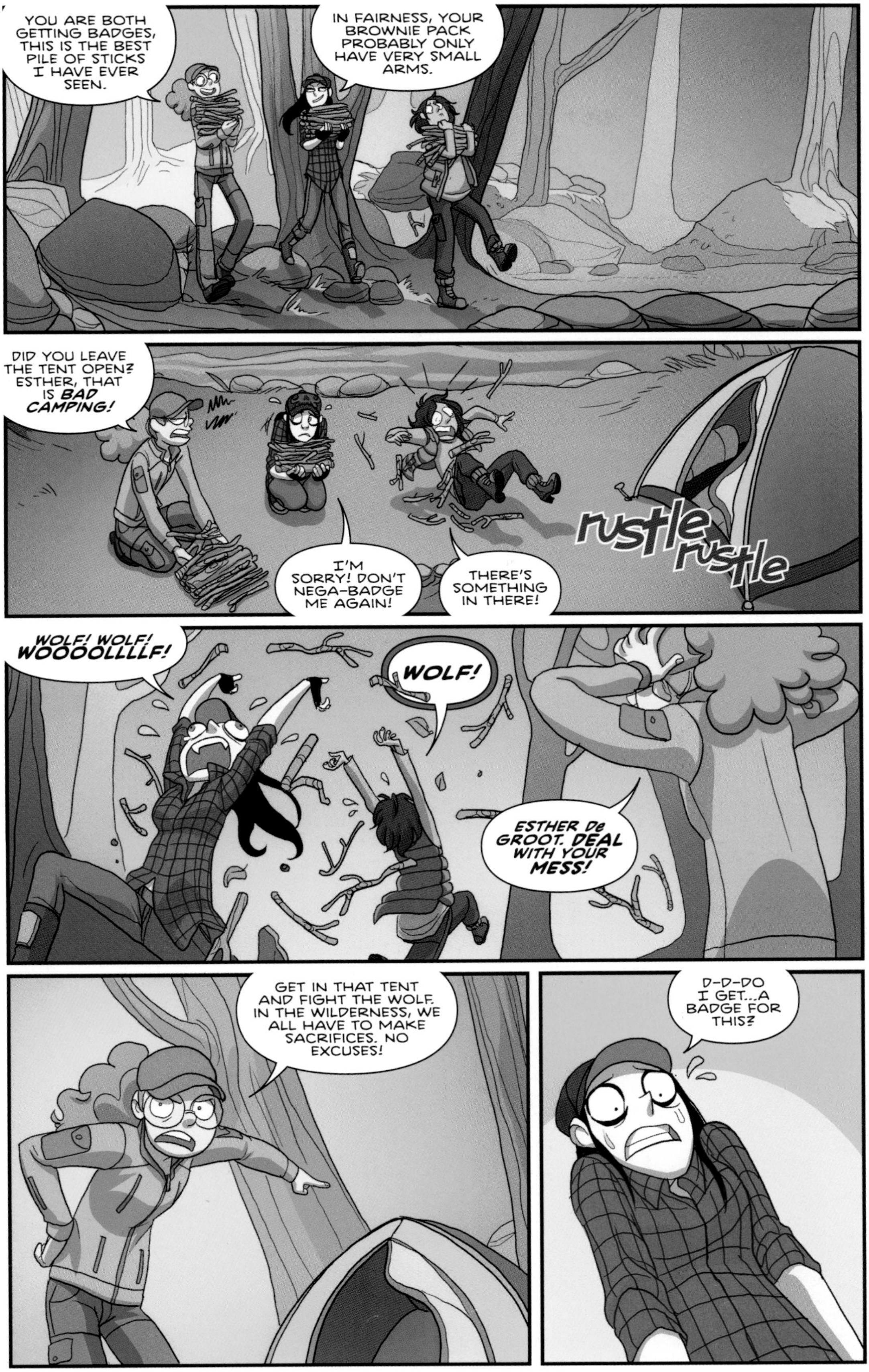
YOU ARE BOTH GETTING BADGES, THIS IS THE BEST PILE OF STICKS I HAVE EVER SEEN.
IN FAIRNESS, YOUR BROWNIE PACK PROBABLY ONLY HAVE VERY SMALL ARMS.
DID YOU LEAVE THE TENT OPEN? ESTHER, THAT IS BAD CAMPING!
I'M SORRY! DON'T NEGA-BADGE ME AGAIN!
THERE'S SOMETHING IN THERE!
rustle rustle
WOLF! WOLF! WOOOOLLLLF!
WOLF!
ESTHER De GROOT. DEAL WITH YOUR MESS!
GET IN THAT TENT AND FIGHT THE WOLF. IN THE WILDERNESS, WE ALL HAVE TO MAKE SACRIFICES. NO EXCUSES!
D-D-DO I GET...A BADGE FOR THIS?

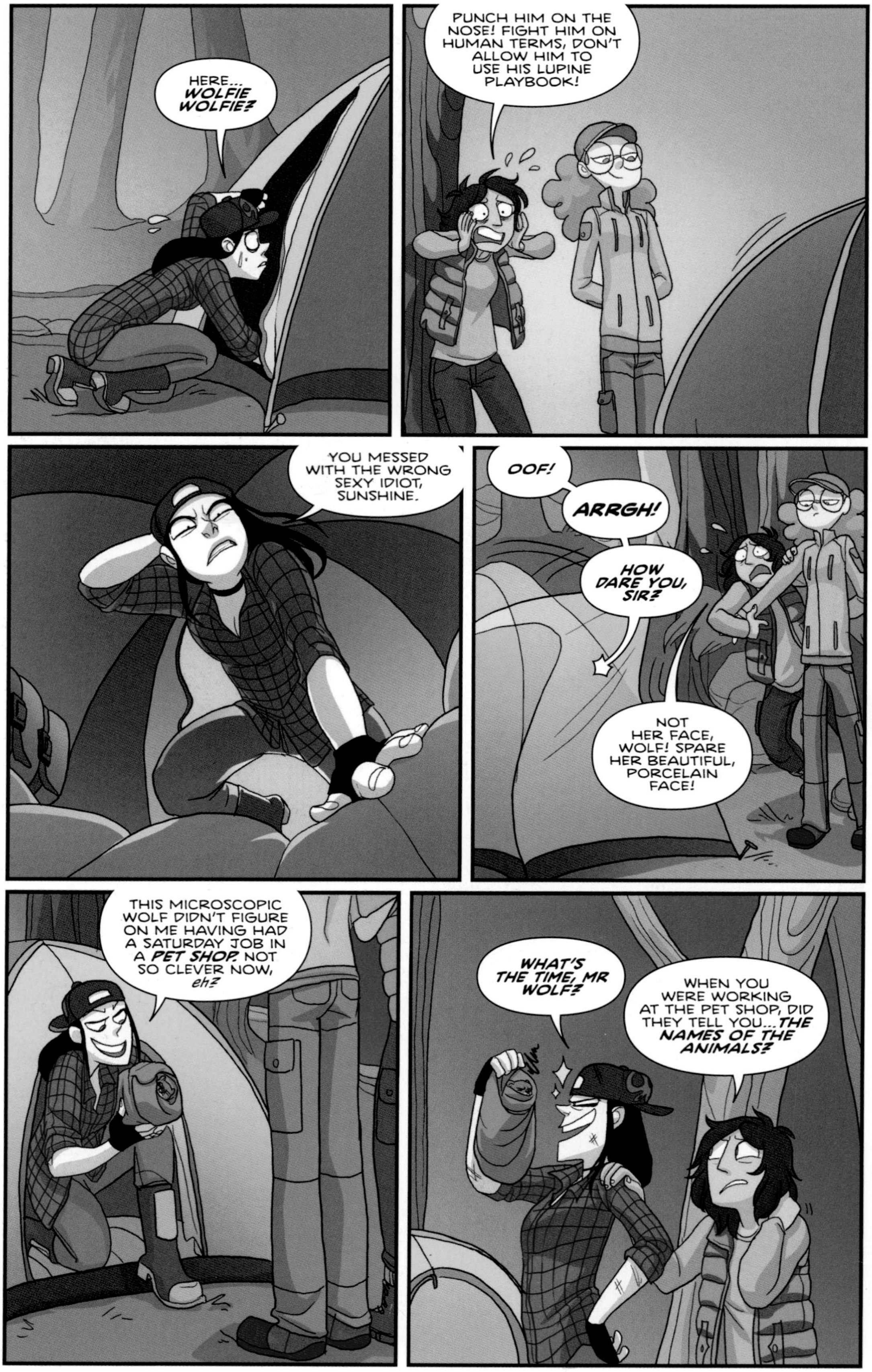
HERE... WOLFIE WOLFIE?
PUNCH HIM ON THE NOSE! FIGHT HIM ON HUMAN TERMS, DON'T ALLOW HIM TO USE HIS LUPINE PLAYBOOK!
YOU MESSED WITH THE WRONG SEXY IDIOT, SUNSHINE.
OOF!
ARRGH!
HOW DARE YOU, SIR?
NOT HER FACE, WOLF! SPARE HER BEAUTIFUL, PORCELAIN FACE!
THIS MICROSCOPIC WOLF DIDN'T FIGURE ON ME HAVING HAD A SATURDAY JOB IN A PET SHOP? NOT SO CLEVER NOW, eh?
WHAT'S THE TIME, MR WOLF?
WHEN YOU WERE WORKING AT THE PET SHOP, DID THEY TELL YOU... THE NAMES OF THE ANIMALS?

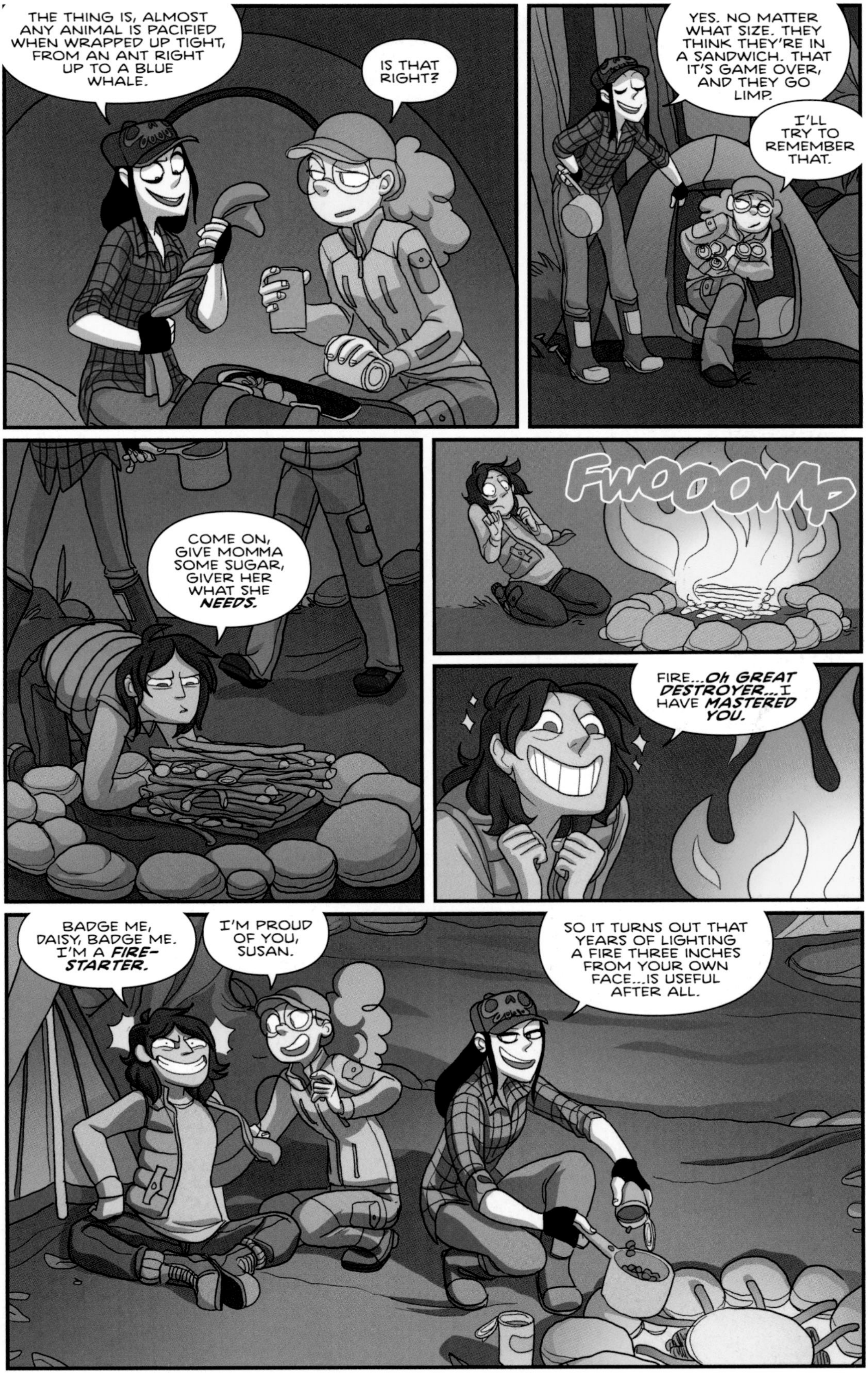
THE THING IS, ALMOST ANY ANIMAL IS PACIFIED WHEN WRAPPED UP TIGHT, FROM AN ANT RIGHT UP TO A BLUE WHALE.
IS THAT RIGHT?
YES. NO MATTER WHAT SIZE. THEY THINK THEY'RE IN A SANDWICH. THAT IT'S GAME OVER, AND THEY GO LIMP.
I'LL TRY TO REMEMBER THAT.
COME ON, GIVE MOMMA SOME SUGAR, GIVER HER WHAT SHE NEEDS.
FWOOOMP
FIRE...OH GREAT DESTROYER...I HAVE MASTERED YOU.
BADGE ME, DAISY, BADGE ME. I'M A FIRE-STARTER.
I'M PROUD OF YOU, SUSAN.
SO IT TURNS OUT THAT YEARS OF LIGHTING A FIRE THREE INCHES FROM YOUR OWN FACE...IS USEFUL AFTER ALL.

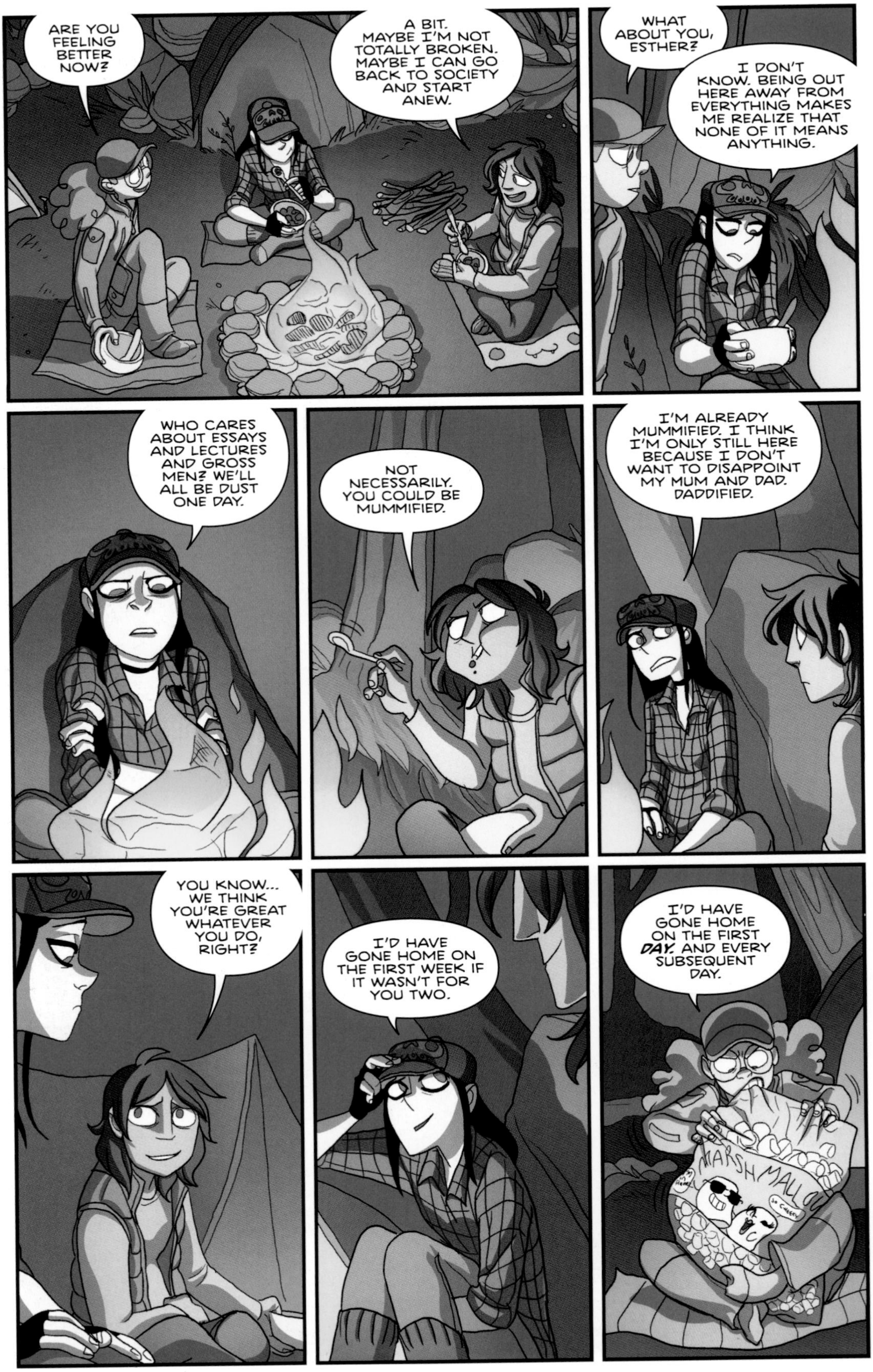
ARE YOU FEELING BETTER NOW?
A BIT. MAYBE I'M NOT TOTALLY BROKEN. MAYBE I CAN GO BACK TO SOCIETY AND START ANEW.
WHAT ABOUT YOU, ESTHER?
I DON'T KNOW. BEING OUT HERE AWAY FROM EVERYTHING MAKES ME REALIZE THAT NONE OF IT MEANS ANYTHING.
WHO CARES ABOUT ESSAYS AND LECTURES AND GROSS MEN? WE'LL ALL BE DUST ONE DAY.
NOT NECESSARILY. YOU COULD BE MUMMIFIED.
I'M ALREADY MUMMIFIED. I THINK I'M ONLY STILL HERE BECAUSE I DON'T WANT TO DISAPPOINT MY MUM AND DAD. DADDIFIED.
YOU KNOW... WE THINK YOU'RE GREAT WHATEVER YOU DO, RIGHT?
I'D HAVE GONE HOME ON THE FIRST WEEK IF IT WASN'T FOR YOU TWO.
I'D HAVE GONE HOME ON THE FIRST *DAY*. AND EVERY SUBSEQUENT DAY.

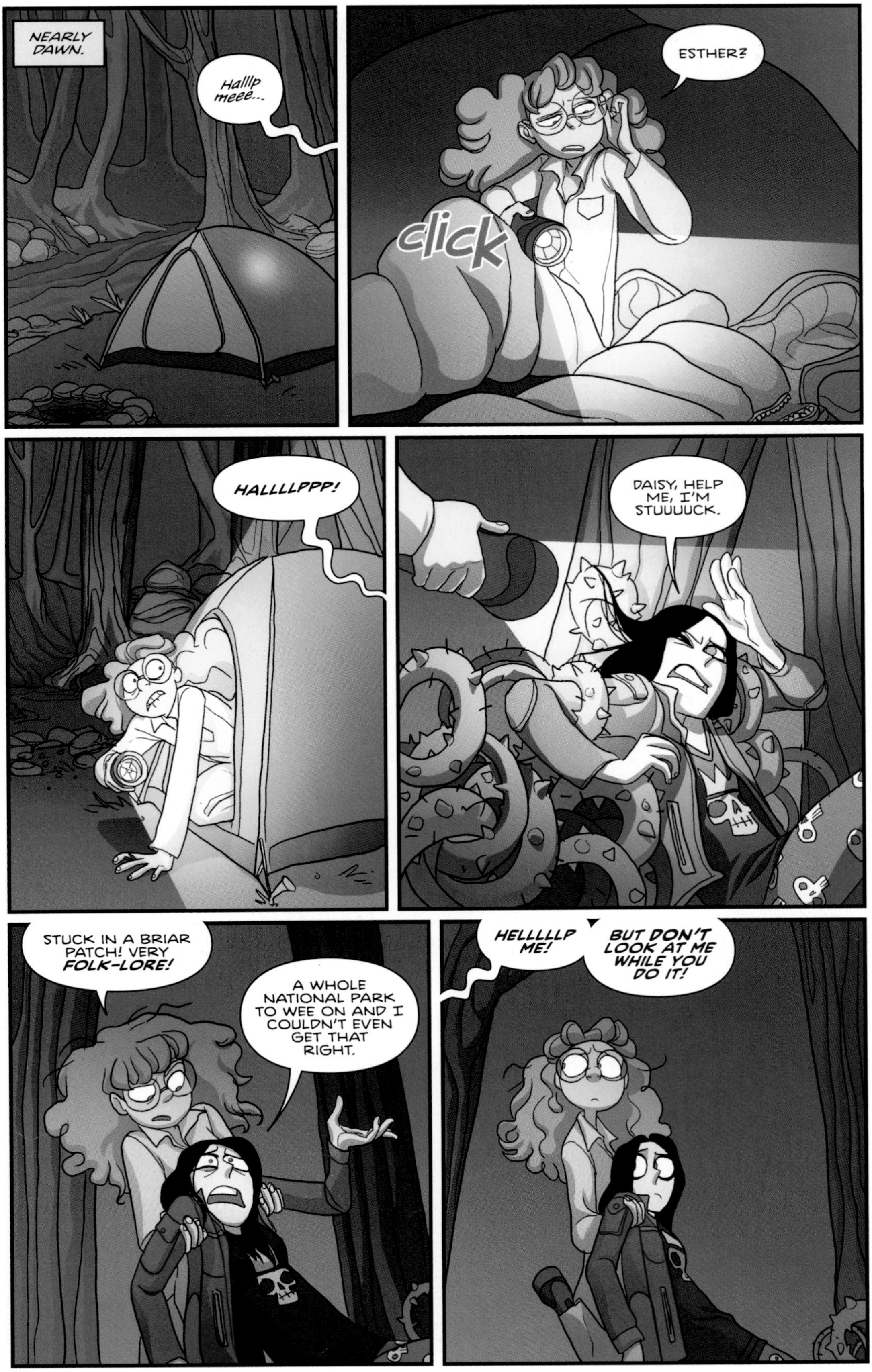
NEARLY DAWN.
Halllp meee...
ESTHER?
click
HALLLLPPP!
DAISY, HELP ME, I'M STUUUUCK.
STUCK IN A BRIAR PATCH! VERY FOLK-LORE!
A WHOLE NATIONAL PARK TO WEE ON AND I COULDN'T EVEN GET THAT RIGHT.
HELLLLLP ME!
BUT DON'T LOOK AT ME WHILE YOU DO IT!

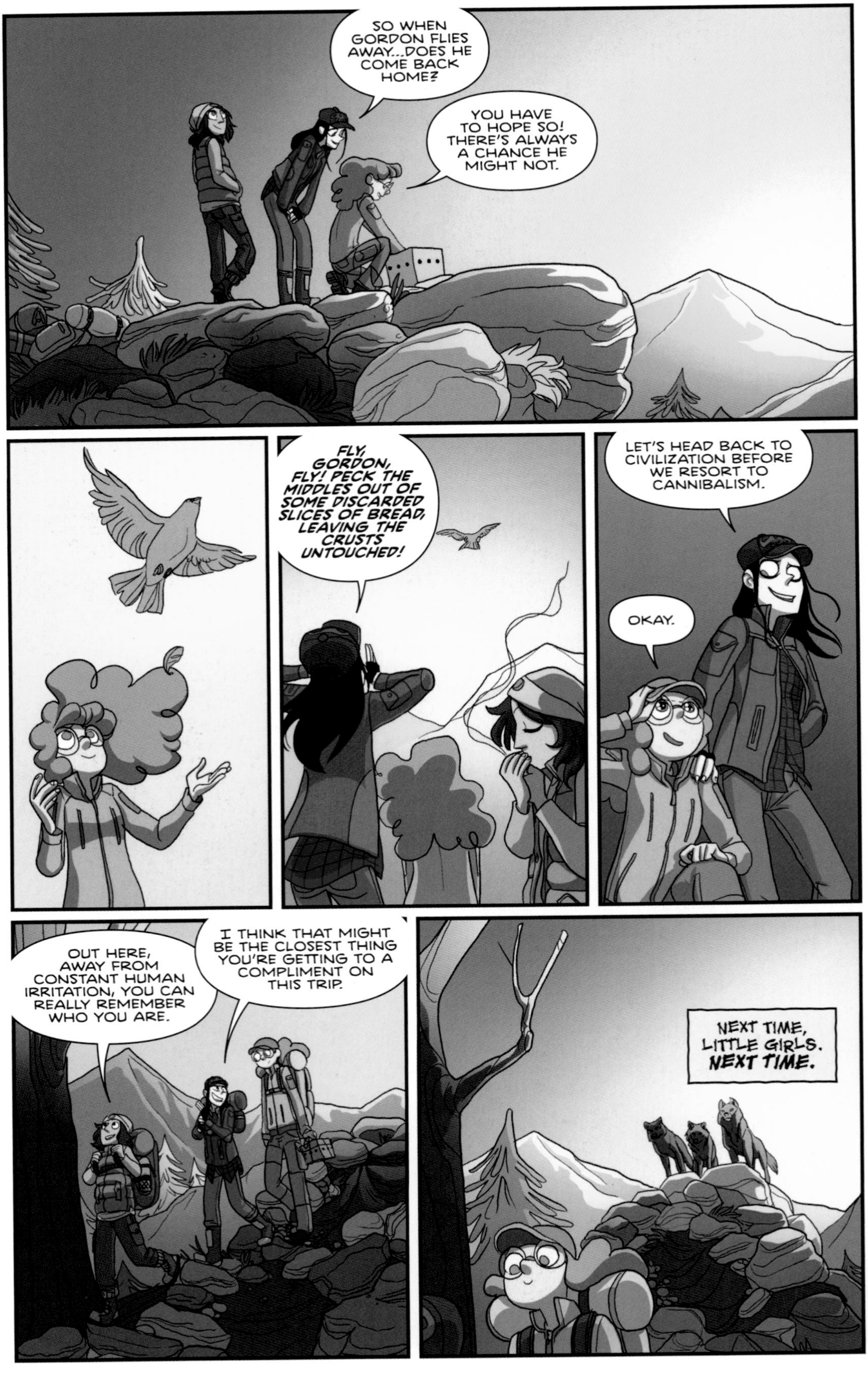
SO WHEN GORDON FLIES AWAY...DOES HE COME BACK HOME?
YOU HAVE TO HOPE SO! THERE'S ALWAYS A CHANCE HE MIGHT NOT.
FLY, GORDON, FLY! PECK THE MIDDLES OUT OF SOME DISCARDED SLICES OF BREAD, LEAVING THE CRUSTS UNTOUCHED!
LET'S HEAD BACK TO CIVILIZATION BEFORE WE RESORT TO CANNIBALISM.
OKAY.
OUT HERE, AWAY FROM CONSTANT HUMAN IRRITATION, YOU CAN REALLY REMEMBER WHO YOU ARE.
I THINK THAT MIGHT BE THE CLOSEST THING YOU'RE GETTING TO A COMPLIMENT ON THIS TRIP.
NEXT TIME, LITTLE GIRLS. NEXT TIME.

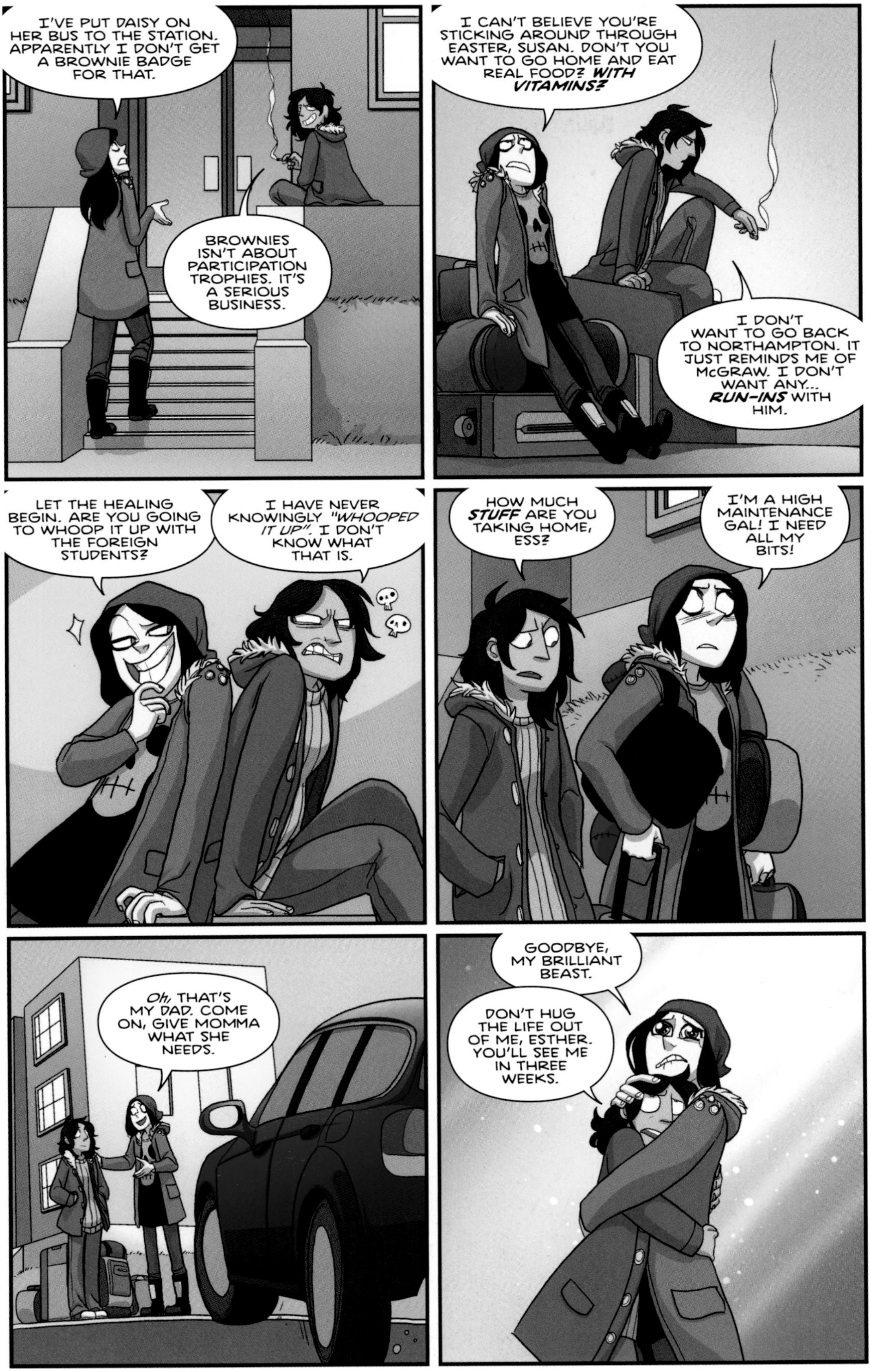
I'VE PUT DAISY ON HER BUS TO THE STATION. APPARENTLY I DON'T GET A BROWNIE BADGE FOR THAT.
BROWNIES ISN'T ABOUT PARTICIPATION TROPHIES. IT'S A SERIOUS BUSINESS.
I CAN'T BELIEVE YOU'RE STICKING AROUND THROUGH EASTER, SUSAN. DON'T YOU WANT TO GO HOME AND EAT REAL FOOD? WITH VITAMINS?
I DON'T WANT TO GO BACK TO NORTHAMPTON. IT JUST REMINDS ME OF McGRAW. I DON'T WANT ANY... RUN-INS WITH HIM.
LET THE HEALING BEGIN. ARE YOU GOING TO WHOOP IT UP WITH THE FOREIGN STUDENTS?
I HAVE NEVER KNOWINGLY "WHOOPED IT UP". I DON'T KNOW WHAT THAT IS.
HOW MUCH STUFF ARE YOU TAKING HOME, ESS?
I'M A HIGH MAINTENANCE GAL! I NEED ALL MY BITS!
Oh, THAT'S MY DAD. COME ON, GIVE MOMMA WHAT SHE NEEDS.
GOODBYE, MY BRILLIANT BEAST.
DON'T HUG THE LIFE OUT OF ME, ESTHER. YOU'LL SEE ME IN THREE WEEKS.

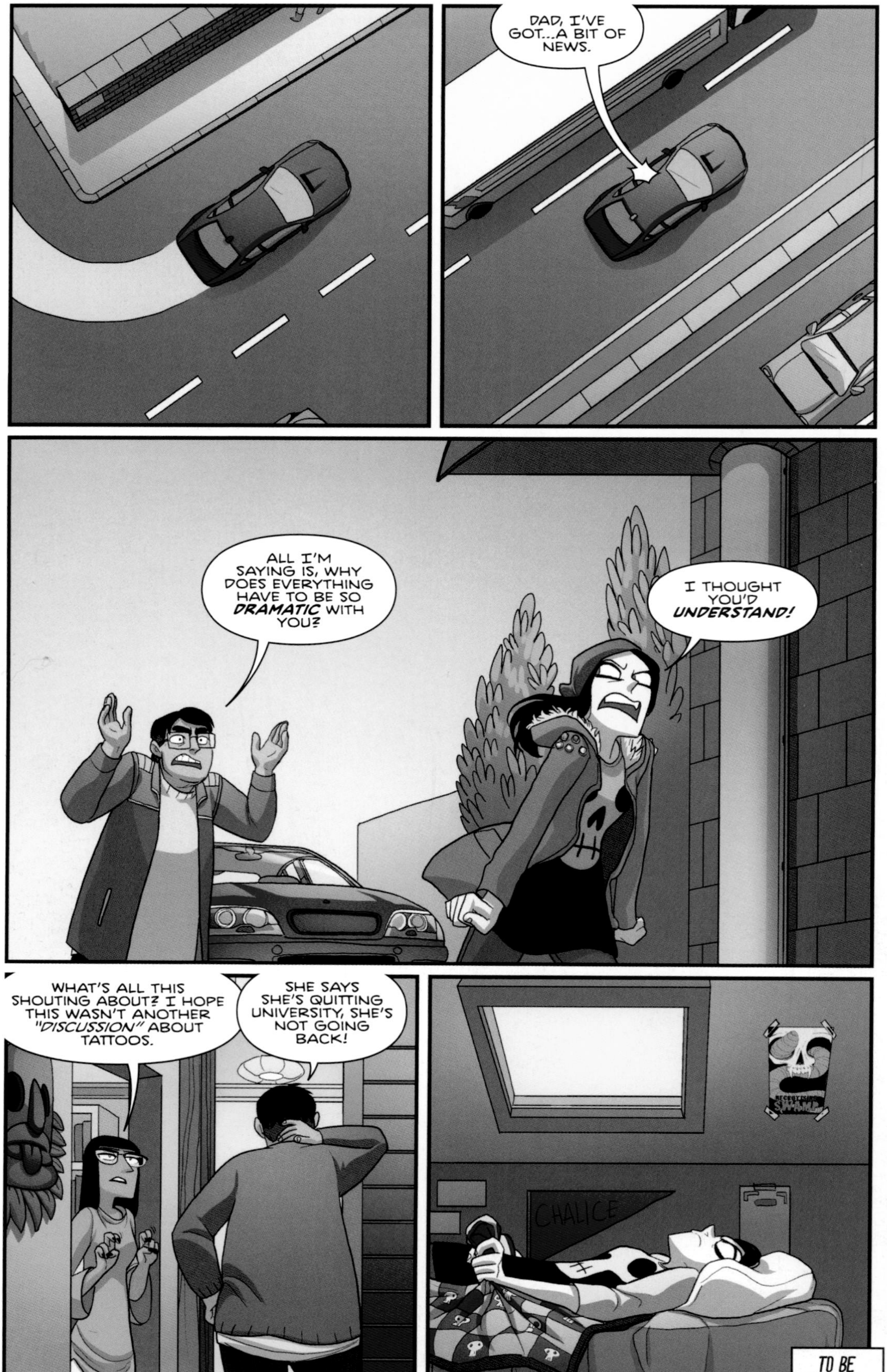
DAD, I'VE GOT...A BIT OF NEWS.
ALL I'M SAYING IS, WHY DOES EVERYTHING HAVE TO BE SO *DRAMATIC* WITH YOU?
I THOUGHT YOU'D *UNDERSTAND!*
WHAT'S ALL THIS SHOUTING ABOUT? I HOPE THIS WASN'T ANOTHER *"DISCUSSION"* ABOUT TATTOOS.
SHE SAYS SHE'S QUITTING UNIVERSITY, SHE'S NOT GOING BACK!
CHALICE
TO BE CONTINUED...

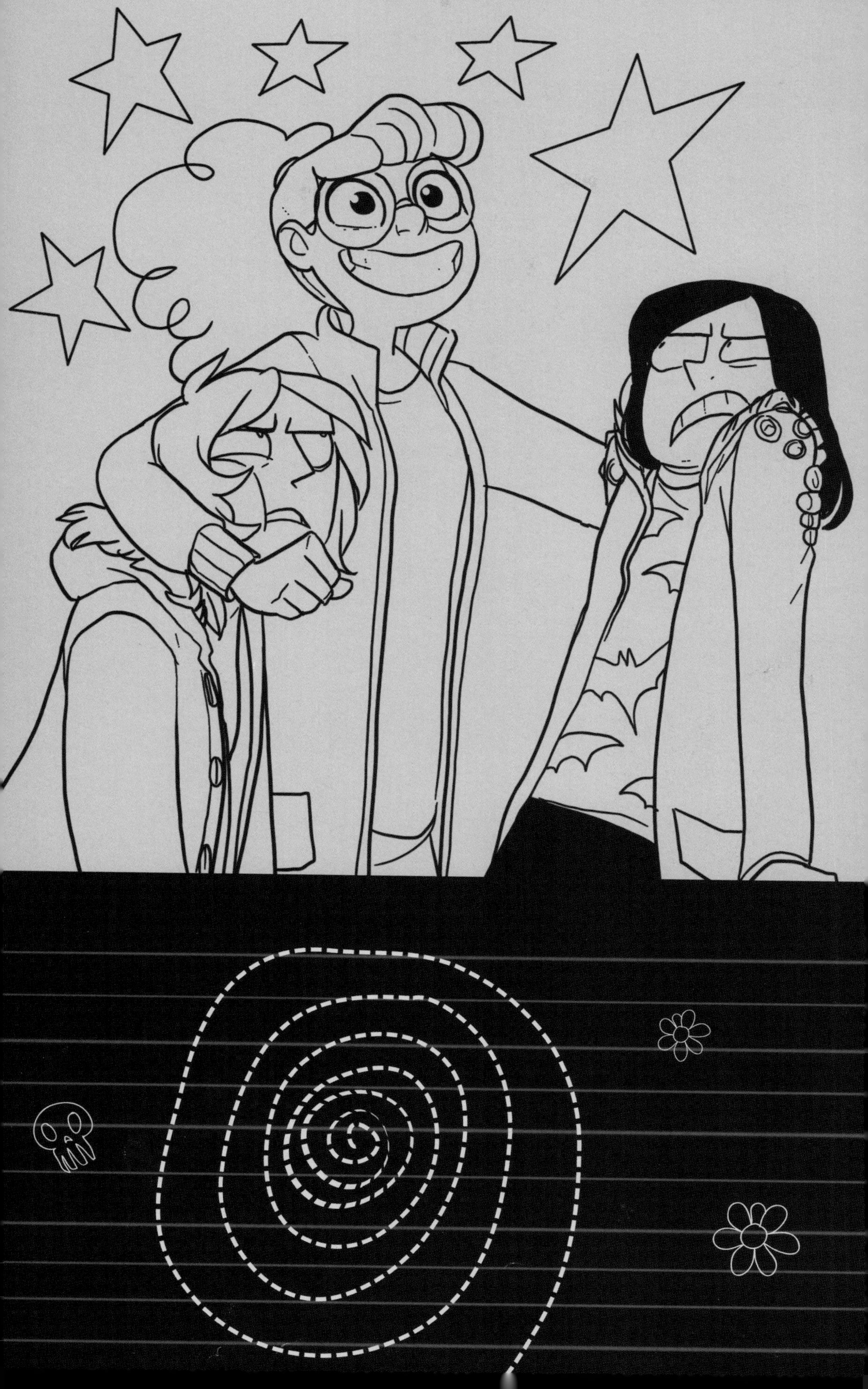

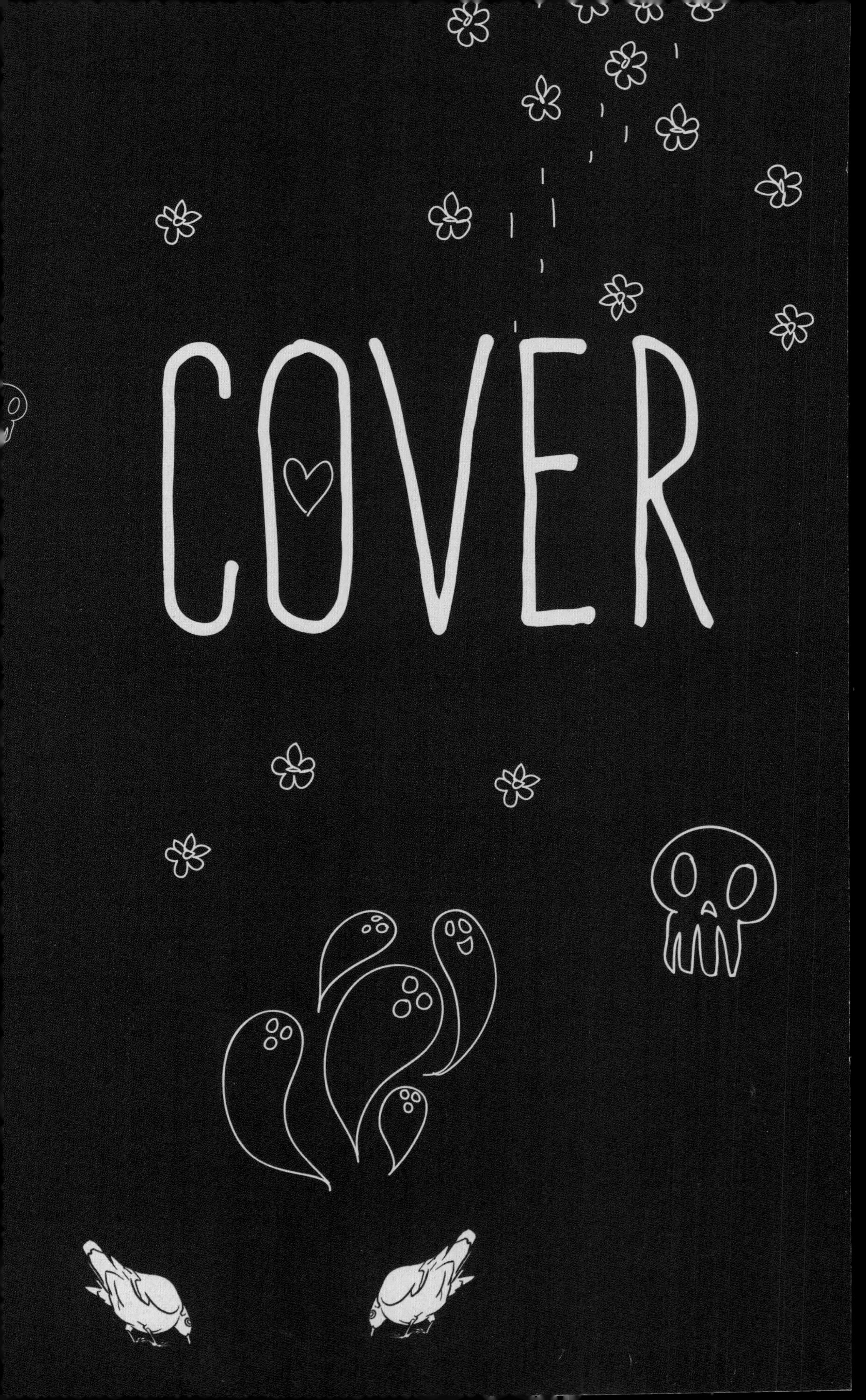
COVER

GALLERY

ISSUE #9 COVER
LISSA TREIMAN

#10 COVER
A TREIMAN

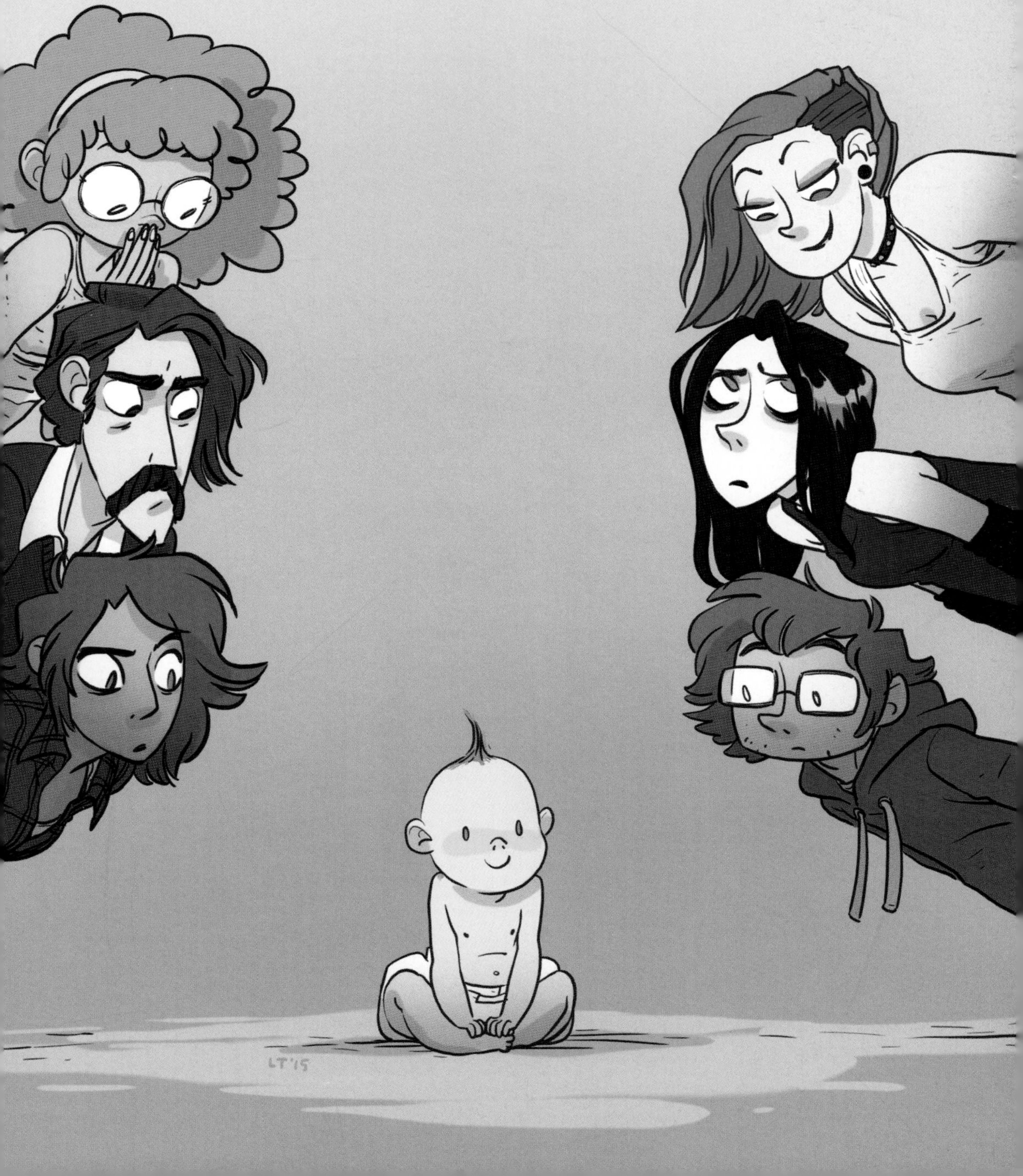
LT'15

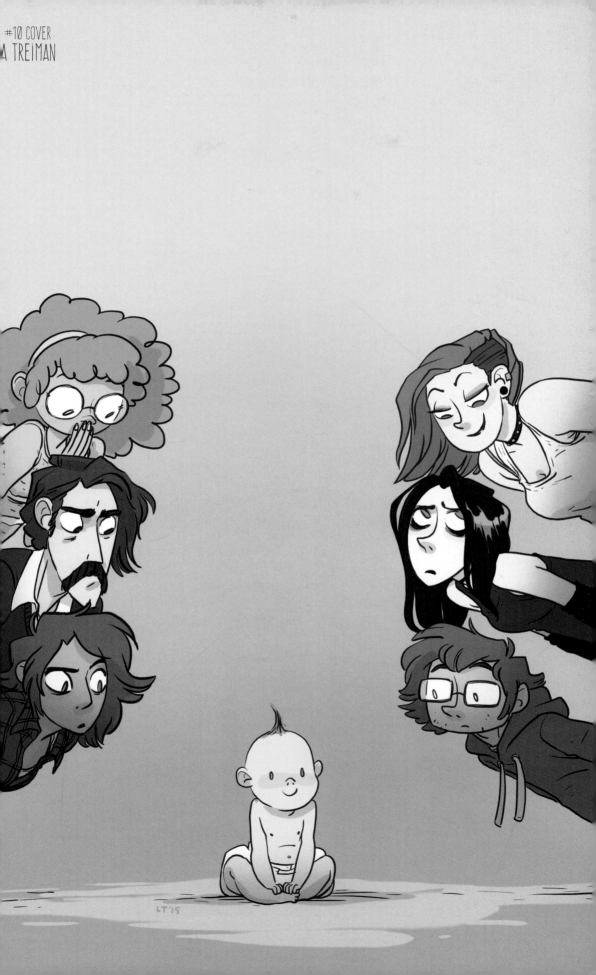

ISSUE #11 COVER
LISSA TREIMAN

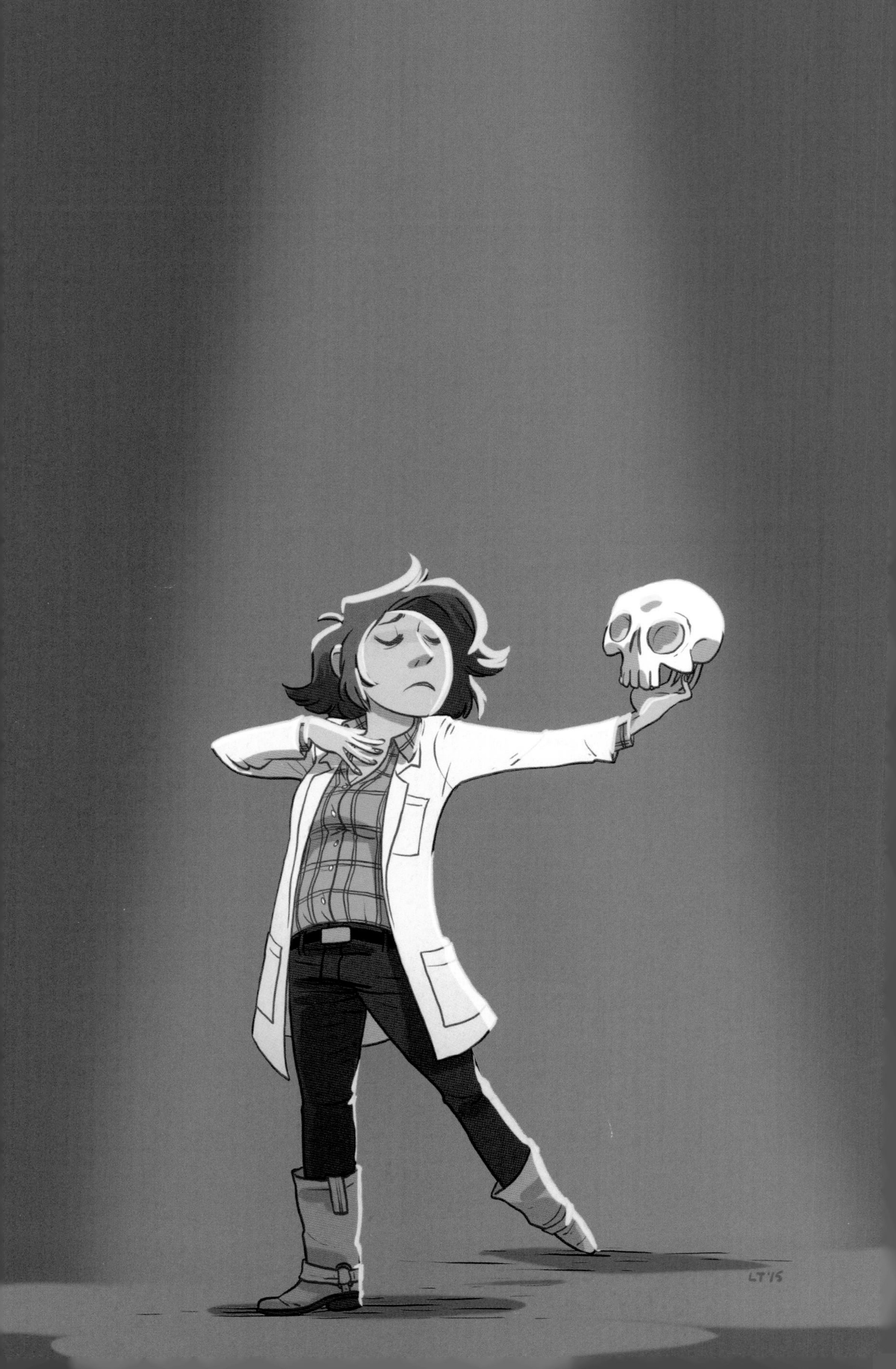
LT'15

#12 COVER
A TREIMAN

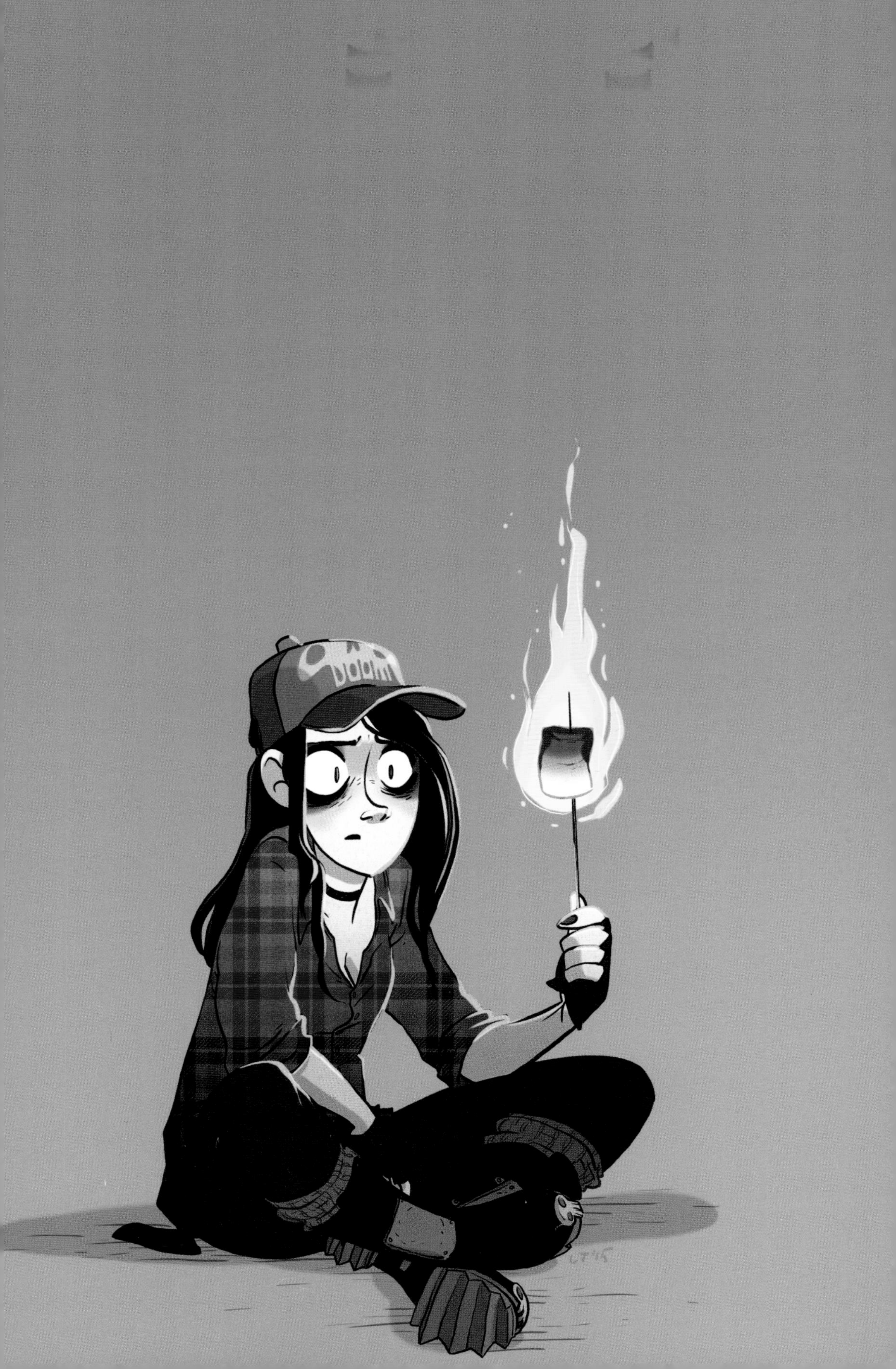

SKETCH GALLERY

SKETCHES BY JOHN ALLISON

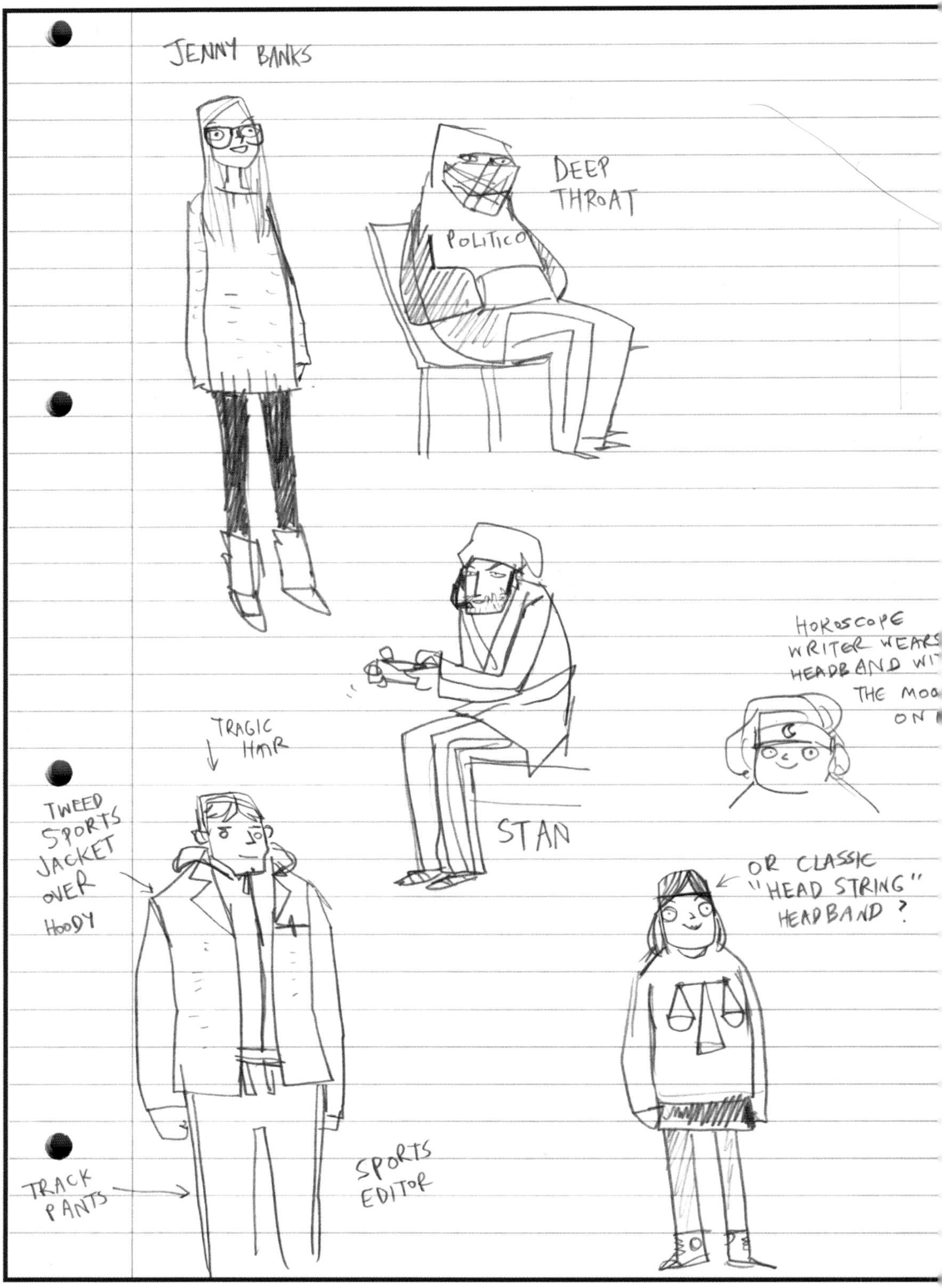

JENNY BANKS
DEEP THROAT
POLITICO
HOROSCOPE WRITER WEARS HEADBAND WI THE MOO ON
STAN
TRAGIC HAIR
TWEED SPORTS JACKET OVER HOODY
OR CLASSIC "HEAD STRING" HEADBAND ?
TRACK PANTS
SPORTS EDITOR

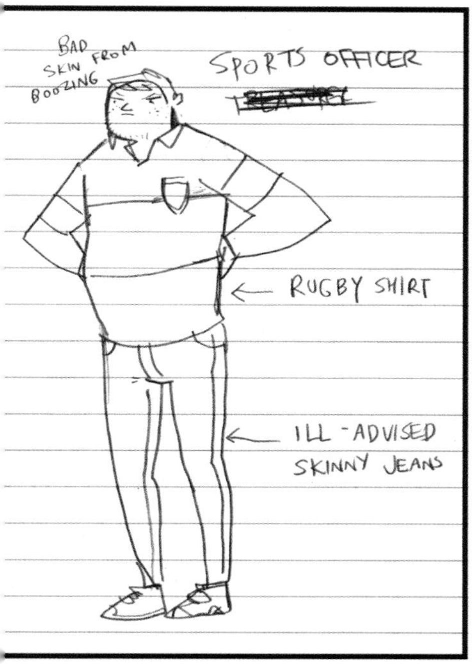
BAD SKIN FROM BOOZING
SPORTS OFFICER
TREASURER
RUGBY SHIRT
ILL-ADVISED SKINNY JEANS

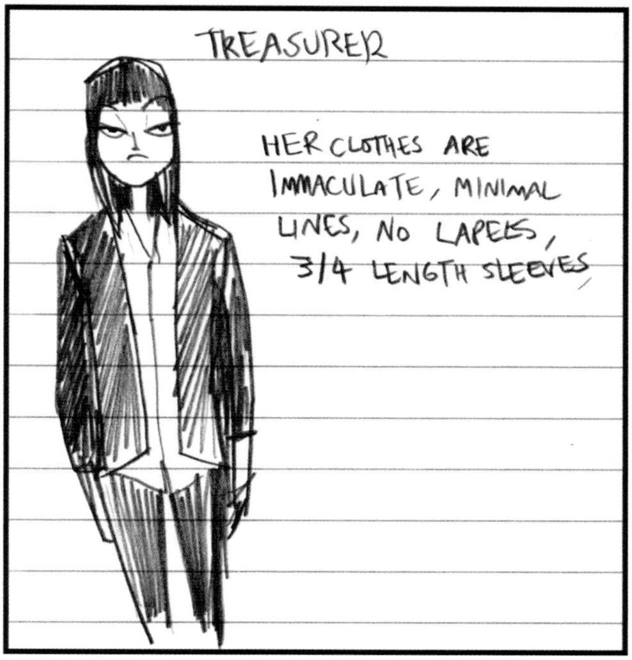
TREASURER
HER CLOTHES ARE IMMACULATE, MINIMAL LINES, NO LAPELS, 3/4 LENGTH SLEEVES

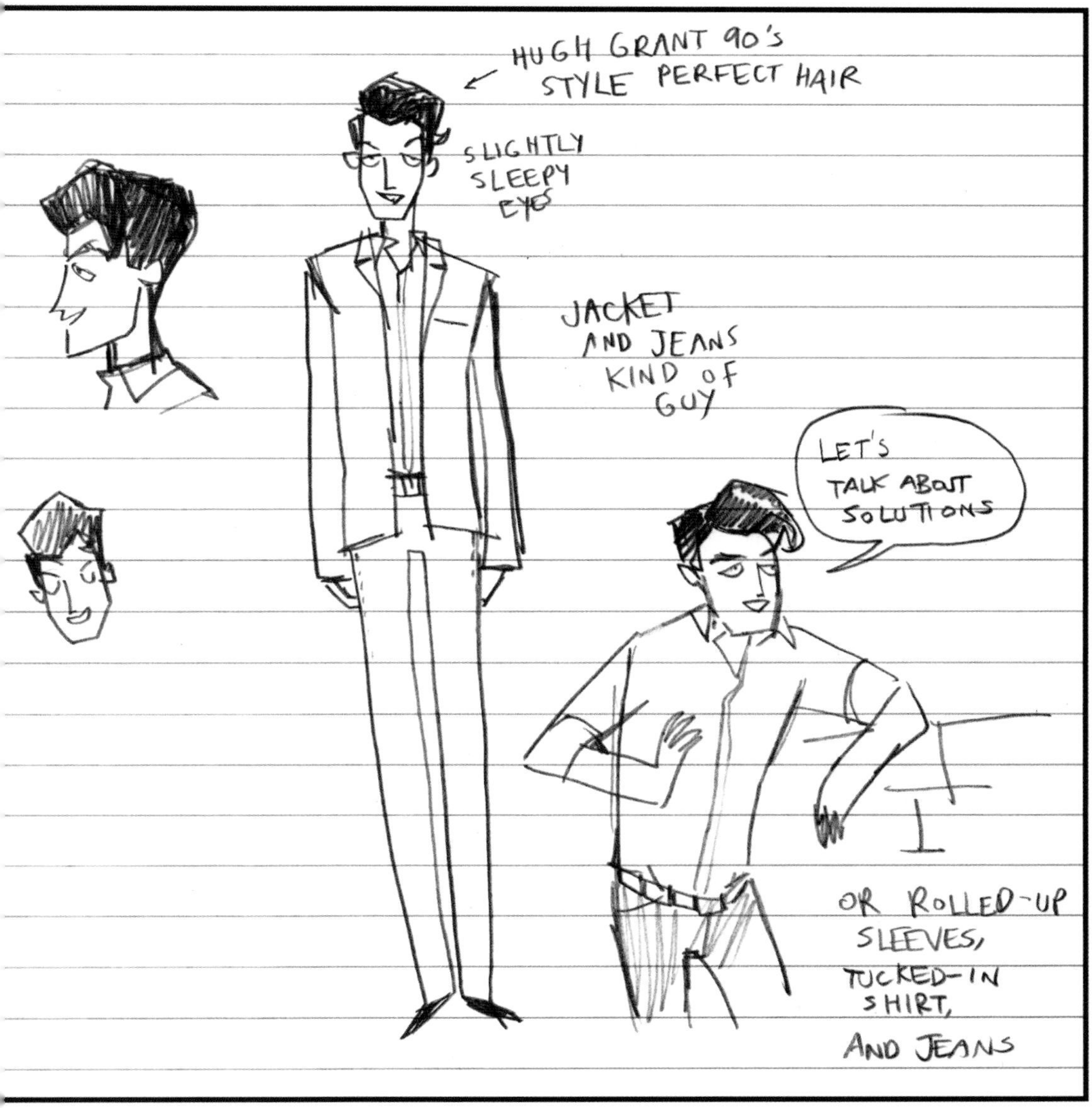
HUGH GRANT 90's STYLE PERFECT HAIR
SLIGHTLY SLEEPY EYES
JACKET AND JEANS KIND OF GUY
LET'S TALK ABOUT SOLUTIONS
OR ROLLED-UP SLEEVES, TUCKED-IN SHIRT, AND JEANS

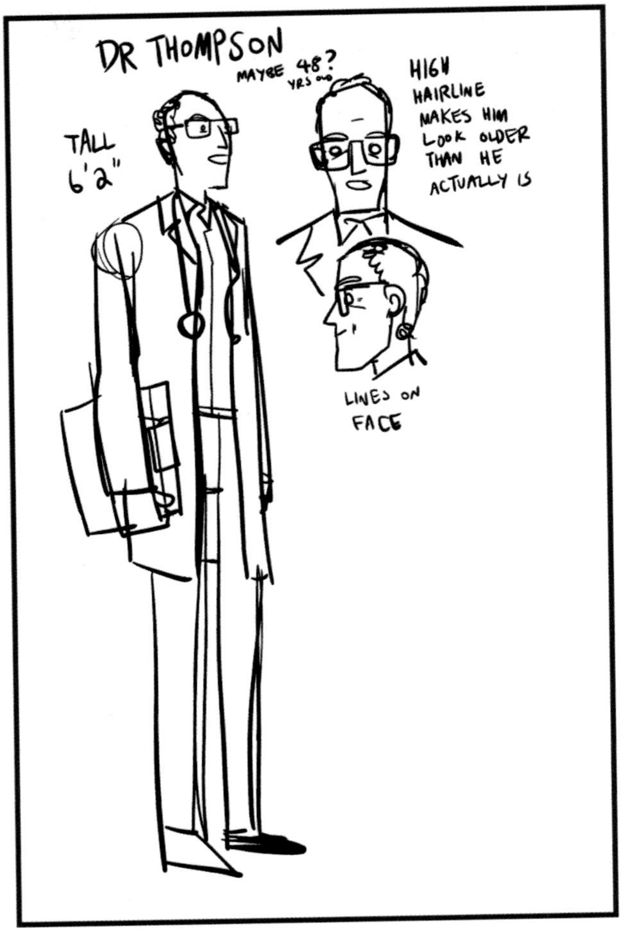
DR THOMPSON
MAYBE 48? YRS OLD
TALL
6'2"
HIGH HAIRLINE MAKES HIM LOOK OLDER THAN HE ACTUALLY IS
LINES ON FACE

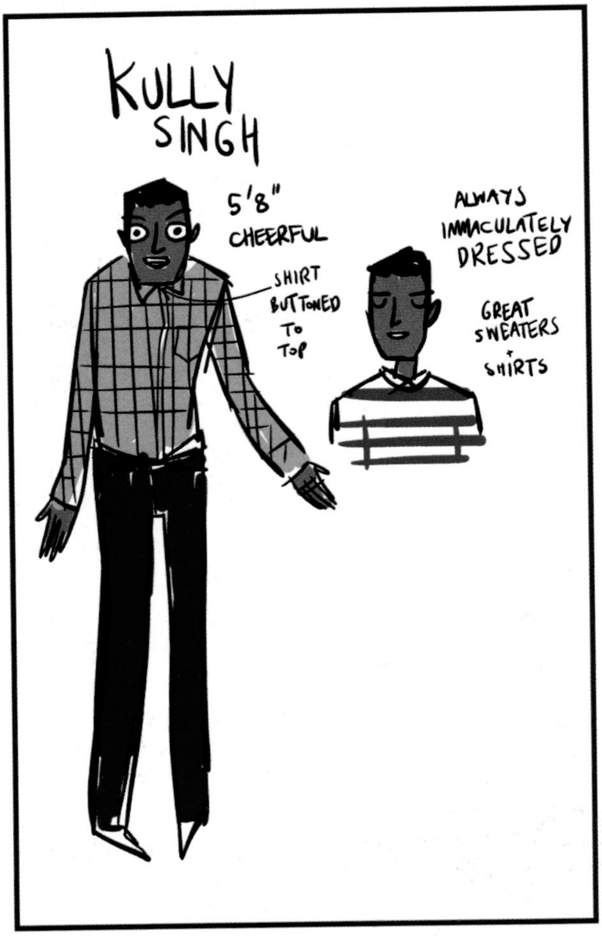
KULLY SINGH
5'8"
CHEERFUL
SHIRT BUTTONED TO TOP
ALWAYS IMMACULATELY DRESSED
GREAT SWEATERS + SHIRTS

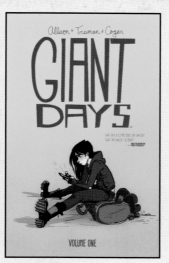

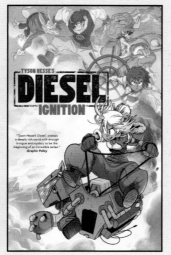

BOTTOM